BETHLEHEM'S CRY

BY

BARBARA N. STEWART

Then Herod, when he saw that he was mocked of the wise men, was exceeding wroth, and sent forth, and slew all the children that were in Bethlehem, and in all the coasts thereof, from two years old and under, according to the time which he had diligently inquired of the wise men. Then was fulfilled that which was spoken by Jeremiah the prophet, saying, In Ramah was there a voice heard, lamentation, and weeping, and great mourning, Rachel weeping for her children, and would not be comforted, because they are not.

Matthew 2:16-18

PART I

Chapter One

THE SHEPHERDS' HOPE

The small group of shepherds huddled close to the fire to ward off the chill of the night. Two were very young, yet to grow facial hair. The oldest one in the group prodded the embers with a long stick as the light danced in his eyes. He gazed at the two younger shepherds.

"Are you sleepy, Simon?"

"Yes and no. I'm tired, but I want to stay awake as long as I can. I can't be a real shepherd like you and my father until I can stay awake all night." The young lad pulled his cloak tighter around his thin frame and yawned expansively.

"True, but this is only your first time coming with us. I think you've done quite well in tending the sheep and keeping them from wandering off. You're going to be an excellent shepherd."

"The night watch is pretty scary, if you ask me," contributed the other lad. "When I finally get my chance, sheer fear will keep me awake!"

"Very wise observation, Son," stated the older shepherd as he threw another log on the fire. "I don't think it will be long before you'll be given the opportunity."

"Well, Eleazar and Rufus, dear cousins that they are, seem to get to tend the sheep all the time, and I don't know when Uncle Thaddeus will let me have the night watch with them even though I'm fourteen years old now."

"They're several years older than you, Benaiah," stated his father, Reuben.

"And I'm even younger than you, Benaiah, so it will be years before I can take the night watch," moaned Simon, disappointment written all over his face.

"I don't think you should complain. Your father talked your mother into letting you come, Simon, and that wasn't easy." Reuben laughed softly, and the wrinkles on his face deepened in the muted light.

"I'm tired of being the errand boy for the rest of you," Simon emphasized with a wave of his arm. "Here, Simon, take your father this water – take this food to Eleazar – take this twine to Uncle Reuben – take, take, take! That's all mother has me do! When can I get to do real work?" He dug at the dirt with his sandaled foot.

"And what are we supposed to do if you don't bring us the food, water, twine and other things that we need when we're in the fields all day? Your job is more important than you know." Reuben rubbed Simon's head affectionately.

"He's right," interjected Benaiah.

Simon hung his head and sighed heavily as he suppressed another yawn.

Suddenly, shouts and the baaing of many sheep reached their ears, and the shepherds quickly rose. Reuben gazed into the darkness beyond the light as the noises continued. He called out.

"Thaddeus! Eleazar! Rufus!"

The sheep were running in frantic circles, bleating and terrified.

"Reuben, come quickly! There's something in the brush, maybe a lion!" His brother's voice pierced the darkness. Reuben quickly responded.

"You stay here," he ordered Simon and Benaiah.

"No! I want to come with you!" Simon argued.

"You do as I say!" Reuben ordered as he shot a threatening glance Simon's way.

"Here, here," cajoled Benaiah. "Obey my father, Simon, and stay here. It's not safe for you to be out there if there's a lion lurking about. Don't you know that they'd just as soon pick you off as kill a helpless sheep?"

"Oh, Benaiah!" Simon whined. "You know I've helped kill a lion before!"

"That's true, but that was during the daylight hours. It's much more dangerous during the night, Simon." He motioned for Simon to sit down beside him as he cast furtive glances at the darkness beyond the circle of light. He spoke quietly.

"Simon, don't be in a hurry to go after a lion or bear in the dark. Remember when my father was just a little older than you, he tried and almost got himself killed. You know the story well; he's told it many times. Let those who are older and stronger and wiser stalk the lions."

"But I want to see what's going on!" protested Simon as he reluctantly sat down on a rock next to Benaiah.

"I do, too, but waiting and listening is all we can do for now. If it's nothing, everyone will return shortly. If it is either a lion or a bear, we'll know soon enough."

A hush fell over the young shepherds as they looked into the deepening blackness that now surrounded them, made more intense by the light from the fire. Benaiah opened a bag made of rough homespun material and retrieved a loaf of bread and a slab of cheese.

"Here, eat a little before you go to bed. It's time to call it a day."

Simon tore a large chunk of bread from the crusty loaf and stuffed it into his mouth just as voices reached their ears. They quickly stood to their feet.

Simon's father emerged from the blackness as the sheep closed the gap caused by his passing.

"It was just a wild boar roaming about," explained Thaddeus as Reuben joined him. "He's gone now. Eleazar and Rufus will stay out for the night watch; they're putting the sheep in the fold right now. Benaiah," he said as he seated himself next to Simon, "would you like to sit up with them also?"

Benaiah's mouth dropped open in surprise. "Yes, Uncle, I'd love to join them."

"Well, then, off with you, but be sure to take extra tunics for all of you. It's getting rather cold tonight."

Benaiah quickly retrieved the tunics from their bags and ran off to find the others in the ever deepening darkness. He cast a smile his uncle's way as he stepped out of the firelight. Calling for Rufus and Eleazar as he crossed the field among the sheep, he joined them and finished guiding the sheep into the enclosed fold.

Reuben threw some more wood on the fire, sending sparks spiraling skyward in the updrafts created from the heat of the flames, which soon grew and chased away the night chill. The sounds of their sons calling and guiding the sheep into the fold pierced the intense quiet of the night. Reuben, Simon and Thaddeus said little as they ate and listened to the familiar night sounds. Crickets chirped, owls hooted, and an occasional wolf could be heard howling in the distance.

Thaddeus lay on the ground and watched the embers from the fire as they danced and circled their way upward. The sky was black, littered with thousands of tiny pinpoints of light. He had never seen a diamond, but he often imagined that they would look like stars – brilliant and sparkling. The moon hung over the horizon, just a sliver of itself, waxing toward its full luminescence. Out here, away from every village and town, they were alone under the vast canopy spread above them, clear evidence of the handiwork of God.

Faint lights on a distant hill revealed the small town of Bethlehem, on the outskirts of which Thaddeus had a house. His wife of many years, Kezia, was in their house right now, probably retiring in their comfortable bed. Gazing upon the distant, dim lights of Bethlehem, Thaddeus longed for the comforts of wife and home.

Simon, laying close by his father's side, gazed into the heavens. It was only a moment before Simon asked a question; Simon never went long without asking questions. "Father, how many stars are there?"

Thaddeus smiled broadly and shook his head. "Only God knows that, Simon. I imagine that there are as many stars as there are grains of sand on the seashore."

"How many grains of sand are there?"

Thaddeus laughed softly and put his arm around his youngest son. "That's also something only God knows."

"Have you ever been to the seashore?"

"Oh, yes, several times before I married your mother."

"What's it like?"

"Well, there's so much water that you can't see the land on the other side, it's so very far away. The water moves in waves that make a wonderful sound when they hit the shore, and the shore is made up of tiny grains of sand, and when you pick them up in your hand, they fall through your fingers. It's fun to take off your sandals and walk in the sand and leave your footprints there."

"Will you take me to the seashore someday, Father?"

"I'll certainly try."

"I haven't been to the seashore either," interjected Reuben, who had been quietly listening to the conversation between father and son. "I've been pretty much landlocked all my life. The only sea I've seen is the Dead Sea, and that's not much to brag about. There aren't even any fish in the Dead Sea."

Simon quizzed his uncle. "Is that why they call it the Dead Sea?"

"Absolutely. It's so salty that nothing can survive in it. The only good thing that comes from the Dead Sea is salt."

"Why did God make the Dead Sea? Wouldn't it have been better to make a sea with fish in it?"

Thaddeus and Reuben laughed. "It certainly seems like that would make much better sense, but I guess God had his reasons for creating the sea the way he did," responded Thaddeus. "Maybe when the weather warms again, I'll take you to the Dead Sea. It's only about 15 miles from here."

"That would be wonderful, Father, but right now, I'm awfully tired."

"Well, let's get you to bed. Reuben and I will join you shortly."

Thaddeus led Simon to the simple shelter outside the circle of light cast by the fire. Simon lay down on his mat, and Thaddeus threw two warm blankets over him. "We'll be going home tomorrow. The grass in the pastures close to home should be recovered by now. Besides, your mother is most certainly lonely now that your sister is married." He tucked the blankets under Simon's chin.

"I miss Deborah," drowsily stated Simon. "Even though she lives in Bethlehem, I don't get to see her much anymore."

"I know. I miss her too, but she and Gedaliah are happy together. We'll see them shortly after we get home. I promise." He knelt down and kissed Simon's forehead.

"Goodnight, Father."

"Goodnight, Simon."

Thaddeus returned to the fire where his brother was adding big logs to ward off the chill of the night during the coming hours, as well as to keep any predatory animals at bay. Long fingers of flame reached for the sky, and dark shadows stretched endlessly away from the fire, finally being swallowed up by the darkness that surrounded them.

"I imagine Simon's already asleep," Thaddeus stated as he sat down on the ground across from his brother. "He's exhausted."

"As are all of us. I'm ready to go back home. Five nights out is long enough for me."

"Shearing time is just around the corner. The wool looks good this year, nice and thick. It should fetch us a good price from the weavers."

"How many more sheep are in the flock this year? I've forgotten the number we had a year ago."

"I let it grow by 20, so we'll have a nice increase in the wool production."

The two brothers sat in silence for a few moments. The only sounds that could be heard were the distant voices of their sons and the occasional baaing of the sheep. Oftentimes, they would sit by the fire for hours without saying a word, and neither would be offended by the other's silence.

Thaddeus eventually broke the relaxed silence. "Reuben, when do you think the promised Messiah will come?" He didn't raise his eyes from the dancing flames of the fire.

Reuben didn't respond immediately. "Why do you ask such a question? Do you long for him to come?"

"Oh, yes, don't you?"

"Of course! You should know that above everyone else!" retorted Reuben as he took a stick and held it in the flames, watching the fire ignite the tip. "I've had enough of these dastardly Romans, and I long to be free of them. They've deprived us of our way of life and have taken away our freedom to govern ourselves and run our own affairs. I long for freedom, which is something you and I have never experienced. But we must wait on the Messiah to appear before the Romans are swept away from our land. We have to endure their presence until then." He paused and gazed into the fire.

"I wonder what it was like to live before the Romans conquered our land," Reuben continued in a more subdued tone of voice. "Generations have existed and died under Roman rule, and yet we see no end in sight for ourselves or for our children." He paused momentarily and glanced at his brother. "I know you've often wondered why I've never married again after Micalah died. If I were to marry again, I would just bring more children into the world, more children that would have to exist under the thumb of Rome, and I don't want to do that."

"So that's why you've remained single all this time. I always thought it was because you just couldn't get over your love for Micalah."

"That's partly true. Micalah was my life, a wonderful wife, full of laughter and joy for living. She was taken all too quickly from me, and I'm still angry at God for taking her. But life came from her even as she died, and I wouldn't trade Benaiah for the world.

Now that I have Benaiah, could I give him up in order to get Micalah back? No. When Micalah was alive, I couldn't imagine my life without her, but now that I have Benaiah, I can't imagine my life without him. I love both of them, but I've had to live my life with only one of them at a time. They passed each other as their souls moved between heaven and earth, and I've often pictured Micalah talking to Benaiah as their souls passed, and I see her lecturing Benaiah about being a good boy, obeying his father, and loving God. Believing that she was able to see him comforts me." He picked up the stick and watched as the smoke from the tip spiraled skyward. "So, my dear brother, I will never take another wife. To do so would ensure that I bring more children into this world which would have to live as we do. I will not be responsible for giving Rome more people to persecute."

Thaddeus raised his gaze from the fire and looked at his younger brother. He knew Reuben was a hothead and lost his temper easily, but he loved him more than he cared to admit. He'd taken Reuben into his house, along with Benaiah, when Micalah had died. Oh, there had been times when he wished he would leave, but those times never lasted long and were usually caused by one or the other being strong-willed and stubborn. And now their sons had become inseparable, growing up together and becoming young men before their eyes.

Thaddeus sighed heavily as he brought his mind back to the conversation at hand. "I agree with you wholeheartedly about the Romans, Reuben. We're forced to pay taxes time after time, never knowing when they'll come pounding on our door for more. Roman soldiers are everywhere. And even worse, their lifestyle has infiltrated our people, polluting our race and indubitably angering Jehovah. I often wonder how long it will be before he raises up a prophet to speak out against the adultery of our people again. History proves that God won't tolerate an adulterous generation for long. He's always been swift to punish in the past."

"But the promised Messiah will free us from all of this, won't he?"

Thaddeus looked into Reuben's questioning eyes. "I certainly hope so." He paused as he gazed at the distant lights of Bethlehem. "I often think of the prophet Micah's words that a ruler will come out of Bethlehem, a man who will rule in Jerusalem. It seems so improbable at times, especially the way things stand now, with Herod Antipas ruling in Jerusalem, yet I cling to that prophecy."

"If I could raise an army," vehemently stated Reuben, "I would attack Jerusalem and kill Herod myself. He's nothing but a vile heathen, an enemy of God." He tossed the stick he had been holding above the fire into it and watched as it was engulfed by the flames. "Herod will burn in hell for the crimes he's committed against our people."

"I wish I could kill Herod, too, but to attempt to do such a thing would be to commit suicide. We must wait until the coming Messiah arrives and claims his rightful throne."

"But how will we know who he is? And how can someone so mighty and powerful come from our little town of Bethlehem? We don't have an army and certainly don't have the means by which to raise one. The Romans would kill everyone who would attempt to do such a thing. How could it even be possible, Thaddeus?" He ran a hand through his hair and then down through his beard in frustration.

"I don't know, I just don't know. But I truly believe that when the Messiah does come, we will know it. Who knows but that there might be a small child living in Bethlehem right now who will become our Messiah. Only time will tell. In the meantime, we'll do what we've been doing – caring for sheep. Life is still good, dear brother."

Reuben stared into the fire, watching the changing colors leaping from the red hot coals. The stars moved through the heavens as the two brothers sat in silence. The prophets were God's voice in their land, and even though much of what they had said had not yet come to pass, they still believed that God would reckon harshly with those who oppressed his chosen people. But the prophets had been silent for several hundred years, and the Jews felt that God had turned his back on them, especially now that they were under cruel foreign rule.

Thaddeus retrieved two more large logs from the pile of wood and placed them on the fire, sending a cascade of sparks upward. "But we have hope, Reuben, we still have hope, and we will always have hope as long as we live."

"But who wants to live their entire life under the rule of Rome? I can't think about it without getting all riled up! Our only hope is the Messiah, but I don't know if I can wait that long. We suffer through year after year, hoping and praying that the promised Messiah will come, and we are disappointed year after year!"

Reuben stood and turned his back to his brother as he fought to control the anger and frustration that rose within him. Balling his fist, he pounded it several times into the palm of his other hand.

Thaddeus stood and came up behind him and placed his hands on his shoulders. "We must try to find our hope and peace in the Lord, Reuben. If we can't, hatred for the Romans will eat us alive. We've been able to function for many years with a relatively peaceful life, and we can continue to do so. We have our farm, our sheep, our children and extended family. We have much for which to be thankful."

Reuben turned and faced him, black eyes sparkling in the firelight. "I know you're right. My heart just cries out at times for the pain and suffering of our people. But the Messiah will come, someday, he will come."

Thaddeus patted his brother on the back and quietly said, "And therein lays our eternal hope. Goodnight, Reuben."

"Goodnight, Thaddeus."

Thaddeus turned and stepped away from the warmth of the fire and joined Simon in the crude shelter, covering himself with as many blankets as he could to ward off the cold, damp air. Sighing heavily, he forced his mind to dwell on more pleasant thoughts of his wife and their reunion tomorrow.

Chapter Two

RETURN FROM THE FIELD

After the shepherds ate a hearty meal cooked over the open fire in the morning, the sheep were released from the fold which had protected them during the night. Benaiah, despite his best efforts, had finally succumbed to sleep in the early hours before daylight. Because Eleazar and Rufus had known they would have the night watch, they had slept during the day before and were able to stay alert the entire night. Even now, as Benaiah and the others let the sheep out, Eleazar and Rufus were teasing Benaiah.

The sheep responded to the voice of Thaddeus as he called them, moving out in an orderly fashion. The others had their staffs in hand to guide the flock as it followed Thaddeus, and so the long walk to the outskirts of Bethlehem began. The early-morning chill quickly evaporated in the warm rays of the sun, and even though Thaddeus wished for rain, he didn't want it on the day they had several miles to cover.

As Thaddeus led the flock, the others kept it together. The way was rough, the land strewn with rocks and boulders and interspersed with brush and grass. Simon, whose feet were aching, had never traveled this far from home before, and when Thaddeus had announced the necessity of going to distant pastures to graze the flock, Simon had pleaded with his mother to allow him to go. Kezia had been reluctant.

"But, Mother," Simon had pleaded, "I'm almost nine years old, and I'm growing bigger and stronger every day. If I don't go, I won't know what to do with myself while everyone else is gone. Please let me go!"

Kezia sighed heavily and looked questioningly at Thaddeus, who just nodded his head. "I think he'll be fine, Kezia; all of us will look after him"

"But I know how young boys can be," Kezia had countered. "Simon can sneak away among the rocks and be lost without you even knowing it."

Thaddeus put his arm around his wife as she continued. "Simon is quick, Thaddeus, and he could get lost without even meaning to leave your side. Boys have the tendency to explore everything."

Thaddeus gently hugged her, doing his best to reassure her. "We'll watch over him as well as we watch over the sheep, for he means much more to us than the sheep, Kezia. He'll be fine."

"I will, Mother," Simon assured. "I'll stay close to Father; I promise."

Knowing she wouldn't win, Kezia had given in to Simon's pleas to go with Thaddeus and the others. Now, as the long walk back home with the sheep was in progress, Simon realized his feet hurt terribly and that he wasn't having much fun at all.

When they stopped to rest, Thaddeus noticed that Simon was subdued, so he came to him and offered him a pomegranate. "Are you getting tired, Simon?"

Simon gratefully took the fruit. "My feet hurt very badly. If I'd stayed home, I could be out exploring and playing with my friends, or I could be helping Gedaliah with running the inn. This hasn't turned out to be as much fun as I thought it would be."

"Well, Son, it has been a long walk, and we're only about half-way home. I don't think you've done too badly for your first time out. Do you think you can make it the rest of the way?"

Simon let the bite of fruit slide down his throat before replying. "I'll have to make it, Father. The donkey has enough to carry as it is, and I don't want to add to its burden."

"Well, it's not easy being away from the comforts of home, but until we get substantial rains, we'll have to keep doing this. However, the sky is becoming overcast even now, so maybe there will be a change in the weather. We'll see."

Simon struggled to keep pace with the others the remainder of the trip. What had started out to be an adventure had now turned into a severe trial. His legs ached with each step, his feet were blistered and dirty, and his arms were exhausted from picking up and placing his staff in front of him with every step. His bed would certainly be a welcome sight tonight.

After what seemed an eternity, Simon saw his home in the distance. The last mile seemed to take forever, but the sheep even knew they were almost home as they scurried over the rocks and into the familiar fold. Clouds now covered the sky, bringing on dusk earlier than usual.

Kezia appeared in the doorway when she heard the noise of the excited sheep. Thaddeus waved to her after he counted the sheep and secured the gate to the fold.

"A job well done," he said to the others as they headed toward the house. He reached down and picked up Simon, throwing him over his shoulder. Simon laughed as he was carried the last hundred yards to his home.

"Wife," shouted Thaddeus, "I have an exhausted lad here, who would probably love to have a bath and crawl into his warm bed." As he reached Kezia, he handed Simon over to her.

"My goodness, Simon!" exclaimed Kezia as his full weight fell into her arms. "You're getting too big for me to carry." She gave him a hug and a kiss and then set him on the ground. Eleazar and Rufus greeted their mother with an embrace and kiss, and then Thaddeus took her in his arms and kissed her soundly, causing her to blush.

"It's always good to see everyone home safely. And the sheep, have all of them returned safely, too?"

"Every last one," replied Reuben. "Not one was lost on this trip."

"We thought there was a lion or bear last night," interjected Simon excitedly, "but it was just a wild boar crashing through the bushes. I wish it had been a lion though."

"That's what you say," Thaddeus stated as they entered the house, "but I personally was rather glad it was just a wild boar."

"I expected you home tonight," stated Kezia, "so Helah and I have prepared a feast. Come, wash your hands and feet while we set it out."

Kezia and the servant girl, Helah, who had placed several jugs of water next to large basins near the door, went into the kitchen and began carrying trays of prepared breads, cheeses, meats, fruits and vegetables into the dining area. They soon had the long table spread with food and wine.

The house had been built by Thaddeus's grandfather and had been improved upon by his father and now boasted a bath, an invention adopted from the ingenious, although despised, Romans. The room was located at the far end of the house, next to the kitchen area. Thaddeus's grandfather had dug a well when he acquired the land and had wisely built the house around the well, which was situated in a corner of the kitchen area. This allowed them to draw water whenever they needed it without leaving the home. The earthen hearth in the kitchen was used to heat the water for bathing and washing. Few people in the area had such a luxury, and Thaddeus was considered wealthy because of it.

The main hall floor was comprised of stone hewn from rocks in the surrounding hillsides and was worn smooth. Five sleeping chambers were situated around the hall, as well as the dining area and the kitchen. Helah had a small chamber in the kitchen to call her own, which allowed her to rise early and start meal preparations without disturbing family members. Heavy curtains of varied colors covered the entrances to each sleeping chamber, and the wall along the front of the house boasted many pegs on which to hang outer garments. Hand-woven rugs were strewn across the floor beneath each curtain, insulating the stone floors.

"Here, Simon," stated Thaddeus as he lifted his son onto a stool, "let's get those sandals off and wash those feet of yours." He gently lifted each foot and slid Simon's sandals off, and then placed his feet in a basin and poured water over them.

"I think I have blisters, Father."

Thaddeus dried Simon's feet with a cloth and turned them over. "You certainly do. Let's get some ointment to put on those."

Thaddeus went into the kitchen area and retrieved a jar of ointment and returned, spreading some on the bottom of Simon's feet. He then wrapped strips of cloth around them and carried Simon into the dining area, easing him down on the long bench.

Kezia saw the bandages on Simon's feet. "What happened?"

"Oh, just blisters from so many steps taken today," replied Thaddeus. "They'll be fine in a day or two."

Everyone sat around the table on huge cushions, including Helah, who, although a servant, was treated as one of the family.

"So, how is our daughter, Deborah?" questioned Thaddeus as he helped himself to a slab of mutton.

"She's fine, happy to be with Gedaliah. She adores him and loves to help him run the inn. She's so busy that she hardly has time to come out here and visit."

"Oh? What keeps her so busy?"

"Well, right now she's making new covers for some of the beds in the inn. Several of them are worn out and rather tattered, and because the inn is doing so well, Gedaliah had the money to spend on new covers. You know Deborah is an excellent seamstress, so she told Gedaliah how much material to buy when he went to Jerusalem recently. I went in to town to see them just after you left, and I must say that Gedaliah found some beautiful fabric. Deborah was very excited about it. He even bought her material to make a new dress."

"The reason the inn is doing so well," piped up Reuben as he waved a leg of lamb in front of him, "is because of the Romans. They constantly house their captains and centurions at the inn, often at the expense of our own people having no place to stay. I just wish the whole lot of them would simply pack up and go back to Rome and leave us alone here in Judea. We certainly don't need them."

Eleazar, the oldest son, voiced his opinion. "As long as we don't cause any trouble and do as they say, they don't bother us."

"Ha!" shouted Reuben. "And if we were to rise up against them, they wouldn't hesitate to kill every man, woman and child, nor would they hesitate to rape every woman before they killed her. They are nothing but savages, I tell you!"

"I agree with Eleazar," timidly interjected Rufus. "The Romans have given us many good things, like the public and private baths, and they've paved roads all over Judea and every other country they rule."

"And that makes them good?" bitingly questioned Reuben.

Rufus felt all eyes on him as he swallowed hard. "Well, not necessarily," he replied, "but they aren't all bad. They've brought some good to our land."

"True," Thaddeus slowly agreed, "but we must always look at the Romans through the eyes of God. We are God's chosen people, and Rome has set us under its feet, conquered us, and now rules over us. True, Herod rebuilt the temple in Jerusalem, but that doesn't make him a good man. Evil men can do good things, and good men can do evil things."

Simon, always hesitant to contribute to such an adult conversation, could contain himself no longer. "When my friends and I play, we often pretend one of us is King Herod, and then we pretend to kill him with our swords. I think he's evil, too."

Thaddeus smiled at his youngest son. "He is, as are all the Romans. The Romans are pagans and have multiple gods, and they offer sacrifices to them daily. Jehovah will not allow the Romans to rule over us forever."

"And so we wait for the Messiah," quipped Reuben, "the long-awaited, promised Messiah, in hopes that he will free us from Roman oppression."

"How can one man, a Hebrew, raise an army and defeat Rome when we are surrounded by well-equipped, well-trained Roman soldiers?" questioned Kezia.

"We don't know," answered Thaddeus. "But Reuben and I were talking around the fire last night, and we remembered that the prophet Micah prophesied hundreds of years ago that a ruler would come out of

Bethlehem and that he would rule in Jerusalem. What better time for him to come than now."

"If he were to come now, we could be in his army, Rufus," excitedly stated Eleazar.

"Who said I wanted to fight?" asked Rufus. "Maybe I just want to tend sheep and have a quiet life."

"What are you, a coward?" taunted Eleazar.

"Of course he's not," quickly interjected Thaddeus. "All of us are different, and just because you and Reuben wish to go off and fight, if you could, that doesn't mean that Rufus is less of a man than either of you."

"So, when will our Messiah come?" quietly asked Kezia after a brief pause in the conversation.

"He can't come soon enough," replied Reuben. "I want Benaiah to enjoy life without Roman rule; I don't have a clue what that's like. We've all lived our entire lives under the thumb of Rome, and I don't want to live like this any longer."

"But, Father," interrupted Benaiah as he licked his fingers, "who in this small town of Bethlehem can possibly qualify to be our Messiah? Who do you think it would be out of all the people we know?"

Silence descended on the group as Benaiah's question fell heavily on their ears.

"We must wait and see what Jehovah will do," quietly replied Thaddeus as he finished his meal. "Even though we cannot see a way, God can make a way just as he did when the Israelites came upon the Red Sea with the Egyptians in pursuit, wanting to kill them all. He made a way then, and he will make a way when the time is right. Until then, there's nothing we can do but wait and pray."

The room had become very dark during the meal, and Helah arose and lit several oil lamps. Suddenly, there was a brilliant flash of light followed quickly by a loud clap of thunder, and the sound of rain could be heard on the slate roof.

"Praise God – rain," stated Thaddeus as he listened to the drumming of the drops.

"Is there anything that you need taken care of outside, Mother?" asked Eleazar.

"No. I saw the clouds rolling in this afternoon, and Helah and I took care of putting things in the stable in hopes that it would rain."

"Well, Simon, let's get you that bath I promised, and then off to bed with you." Thaddeus rose and lifted his youngest son in his strong arms. "Helah, could you heat some water for the bath?"

"I already have some on the hearth; I'll bring it right in." Helah moved quickly to do Thaddeus's bidding.

"Here, let me help you," offered Rufus, rising so quickly that he almost knocked over the table. Helah scurried into the kitchen.

"Ah, yes, Rufus has a crush on Helah," taunted Eleazar.

"Hush, Eleazar," reprimanded Kezia.

Eleazar laughed as Rufus set off to assist Helah, taking the jar from her hands and lowering it into the well. Helah stepped back slightly, knowing that to touch his skin would set hers on fire. Ever since Helah had come to work in the house, her heart beat wildly whenever she was around Rufus. She often thought he felt the same way, but she wasn't sure. Sometimes she'd find him looking at her in a way no other man had ever looked at her before, but after all, she was still the family's servant, despite the familial way in which Kezia and Thaddeus treated her.

After the jar was full, Rufus offered to take it to the bath, but Helah took it from him. "It's my job, Rufus, but thank you for offering." She looked at him from under her dark lashes, and their eyes locked for an instant. Rufus stretched out his hand as if to touch her face, but Helah quickly turned and headed to the bath with the jar of water, her heart thumping wildly in her chest. Upon her return to the kitchen, Rufus drew two more jars for her, yet not a word was said between them. Each time she waited for him to fill the jar, Helah kept her distance even though her flesh burned with the desire to simply touch him.

"Thank you, Rufus," Helah said softly. "That's all that is needed. You can go join the others now." Rufus quietly walked slowly past her, never taking his eyes off her until he was out of the room.

Helah exhaled slowly, trying to control the racing of her heart. She hurriedly poured the last jar of cold water into the bath, and then poured in the hot water to complete the bath. A few minutes later, Simon eagerly climbed in, wincing with pain as his blistered feet touched the warm water.

Kezia washed the dirt from his youthful, lithe body. She scrubbed him clean with soap made from olive oil, then dried him off and applied more ointment and fresh bandages to his blistered feet. Simon was almost asleep before he was in his bed despite his desire to stay up and talk about the promised Messiah.

Thaddeus, Reuben, Eleazar and Rufus relaxed in the dining area, where they settled on large pillows in one corner of the room. Helah busied herself in the kitchen, cleaning up from the evening meal and organizing herself for what she needed to do in the morning. Secretly, she hoped Rufus would come in and see her again, but simultaneously, she prayed he'd stay away – far away. Even though she'd known Rufus casually through the years, she had no idea being close to him would have such an impact on her at this stage of her life.

Helah had gone to work to relieve her elderly, ill parents of responsibility for her until she was married. Her father was weak and ill, and her mother, also very frail, barely made ends meet with the little money that they had put away. Thaddeus and Kezia were friends with her parents and hired her when they saw their need, paying her by providing room and board; they treated her very well, more like a friend or family member than a servant girl.

Helah heard the men speaking in the other room as she worked. "Shearing time is just around the corner," declared Thaddeus. "We've been very fortunate to have such a healthy flock this year. I expect that the wool will bring a good price at the market in Jerusalem."

"Do you intend to sell the lambs again?" asked Reuben.

"That's a necessity, as usual. If we don't sell them, our flock becomes too big, and our pastures can't sustain them. Besides, the temple in Jerusalem is always in need of perfect lambs for sacrificing. We should decide how many we want to take when we go again, and we probably should do that within the next week or two."

"Father," offered Eleazar, "would you let me and Rufus take the lambs to Jerusalem?"

"I think the best thing would be for all of us to do the shearing, starting in three days. Then when that is finished, Reuben and Rufus should go to Jerusalem with the lambs."

"Why not me?" questioned Eleazar rather irately.

Thaddeus flashed an impish smile toward Rufus. "Because we need to keep Rufus away from Helah."

Even in the diminished light, Rufus was sure that everyone could see that he had turned many shades of red. His father reached over and slapped him on the back good-naturedly. Rufus relaxed and laughed, and the others joined in.

"I thought it was my own little secret," he said softly. "Please don't embarrass Helah by saying anything to her. Please!"

"We won't," assured Thaddeus. "I remember when I was young."

"So Rufus gets to go to Jerusalem and I have to stay because he has eyes for Helah?" Eleazar questioned, astonished.

"That's probably best," assured Reuben. "Besides, you never know, Eleazar. You might see a pretty young thing in Jerusalem if you were to go, and we can't have two young men infatuated at the same time. That would be unbearable!"

"Hey, I'm the oldest!" replied Eleazar. "Shouldn't I be the one falling in love first?"

"I'm not in love," emphatically exclaimed Rufus. "You act like we're betrothed or something."

"Well, maybe you should be."

"All that in due time," interrupted Thaddeus. "Meanwhile, I want you to go into town tomorrow, Eleazar, and purchase twine from Gibea's shop. We'll need it to bind up the hay sometime soon, and I don't think we have enough on hand. I may not remember later to ask you do that, so I'm asking you now."

Kezia entered the room and sat down on a cushion next to Thaddeus. "Simon was asleep before his head hit the pillow, I think. He was utterly exhausted."

"Father," interjected Rufus in an effort to change the direction of the conversation, "did you ever discover where Gibea's brother went? You remember he was trying to incite people in town to take up arms against the Romans. I haven't seen him since then."

"The last I heard, Gibea told me that Heber had gone off into the hills. The Romans had somehow found out that he was talking insurrection, and for fear of his life, Heber left town and is apparently living in the wilderness."

"Maybe he's destined to be the Messiah," offered Reuben. "He might be the one to come back to Bethlehem and gather an army."

"What kind of talk is this?" asked Kezia. "Who could possibly raise an army to go against the Romans?"

"It's just talk, that's all," assured Thaddeus.

"But the Messiah is supposed to come out of Bethlehem," Reuben countered, "so why can't it be Heber? He was born in Bethlehem and wants to overthrow the dastardly Romans as much as any one of us."

"To even consider a thing would be suicidal," insisted Thaddeus. "The Romans have equipment and manpower that would squash any rebellion before it could even become a rebellion."

"If Heber were to come back and ask for volunteers to join an army," quipped Eleazar, "I would certainly go."

"You most certainly would not," loudly insisted Kezia. "You are too young to fight."

"Mother, I'm nineteen years old, old enough to marry and work, and certainly old enough to take up the sword if need be."

"Thaddeus, don't let him do it," Kezia pleaded.

Thaddeus reached over and took her hand. "Don't worry, Kezia, dear, it's all just talk, and I'm sure nothing will ever become of it. It's too improbable to even think about, really."

Silence enveloped the room as each was lost in his own thoughts; the only sound was the occasional clap of thunder in the distance and the pounding of the rain. The air had freshened and cooled with the downpour, and Kezia stood and pulled the cover over the window.

"It sounds as if we're getting a thorough drenching," observed Thaddeus. "At least it will be enough to revitalize the grasslands again." He stood and stretched. "Well, I'm off to bed. I imagine the rest of you are as exhausted as I am."

Amidst mumbled agreements, everyone said goodnight and retired to their rooms. Thaddeus followed Kezia to their bedchamber, noticing the sweet smell of her body.

"Is the water still in the bath?" he asked.

"Yes, I believe it is; Helah was going to drain it in the morning."

"I think I'll go wash off before coming to bed; I'll only be a few minutes. It doesn't matter that the water has cooled by now. It will still be warmer than the creek." He quietly left the room.

Kezia took down her hair, letting it fall down her back, and brushed it out. She had a looking glass, a gift from Thaddeus on her last birthday. She had never seen an image of herself before and had been delighted to have such a fine gift. Looking into it now, she saw all the gray hairs that were appearing in the midst of her black hair. She was almost 39 years old, and yet she didn't feel that old at all. The years had passed all too quickly. And now she had a son-in-law, and she welcomed the fact that she would become a grandmother sometime soon. She prayed that Eleazar and Rufus would marry before too long; it would secure her future in case Thaddeus died before she did. How she dreaded the thought.

Thaddeus reappeared, a towel wrapped around his waist, his hair glistening and wet. Kezia still marveled at the male body, and her heart raced as he approached her. Pulling the doorway drape closed, he came to her and lifted her up into his arms. Kezia responded, wrapping her arms around him as he laid her down on the bed. He helped her slide out of her dress and then slid beneath the covers with her. She ran her fingers alongside his face, tracing the creases around his eyes.

"Do you know how much I miss you when I'm gone?" Thaddeus asked as he looked into her eyes so close to his.

"Probably as much as I miss you when you're gone," Kezia whispered back.

Thaddeus took her more fully into his arms, and as their bodies intertwined, he knew he was the most blessed man on the earth.

The falling rain muffled the sounds of their love as the sky continued blessing the land with refreshing rain.

Chapter Three

THE DECREE

It didn't take long before Eleazar and Simon's sandals became covered in mud as they navigated the path to Bethlehem the next morning. The deluge of the night before had finally ceased in the early morning hours, and the abundant rain had turned the path into a slippery quagmire.

"What do you have to get in town?" Simon asked.

"Two bundles of twine from Gibea's shop. We don't have much on hand, and Father doesn't want to run out."

"Can I stop and see Deborah while you go to the shop?"

"Sure, Simon. And after I buy the twine, I'll stop for a brief visit myself. I'm still not used to having Deborah gone from our house. She's an old, married woman now!" He and Simon laughed as they slid along the path as they walked further into town

The houses and businesses existed side by side, which was an easy way for business to be conducted at all hours of the day. Merchants were already opening up their shops. Several called out greetings to the boys as they passed.

"Good morning to you, Eleazar!" shouted Amnon, a weaver of rugs. "Do you think the rain is over?"

"Yes, the clouds are moving away."

"Your father must have been happy to see the rain."

"Yes, he was."

"Tell your father I send my greetings."

"I will, Amnon."

"Can I run off to Deborah's now?" Simon asked as he came to the street that led to the inn.

"Sure, but stay there until I come."

Simon bounded off like a jackrabbit, mud flinging from his sandals. He seemed to have forgotten all about his blisters from the long walk the day before.

He quickly reached the door to the inn and slowly opened it and then carefully removed his sandals while still outside and held them in his hands. Sticking his head through the door, he called for Gedaliah.

"Is that you, Simon?"

"Yes! May I come in? My feet are awfully muddy!"

"I'll be right there with a basin of water. Step onto the rug and leave your sandals there."

Simon dropped his mud-caked sandals on the rug as he planted his soiled feet next to them. The inn was quiet right now, with only one man in the entrance area. He was counting the money in his pouch and didn't even notice Simon.

"Here you go, Simon," Gedaliah said as he entered, carrying a large basin and a jug of water. "Let me pour this for you. My goodness, your feet are absolutely filthy!" he exclaimed as he set the basin down by Simon and filled it with water.

"I know, and I even had a bath last night. Mother gave it to me because I smelled as bad as the sheep I'd been with for five days."

Stepping into the basin, Simon rinsed his feet and stepped out onto the towel that Gedaliah placed on the floor. He quickly dried his feet and stepped onto the cool stone floor. The inn was clean and attractive, but the furnishings were plain and simple, offering a respite for a weary traveler and a bit of comfort.

Cushions adorned the padded benches, and several small tables held jars and bowls. Gedaliah had taken over the business of running the inn when his father had died two years earlier, and then he had set out to get a wife. Once he had the responsibility of running the inn, he knew he should have a wife to help him, and it wasn't long before he and Gedaliah were betrothed.

"Where is Deborah? I came to see her . . . . . and you, too," Simon added with a smile.

"She's upstairs having breakfast with my mother, and you may certainly go up and see her."

Simon padded through the room and down the hall, passing several sleeping chambers as he went, and climbed the stairs at the end of the hall. The inn contained twelve sleeping chambers, and almost every one of them was used each night.

As he climbed the stairs, he heard Deborah's voice. "Mother Eglah, how did you manage to do everything when you helped run the inn? I find it's difficult to keep up with everything each day."

"It just takes experience," Eglah answered. "Please give yourself time to learn it all. You haven't even been married for four months yet."

Simon cleared his throat to make them aware of his presence.

Deborah turned, surprised. "Simon! How good to see you!" Quickly rising from her chair, she ran to Simon and embraced him. "Look at you! You seem to have grown taller every time I see you!"

Simon glowed under her lavish praise. "Mother says the same thing. I think I'll be as tall as Rufus when I grow up. He's taller than Father, you know."

"Come up here and sit with us," offered Eglah, "and tell us what you've been up to."

"I just returned from a trip with Father and the others to take the sheep to green pastures. The ones close by were grazed down. It was fun at first, but the trip home was awfully long."

"How long were you gone?"

"Five whole days," moaned Simon, "five very long days. I was so excited to be able to go at first, but after a few days, I wished I had stayed home and played with my friends. It isn't a whole lot of fun watching a bunch of sheep all day long."

Deborah and Eglah laughed at Simon's expression. "Well, here, eat this freshly baked bread. I imagine you've already had breakfast, but a growing boy like you can always find more room to put food in his stomach."

Simon took the proffered bread, savoring its richly blended flavors. Eglah had a way of making bread with herbs, twisting it into wonderful shapes and baking it to a golden brown. He added some goat cheese from a jar.

"How's everyone at home?" inquired Deborah.

"Fine. Eleazar is buying twine at Gibea's shop and will be stopping by when he's done."

"Wonderful!" exclaimed Eglah. "I love to have visitors."

"I've got to get busy helping Gedaliah," explained Deborah as she rose from her chair. "I'll talk to you some more later, but stay here and visit with Eglah until then." Simon nodded as he stuffed another chunk of the savory bread into his mouth.

Deborah hurried down the stairs and found Gedaliah as he was checking out two of their guests.

"Was your stay pleasant?" asked Deborah as she smiled at the men.

"That was one of the most comfortable beds I've slept on outside of my own," replied one of the guests. "I'll certainly recommend this place to any of my business associates who should need to travel this way."

"Thank you," smiled Gedaliah. "We're glad you came. Have a safe trip."

The two men left, commenting on the muddy conditions of the street as they opened the door.

Deborah went to the vacated room and made the beds; the linens would get washed after a few more nights. She tidied up the room and opened the window so it could air out. She emptied the wash basin and threw the soiled water out the open window into the area behind the inn. Then she went to a room where they stored large jugs of water and filled up the jug from the room and returned it to the shelf where it waited, ready for the next guest.

As Gedaliah checked out other guests during the next few hours, Deborah repeated the same tasks. She was soon hot and sweaty, tired and hungry, and yet she somehow enjoyed her work, which she did because she loved Gedaliah. Eglah had helped Gedaliah's father for years, and they had raised a family at the same time. Of course, once the children had become old enough to help, they had assisted their parents in the running of the inn. Gedaliah had been the only one who had really wanted to manage the inn when he grew up; his brothers had pursued their own businesses, and his two sisters had married. He had worked several years with his father before he had died, so he knew the business well.

Eleazar arrived while Deborah was in the midst of all her cleaning, so he visited with Gedaliah when he wasn't dealing with guests. He noticed all the work Deborah was doing, so he mentioned this to Gedaliah.

"I've offered to have someone help us," his brother-in-law explained, "but Deborah wants to see if she can handle it by herself first. I say she's being a bit stubborn about it, if you ask me. The woman who helped Mother is more than willing to return and help Deborah, but she won't stand for it, at least not yet. I think she'll change her mind before too long, especially now that she's with child. It's hard work."

"Maybe she's jealous and doesn't want another woman around you," teased Eleazar.

"My goodness, the woman who helped Mother is as old as my oldest sister!"

"Ah, but a newly-married woman can be quite jealous, so I've heard."

The sound of galloping horses reached their ears, followed by shouts and curses being hurled at their riders as pedestrians scurried out of the way. Hurrying to the door, Gedaliah and Eleazar saw Roman soldiers as they passed by on their spirited steeds, mud from the horses' hooves splattering in all directions and adhering to the simple houses. The lead soldier was carrying a scroll, and the unit reined in their horses at the intersection of the narrow streets right next to the inn. The soldier with the scroll shouted as he read from it in a loud voice as he sat astride his prancing steed. People stopped and listened, anger and frustration in their eyes.

"Caesar Augustus, Divine Emperor of Rome, has decreed that everyone in the Roman Empire is to return to the birthplace of their fathers, to be registered and counted. Everyone is to leave their homes and reach their destinations within a fortnight. Anyone who does not obey the command of Caesar shall be put to death."

The mounted soldiers continued on their way down the street, stopping periodically to proclaim the announcement over and over again, as shouts of dissention followed them. People started pouring out of their homes, raising their fists at the backs of those who had brought such unfathomable news.

Deborah stood in the doorway, Simon by her side. They watched as children picked up chunks of mud and hurled them at the receding backs of the Roman soldiers, a small attempt to show their outrage.

"What Caesar really means," angrily stated Gedaliah, "is that he wants to count us so he can tax us again!"

The voices of those on the streets created an ever increasing crescendo pulsating with anger.

"This is insane!"

"We'd rather die first!"

"Let Caesar come and count us himself!"

"How can he possibly do this to us?"

"What does all this mean?" quietly questioned Deborah as she looked at her husband.

Gedaliah put his arm around her and drew her close. "All of King David's descendants must return here, to Bethlehem. I can't imagine how that will be possible. The town will burst at the seams with people. Fortunately, we are of David's lineage, so we won't have to travel."

"But you'll have to prepare to be overrun by people coming here," stated Eleazar. "It looks as if you'll have more business than you know what to do with during the coming days, maybe weeks."

Gedaliah and Deborah looked at each other, and Deborah's heart sank. Gedaliah immediately noticed the panic in her eyes.

"That does it. We're getting Selma back to help you."

"And you'll be overwhelmed with guests checking in every day, so you won't be able to clean the stable for our guests' donkeys. What are we to do about that?" Deborah posed.

"I could clean the stable every day. You let me do it when I'm here for visits, so why can't I do it every day?" offered Simon.

Gedaliah bent down and looked directly into Simon's eyes. "It will be a big responsibility, Simon. The stalls will need to be mucked out, the mangers filled with fresh hay, and the water troughs constantly filled with fresh water. And you will have to curry down any animals that a traveler wants you to tend. Are you sure you want to do all that?"

Simon nodded vigorously.

"He could make quite a bit of money from travelers who appreciate his services," interjected Eleazar. "Some people are very particular about their donkeys and horses."

"You mean I'd get paid?" Simon asked in astonishment.

Eleazar and Gedaliah laughed at Simon's reaction. "Yes, you would."

"But how are we supposed to prepare for all of this?" asked Deborah. "Just the thought throws me into a panic."

"We have time to think and plan," assured Gedaliah.

"We'd better be getting back home," interrupted Eleazar. "I wonder if the soldiers went close enough to our home for Mother or Father to hear of this required 'registration.' Come, Simon."

He and his young brother headed off toward home amidst the angry people gathered in the streets. Once again, they were being forced to do something that would create extreme hardship for many people.

Simon bombarded Eleazar with endless questions on the short walk back home. "When will the people start arriving in Bethlehem?"

"Probably in about a week or so."

"How many people will come?"

"Possibly hundreds."

"Where will they all stay?"

"That's the biggest question of all, Simon. I imagine that, once the inns are full, many of them will have to stay out in tents in the countryside surrounding Bethlehem. I can't possibly imagine what other accommodations can be made."

When they finally arrived home, they found Kezia and Helah going about their business as usual. They obviously hadn't heard the upsetting decree.

Kezia turned toward the door when she heard Simon and Eleazar enter, sliding off their sandals as they did so and stepping into a large basin of water prepared for them.

"You'd never guess what's happened, Mother."

"What is it?"

"Caesar has made a decree that every citizen of the Roman Empire must return to the birthplace of his forefathers, to be counted and registered, in other words, taxed." Eleazar dropped the soiled towel into a large container by the basin. "That means that everyone who is of the house of David must return to Bethlehem. Hundreds and hundreds of people will be descending on our little town."

Kezia's eyebrows came together in a deep furrow across her forehead. "That's impossible! Where are all of the people supposed to stay? How can they all be fed and supplied with fresh food and water?"

"My concerns exactly," stated Eleazar.

"Does Gedaliah know?"

"Yes. I was with him and Deborah when the soldiers tore through the town on their fancy horses, terrorizing the children and citizens in the streets. One soldier simply read the decree from 'The Divine Emperor of Rome' as he rode through the town."

"That means that Gedaliah and Deborah will be overrun with people at the inn."

"Exactly. Gedaliah will be hiring Selma back to assist Deborah in the day-to-day operations of the inn. It's almost too much for Deborah as it is right now."

"And I'm going to take care of the stable and any animals that stay there," piped up Simon, who had been quietly listening until now. "I'll even be able to make some money of my own!"

"That's wonderful!" exclaimed Kezia. "I'm sure Gedaliah will need all the help he can get. I'll check with Deborah and see if she needs me to help her also. Things around here can run smoothly without me; Helah is quite capable."

Eleazar picked up his mud-caked sandals and stepped back outside and slid them onto his feet after shaking off as much mud as possible. "I'm going to tell Father and Uncle Reuben now. I don't imagine that this whole thing will upset or change our schedule around here very much. We are but simple shepherds and farmers."

Leaving the door ajar, Eleazar headed off toward the fields to find the others. The sky had brightened considerably, and patches of blue could be seen between sweeps of clouds. The water-soaked ground was quickly drying out, leaving only a few low-lying spots that were muddy and slippery. Eleazar walked carefully lest he slip and fall and injure himself on the many rocks. They couldn't afford to have any one of them laid up with any kind of illness or injury at this, or any, time of the year. There was always too much work to do, and if one was unable to work, that meant more work for the others.

Eleazar loved living in the hill country. Bethlehem was an elevated town, rising 2000 feet above the Dead Sea just a day's walk south and east of Jerusalem. From several rises, he could see the surrounding countryside, the gentle slopes and the deep valleys, with the City of Jerusalem shining in the distance. Israel had been a land of peaceful living until the Romans, with their lust for power and blood, had overrun their small country, and now they ruled it with an iron hand. But the Messiah would come soon; he would have to come soon, to deliver them from all the restrictions forced upon them by Rome.

Around the dinner table that night, all talk was of the coming census and how it would affect the small town of Bethlehem. Surely this would mean the greatest number of people in Bethlehem at one time that the town had ever experienced. There were only two inns in town, and they would be stretched to the limits with guests. It was inevitable that many would have to be turned away, and the very wealthy would make sure they were the ones staying in the inns, not camping out on the hillsides with the riffraff of society that was certain to show up.

But Kezia's thoughts were centered on those who wouldn't be able to stay at the inns, which would undoubtedly mean hundreds of people. The nights were cold and damp at this time of year, making living outdoors an unpleasant challenge. What of the frail and infirmed? What of the elderly? What of young mothers with new babies? What of those young women who were with child and about to give birth? She could easily see that there would be an unprecedented number of situations descending on Bethlehem, and it would all start very, very soon. Kezia saw no particular way to prepare for such an influx of people and felt that there was little she could do at the present time, but with so very many people sure to arrive in Bethlehem during the coming days and weeks, the need to assist someone would certainly arise.

As she drifted off to sleep in the strong arms of her husband, Kezia prayed that God would use her to help those in need during the coming weeks.

Chapter Four

PREPARATIONS

The town of Bethlehem was buzzing with activity from that day forward. Many of the residents of the town were merchants who were of foreign origin, Syrian and Greek, who would have to travel countless miles to the homes of their forefathers, while others were Levites, who would have to travel the short distance to Jerusalem. No matter the distance to be traveled, not one person had one positive word to say about being dislocated and thrust into the masses forced to return to places they'd never been to before, despite their ancestors having lived there.

Outside of the town, Reuben and Thaddeus were busy in the fields with Rufus and Eleazar, gathering and tying the hay for storage for feeding the sheep during the winter months. The grass didn't grow much at this time of year, and the sheep, with the habit of grazing down to the dirt, needed a great deal of feed to get them through until the warmer weather arrived to produce green grass again. There would always be grass in the fields, but the rate of its recovery was greatly reduced by the diminished daylight hours and cool temperatures.

The work was hard, and the men sweated profusely even though the day was cool. The recent rain had done much to replenish the land, but it had prevented the hay, which had already been cut, from drying out for several more days. The twine that Eleazar had purchased from Gibea's shop was being put to good use as they gathered the hay and tied it in great bundles, and then they loaded it on a cart which was pulled by a donkey to the storage barns close to the house.

"I suppose we'll begin to see people arriving for the great census within the next day or so," Reuben stated as they took time to rest and eat the marvelous lunch that Kezia had packed in a basket.

"Several from our own town have already left for their countries," stated Thaddeus. "I know Amnon has returned to Damascus, as he is Syrian. Shimon has to travel to Israel. Mehir, the Greek merchant who makes that beautiful pottery, left for Greece days ago. He had no idea how he can arrive at his destination in time, and that bothered him a great deal when he left."

"When did you talk to him?" questioned Rufus.

"I was in town to see Deborah and Gedaliah the other day, and on my way, I passed Mehir's shop. All the activity caught my attention. They were loading their donkeys for the long journey, taking as many provisions as they could with them. His wife was quite upset about the whole thing. She's afraid her house will be occupied by someone else when they return, but Mehir took me aside and told me that he may not even return. The thought of traveling so far and then returning was more than he could take. So I won't be surprised if they stay in Greece."

"What will happen to their house?" asked Reuben. "I mean, if a home is empty and all these people will be coming here, won't someone find it and just move in?"

"Probably," agreed Thaddeus as he pulled a cluster of grapes from the basket of food. "I heard Mehir's neighbors assuring his wife that they would make certain that anyone who stayed in the house during the census did not establish permanent residency. But Mehir also told me that he was angry that he wouldn't be able to sell his house because he didn't have time to do so. Not wanting to upset his wife with the probability that they won't be back, he just let the neighbors assure her they would watch over it for them."

Eleazar, quiet until now, swallowed a chunk of bread and cheese. "What will we do if people set up tents on our fields?"

Thaddeus waited briefly before replying. "There isn't much we can do, Eleazar, except move the flock to a pasture farther from the town. As long as people are well-behaved and civil, I don't mind if they stay in our fields. I know how I would feel if I had to travel from home and didn't have a place to stay."

"Ah, gone are the days when Bethlehem's population was mostly Hebrew," mused Reuben. "The roads built by Roman slaves opened the doors for easy travel, and now our race is anything but pure. This census is just another outrageous scheme of Caesar's to bring our race together again, probably in an effort to wipe us out. Get all the Jews together and then slaughter them -- that wouldn't surprise me one bit." His bitter tone didn't go unnoticed by others in the room.

"But why can't the Romans just go to every town and count the people? Why does everyone have to go to the town of their forefathers?" asked Rufus as he bit into a pomegranate, keenly aware of the anger boiling inside his uncle.

"Only God knows," clipped Reuben. "They must like to make life miserable for everyone."

"Well," interrupted Thaddeus, "I'm grateful that we don't have to travel. It would be a hard trip, and I don't know what we would possibly do with our flocks. Thank Jehovah for that blessing."

"Gibea has to travel to Jerusalem," quietly stated Rufus, "and so must Helah and her parents. The trip, even though short, is going to be very difficult for them in their condition."

"When will they be leaving?" asked Thaddeus.

"Not for another day or so. Helah expects that they can make the trip in just one day, but she doesn't want to hurry because of the health of her parents. Thank goodness her older brother, Caleb, will be going with them also."

"And what will you do without your precious little Helah, Rufus?" taunted Eleazar. He threw his hands to his chest and tilted his head to one side, batting his eyelashes at his brother.

Not in the mood to take such bantering, Rufus threw some pomegranate seeds at his brother, hitting him in the head and leaving a splash of red. "Can't take it, can you?" teased Eleazar. "I'll bet you'll lie awake for hours just thinking about Helah when she's gone."

"And what if I do?" Rufus shouted as he stood up and headed off to work again. "What business is it of yours?" He stomped off as he grabbed a scythe, gripping it in his hand and secretly wishing he could cut off his brother's head with it.

Eleazar laughed at Rufus's back as he enjoyed the torment he was dishing out.

"You shouldn't be so hard on your brother," reprimanded Thaddeus.

"Oh, Father, it's all in fun."

"You know that, but Rufus doesn't think it's funny. It hurts him to have you tease him like that. How would you feel if it were you who liked Helah or another girl? Would you like to be teased unmercifully?"

Eleazar stopped laughing. "I suppose you're right, Father. I'll try not to tease him any more."

"Good. Now it's back to work. If we don't get this task accomplished today, we may have more rain to slow us down. Besides, I want all this hay secure in the barn before people start arriving for the census."

As they headed back to the field, Reuben asked Thaddeus, "I wonder how Benaiah is doing in the barn. That was a lot of work to leave to his responsibility."

"I know," agreed Thaddeus as he picked up the bundle of twine. "But I'm sure he'll have the barn in good order when we take this load of bundled hay back. I think he's old enough to handle the work by himself."

The rest of the afternoon passed quickly as they worked, the sun beating down on their backs. Thaddeus and Reuben felt their years as they worked, while Eleazar and Rufus didn't seem to be bothered by the heavy manual labor in the least.

Kezia could see them working in the fields from the house. Even though they weren't far away, she had packed a large lunch for the four of them so they could avoid walking back to the house. Binding the hay was work enough for one day; no sense walking half a mile if one didn't need to. Benaiah had returned to the house for his mid-day meal, thankful to be out of the darkness and dust of the barn and to have a conversation with someone. Working alone made the day seem interminably long.

Off in another direction, Kezia watched Simon as he tended the flock of sheep with his friend, Obed. Kezia knew the sheep were safe with the boys because they were close to the house and it was during the day, but the boys were so proud to be able to tend the flock by themselves.

Outside, Simon and Obed laid down on a rock and gazed up at the azure blue sky. Wisps of clouds were brush strokes on the canvas above their heads, and the sun's rays warmed their skin.

"I'm glad we don't have to travel somewhere for the census," stated Simon as he watched the birds flitting through the sun-drenched atmosphere.

"Me, too. It would be scary to leave home and travel to Damascus or wherever. I wouldn't know when I'd see you again, but I'm glad I'm not leaving."

"Do you think there'll be any boys our age coming here to Bethlehem?"

"Probably. It seems like whole families will be traveling, so lots of children should be coming to Bethlehem, too."

"I'm going to help Gedaliah take care of his stable once the people start arriving," proudly stated Simon. "I get to muck out the stalls, fill the mangers with fresh hay, empty and refill the watering troughs, and even curry some donkeys or horses if need be. And the best part about it is I'll even get paid for it."

"You will?"

"Yes. I've never had my own money before, so I don't know what I'll do with it. Maybe I'll buy Mother a present or something. I don't know; I just haven't thought about it much yet."

"I don't get to do anything exciting like that."

"Well, I could ask Gedaliah if you can help me. It might be more work than I can handle by myself once everyone arrives."

"Really? You'd do that?"

"Sure."

The boys continued looking up at the sky, watching a hawk as it glided effortlessly on the air currents. The sheep were quietly grazing or lying down, and there was hardly a noise to be heard from their location. Warming rays of the sun made them sleepy, but they didn't fall asleep. Life was good for them, and their friendship had grown since they were very small children. Even though Simon lived outside the town, he played with Obed as often as he could. Not having a brother close to his own age, Obed had become for Simon a brother. Sometimes they even fought like brothers, but they were always quick to make amends and never held a grudge against each other. They seemed to know each other's inner thoughts and feelings, and doing things together just came naturally.

"Do you like the Romans?" suddenly asked Obed.

Simon didn't hesitate to answer. "No, I don't, Obed; I hate them. Father says they are heathen, and Uncle Reuben calls them swine. If they don't like them, why should I?"

"My father feels the same way," replied Obed as he swatted a fly from his nose.

"When I grow up, I'm going to fight and kill them. My father thinks the Messiah will come soon to rid us of the Romans, and I'll be old enough to fight before too long."

Obed quietly observed his close companion. "You have a lot more courage than I do. I don't think I could ever kill someone, not even a Roman soldier. I'd rather read at the temple than be out fighting soldiers and worrying about getting killed. Ever since Rabbi Samuel taught me to read, I love that more than anything. This talk of killing Romans bothers me."

They lay in silence for a few minutes, each absorbed in his thoughts.

"What if the Messiah doesn't come while we're alive? What if he comes 100 years, or even 1000 years, from now?" questioned Obed.

"I'll still do my best to fight against the Romans any way I can when I'm grown." Simon rolled onto his side and looked at his companion. "Do you remember Heber?"

Obed nodded.

"Well, Heber's off hiding somewhere in the wilderness with a bunch of other men, and their only purpose in life is to kill Roman soldiers, or Roman citizens, whichever they happen to find. They are called Zealots. Heber can't even come back to see his brother Gibea for fear that a Roman soldier will recognize him and kill him. I heard that the Zealots have killed thousands of soldiers, and that's why his very life is in danger."

There was a rustle among the sheep, and Simon and Obed sat up. "It looks like the sheep want to move a little bit," stated Simon. "Let's go."

The boys clambered down the rock on which they had been lying and retrieved their staffs, then slowly walked behind the flock as it moved about 100 feet. They occasionally had to hook the end of the staff around the neck of a wandering lamb and pull it back into the safety of the flock. They walked in silence, each absorbed in their own thoughts of what the future could possibly hold.

From her position at the house, Kezia watched as the flock moved slightly north, and then she turned and went inside. Returning to the kitchen area, she resumed kneading the bread dough that had been resting on a slab of stone. Helah was busy cutting vegetables to go into a stew for the evening meal. Kezia flipped the dough over, punched it together with the heel of her hands, turned it and repeated the process. She found great satisfaction in making bread, something that was eaten every day by everyone. It was the mainstay of their diet.

Kezia glanced over at Helah, her quiet, efficient servant girl. The young girl's black hair was tied back in a long braid reaching almost to her waist. Her skin was perfect, and her face was oval-shaped with a classic Hebrew nose. Her lips were full, and her eyes were almost as black as her hair. Kezia could easily see why Rufus was sweet on her.

Turning her eyes back to the dough, Kezia asked, "How do you feel about having to travel to Jerusalem for the census?"

Helah didn't look up from the work at hand. "I don't want to go. I'm afraid of how it will affect Mother and Father, particularly Mother. I think she is too frail to make the journey. That's why I'm so thankful that Caleb will be going with us. He arrived from Bethany yesterday, knowing how difficult it would be for me to get both Mother and Father to Jerusalem. Of course, it would have been much easier for him to have gone to Jerusalem directly from Bethany, but he was very gracious about coming here and helping me with our parents."

"He still hasn't married?"

"No. He said he wants to be a good potter before he takes a wife so he can provide for her, and so he continues his training with Lahad."

Kezia finished punching down the dough and set it aside to rise. She wiped her hands on a towel draped through the cord on her dress, and then she laid her hand gently on Helah's arm. "God will go with you, Helah, and make a way for you and Caleb to return quickly and safely. I know he will."

Helah paused in what she was doing. "I know, Kezia, but I'm afraid for both of my parents. They are both so very sick and frail that they may not survive the journey. Besides, it will take me away from here for several days, and that makes me very sad."

"Ah," observed Kezia, "you must mean that you will miss Rufus." She smiled in spite of herself.

Helah blushed unashamedly. "He's a fine young man; you must be very proud of him."

"But how do you feel about him?" gently probed Kezia.

Helah looked up at her from under her long, lush black lashes and felt the heat rising to her face. "If you'd allow me to speak the truth, dear Kezia, my heart races every time he is with me in the same room." She lowered her face. "Even now, just talking about him makes my heart flutter."

Smiling broadly, Kezia put her arm around Helah's slim waist. "When you return, I think it would be wise for Thaddeus to speak to your parents about you and Rufus becoming betrothed. It will be better for both of you."

"Oh, please don't force Rufus to marry me!" exclaimed Helah. "He hasn't expressed his feelings for me, if he has any at all."

"My sweet girl," chided Kezia, "all one has to do is look at Rufus when he's near you! There's no doubt about his feelings for you!"

Helah lowered her head and resumed the task at hand. "Then as you wish, my lady."

Brushing thoughts of the future aside as best she could, Helah worked alongside Kezia the rest of the day, preparing the evening meal, but she found it impossible to not think of what Kezia wanted to do. She fervently prayed that Rufus wouldn't be ashamed to be betrothed to her.

Simon and Obed could still be seen on the hillside, watching the sheep. Kezia knew the sheep would soon return to the holding pen when the sun began to set. The boys would return and join in the evening meal, and Obed would go home; his mother had just given birth to a baby girl just a few days ago, and Kezia was glad to take Obed off her hands for the day so she had one less child to attend.

When the cart laden with hay and pulled by the donkey could be heard approaching the barn, Kezia and Helah readied the basins for washing hands and feet, and then they arranged the food on the table. Soon the entire family was seated, and they feasted on lamb stew, freshly-baked bread, cheese, pomegranates, grapes, and lentils with spices. The conversation was once again centered on the census and those who had to travel to distant towns. Kezia brought up the subject of Helah's pending trip.

"Helah will be returning to her home tomorrow and will be leaving the next morning for Jerusalem. We'll need to pray for her and her parents. It will be a difficult trip for them."

Rufus had his eyes fixed on Helah, seated next to his mother. His heart pined for her. The allure of her smile simply melted his heart. Thinking about her being gone for several days made his heart race and a knot form in his stomach. These feelings were so new to him; for the first time, he was more than just sentient. He fervently longed to be with Helah, to touch her skin, to feel her close to him, to feel the heat of her flesh.

Rufus realized that his mother had been speaking to him, and he hadn't heard a word. Blushing profusely, he mumbled an excuse.

"As I was saying, Rufus, please assist Helah in the kitchen this evening. I'm not feeling up to it tonight." She smiled coyly across the table at him, and at the same time, Thaddeus glared at Eleazar to keep his mouth shut, and he quickly understood the unspoken warning.

"Yes, Mother," quietly stated Rufus as he rose and followed Helah into the kitchen with the dishes they gathered from the table in their hands. Conversation among the rest of the family resumed when they left the room, and Rufus breathed a sigh of relief that no words of torment and teasing came from his brother.

Awkward silence enveloped Helah and Rufus as they began to wash the dishes. As usual, Helah had hot water ready on the fire, and it took little time to establish the routine. As Helah handed Rufus a plate, their arms touched, and Helah was filled with a burning fire. She felt her heart racing inside her chest and the color rising in her cheeks. Methodically and slowly, she washed each dish and bowl and cup, then rinsed them and handed them to Rufus, who carefully took them from her hands. Despite her best efforts, her hands shook with the transfer of each dish.

Rufus carefully took each dish from Helah, hoping he wouldn't drop one and make a complete fool of himself. He watched Helah's hands as they worked, noticing her long and slender fingers. Her arms were graceful yet well-toned from the work she did every day, and she smelled sweet like the flowers in the fields. He wondered what it would be like to actually touch something so beautiful. Trying desperately to keep his mind on the task at hand, Rufus tried to steady his breathing and his heart as he worked with Helah. Soon the last dish was washed and dried.

Unable to contain himself any longer, Rufus put down his towel and took one of Helah's wet hands in his, immediately noticing its smallness compared to his, and gently turned her toward him and ran both of his hands along her arms.

Trembling from head to toe, Helah looked at the floor where his feet were close to hers as Rufus's touch ignited the blood in her veins. She placed her hands on his waist as she melted at his touch, his hands caressing her arms, fanning the flames that burned within her. Her heart threatened to thump out of her chest, or so it seemed, and she was afraid that she would simply drop dead with anticipation and longing.

Amazed at the softness of her skin, Rufus wanted the moment to last forever. Helah was tall and slender, but not as tall as he, and her raven black hair outlined her beautiful oval face. Her dark lashes lay close to her cheeks; her eyes were hidden from him as she continued to look at the floor. But he didn't want her to look at the floor; he wanted her to look at him. Slowly, ever so slowly, he raised his hand and laid it alongside her face, cupping her chin in his palm. Rufus felt the heat from her body and heard her shallow, fast breathing, which was in tune with his own.

Helah gasped at his touch and quickly raised her eyes and looked into his, inches from her own.

Rufus slid his arm around her waist as he cradled her face, and then he slowly drew her body close to his, never averting his gaze from her dark brown eyes. He felt the trembling of her body beneath his hands and knew it wasn't from fear.

Finally speaking softly, Rufus whispered, "I'm going to miss you so very, very much, my little Helah. Do you mind if I call you 'my little Helah'?"

Still trembling beneath his gentle hands, Helah wasn't able to speak, and so she nodded her head.

"For that is what you are, Helah, mine. I want Father to speak to your parents and ask for your hand in marriage. I don't have much to offer you right now, but I'll be a good husband to you. I just can't live without you any longer. I need to be near you, not just see you from a distance. I want to spend my whole life with you." He ran his thumb alongside her face.

Helah gently leaned into the heat of his touch. She felt the breath of every word Rufus spoke as if they were caresses delivered on a warm summer breeze. But this breeze didn't cool, but instead fanned the flames of the feelings burning within her. She was captivated by Rufus's touch, certain that if he let go of her, she would simply crumple to the floor in a dead faint.

Rufus continued to run his thumb along the side of her face, and Helah closed her eyes as she enjoyed every gentle stroke. The fire of young love was much more intense than she had ever imagined it would or could be, and she never wanted it extinguished.

"Helah," whispered Rufus, "may Father speak to your parents? I don't want him to if you don't want to become betrothed to me." He found he had a lump in his throat as he waited for her answer.

Still unable to speak, Helah again nodded in agreement as she gazed longingly at him with her dark, sparkling eyes. Rufus felt his heart leap when he realized that she had agreed, and he held her face so close to his he could feel the heat. "As soon as you return, Father will do just that, my little Helah. I don't want to waste any time, for I love you."

Loud noises emanating from the eating room suddenly reached them, causing them to instantly pull apart. Helah quickly immersed her hands in the basin of water and searched for another dish, only to realize that they were all done. Rufus watched her scramble for something to do, and laughed softly at her frustration. Hoping beyond hope that no one would enter the kitchen until she had regained her composure, Helah quickly grabbed the basin to carry it outside and empty its contents.

Casting a glance at Rufus, she noticed a glow about him that hadn't been there before. She broke into a broad grin as they silently agreed to keep their secret, and Helah felt the color creeping up from her ears and across her face.

Simon suddenly burst into the room, almost knocking Rufus over.

"Rufus!" he shouted. "Obed and I are going to the barn; do you want to jump from the loft into all the hay like we used to? It's all fresh and soft, just waiting to be jumped on!"

With his eyes still on Helah as she carried the basin out the door, Rufus replied, "No, Simon, you'll have to jump with Obed. I have other things on my mind."

* * * * * * *

Back in Bethlehem at the inn, Gedaliah and Deborah had just rented their last room for the night. As they headed to their own living quarters above the inn, Gedaliah drew Deborah to him, holding her close.

"Do you know how much I love you?" he asked softly in the muted light from the oil lamps.

Deborah smiled up at him, feeling the warmth and closeness of his body. "Yes, I believe I do. And don't ever stop."

As Gedaliah began walking with his arm around her waist, he replied, "Roman soldiers threatening my life couldn't make me stop loving you. Not even a census ordered by the' Divine Emperor of Rome' could make me stop loving you! Wild stampeding camels couldn't make me stop loving you! A flock of wild vultures pecking at my head couldn't make me stop loving you!" Each phrase of his undying devotion became louder, and Deborah couldn't help but laugh. Finally, she reached up and put her hand over his mouth and held it there as they climbed the stairs, Gedaliah's muted words combining with Deborah's suppressed giggles.

After seeing that his mother was settled in, Gedaliah entered their bedchamber. The oil lamps were turned down low, and Deborah was already under the silky cover that had been given to them as a gift at their wedding. Slowly Gedaliah loosened the belt of his tunic and let it drop to the floor. Gedaliah approached his wife in only his loincloth. He would never adjust to having such a beautiful wife, and her looks weren't all that was beautiful about her – she was also a beautiful person inside. Her hair spread across the pillow, creating a sea of dark waves on which rested her head. One arm was laid above her head as it rested on the sea of waves created by her hair.

Gedaliah slid under the covers beside her and drew her yielding body to himself. He found her neck and lost himself in the scent of her as Deborah's arms wrapped around his body, eagerly drawing him ever closer. Their kisses were full and long, and they enjoyed the pleasures granted them by God as they came together.

Later, as they lay resting in each other's arms, Deborah whispered softly to him as she stroked his hairy chest. He gently placed his hand on her stomach, which was just beginning to show a slight bulge because of the new life already growing within her, and lovingly embraced his wife as they drifted off to sleep.

Chapter Five

STRANGERS IN BETHLEHEM

"Thank you, Selma," Deborah said gratefully as they finished spreading the new coverlets on the beds. "Without you and your mother helping with the sewing, these wouldn't have been finished in time for the influx of guests for the census."

Selma ran her hands over the coverlet, smoothing it out even more. "That dear husband of yours certainly picked beautiful material for these; they should last for years."

"I hope so; I don't want to have to make these again for a very long time." Wiping the sweat from her brow, Deborah sighed heavily. "Let's go check with Gedaliah."

As they headed back to the entryway, they heard Gedaliah speaking with a firm but controlled voice.

"I can only allow you to stay in the rooms for an extended period of time at a higher rate. Many people will need shelter during the next weeks, and if you stay here, you will have to pay the premium rate. I'll have to turn away many guests because every room will be occupied. Consider yourselves fortunate that you've arrived early."

"Well," stated one portly man as he dropped his pouch down on the table, "I certainly don't want to be left out in the cold or in the fields with the rats of society, so I don't mind paying the premium rate. At least we'll have a solid roof over our heads."

Another well-dressed man standing by his side spoke up. "I don't mind paying the premium price, either. I much prefer it to spending days in a tent on the hillsides."

"Well, then, how long do you plan to stay?" asked Gedaliah.

The two men looked at each other, and then the portly one replied, "At least five days. Of course, our wives are with us. Thankfully, the children are grown and must get here by themselves. I don't know what we'd do if we had our five children in tow."

"So I'll book you for five days," Gedaliah stated as he wrote on a tablet, "and at two denarius a day, the total for each of you is ten denarius. Payment must be made in advance."

"We have a boy holding our donkeys outside. I certainly hope you have a stable where they can be kept."

"I do. There is a stable out back, and my wife's young brother will be there shortly to tend your animals."

"And the fee?"

"Four farthings each for the donkeys, and whatever you wish to give the young lad for his work. He will feed and water them every day, even brush them down if you'd like."

"That sounds reasonable enough," agreed the portly man.

"I'll have Simon take your donkeys around back."

As the men opened their money pouches to pay, Deborah approached their two wives, who had been standing quietly near the doorway, and introduced herself. "Please let me know if you need anything during your stay, or Selma, also," she added as she indicated Selma by a wave of her hand.

"Thank you for your kindness," stated one woman, obviously tired and dirty from the long trip. "We've traveled all the way from Sepphoris, and we're utterly exhausted. May God curse Caesar for burdening us with this census!" The other woman agreed with her as she mopped her brow with a delicate piece of fabric. "You don't happen to have public baths in this tiny town, do you?"

Deborah smiled softly and responded, "No, we don't. But there is a large jug of water and basin in your rooms for freshening up. If you'd like, I could warm some water for you."

"Thank you, I'd like that very much." Deborah nodded to Selma, who scurried off to do their bidding.

The two men were completing their business with Gedaliah. "Thank you for your kindness and reasonable prices," stated the portly gentleman. "The only other inn in town had prices that were absolutely outrageous. It's bad enough that we had to travel here just to be counted and taxed by these heathen Romans, but to be robbed by a fellow Hebrew is unconscionable." He secured his pouch in his money belt.

Gedaliah led them to their rooms, and when he returned, Deborah was welcoming more guests.

"Where do we go to be registered and counted?" asked one man as he elbowed his way between the people in the room, which was becoming quite crowded. "We've been traveling for three days and wish to get this over with as soon as possible so we can return home and get on with our lives."

"I believe the Romans have established a tented area on the south side of the town. I hear that they aren't beginning to take names until tomorrow; at least, that's the word around town. I could be wrong."

"Thank you for the information. I'll find a place to erect my tent for the night; I can't afford to stay here or anywhere else. I have four small children and my wife. We will stay somewhere outside the town and register tomorrow, hopefully. Then we can go home and resume our lives. Leave it to Caesar to find another way to make our lives miserable."

Leaving through the door, he left it slightly ajar, and the noise from the street flooded in. Even as they greeted people and took payment, Deborah and Gedaliah could see that the street was crammed with people – some walking, some riding donkeys, some leading donkeys, and all of them very talkative and frustrated. The din was incredible. The mud of several days earlier had totally disappeared, and the many feet stirred up the dry, compacted soil, making it rise on the breeze in choking clouds. The masses pushed and shoved their way to wherever they were going, often cursing anyone who was in their way. Worshippers of Jehovah were debasing themselves as they let the situation get the best of them. Donkeys brayed at the commotion and often balked at moving against the pressing tide.

"It's hard for me to believe this many people have to come to Bethlehem," observed Gedaliah as he returned from taking more guests to their rooms. "All of our rooms are already booked, and not one of them will be available tomorrow either. Guests won't leave until they're through with this insane census. This is really turning into a big mess."

"Did you see that old man over there?" asked Deborah as she pointed to a white-haired, elderly man in the crowd. "He almost fell down just a moment ago; he doesn't seem to have the strength to walk against all these people."

They watched as the old man fought to stay on his feet as he was pushed along by the crowd. Soon he was out of their sight, and they could only hope that he was able to make it to his destination without injury.

"We need to get Simon here as soon as possible," Gedaliah stated as he closed the door against the commotion and confusion in the street, noting the young village boy still patiently holding the donkeys. "That boy can't hold those donkeys forever."

"I'll go to Mother's and bring him back with me," offered Deborah. "I'll use the back way by the stable; it isn't as crowded out there."

Gedaliah gently grabbed her around the waist and pressed his hand on her stomach. "Yes, you have to be very careful about falling or being pushed down now. We don't want anything to happen to the little one within you," he said as he gently brushed his lips against hers.

"I'll be very careful, don't worry," Deborah whispered with a smile as she placed her hand over his. "I'll not let anything happen to our baby."

Deborah quickly left by the back door, and Gedaliah returned to the front to watch the weary travelers. So many people, of all ages and sizes, were being jostled in the narrow streets that it made his head spin. Never had he seen so many people in Bethlehem at one time, and he probably would never see such crowds again. People continually came up to him and asked him if he had any available rooms, but each time, he had to turn them away.

As Deborah walked toward her childhood home on the outskirts of town, she heard the din from all the travelers fade away, and she was grateful that her parents' house wasn't in town, but outside where it was more peaceful. As she climbed the hillside, she saw the main road into Bethlehem, and it was congested with travelers. Roman soldiers were everywhere. Turning to look back, Deborah saw the group of tents that the soldiers had erected on the south side of town, preparing for the census. People were milling about in large groups, but it was apparent that no registering would take place until the next day. Numerous families had already established temporary shelters on the hillsides, and children were frolicking in the sunshine, still full of energy despite a long journey for many of them. The smoke from the many fires outside the tents drifted into the sky, swept along by the gentle breeze. She observed mothers preparing meals over those fires, doing their best to deal with the difficult circumstances forced upon them by Rome. But what did it matter to Caesar, who sat in his royal palaces in a place far removed from Bethlehem and Judea, if he imposed hardships on his subjects? He probably didn't even consider the difficulties he would bring upon others when he made his hideous decree.

Deborah hiked up her dress as she traversed the rough terrain, thankful that she didn't need to go to another town to be counted. She couldn't imagine packing up and traveling to some distant town with Gedaliah, especially now that she was pregnant. Her heart went out to all that were camped on the hillsides.

As she approached the house in which she was raised, Simon, who was out chasing the chickens, saw her. "Deborah!" he shouted in greeting as he ran to her and threw his arms around her waist.

"Oh, Simon, you're getting so tall!" She rubbed her hands through his unkempt hair. "Where's Mother? It's time for you to come and stay with us and take care of the stable. People are arriving in droves."

"I know; I can see them from up here. I was hoping you'd come for me soon." Simon danced circles around her as they went into the house.

"Mother!" he shouted as they entered. "Deborah's here! They need me down at the inn now!"

Kezia entered the main hall from her bedchamber where she had been putting away clean clothes. Going to Deborah, they embraced and kissed. "So, how is the mother-to-be doing?"

"I'm feeling fine, Mother. That little sickness I had has passed, and I'm just fine now."

"So it's time for Simon to help? He's been badgering me for days to let him go down, but I wouldn't until you came for him. It's easy to see that the town is getting very crowded."

"True. The people started arriving in hordes today. Our inn is full, and I suspect the other is as well. Of course, we've heard that Azor has been setting exorbitant prices, and we didn't, so our inn was probably booked up before his. We won't have any empty rooms for several days, and there are animals that Simon must attend to in the stable."

"Do I get to sleep in the stable?" eagerly questioned Simon.

"Do you want to?"

"Oh, yes, I think that would be wonderful! I love sleeping in hay, and I'll bet the donkeys are nice to sleep with, too."

Kezia and Deborah looked at each other skeptically.

"Alright," agreed Kezia. "Let's go get those things that we rolled up for you. It's too bad your father and the others are so far away from the house right now; they won't be able to say goodbye to you."

Simon took the roll from his mother's arms. "I'm only going into Bethlehem, Mother, not all the way to Jerusalem, and I'll be with Deborah and Gedaliah."

"We'll make sure he's safe and warm, Mother, and we'll certainly feed him well. Don't worry."

After goodbyes were said, Deborah walked back to the inn while Simon bounced his way there.

"Wow!" he exclaimed as they came into full view of the town. "Look at all the people! Where did they all come from?"

Deborah laughed as she gingerly picked her way down the rocky slope. "From everywhere, Simon, and just think, they're all from King David's line, just as we are. In some distant way, all of these people are related to us. It's hard to imagine, isn't it."

They stopped and looked in the stable when they arrived at the inn and found that it contained three donkeys and several sheep and two cows. Upon further inquiring of Gedaliah about all the animals, he said that several travelers didn't want to lose their animals, especially the cows, and had brought them with them in order to keep them safe until they were ready to return home.

"So I have donkeys, sheep and cows to take care of!" exuberantly exclaimed Simon. "This will be so much fun!"

"You won't think it's much fun after working all day cleaning up after them," reminded Gedaliah. "You might want to see if Obed wants to help you."

"I'm sure he will, because we talked about me taking care of the stable animals just the other day. Besides, he's my best friend, and I like having him around."

Gedaliah addressed his wife. "While you were gone, I put a sign on the door, telling people that we have no more rooms. Of course, most of the people can't read, but it's highly unlikely that those people could even afford a room anyway, but the sign being there should be a clue that the inn is full. We shouldn't have to keep telling people that we have no more rooms from now on."

"That's a good idea. I was wondering if we were going to get any sleep tonight with people constantly pounding on the door and inquiring about rooms."

Gedaliah stretched out his arm to Deborah and Simon and directed the way to the stairs. "Come, let's

63

go upstairs and see how Mother is doing. She was working on mending a garment of mine earlier today. She's probably finished by now."

Eglah had finished the garment and was busily working in the kitchen, one of her favorite places, preparing the evening meal. "Oh, Mother," exclaimed Deborah, "you should have allowed me to cook tonight." Deborah went over and started helping her chop some vegetables.

"What? After all the work you've done today and all you're going to be doing for the next few weeks? I know how difficult it is to do everything, especially when expecting a child, so let me cook until this registration madness is over."

"Simon will be joining us until then also," Gedaliah informed his mother.

"I get to sleep in the stable!"

"But not tonight," added Deborah.

"Aw, Deborah, why not tonight?"

"Because it's almost dark, and there's no bed for you out there. We'll get you set up tomorrow morning."

"But I want to sleep there tonight!"

"Don't argue with your sister," interjected Eglah. "She's right about this. You'll be glad to sleep in your own bed by the time everyone returns to their homes. You may think sleeping in the stable is fun now, but you'll change your mind before long."

As evening fell, the masses that had clogged the streets of Bethlehem settled into the inns, onto the hillsides in their tents, or into the homes of friends or relatives. The noise and confusion of the day faded into quiet and rest as people fed their children, who then drifted off to sleep on the hard ground inside their tents. Babies cried and mothers tried to console them. Occasionally, a conversation would become loud and volatile as the displaced people tried to settle their differences in their makeshift homes. The light in the sky yielded to darkness as the sun dipped below the horizon, and stars speckled the heavens above. Night enveloped the town and the surrounding hillsides like a dark cloak, and the streets of Bethlehem became quiet.

But there then appeared two lone figures, one riding a small donkey, weary and worn. They passed by some people on the outskirts of town and inquired where they could find an inn.

"The inns are full, as I understand it," was the gruff, impatient reply, "but I guess it wouldn't hurt for you to try the one down the street."

The man leading the donkey graciously offered his thanks, and he slowly turned his exhausted little animal and headed down the street. The other figure, a woman riding the donkey, cried out.

"We're almost there, Mary," he quickly assured her as he patted her shoulder. "Please try to hold on just a little longer. The donkey is exhausted and can't travel quickly. Please hold on just a little longer."

The woman laid her hand across her abdomen. It was clearly evident that she was heavy with child.

"I'm trying, Joseph, I'm really trying."

They passed two more people in the darkness of the streets as they approached the inn. To Joseph's dismay, there was a sign posted on the door, stating that all the rooms were occupied.

"It's full, isn't it?" Mary asked as a tear trickled down her cheek.

Disregarding the sign, Joseph climbed onto the step and pounded on the door.

"Joseph, it will do no good; the inn is full."

"I realize that, but maybe they can tell us where to stay." He raised his strong arm and pounded again on the door, determined to awaken whoever was on the inside. He had to get Mary off the donkey and into a safe place.

Gedaliah heard the pounding from upstairs as he and Deborah were relaxing with Eglah and Simon before retiring for the night. He shook his head in disbelief.

"Wouldn't you know it? At this hour of the night, we get someone who can't read or figure out that we have no more room."

"Aren't you going to answer it?" questioned Deborah.

"No, they'll leave soon enough once they realize the place is full."

The pounding came again, harder and more earnest this time. Deborah and Gedaliah looked at each other as they waited for the incessant pounding to cease. After another short spell of quiet, the pounding knock came a third time, more intense and demanding.

"I think you should answer it," advised Deborah. "Someone may need help."

Gedaliah reluctantly rose to his feet and hurried into the hall and down the stairs. Several guests had stuck their heads out of their rooms, wondering what all the commotion was about. Gedaliah quickly indicated to them that he was taking care of it and they had nothing to be concerned about.

When he reached the door, Gedaliah threw it open, ready to holler at whoever it was that was so insistent, but God stayed his tongue when he saw who stood outside his entrance. The man was clearly anxious and was holding the tether of a donkey, on which sat a woman. Even in the darkness, Gedaliah saw that she was heavy with child. A painful, subdued moan reached his ears as the woman laid her hands across her swollen belly and rested her chin on her chest.

The man broke the awkward silence. "Please, sir, my wife is in labor. Do you have a room, any room at all?"

"I'm so sorry," stuttered Gedaliah as all anger drained from his bones, "but all of my rooms are full, every last one of them. I don't have any idea where you can find lodging."

"Is there another inn in town?" questioned Joseph as he gazed pensively at his wife and offered a comforting hand on her shoulder.

"Yes. I will take you there if you like," offered Gedaliah as he stepped down from the door stoop. "But I'm sure they will be just as full as I am. But wait, I have a better idea," he said as his sandals touched the street. "I have a stable behind the inn. It's clean, and there aren't too many animals in there. There's plenty of fresh hay also. It would be much more comfortable in there than sleeping outside on the ground, which is where I'm sure you'll end up."

Joseph looked at Mary, who eagerly nodded her head in agreement. Her eyes were wide with pain and fear as she clutched her abdomen again. "Anything, Joseph, anything. Please hurry!"

"Follow me." Gedaliah quickly led them around the back of the inn and into the stable, warm from the heat of the animals. "Wait here," he said, "and I'll get an oil lamp."

Joseph gently helped Mary slide off the small donkey, and he held her in his arms. She leaned heavily into him as another contraction hit and buried her head in his chest as she moaned. Gedaliah soon returned with the oil lamp, which he set on a barrel next to the doorway.

"Thank you," whispered Joseph. "I think we'll be fine now."

Confused and concerned, Gedaliah nodded quickly and left the stable. Returning to his living quarters, Deborah was instantly aware that he was anxious about something, before he had the chance to speak.

"What is it? Who was at the door?"

"A man and his wife, who is obviously in labor. I put them up in the stable; that was the best I could do." Gedaliah ran his hands through his hair as he paced back and forth across the room.

"She's in labor?" asked Eglah

"Oh, yes, no doubt about it."

"She'll need help," Eglah exclaimed. "But my legs won't hold up long enough to get me to the stable."

Deborah grabbed Simon's shoulders. "Run and get Mother, Simon. Tell her that she's needed here right away!"

"Don't run too fast in the dark," advised Gedaliah as Simon raced down the stairs. "You don't want to fall and hurt yourself!"

Simon ran out the back door and past the stable, where he could see the faint light from the oil lamp and two shadowy figures moving about.

"Mother Eglah," worriedly stated Deborah, "what can I do? I've never attended a birth before."

"Well, it won't be long before you attend your own, so you might as well see your first tonight. Take as many clean cloths as you can to her, and also take a jug of water and a large basin. Your mother will help you when she arrives."

They set about collecting all the clean clothes they could find in their living quarters, tearing some of the larger ones into small strips. Deborah gathered them in her arms and retraced Gedaliah's steps to the stable, taking another oil lamp with her to light her way. Gedaliah followed her carrying a jug of fresh water and a basin. Her heart was racing with the fear of the unknown, fear that she wouldn't be any help at all to the young woman in labor. She knew nothing! She'd been just a young girl when Simon had been born and wasn't allowed to watch the birth. She'd

68

been exposed to a lot of talk, but she was far from able to deliver a child without assistance. Frantically, she offered up a prayer for God to hasten her mother's arrival.

When she entered the stable, Deborah saw the woman lying down on a pile of hay, her husband kneeling by her side. Her abdomen was swollen with child, and her brow was covered with perspiration. Slowly approaching the couple, she quietly said, "My name is Deborah, and this is my husband, Gedaliah. We will help you any way we can."

She hung the oil lamp from a hook on a beam of the stable and then set the cloths in the basin after Gedaliah set it on the floor. He looked furtively at his wife, who nodded and smiled, and Gedaliah retreated and was swallowed up by the darkness.

"My brother has gone to fetch my mother," stated Deborah as she approached the woman. "She'll know what to do. I've not yet attended a birth, although I'm expecting my first child in about six months."

The woman looked up at Deborah and said through gritted teeth, "Thank you so much." Deborah's heart lurched when she saw the woman's eyes, for they revealed both pain and fear, and the seeing set Deborah's heart pounding. Swallowing hard, Deborah once again prayed for her mother's quick appearance.

Joseph pulled the hood of his wife's cloak back from her face, and for the first time, Deborah saw that this was not just a woman, but a very young woman, probably close to her own age. What a horrid place and time to have your first child, thought Deborah – far away from home and family and in a stable full of animals with no one present other than her husband and someone she didn't even know.

"My name is Joseph," said the man as he introduced himself, "and this is my wife, Mary. We've traveled from Nazareth for the census, and the timing couldn't have been worse. My main concern was that we wouldn't arrive in Bethlehem in time and Mary would give birth alongside the road."

"Well, you've made it, so we'll do everything we can to help," Deborah said as she poured water into the basin, moistened a cloth and placed it on Mary's forehead.   Mary whispered, "I'm thirsty."

Joseph quickly reached into a nearby pack and pulled out a flask of water and offered it to her. He loosened her clothing and tried to make her more comfortable.

Outside the town, Simon dashed down one hillside and up another to his home. He had traversed this path numerous times and knew it by heart, so he wasn't going to worry about falling. He saw the faint light escaping from the windows of his home, and he knew his mother and father would be gathered in the eating room, reclining on the pillows and discussing things. Because of the crowds for the census, Reuben, Rufus, Eleazar and Benaiah had taken the sheep to a hillside for grazing and wouldn't return until the morrow.

He burst through the door and sent it slamming against the wall. "Mother! Father!" he called at the top of his lungs. "The inn is full and a woman and her husband came and Gedaliah took them to the stable and the woman is going to have a baby right away! You must hurry, Mother! Deborah needs your help!"

"Whoa!" shouted Thaddeus as he hurried into the main hall and practically bumped into Simon as Kezia followed him. "Slow down, Simon."

"You said a woman is going to have a baby?" questioned Kezia as she knelt down before Simon.

"Yes! She's in the stable, right now, and Deborah sent me to get you so you can help her."

Kezia sprang into action. She picked up her scissors and some twine from her work basket, then grabbed her tunic and wrapped it around herself. "I don't know when I'll be back, Thaddeus. This could be a long night if it's her first child. Only time will tell."

Kezia followed Simon as quickly as she could through the blackness of night. They were soon at the stable, where they found the young woman and her husband, as well as a very anxious Deborah. Kezia immediately saw that the young woman's labor was advanced. Simon disappeared into the shadows next to the stall containing the sheep, hoping no one would discover him. His heart was still racing from the run up and down the hills, and he wasn't about to leave now and miss all the excitement.

"How long has she been like this?" Kezia asked Joseph.

"Since mid afternoon," he replied as he wiped his wife's brow again.

"I must see if the child has entered the birth canal and if it's in the right position," explained Kezia. "This will be a little uncomfortable, uh ...."

"Mary, her name is Mary," whispered Deborah as she knelt close to her mother.

". . .Mary, but it will be for just a moment." Kezia lifted Mary's garments and made her examination. As she washed her hands, she stated, "The baby is ready to come in a very short time, Mary, and things look good. Just keep doing what you're doing, and nature and God will do the rest."

Joseph sat at Mary's head, cradling her gently as the contractions came and went, each stronger than the last. Mary often moaned in pain and anguish as the birthing process advanced, and Deborah stood and watched in awe. This miracle called birth would happen when her child was born. She watched Joseph as Mary labored to bring his child into the world, and she saw love and tenderness in his gaze.

Mary cried out, and Kezia examined her again. "It's time," she said matter-of-factly. Kezia had attended many births of other babies in the town, besides having given birth four times herself; she lifted Mary's dress and helped her rise onto her feet in a squatting position. She quickly reached into the basin and retrieved a large, thick cloth and placed it under Mary.

"Hold onto her arms, Joseph," directed Kezia. "That will be easier for her." Joseph did as he was told, and after one big push, Kezia felt a head of hair, which was soon followed by a slippery, tiny body. Kezia caught the child as it entered the world and pulled it out from under Mary. Grabbing her scissors, she cut the umbilical cord and then laid the new infant on Mary's chest as she settled back on the hay. It was a boy, and he immediately started to make his presence known in the world. His cry was plaintive, lusty and strong, and Mary gently reached down and touched him. Her eyes were filled with wonder and joy, and Joseph was also caught up in the moment, marveling at the tiny hands and feet of their child, their newborn son.

"He's absolutely gorgeous," glowed Mary.

"That he is," heartily agreed Kezia. "While you marvel at the birth of your son, you will have a few more contractions, and the afterbirth will be discharged. Then we can clean you up and get the two of you settled down for the night."

Suddenly, Kezia felt an awesome Presence in the stable, and she quickly turned, fully expecting to see someone, but no one was there. Glancing at Deborah, their eyes met, and she knew Deborah sensed the same Presence. A strange, wonderful, inexplicable feeling of peace settled upon her, and Kezia knew that God was in the stable. What was so special about this child that God was present at his birth? She had attended many births and had never felt anything like this when a child was born, but this one, for some unknown reason, was different.

Kezia's heart raced as she softly whispered so only Deborah could hear her, "God is here." Deborah's eyes turned to the rafters above their heads as she wondered at the Presence that was saturating the small stable. She was both comforted and shaken.

Quickly returning to the task at hand, Kezia motioned for Deborah to come to her side. "Take this cloth and clean the infant. Don't mind if he cries; crying is good for him. Then help Mary wrap him in these swaddling clothes."

Deborah did as instructed, wiping the marks of birth from the tiny child. He was perfect, a miniature human, yet he was so very helpless and completely dependent. The more he cried with the brisk rubbing, the redder he became, and she tried to shush his crying with gentle words and coos. Deborah soon had the child wrapped and back into his mother's gentle arms.

Simon watched from the shadows as he marveled at what he had seen. Was that how he came into the world? He was glad he didn't remember any of it. He didn't think it was a very pretty or dignified process, but it was certainly amazing.

Oddly, the animals endured the disruption without any concern. The cows continued to chew their cud, and the sheep were curled up into mounds of wool, fast asleep. The donkeys were standing, asleep on their feet.

Deborah and Kezia took care of everything as the afterbirth was passed, and then made a fresh bed of hay for Mary on which to sleep. Kezia showed Mary how to hold the baby so it could nurse, and the little child eagerly suckled, taking his first nourishment as he lay cradled in his mother's arms.

"What will be the child's name?" asked Kezia as she gathered up the soiled cloths and put them in the basin.

Mary and Joseph exchanged tender glances. "His name will be Jesus," Joseph replied quietly.

"That's a good name," Kezia said. "Now, Mary, try to get some sleep. Jesus will wake often for feeding, but you can sleep when he sleeps. And Joseph, I'm sure you could use a good rest yourself. All is well now."

"Thank you for all you've done," Joseph said, and Mary sleepily nodded her agreement.

"I was glad to be of help," Kezia stated as she stood up with the basin in her hands. "Just the other night, I was wondering how I could help someone in need during this time of the census. You are the first that God has given me to help. I'm sure there will be more."

Simon shifted his weight, and as he leaned over the gate to get a better look at the baby in Mary's arms, it flew open, and Simon tumbled into the hay on the stable floor.

"Simon! What are you doing here?" harshly questioned Kezia. "I thought you were back in the inn."

Simon stood up and dusted the dirt and hay from his tunic. "I'm sorry; I was just too excited to leave."

Kezia sighed heavily. "No matter, Simon, I guess no harm was done." She stretched her arm out to him. "Please put some fresh hay in the manger so Mary can lay Baby Jesus in it for the night. He will be comfortable there."

Simon ran and emptied the remaining hay from the manger, and then went to the fresh bundle of hay, tore a chunk from it, fluffed it and spread it in the manger. He smiled warmly at Mary, and her kind smile in return warmed his heart. He paused and gazed into her eyes and then lowered his gaze to look down at the baby, keenly aware of the strange aura that permeated the stable.

Kezia touched his shoulder and gently turned him toward the door as she handed the basin of soiled clothes to Deborah. Together they left the stable and entered the inn, where they told Eglah and Gedaliah the wondrous story of the new baby in the stable.

Eventually, Kezia returned home, careful to watch her footing on the way up the rocky hillside. Even though she was exhausted, she was glad that she'd been able to help a young woman in need.

She roused Thaddeus as she climbed into bed, and he was eager to hear the entire story as they lay in bed together. As Kezia came to the end of the story, she said, "But this was no ordinary birth, Thaddeus. For some strange reason, I had a strong feeling that God was present. Deborah felt it, too. And Mary – I can't begin to describe what showed in her face, even in the way she smiled. She is so young, Thaddeus, probably the same age as Helah or Deborah, and Joseph is several years older. But he loves her dearly; I could see it in his eyes." She turned to look at Thaddeus in the dim light. "This is no ordinary couple, and I believe this is no ordinary baby. I can't tell you why I feel that way; I just do."

Kezia stared at the ceiling over her head as she tried to go to sleep, but to no avail. She couldn't forget the Presence she felt in the stable; it wasn't here with her now, but it had definitely been present in the stable, so much so that Kezia felt she could touch it if she could see it. Amazed and in awe, Kezia wondered at it all as she finally drifted off to sleep, unaware that Reuben and the others in the field with the sheep were being greeted by heavenly messengers on a hillside outside Bethlehem.

Kezia was right. It was no ordinary birth.

Chapter Six

ANGELIC VISIT

On a hillside outside Bethlehem, Reuben, Eleazar, Rufus and Benaiah were huddled around a small fire to ward off the chill of the night. Seeing all the hordes of people encamped on the hillsides surrounding Bethlehem, they had opted to take the flock a short distance and spend the night there. The fields close to the house had been heavily grazed in the last few days as they had bound and stored the hay for the coming months, and the sheep needed green grass. So, coupled with the invasion of innumerable people, they had traversed the hills and gone about a mile and a half from Bethlehem.

"It seems very quiet, very peaceful out here tonight, moreso than usual," observed Eleazar. "Of course, with all the people arriving in Bethlehem, I feel as if I've been overrun. There doesn't seem to be any room to breathe."

"I agree," quietly replied Rufus. "I was beginning to feel smothered."

Reuben tossed another log onto the fire. "More people have arrived than I imagined, but so much for Roman ingenuity. They probably don't have any idea how many people would be traveling for this cursed census. The Roman army itself will probably be overrun by the masses."

"Father, just think of all the people that are descendants of David," interposed Benaiah. "Thousands and thousands of people have been born through the centuries, and if they are in the Roman Empire, they must travel here, to Bethlehem."

"But how will the Romans know if everyone obeys Herod's order?" asked Rufus.

"They won't," retorted Reuben. "They just believe that the threat of death will force everyone to do their bidding."

The group was quiet around the fire, only the occasional baaing of a sheep disrupting the silence. The air was chilly, biting through their warm cloaks. Benaiah tucked his feet underneath his cloak in an attempt to warm them.

Reuben once again found himself gazing up at the stars in the velvet canopy above. "It seems as if the sky is more brilliant tonight than I have ever seen it," he observed as the others followed his gaze. "Lord Most High, creator of the heavens – who is man that Thou art mindful of him."

Silence wrapped around them closer than their cloaks as the heavens glittered and sparkled above them. The stars looked like diamonds on black velvet, the moon like a glowing ember of a fading fire. Trees were dark shadows, casting even darker shadows underneath their branches in the faint light of the moon. The sheep appeared as gray rocks in the opaque light, mounded together in groups of five or more for warmth and safety. The only significant source of light came from the fire, and it cast long shadows that reached into the darkness like gnarled fingers. The fire crackled and hissed as it burned, and sparks danced upward until they disintegrated into ash and descended unseen to the ground.

Without warning, this dark and obscure corner of the world was suddenly, unexpectedly ablaze with vibrant light so intense that the fire cast a shadow in its presence. The surrounding hillsides were greener than during the daylight hours, and the shadows from the trees and rocks were dark as night in comparison to the brilliant light. Stunned and terrified, the shepherds huddled together and raised their arms over their heads in an effort to protect themselves from the unknown source of unspeakably bright light, but oddly enough, the sheep weren't disturbed by the light in the least and remained huddled and content.

"Father!" loudly cried Benaiah, "what is it?"

Reuben huddled with the others, fear galloping through his body as he quaked from head to toe. He felt utterly helpless as he cowered on the ground with his family members.

"Lord God save us!" he cried as he reached his arms around his family as his stomach threatened to forcibly empty its contents.

Suddenly, out of the midst of the glorious light came a voice, pure and deep, cascading through the heavens like a powerful waterfall.

"Don't be afraid," said the voice from heaven.

Reuben relaxed his hold on the others as the fear started to drain from his quaking body. Slowly, arms shielding his eyes from the penetrating light, he and the others hesitantly gazed heavenward. Immediately they saw the one who had spoken, and the sight made them gasp in amazement and fall to their knees. A heavenly being was the center of the light, and he was suspended above the hillside, gazing down at them with eyes that sparkled and danced. His countenance was like daylight multiplied many times over. He continued to speak, his voice like a gentle rain on thirsty ground.

'Don't be afraid, for I have come to bring you tidings of great joy, which will be to all people. Tonight, in the City of David, a child is born to you, a Savior, who is Christ the Lord. And this will be a sign that you have found him. He will be wrapped in swaddling clothes and will be lying in a manger."

Suddenly, a multitude of angels joined the one who had made the announcement, and they began to praise God, their voices washing over the shepherds and warming their hearts. A crescendo of joyous sound that was beautiful beyond belief reverberated through the hills.

As the shepherds watched in holy wonder, the angels shouted praises in unison, "Glory to God in the highest and on earth, let there be peace and good will toward all men!" The heavens resounded with their praises, and yet the sheep still continued to sleep, oblivious to the heavenly display above them.

Just as suddenly as they had appeared, the angels disappeared into the heavens, their glorious light vaporized, the darkness once again cloaked the sky, and the stars glistened like diamonds on black velvet. Once more, the trees were dark shadows and the fire had its own light. It was as if nothing had happened at all. The silence left by the vanished angels was deafening.

Reuben simply stated softly, "They're gone."

All of them gazed heavenward, each longing for the messengers of God to return, but only a holy, awestruck silence remained.

Slowly rising from his knees, Reuben stared into the sky as his heart hammered wildly in his chest. He finally broke the silence as his voice cracked with emotion. "The long-awaited Messiah has come -- our Savior, who will free us from the iron grip of Rome."

"The angel said he was born in Bethlehem tonight," whispered Rufus as he stared into the sky. "How can we find a newborn baby tonight? There are hundreds of people in Bethlehem and camped out on the hills. How will we know where to look?"

Reuben continued to gaze upward, his mind racing as he tried to process what had just occurred. It had been hundreds of years since God had spoken to his people, Israel. Could it be that the long silence was finally over? He turned and faced the others.

"The angel said that we would find the baby lying in a manger. Mangers are found in stables, and stables are found behind inns." He looked intently at the others, whose faces still reflected the glory of the angelic visit.

"Maybe it's Gedaliah's stable!" exclaimed Eleazar excitedly. "Maybe they put someone up in the stable because the inn is full! That sounds like something Gedaliah and Deborah would do; they would never turn away someone, especially a woman about to have a baby!"

Reuben stood and retrieved his staff, and then turned to the others. "Let's go into Bethlehem and see if we can find the baby, just as God has told us."

"But what about the sheep? Who will watch over our sheep?" Benaiah asked with a worried frown.

Reuben answered, "Surely He who has told us this wonderful news will watch over our sheep for us and see that no harm comes to them." He motioned to the others. "Come, let's hurry."

The others wasted no time as they followed Reuben to Bethlehem. The moon provided just enough light to ease their way, and their glad and expectant hearts carried them speedily to their destination.

Reuben's heart overflowed with unspeakable joy as questions raced through his mind. Tears flowed down his cheeks as he hurried over the rocks and through the trees, eager to reach the stable. If it wasn't Gedaliah's stable, then they would seek out the other inn. He had to find the One for whom all of Israel had waited so long.

The three boys talked among themselves as they scurried along behind Reuben, excitement overriding exhaustion. If the angelic announcement had not come, they would be sleeping in their shelters or watching the sheep right now, oblivious to the birth of the child, the Messiah, the Savior!

"Why do you think the angels told us, of all people?" questioned Rufus as they struggled to keep pace with Reuben, who was covering the trail like an agile goat. "Why didn't they announce it to the Pharisees? That would make a lot more sense to me."

"I don't know," replied Reuben as he shook his head. "It baffles me, too."

The smoldering fires from those encamped around the town came into view as they reached the crest of the last hill. Reuben paused momentarily to get his bearings, and then quickly descended, meandering through the tents and shelters as he made his way into the town. With the others following behind, Reuben hurried, sure of where he was going now, nothing impeding his progress. When they reached Gedaliah's inn, all was quiet and dark. Reuben motioned for the others to follow him down the side of the inn and behind the rear of the building where the stable was located. As they turned the corner and it came into view, they stopped, hoping beyond hope that this was the place.

As they stood there, Benaiah asked, "Why would our Messiah be born in a stable, of all places? Don't you think that's rather odd?"

No one answered him. They paused only momentarily before Reuben stepped forward. A soft light could be seen through a crack in the doorway. Ever so slowly, he pulled the heavy door. It creaked on its rusty hinges, but yielded to his strength. All heads came together as the door opened enough for them to see inside. Instantly they knew they would have to search no further.

Light from an oil lamp cast soft shadows and washed the stable and its occupants in muted colors. The air was warm and pungent with dung and animals' breath. A man and a woman huddled closely around a manger, where an infant lay, and the man had his arm around the woman, who was singing softly to the baby. Upon hearing the door creak, they turned anxious faces toward the sound. The man moved in front of the woman and her baby and took a step toward the entering shepherds.

Reuben stepped into the dimly-lit stable. "We mean no harm," he said softly. "My name is Reuben, and we are humble shepherds. We have come to see the baby. May we enter?"

Surprised, Joseph turned and looked at Mary and then motioned for them to step inside.

Reuben slid through the doorway, and the others quietly followed. They sensed a holy Presence in the midst of the hay and barnyard animals as they tiptoed toward the woman and the manger, which held the infant. Upon closer scrutiny, Reuben saw that the woman was very young, probably just a year or two older than Benaiah, yet she had a maturity and grace in her face that belied her youth. Her husband was very attentive to her, very protective of her and the child.

"Come," Joseph stated as he welcomed the unexpected visitors with a warm smile and a wave of his arm, "see the child. He is but a few hours old."

Reuben and the others approached the sleeping infant and his young mother, curiosity and excitement dancing through them. This was the promised Messiah! A baby, born in a stable! He was beautiful, his cherub face framed by the clothes in which he was tightly wrapped. He slept peacefully, gently breathing the musky air. All of them knelt beside the manger in awe. This was the child spoken of by the angel.

Mary asked inquisitively with a smile, "How did you know where to find us?"

Reuben quickly responded as his hand gingerly reached out and touched the child's wraps. "We were watching our sheep outside Bethlehem when an angel of the Lord came to us." He relayed the story of the magnificent visitation.

Mary and Joseph listened in rapt attention. A warm, understanding smile slowly crept across Mary's face, and her eyes glowed with a heavenly peace. Occasionally, she and Joseph exchanged knowing glances, privy to a secret that no one else knew.

"He's so tiny," exclaimed Benaiah. "Was I that small when I was born, Father?"

Reuben laughed softly. "Yes, Benaiah, everyone is that small when born."

Rufus looked at Joseph. "This child will be special; the angel told us so." His eyes turned to Mary, who nodded.

All was quiet as they marveled at the tiny infant sleeping in the manger, a place to hold fodder for livestock. They realized it was a very humble beginning for one who would lead an army to crush the Roman imperialists! But it would be years from now, for the child must grow up in order to accomplish his task.

"What is the child's name?" asked Eleazar.

Mary softly replied, "His name is Jesus."

"Jesus," repeated the shepherds in unison, which caused them to laugh softly. They continued to gaze upon him in awe for several more minutes, and then they reluctantly bade farewell to Mary and Joseph. Turning slowly, they left the stable and didn't speak until they were outside and the door closed behind them. As they shut the door tightly against the cold night air, they sighed, a sigh of relief for Reuben, glad that the days of Rome were finally numbered. A tear of joy trickled down his weathered cheek and into his beard, where it glistened in the moonlight.

No one spoke a word during the return trip; each of them had thoughts too deep to share. They were simple shepherds, yet the God of the universe had chosen to announce the birth of his Son to them as they tended their sheep. He hadn't chosen the Pharisees or the religious leaders, but them, humble shepherds. Why? So many questions plagued their minds that they dared not share them, and so they walked slowly back to the sheep, reluctant to leave behind the child they had just visited.

It was almost dawn when they returned to the flock, and, as Reuben had predicted, the sheep were as they had left them; not one was harmed. The fire had almost grown cold, so Reuben set about stirring the coals and adding tinder to rekindle the fire.

As the fire began to consume the wood, Reuben and the others gathered around, warming their hands. Dawn began to brighten the sky in the east, and birds began to sing, welcoming the new day. Overcome still with wonder and joy at what the last few hours had brought them, they spoke little. Each was absorbed in his own thoughts, even his own confusions. The whole night seemed surreal, but at the same time more real than their own heartbeats.

As the light from the rising sun cast its rays across the hillsides, the trees changed from gray to green, the sheep were once again white, and the sky whispered its way from black to azure blue. Still silent, the men retrieved food from their packs and ate the meal that Kezia had provided for them, slowly savoring each bite as they warmed themselves by the fire. By the time they finished, the sun was warming them also, chasing away the weariness and chill from their bones.

Reuben kicked dirt on the fire to extinguish it, signaling to the others that it was time to head back to the house with the sheep. As the smoke escaped through the dirt, Reuben said, "Let's hurry home and tell Thaddeus and Kezia what happened last night and that the long-awaited Messiah has finally arrived."

By mid-morning they reached the house. From a distance, they saw Thaddeus spreading hay in the mangers inside the sheep fold, where they would be left while they registered. Thaddeus waved a greeting when he saw them coming, and as they got closer, the sheep quickened their pace and hurried through the gate. Thaddeus and Reuben greeted each other with a brotherly hug.

"So," questioned Thaddeus, "did you have an uneventful night?"

The others exchanged quick glances. "Hardly," replied Reuben. "You probably won't believe this, but let's go inside so Kezia can hear also. I don't want to have to retell it to her later."

They entered the house and were soon seated around the dining table, where Reuben and the others relayed the events of the night. Kezia and Thaddeus listened attentively, and Kezia couldn't help but smile through the whole telling; it was difficult for her to contain her excitement. When Reuben finished speaking, Kezia stated simply, "I was at the birth, Reuben. I attended Mary, along with Deborah."

"Then you knew this was the long-awaited Messiah before we did!"

"No, I didn't."

"But you said you were there."

"Yes, I was, but I didn't know until now that this child is the long-awaited Messiah. I knew there was something special about him – I even mentioned to Thaddeus last night that I felt the presence of God in the stable – but I didn't know that this child is the promised Messiah. How wonderful is our God!" Kezia closed her eyes as she inhaled deeply.

"We can finally see an end to Roman rule here in Judea! This child will have to grow up before any of this takes place, but at least he is here! Twenty years or so from now," exclaimed Reuben excitedly as he got up and paced the floor, "he will gather an army that will defeat the Romans and drive them from our land! He will then be placed on the throne in Jerusalem where Herod now reigns! The throne will finally be returned to King David's line as the prophets prophesied!"

His excitement spread among the others, and they spent the rest of the morning imagining what the years ahead would be like. As they talked, they prepared to go into town to the registering tents. It would be a long day of waiting in line and dealing with the throngs of people, and none of them looked forward to it.

Early that morning, Deborah went to the stable with fresh water and warm bread and fruit. She knocked softly on the door. As she entered, Joseph approached her in greeting and took the water jug from her hands. Deborah saw that Mary was asleep on the hay, Baby Jesus cuddled next to her.

Joseph anticipated her question. "Yes, Mary's asleep. The baby kept her awake often, but they are both asleep now."

"And you," Deborah asked, "were you able to sleep?"

"Yes, a little, even though it was a busy night after you left."

"What do you mean, a busy night?"

"Not very long after you and your mother left, we were visited by four shepherds from the hillsides. They came to see the baby."

"But how did they know about the baby? My mother and I – and Simon – were the only ones present at the birth, and we all went home and went to bed."

"True. The shepherds said they were visited by angelic hosts that told them of the child's birth and where to find him."

"Indeed," Deborah puzzled. "You said four shepherds. Do you remember any of their names?"

Joseph paused momentarily. "I believe that the oldest said his name was Reuben. I don't recall that I heard any of the others' names."

Deborah gasped as her hand went to her mouth. "That was my Uncle Reuben," she exclaimed as she removed her hand from her mouth. "And those with him were my brothers and my cousin."

The baby started crying, and Mary stirred. She gently and lovingly reached over and took him in her arms, then quieted his cries by holding him to her breast. Seeing Deborah, she greeted her warmly, and Deborah approached her with the food she had brought.

"Thank you so much, Deborah," quietly said Mary. "After yesterday, I'm quite famished. And thirsty. I could drink a jug of water myself, I think."

They laughed together as the baby nursed, and Joseph set about unwrapping the food and cutting it up. As they ate, the conversation continued.

"I think I remember you saying last night that you are newly married," recalled Mary.

Deborah smiled bashfully. "Yes, and we are expecting our first child, but it won't be until the beginning of summer."

"How wonderful! I can tell that you're very excited about becoming a mother soon."

"Yes, and so is my husband, Gedaliah. He wants lots of children, or so he tells me."

"I must go and thank your husband for allowing us to stay here last night," interjected Joseph. "If he hadn't let us stay here, I don't know what would have happened to us."

"You'll find him in the greeting room at the inn; there really isn't much to do in the way of checking guests in and out because everyone who has a room won't be leaving until they are registered, which Gedaliah and I also have to do today."

"Mary, do you mind if I go see Gedaliah for a few minutes and thank him for all he's done for us?"

"I don't mind, Joseph. Deborah's here with me."

Joseph left the stable, leaving the door ajar, allowing the morning sunshine to cast its rays into the stable. The shafts of light exposed the particles of dust floating in the air. The cows and sheep and donkeys were getting restless, eager to be released from the confines of their stalls.

"When Joseph returns, I'll send my brother, Simon, to tend the animals. He'll take them outside and tether them on the railing while he cleans their stalls."

Mary finished nursing the baby and changed his soiled undergarment, which Deborah put into a sack she found hanging on a peg by the door. "I'll make sure these are washed and returned to you as soon as possible. I'll also see what other things we can find for you to use."

"We didn't come totally unprepared," stated Mary. "We knew the baby would arrive while we were on this trip, so we brought infant clothes and blankets and other necessities. But we couldn't bring much without overloading our poor little donkey."

Mary rose and placed Baby Jesus in the manger, then went to the stall where the donkey was tethered and gently patted its head. So much of what had happened during the last few months was beyond her comprehension, yet she held everything close to her heart and pondered it. Now, as she patted the donkey that had so carefully and faithfully carried her, swollen with child, all the way from Nazareth, over the rocky roads for many days and many miles, Mary's joy could be contained no longer. She quietly began to sing a hymn of praise, and Deborah listened in rapt attention as Mary's voice swelled in volume.

When her last chord faded into the rafters of the stable, Mary turned and faced Deborah, who saw a holy light shining from her eyes.

Mary spoke softly as she gazed upon the tiny child in the manger. "Deborah, the birth of my child is a miracle. An angel of the Lord came to me many months ago and told me that the Holy Spirit would come upon me, and I would give birth to a son, who would be called the Son of the Highest. God would give him, my child, the throne of his father, David, and he would be called the Son of God." She turned and faced Deborah. "I have not known my husband yet."

Deborah looked steadfastly at Mary, stunned by her words. Her heart raced. "I can believe your child is special because of the angelic visit announcing his birth to my uncle and cousins, but it's a far greater thing to believe that he's the Son of God."

"Do you believe, Deborah?" Mary whispered as she gazed at her.

Deborah hesitated, her heart hammering in her chest. It made no sense, really, but she couldn't help but recall the feeling that had permeated the stable when Mary was in labor which, coupled with her family showing up during the night, compelled her to grasp faith.

Nodding her head, she replied, "Yes, I believe, for to see you and the child is to believe." She fell down on her knees at the side of the manger as Mary's hand gently rested on her shoulder. The baby slept peacefully, cradled in the hay and wrapped in swaddling clothes.

Chapter Seven

REGISTRATION

Joseph entered the inn after pressing his way through the throngs of people in the narrow streets. He waited patiently until Gedaliah was finished speaking with some people, and then approached him. He bowed slightly in greeting.

"Gedaliah, good morning to you."

"Good morning, Joseph, isn't it?" Gedaliah nodded in greeting also as he smiled warmly. "My wife tells me that you have a beautiful baby boy."

"Yes." Joseph's smile was broad.

"And all is well?"

"Very, and I just want to offer my deep deepest gratitude for allowing us to say in your stable last night. I don't know what we would have done if you hadn't."

"It was my pleasure," replied Gedaliah as he laid his hand on Joseph's shoulder. "I only regret that I had nothing better to offer you."

"It was very much appreciated. And the help your wife and mother-in-law gave Mary - - - - well, there is no way we can adequately thank you. You don't even know us, yet you've shown us so much kindness."

"Well, I know what I'd want someone to do if I were in the same situation that you and Mary were in last night. It was the very least I could do."

"How can I repay you? What is the charge for the stable for the time we've stayed there?" Joseph reached into his money pouch.

Gedaliah quickly held up his hand in protest. "Joseph, there is no charge for staying in the stable. We were more than glad to let you stay there and we'd gladly do it again. Please, put away your pouch."

Reluctantly, Joseph replaced his pouch.

"Is my wife with Mary now?" questioned Gedaliah.

"Yes, she's visiting and enjoying the baby, I'm sure."

"Well, I know Deborah would agree with me about you joining us for our evening meal tonight so you don't have to worry about buying and preparing food. The stable is not much of a place to fix a decent meal. I insist that you join us and my mother, Eglah."

Joseph started to protest, but Gedaliah stopped him by upholding his hand. "I'll not take no for an answer, Joseph. I insist. Bring Mary and the babe and join us just before sunset this evening."

"Thank you for your continued generosity," Joseph said as he turned to leave. "I'll tell Mary about your invitation. She'll be most grateful, I'm sure."

"Deborah and I must register today, so we may not see you again before this evening."

Joseph returned to the stable, and he passed Deborah as she returned to the inn, where she found Gedaliah filling water jugs for the guest rooms.

"Gedaliah, we must do something for Mary and Joseph and Baby Jesus. They can't stay in the stable the whole time they're here in Bethlehem. The baby might become ill, and Mary needs a comfortable place to stay also in order for her to recover."

"I agree. Maybe we could put them in Mehir's house; Joseph and Mary will certainly return to Nazareth before Mehir returns from Greece, if he returns at all."

"That's a wonderful idea! Why didn't we think of that last night?"

"It was almost the middle of the night when they arrived," Gedaliah reminded Deborah. "Besides, the stable was much closer, and Mary's need was imminent."

He finished filling the last of the small jugs. "We'd better go to the south side of town for the registration process now. Are you ready?"

"Yes, as much as I hate to go. I feel like a sheep being counted by the shepherd, but in this case, the shepherd is not kind to the sheep. But first let me go tell Eglah that we're going. I just hope the authorities don't make us come back and get her; it would be far too great a strain on her."

When Deborah returned, Gedaliah opened the door for her to pass through, and they stepped into the streets, still more crowded than usual. Dust was thick in the air, pregnant with a multitude of odors - - donkey and sheep dung, freshly-baked bread, and the sweat of countless unwashed bodies among them. Deborah quickly put her cloak over her mouth to ward off the desire to vomit, which came easily now that she was pregnant. Gedaliah gently put his arm around her and guided her along through the swarming crowds, which were almost overwhelming. Good for business, yes, but still overwhelming.

As they reached the south side of town, they could see the Roman tents erected in a cluster. Several soldiers stood guard, their mere presence enough to squash any thoughts of confrontation. The crowds waited in line, whole families, while parents desperately tried to keep their young children under control, fearing a short-tempered soldier.

The wait was long and tedious, and Deborah became quite tired. Although it was a cool and pleasant day, the sun beat down mercilessly, and she pulled her cloak over her head in an attempt to shield her eyes from the sun. They periodically quenched their thirst with a flask of water that Gedaliah had brought as they snaked their way toward the front of the line, but soon, trouble suddenly developed.

A poor and destitute man was pleading with the Roman registrars. "But I couldn't bring my whole family!" he shouted in frustration.

"And why not?" curtly demanded the registrar. "Caesar's decree stated that everyone was to return to the birthplace of their fathers!"

The man cowered, cringing with fear. The veins on his arms and legs stood out like worms on stone. His hair was gnarled and matted, and his beard was unkempt and greasy. His clothes were rags, and his body was filthy from head to toe. Half of his teeth were missing, and those that remained were brown and rotten. "But I have no money! I'm but a poor farmer, barely raising enough to feed myself and my family!"

"I did not ask for an excuse!" roared the registrar as a few soldiers came to his side. By now the crowd was tense and hushed as everyone watched in fear.

The bedraggled man stood trembling in terror of those that now stood around him. "I came all the way from Bethsaida," he cried as his voice shook uncontrollably. "Do you know how far away that is?"

"I don't care how far away it is!" shouted the registrar as he slammed his fist down on the table in front of him. "You were supposed to bring your entire family, you filthy swine!"

The soldier closest to the man swung his arm at the man, sending him sprawling onto the ground, as his cries for mercy fell on deaf ears. "I had no money to feed us along the way!" he shouted as the soldier kicked him soundly in his ribs.

Gedaliah put both arms around Deborah as she hid her face in his shoulder and cried softly. He felt her tremble in his arms, and his heart was full of rage at what he was witnessing, but to attempt to do something would mean certain death. He sensed that the entire crowd felt the same. He held Deborah close to his chest as he whispered assurances to her even as his rage sought an escape.

The poor, doomed man screamed out in pain as he was dealt another swift kick by the soldier. The registrar, in his fine clothing and jewelry adorning his ample frame, stood and looked down at him. "Take him away. He has disobeyed Caesar's decree. He is Roman property now." The soldiers roughly yanked the scrawny man to his feet and dragged him away as he continued to plead for mercy.

Straightening his robe, the registrar haughtily glanced across the terrified crowd as his gaze challenged anyone to contradict him. After a moment, he lowered his rotund frame back into the chair and simply stated, "Next."

The family in front of Gedaliah approached the table while he waited with Deborah by the guard. Suddenly, Gedaliah regretted the fact that he hadn't brought his mother along, even if he'd had to carry her. Fear gripped his heart. *God help me*, he prayed as he tried to quiet the mad thumping inside his chest.

When the people in front of them moved, he and Deborah stepped up to the table. Without looking up at them, the registrar said, "State your name."

Gedaliah took a deep breath. His legs were shaking beneath his tunic, and his mouth was as dry as sand.

"Gedaliah."

"And this is your wife?"

"Yes. Her name is Deborah."

"And what do you do for a living?"

"I operate one of the inns in Bethlehem."

"And your parents?"

"My father is deceased, but my mother is still living."

The registrar looked up at him with a taunting smirk on his face. "And where does your mother live?"

"Here, with me." Gedaliah looked the registrar directly in the eyes, despite his deep quaking.

"And why isn't she here with you, standing here before me?"

"Sir, my mother is unable to walk; it is impossible for her to descend the stairs in our home. She is frail and in poor health."

The registrar slowly studied Gedaliah, noting the quality of his clothing and that of his wife. It would be far more expedient for Rome to let him continue earning a living and paying taxes. To make him a slave would only cost Rome.

The registrar slowly leaned back in his chair and locked his fingers behind his head. "Any children?"

"No, not yet." Gedaliah's arm was still around Deborah, who was still shaking in fear.

The registrar began to write on a tablet. "Gedaliah, you are to pay a penalty tax of one piece of silver for not bringing your mother with you." He wrote rapidly in the ledger and then looked up. "You have until tomorrow to pay the penalty tax, or you will be imprisoned until it is paid by your family. Do you understand?"

Gedaliah nodded, and the registrar dismissed them with a wave of his hand.

Gedaliah quickly guided Deborah through the line of soldiers and past the long line of restless people, and then they walked swiftly down the narrow street to the inn. Once inside, Deborah turned to him and threw her arms around his neck as she let her tears flow unabated. "Oh, Gedaliah, I was so afraid they were going to take you and beat you like that poor man and then take you away to become a slave!" She buried her face in Gedaliah's shoulder as she clung to him.

Holding her close, Gedaliah whispered softly into her hair, "Thank God they didn't, Deborah. Everything is all right; nothing is going to happen to me."

Deborah frantically clung to him as tears washed away the fear that had gripped her. Cupping her face in his hand, Gedaliah gently kissed her soft lips and said, "Wait until Mother hears that she is worth only one piece of silver to the Romans." He laughed as he wrapped Deborah in his arms again.

"But a whole piece of silver!" exclaimed Deborah. "That's still a lot of money!"

"Yes, it's a tidy sum, but certainly not something that we can't afford to pay. I've put money away, and it won't be a problem to pay the tax tomorrow. I could pay it now, but I want them to think that I was up all night scrounging and borrowing from my friends in order to pay the tax."

They were interrupted by Simon as he ran into the room, sending the door crashing into the wall. "I've cleaned all the stalls, and I've spread fresh hay on the stable floor. The owner of the donkey, the one that doesn't belong to Joseph, paid me a copper coin to brush it! I've never had so much money to call my own!" Simon danced around the floor until Deborah noticed that his sandals were caked with the muck from the stable. She quickly grabbed him.

"Simon, please take off your sandals; look at the mess on the floor!" she reprimanded.

Together, she and Simon cleaned the floor, which gave Deborah time to disassociate from the earlier trauma of hearing the sickening thud of a booted foot into flesh and ribs.

"When are Mother and Father coming to get you for the registration?" she asked as she swept the last of the dirty straw out the door.

"Pretty soon, I think," Simon exclaimed as he put his sandals down on the rug by the door. "Mary and Joseph just left with Baby Jesus. He's a really cute baby, don't you think?"

"Yes, he's absolutely perfect, but he's even more than that, Simon. He's a very special baby."

"And the baby you're going to have will also be very special, won't it?"

Deborah smiled at Simon as she ruffled his hair. "Yes, Simon, my baby will also be very special."

A short time later, Kezia and Thaddeus arrived with the entire family, and Simon joined them. Gedaliah pulled Thaddeus aside and told him what had happened earlier in the day, and Thaddeus thanked him for the information as he headed down the street with the others.

Later that evening, Deborah and Eglah prepared a simple meal of stew, eggs poached in olive oil, cheese, and a loaf of Eglah's savory bread. Mary and Joseph arrived and were led up the stairs to Gedaliah's living quarters after being greeted by Deborah.

"You're fortunate to have such a lovely inn," commented Mary as she followed Deborah with Baby Jesus held closely in her arms.

"Yes, we are. It's really Mother Eglah's home; she is Gedaliah's mother. It will be ours upon her death, of course, but I hope that God grants her many more years with us."

When they entered the living quarters, Mary and Joseph were introduced to Eglah, who was absolutely delighted to hold the baby.

Gedaliah soon joined them with Simon in tow. "Simon just got back from the registration," he explained as they washed their arms and hands in the basins. "Did everything go smoothly for you while registering?"

"Yes, I guess so. It was pretty boring, if you ask me. Nothing to do but wait in line with hundreds of other people, then stand there while the soldiers and this horrible registrar look you over and ask all kinds of questions. I could have had a lot more fun out playing in the hills or even watching the sheep."

Gedaliah's eyes met Deborah's; no mention was made of the horrible event they had witnessed.

As they dined, Mary was particularly pleased with the meal and couldn't compliment the cooks enough. It was wonderful to enjoy a meal with newfound friends, when twenty-four hours ago, she had been sitting astride a donkey in the throes of labor.

Washing down a bite of bread, Gedaliah cleared his throat. "Joseph and Mary," he announced with a bit of flourish, "you are not going to be staying in the stable tonight. We have a house in which you can stay."

Mary looked at Joseph, perplexed. "A house?" she questioned.

"Yes, a house. One of the families here in Bethlehem had to return to Greece, and he indicated to me before he left that it was unlikely that he would return, so you're certainly welcome to use it until you return to Nazareth."

"But it's not our house," protested Joseph.

"No, but it's empty and available, and I think you should use it until you can return to Nazareth. I spoke with the neighbors today and told them of your plight, and they agree that you should use it."

Mary and Joseph exchanged glances. "What do you think, Mary?"

"I think it's a wonderful idea, Joseph. God continues to provide."

"Then it's settled," Gedaliah stated emphatically as he smiled broadly. "We'll help you gather your things after our meal and then take you over to Mehir's house. It's only two streets over, so you'll be close by."

Baby Jesus started to fuss, and Mary picked him up in her arms and whispered, "See how your Father has provided for us, little one? He has provided every step of the way." She pressed his little cheek against her own as she closed her eyes.

In a short time, Mary, Joseph, and the baby were in Mehir's now-empty dwelling. Gedaliah and Deborah helped carry their few belongings, and then surprised them by returning a short time later with baskets filled with several jugs, basins, bowls, blankets, oil lamps, and an ample supply of food as gifts. Mary was overwhelmed to the point of tears.

"Oh, please don't cry," gently implored Deborah. "We're very happy to give you these things. We have more than enough."

Mary put her arms around Deborah and hugged her. "You are a wonderful person, Deborah. Thank you so much."

"You're very welcome," smiled Deborah as she wiped a tear from Mary's cheek. "Now you can sleep well tonight and not be bothered by people coming into the stable in the morning. Some of our travelers will be starting their return trips tomorrow, and many of them will want to get an early start."

"And Simon can sleep in the stable with his friend, Obed, tonight. He's been begging me all day long to allow them to sleep out there," Gedaliah stated.

Joseph smiled at Gedaliah. "God will surely bless you for the kindness you've shown to us."

"It's my pleasure. Do you know when you will be returning to Nazareth?"

Joseph lighted an oil lamp from the lighted one that Gedaliah held in his hand. Dark shadows appeared on the walls, ever larger as they retreated from the source of light. Mary laid the baby into one of the baskets Deborah had brought, not filled with straw or hay, but with soft blankets.

"I'm not sure," replied Joseph as he placed the lamp on a small ledge on the wall. The dim light revealed several sleeping pallets stacked atop each other in one corner and a large table in the center of the room with two long benches. There was another long table along one wall, obviously the food preparation area, and along an outer wall was a fire pit and oven. There was a door at the back of the room, and there were two windows at the front of the house facing the street, covered with heavy drapes to ward off the chill of the night and to provide a bit of privacy. The door was wooden and had a latch to secure it shut. The floor was earthen, packed hard and worn smooth by the many feet that had used it over the years.

"I've been thinking we just might settle down here for a while. Mary has had a very difficult trip from Nazareth, and I don't want to make her endure it again so soon after the baby's birth."

"That would be wonderful," exclaimed Deborah as she raised her hands to her face in utter delight. "We would be so happy if you stayed."

Mary smiled at Joseph. "Yes, it would be wonderful to stay here."

"Well, you must be exhausted after today; I know I am," stated Gedaliah as he turned and retreated to the door. "If you need anything, just let us know. You know where to find us."

As they returned to the inn in the darkness of night, Deborah asked, "Do you suppose they'll stay very long?"

"I have no idea, but I know I'd like them to stay. They could become good friends."

Later that night, Deborah nestled into Gedaliah's arms as they slid under the covers. "Just think. Mary's son and our child will be only about six months apart in age, Gedaliah. They will be playmates if Mary and Joseph stay. What a wonderful thought."

They lay quietly in bed together for a few moments, and then Deborah softly whispered, "Mary told me something this morning when I went out to the stable that has simply taken my breath away. It's so very wonderful."

"What is it?"

Deborah paused for several moments and then told Gedaliah about the shepherds – her family – being told by angels that God's Son had been born in Bethlehem and how they had visited the stable during the night hours to see the baby. Then she told Mary's story of being visited by an angel who told her that she would have a baby who would be the promised Messiah.

When Deborah finished her narrative, Gedaliah stated, "Just think of it! Our child, if it's a boy, will be able to help the Messiah overthrow the Roman Empire! There is hope after all, and that hope is in Jesus! Thank God we can finally see an end to this foreign occupation."

The young couple fell asleep in each other's arms as they dreamed of the future which had suddenly become very bright with hope.

In the small house across the way, Mary gently bathed her baby's tender skin in a basin of water, and then rubbed him down with olive oil and powdered myrtle leaves once more before snuggly wrapping him. He was so perfectly formed and so very tiny. She felt totally and completely unqualified for what she had been chosen to do, but the words of the angel always came back to her. She was 'highly favored among women' and completely and utterly humbled by her assignment. Months ago, she had simply been a Hebrew girl growing up in Nazareth, doing what all other Hebrew girls her age did, and yet somehow she was 'highly favored' of God. Even now, she often had difficulty believing what was occurring in her life, yet she knew that this little child in her arms, this little child that she had carried inside her womb for nine months, this little child was totally human and yet totally God and would change the world forever.

Gently placing Jesus in his basket, she marveled once again at his existence. She stroked his cheek with her finger, lightly touching his eyebrows and the tip of his nose. She knew the truth of his existence more than anyone else; God was his Father. She had yet to be with her husband as a wife; she was still a virgin. To give birth to a child and yet still be a virgin – who would believe her? There was no doubt in her mind that many would not believe because such a thing was impossible. But there would be others, like Deborah, who would believe. Mary leaned over and gently placed a kiss on her baby's tiny forehead and then wiped away a tear that fell unbidden from her eye.

Turning, she saw Joseph in the soft light of the oil lamp, gently smiling at her. He opened his arms to her, and she went to him.

Chapter Eight

BLESSINGS

"Thank you, Caleb, for all your help during the last few days. I don't know what I would have done without you." Helah spread a blanket over her mother as she lay down on her pallet and then quickly tucked it around her. Gazing at her frail mother, Helah quickly suppressed a cry, burying it deep inside. Caleb's strong arm held her as they bid their mother goodnight. Their father had already settled down and was fast asleep even though it wasn't yet dark outside.

Caleb whispered softly, "It's difficult to see our parents so ill and frail, isn't it?"

Helah looked at him as the tears that she had held back ran unchecked down her face.

Caleb guided her into the other room and pulled the drape across the doorway. "You were so very strong the whole time we were traveling and in Jerusalem," stated Caleb as he patted his sister's arm. "I never knew you possessed such strength."

Helah wiped the tears from her sunburned cheeks. "I had to be strong, Caleb, for Mother and Father. I fear that neither of them has many days left on this earth."

Caleb drew her into his embrace and held her, gently rubbing her back. "I think you're right about that."

"Both of them are sick with the same illness, but not one physician can tell us what ails them. There's nothing that can be done."

She buried her face in Caleb's shoulder and cried, letting all the pain and worry flow from her. The walk to Jerusalem had been long and hard for those

104

who were frail or aged. Helah knew that there were sick and elderly people who hadn't survived the trip forced on them by the cursed census. She'd seen death both going to and coming from Jerusalem several times, and she tried to rid her mind of the suffering she had witnessed.

Her parents had ridden in a small cart pulled by a donkey, but the jarring motion of the wagon had taken its toll, and the roads had been so crowded that the going was extremely difficult and slow as people pushed and shoved as they carried their belongings or guided little donkeys, loaded with provisions, along the congested roads.

Once they'd reached Jerusalem, they had to sleep in a tent that Thaddeus had loaned them. Helah and Caleb had tried their best to make their parents as comfortable as possible on the pallets on the ground, but this, too, had been difficult. They were grateful that they'd been able to register the day after they arrived in Jerusalem, which allowed them to leave the next day. They returned to Bethlehem four days after they left, thankful that the wretched journey was over.

As their parents rested in the other room, Caleb put his hands on Helah's shoulders and held her at arm's length as he looked intently into her eyes. "Well, little sister, I'll stay here with Mother and Father. I know you've missed Rufus very much while we've been away, so go and see him. Resume your job, and I'll stop by and let you know if and when I'll be returning to Bethany." He gave her a quick hug and guided her to the door, where she planted a kiss on his cheek.

As Helah hurried through the streets, now almost void of travelers, she noticed the accumulated filth on the street, evidence that little Bethlehem had been overrun with people. Most were finally returning to their own towns, and not one person had anything good to say about the forced census.

Helah scurried up the path to Thaddeus's house as the light faded, shades of red and yellow being swallowed up by the advancing darkness. She knew the trail well, and her heart raced at the thought of seeing Rufus again. It seemed as if she had been gone forever. A field mouse scampered across her path, but it didn't bother her in the least.

Helah soon reached the flat land around the farm, comforted by the sounds of the sheep in the pens for the night. The lights from the house shone softly in the windows, open to the cool night air. She heard familiar laughter as she opened the doorway and entered the main hall.

Slipping out of her sandals, she walked across the stone floor and into the dining area where everyone was gathered. As soon as she reached the doorway and was seen, everyone was on their feet greeting her or hugging her, everyone except Rufus, who stood aside and watched. His mother embraced Helah, and then poured a drink of wine for her and offered her a pillow on which to sit.

Helah watched Rufus as he stood on the side of the room, and her heart raced more than it had from the run up the hillside to the farm. Their gazes met for only a fraction of a second, yet Helah knew that he had missed her as much as she had missed him. Grasping the glass of wine as she sat down, Helah told everyone how very happy she was to be back.

"Tell us about your trip," entreated Kezia. "It must have been extremely difficult to take your parents to Jerusalem, even though it's not very far."

Helah blushed slightly, knowing all eyes were on her.

"If my brother hadn't come to assist me, I don't know how I could have done it. Caleb brought a small cart and donkey for our parents to ride in, but even that was extremely difficult for them." Helah filled them in on the rest of their difficult trip.

"And the Romans," queried Reuben, "I imagine that they were everywhere, as they were here."

"Oh, yes, they were. I found it quite intimidating."

"I often wonder how there can possibly be any soldiers in Rome when there are so many of them here," tartly stated Eleazar. "Every young man in Rome must be forced to become a soldier in order to have soldiers everywhere."

"Ah, but we now know that their days are numbered," reminded Reuben.

"What do you mean, their days are numbered? How can you say that when Rome rules the world?" questioned Helah.

"You wouldn't believe what has happened in our quiet, little town while you were gone, Helah," Kezia said as she smiled and patted Helah's arm. "The promised Messiah has arrived, the one spoken of by the prophets, and Deborah and I were there to help his mother deliver him."

Suddenly, everyone had to tell their story of their whereabouts during the last few days, and Helah was bombarded with stories from everyone simultaneously.

"Whoa! Stop!" shouted Thaddeus with a hand in the air. "Let's tell our stories, one at a time, so Helah can understand what has happened." Reaching over to Kezia, he said, "And why don't you be the first since you were there at the beginning."

"I think Simon should start, because he was the one who brought us the news of the coming birth."

Simon, bursting to tell his story, eagerly obliged them. His animation made everyone laugh as he told of his hurried scamper from the stable to the house.

Then Kezia took over the narrative. Her eyes looked back in time, and her face became radiant as she told Helah of the humble birth in Gedaliah's stable. Then those who had been tending the sheep told of the angelic visit in the night skies, of the announcement and the heavenly beings and how they hurried to find the baby in the stable behind Gedaliah's inn.

A comfortable quiet settled on the group after the accounts were finished, and Helah tried to digest all that she had heard. "So, the Messiah, the one promised by the prophets for hundreds of years, has been born, here in our little town."

"Yes," replied Reuben. "It is as we said. Our Deliverer has come, so that is why we say that the Romans' days are numbered."

"You said they are from Nazareth," noted Helah. "Won't they soon return there?"

"Maybe, but not for some time," replied Kezia. "They're now residing in Mehir's house until Mary regains her strength."

Helah tried to digest the news as the evening wound down, even as her heart longed to speak with Rufus.

When it was time to bed down for the night, Rufus was finally able to speak privately with Helah as the others were preparing to retire to their sleeping chambers. Seeing Helah again after her absence for four days was like seeing her for the first time; her beauty had only increased in his eyes.

"Would you like to take a short walk?" he asked Helah.

They were soon strolling in the dark under the canopy of the sky, adorned with jewels that twinkled and danced. Complete darkness engulfed them occasionally as the moon dipped behind a passing cloud. Helah drew her cloak closer around her even though her blood was like boiling water racing through her body.

Rufus slowed his steps to match Helah's, and they traversed the land around the sheep pens and barn. Helah's black hair, dark as a raven, reflected the shimmering moonlight as she walked next to him. Occasionally, their arms would touch and each time, Rufus felt as if he had been struck by lightning. He was never more alive than when he was with Helah. He couldn't live without her much longer.

Rufus finally broke their electric silence. "Father agreed to speak with your parents once you returned from Jerusalem," he whispered as he reached for Helah's arm.

The heat from his touch stopped her, and she turned as he finished speaking. His look was intense, so tender, so endearing, that she felt like melting to the ground. Rufus was so handsome in the moonlight, his features softened, his youthful beard appearing thicker. His lips were full and tempting, and Helah wondered if she could withstand the fire of his kiss.

"Your father may have to speak with Caleb," Helah whispered in reply. "I don't know if Mother or Father will be able to give consent to our becoming betrothed. They are far from well, as I told everyone tonight."

"Whichever it is," Rufus said as he stood face-to-face with her, "I'll ask him to do it tomorrow, if possible." He reached up and touched a strand of her hair, rubbing it between his fingers. It felt like fine silk, not like his wiry hair.

Helah closed her eyes, bracing for the effect of his touch on her skin. He placed his roughened hand alongside her face, and she leaned into its warmth.

"Helah, I'll be a good husband to you. I love you more than my own life."

Helah attempted to quiet the racing of her heart as she wet her lips and tried to respond. "And I, Rufus, will be a good wife to you, giving you children and taking care of you for the rest of my days." She raised her hand and placed it atop his, and then they clasped hands as they turned and retraced their steps to the house, where each lay awake in their separate beds for a long time before sweet sleep overcame them.

* * * * * * * * * *

"I have everything I need," Mary stated to Deborah as they returned from market the next morning. "Thank goodness Joseph had the foresight to sell his carpentry tools and our belongings before we made this trip. Otherwise, we might not have any money at this point in time." She shifted the baby in her arms as she adjusted the weight of the heavy basket.

Deborah switched her shopping basket to her other hip. "I'm certainly glad this census is over," she stated happily. "I don't care if the inn is empty for days right now, I'm so tired. If Simon and Obed hadn't kept up the work in the stable, we would have been overwhelmed with everything. I'm so thankful that he was willing to do it. And Selma, what would I have done without Selma?"

Mary smiled warmly as she walked along the narrow streets with Deborah, who had become her new best friend. Even though she and Joseph had left family and friends in Nazareth and she knew that she would eventually see them again, Mary sensed in her heart that they wouldn't be returning any time soon.

"Joseph and I are indebted to you for what you've done for us," quietly stated Mary. "We're forever grateful."

"You would have done the same for me. Besides, when my baby arrives, I know you'll help me with the delivery, that is, if you're still here in Bethlehem. And Mother, too, of course. You're the ones I want there when the time comes."

"And that will arrive sooner than you think; you're already getting a little tummy on you," observed Mary.

"Yes, I'm into my fourth month now, and I can feel the baby moving around when I'm quiet. It's simply an absolutely marvelous feeling. My tiny baby is already full of life."

They reached what was now Mary's house, and Deborah unloaded Mary's basket as Mary sat down and nursed the baby. When she was done emptying the contents, Deborah watched Mary in the dim light created from the open windows.

"It's beyond my ability to understand that God, the creator of the universe, fathered your child, Mary. I know how it is when Gedaliah and I come together, yet I cannot imagine what it was like for you."

Mary gazed up at Deborah as the baby suckled. She paused and chose her words carefully. "The angel told me that the Spirit of the Lord would come upon me and that I would conceive a child. Ever since the angel's visit, I've felt a profound presence of God, as if He is part of me. It's terribly difficult to explain, but it's a constant presence, not something that comes and goes. So I don't know the exact moment that the conception took place, but I do know that Joseph and I have not yet come together as husband and wife."

"All this time you have been married, Joseph hasn't touched you?"

Mary shook her head. "No. He's honored God's declaration that I was to be a virgin when I gave birth. No one can question the fathering of this child as I am still a virgin." Mary stroked the baby's face gently as he nursed, her eyes filled with love and wonder.

The front door was suddenly thrown open, and Joseph entered with several tools in his arms. When he saw Mary nursing the baby, he put the tools on the table and came over to her and kissed her gently on the forehead. He placed a tender kiss on the baby's head as Mary detached him from her breast and put him on her shoulder.

"Where did you get all those tools, Joseph?" she asked as she looked up at him.

"I was with Gedaliah, and he took me to Hezron's house. Hezron is a carpenter, but because of his failing eyesight and advanced age, he hasn't been able to work for many months. Gedaliah introduced us, and Hezron was quite excited to learn that I'm also a carpenter. He took me into a small room where he had stored his many tools, and then he gave me some of them." Joseph picked up a well-worn plane and cradled it in his calloused hands, savoring the feel of carpentry tools once again in his hands. "I was stunned that he gave them to me, but when Gedaliah told him of our plight, he insisted that I take them."

"Once again, God has provided," quietly stated Mary.

"Well, if we're going to stay permanently here in Bethlehem, I'll need to set up a business, and soon. We hardly have any money left."

Deborah's eyes widened. "You'll be staying in Bethlehem? You're not going to return to Nazareth?"

Joseph picked up a well-worn carving knife. "Mary and I have talked it over, and we'll be staying here. This is our new home."

"I'm so excited that you're going to stay," exclaimed Deborah as she jumped from her seat. "Our children will grow up together, Mary; just think of it!"

As the days passed, Joseph and Mary settled in Bethlehem, and Deborah and Kezia frequented their home. Joseph set up his shop, although it was sparsely furnished, in the room located behind the living quarters, and he was ready for customers soon after moving into the house. The shop had another entry that faced onto another narrow street, allowing Mary to leave and enter their home without ever going through the shop. It also allowed customers to enter the shop without interfering with Mary's privacy. It was a comfortable and convenient setup, and Joseph was soon producing benches, chairs and tables, as well as an occasional special order, for the people of Bethlehem. Many people who'd gone away for the census chose to stay in their homelands, just like Mehir and his family, which created a void in the economic structure of Bethlehem. Since Joseph was the only carpenter around for miles, he soon established a name for himself as a maker of sturdy, practical furniture.

Reuben, Eleazar, Rufus, and Benaiah were instrumental in informing everyone with whom they came in contact about all the things that they had seen and heard the night of the birth of the baby in the stable. Many believed that the Messiah had finally come, while others doubted that such a child from such a place could possibly be the promised Messiah. Debates were frequent whenever a group of men would gather in or around Bethlehem.

Life was quiet and uneventful for Mary, her days filled with caring for the baby, washing clothes, going to market, baking bread, and preparing meals. According to the Law of Moses, Jesus was circumcised on the eighth day in the local synagogue, with friends attending the ceremony to witness the event.

Also in meeting the requirements of the law, Mary and Joseph were eager to go to Jerusalem to present the child to the Lord, as was the Jewish custom for all first-born male children. She knew in her heart that Jesus would be special, as God had told her, but not in the way everyone hoped. She and Joseph knew that Jesus would save the people from their sins, not from Roman rule, but they could never broach the subject with anyone; they simply wouldn't be able to understand such a thing. All everyone wanted to hear was that Jesus was the promised Messiah and that he would deliver them from the clutches of Roman rule forever.

Mary and Joseph often spoke long into the night during the child's first month about the future of the little baby sleeping next to them. Joseph could never forget that the angel of the Lord had told him that the child would be called Immanuel, which meant 'God with us.' The Holy God of the universe had become human and was sleeping in the basket next to their bed, and he looked to them for his care. It was an awesome, overwhelming responsibility, and Joseph often wondered why he and Mary had been chosen. Neither saw themselves as better than others. They had to rely on God daily to give them wisdom and strength to raise His child.

Joseph cradled Mary in his arms as they lay awake one night. He kissed the top of her head and whispered, "We'll need to go to Jerusalem the day after tomorrow; your days of purification will be accomplished, and we'll need to present Jesus to the Lord at the temple. I know how much you've looked forward to this event; the last five weeks have been full of anticipation for you, haven't they?"

"Yes, but the short trip to Jerusalem will be much easier than the trip to Bethlehem was while I was heavy with child." She laughed softly.

"True, but it will still be tiring. We should be able to make it in one day if we rise early. Of course, you'll ride the donkey again."

Mary rested in Joseph's arms. He'd been so kind and understanding, never forcing his desires on her, but yielding to God in everything. They knew that the Law of Moses required going to Jerusalem and presenting their baby to the Lord and offering a sacrifice. Even though Jesus was God, they would still present him to the Lord in complete obedience.

On the fortieth day after the baby's birth, they left Bethlehem and traveled to Jerusalem, returning very late the same day. Deborah had told Mary to stop at the inn to let her know when they returned, and they did just that.

"Come over tomorrow, and I can tell you all about our trip," Mary said to Deborah as she held Baby Jesus tightly in her arms upon their return to Bethlehem. Gedaliah lead the donkey back to the stable, where it was permanently housed unless Joseph had need of it. Simon often took the little animal out to the fields during the day for exercise and green grass. Now, however, the little donkey was obviously very tired, his hooves hardly able to clear the ground as he placed one in front of the other as he followed Gedaliah to the stable.

Later the next morning, Kezia and Deborah went to market together, accompanied by Helah. After their baskets were full, Helah went off to visit her parents, who were still under the watchful eye of her brother, Caleb.

Kezia and Deborah returned to the inn, where they deposited most of their purchases and, after making a small basket of food for Mary, they walked the short distance through the narrow streets to Mary's house. They found her sitting outside in the sun, warming herself and holding the baby as he slept peacefully.

"Greetings," said Kezia. "We have a few things to share with you and Joseph."

Mary sighed heavily, smiling as she did so. "Thank you so much, but it really isn't necessary for you to bring us food any more. We're able to make ends meet now."

"Then simply be grateful for more than enough and look at it as God's abundant provision," Kezia smiled as she stroked the baby's face with the tip of a finger. "The sun feels good after so many cloudy days, doesn't it?"

"Yes, it does. We were afraid we might get rained on while we were traveling to Jerusalem, but thankfully, we didn't."

"How was your trip? What was it like to present your first-born son to the Lord?" asked Deborah as she settled herself down on the bench next to Mary. The child within her kicked, and she placed her hand on her growing abdomen.

Mary's face lighted up with a smile. "Let's go inside, for I have to tell you everything that happened to us in Jerusalem."

After making themselves comfortable on the benches around the table, with Jesus asleep in his basket, Mary began her story.

Chapter Nine

REVEALED

Mary's eyes were ablaze with excitement as she began her narrative. Her youthful face took on a radiance that expanded the expression of her eyes.

"When we arrived in Jerusalem, we went into the temple as soon as we could. The crowds inside grew rapidly with the rising sun, and there was a man who approached us as we ascended the stairs. He was very advanced in years. His hair was white, and his face wore the wrinkles of countless seasons, but his eyes shone with the light of God, and he knew immediately who we were." Mary closed her eyes as she tried to recall every detail.

"This man came right up to us and told us his name was Simeon. He explained that he had been devoutly waiting for the consolation of Israel and that the Holy Spirit of God had told him he would not see death until he had seen the Lord's Christ."

Mary stopped speaking as she looked into her friends' eyes.

"Please continue," urged Kezia as she sat forward on the bench, her arms crossed in front of her on the table.

Slowly Mary spoke, taking great pains to include as much as she could. "Simeon said that he'd been told by the Spirit of God to go to the temple that day. When he saw us, he approached us and asked if he could hold the baby in his arms. We didn't hesitate to hand Baby Jesus to him, and when he took the child in his arms, his face simply glowed, and he raised his voice and blessed God.

"As we stood there, Simeon said that he could now die in peace, according to God's word, because his eyes had seen God's salvation, which had been prepared in the presence of all the peoples. He said that Jesus would be a light for revelation to the Gentiles and that he would bring honor and glory to Israel."

Deborah and Kezia sat silently. When Mary paused again, Deborah asked, "What did you think about what Simeon said?"

Looking down at her clasped hands resting on her homespun dress, Mary quietly stated, "Joseph and I simply marveled at everything he said. And then Simeon did something very strange," she softly continued. "He blessed Joseph and me, saying to us that this child, Jesus, is appointed for the rising and fall of many in Israel and for a sign which shall be spoken against." A tear suddenly appeared and ran down her cheek and tumbled down onto her dress, where it was quickly absorbed.

Kezia reached across the table and touched her hand. "What is it, Mary? What happened next?"

As she reached up and wiped away the trail of moisture from her cheek, Mary whispered, "Simeon said that a sword would pierce my heart, my soul, in order that the secret thoughts and purposes of many hearts might be brought out into the open."

Silence, thick and heavy, hung in the room as tears continued to spill from Mary's eyes and splatter on her clasped hands. Seconds later, Mary looked pensively at her friends.

"That is all he said. He then kissed the child and laid him back in my arms, continually giving praises to God. He patted Jesus one last time on his head, then turned and walked away."

"What does all this mean, Mary?" asked Kezia, puzzled. "Does Joseph understand it?"

Mary shook her head. "Joseph is as confused as I am. We can understand the blessings, but we can't and don't understand Simeon's last words to us."

Mary slowly rose from her seat and stood facing the wall as she tried to gather her thoughts, deeply troubled at the possibility of death by a Roman sword; what else could it mean?

"Mary, are you all right?" gently asked Deborah.

Mary turned and took her seat again. "I'm fine. It's just that so many things are not yet known about this child, and I must trust God every day to help me understand his purpose and mission in life."

Mary took a deep breath and sat down as she exclaimed, "But Simeon wasn't the only one to greet us in the temple courtyard. There was also a woman, whose name was Anna, who came up to us after Simeon departed. She, too, was very old, even older than Simeon, I think. Although she was quite frail, she told us that she had never left the temple, but stayed there day and night. She'd been a widow most of her life, having been married only seven years when her husband died, and now she served God by fasting and praying daily in the temple. She's done this, day and night, year after year, for many years.

"She told us she was a prophetess of the tribe of Asher, and when she saw us, she did as Simeon did: she gave thanks to God. Then she started talking to everyone about Jesus, to all who were looking for the redemption and deliverance of Jerusalem."

Jesus started crying, and Mary picked him up in her arms, speaking softly to him. "What manner of child is this, that people have awaited his coming! God has showed loving-kindness to those of low degree and has satisfied those who are hungry with good things! He who is the Almighty has done great things for me, and Holy is his Name!" She closed her eyes as she cradled the baby's head in her hand.

Deborah and Kezia were confused by the mysterious things that Mary had told them. The exchanged questioning glances.

Mary sang softly to her child, rocking back and forth as mothers do, relishing the innocent form that kicked and squirmed in his wraps. Kezia watched, remembering the days when she was nursing babies and enjoying the few months that they remained little. Jesus was already rapidly growing; he had lost his newborn look and was now almost six weeks old. He wasn't prone to fussing and crying, but was an easy baby. Watching Mary and her baby made Kezia realize how quickly time had passed; life was much too brief, often filled with unbearable suffering even while being sprinkled with unspeakable joy.

Mary held the baby up in front of her, cooing at him and making him laugh. Her face lit up with a wonderful smile as she said, "After Anna left us, we went into the temple, and the priests performed the dedication ceremony. After we offered a sacrifice of turtle doves, we came home."

Deborah rose from her seat and came over to Mary, taking Jesus from her and cradling him in her arms. "It won't be long now until I become a mother, and I'll also have to go to the temple to dedicate my baby, that is, if it's a male child," she added as she tickled the baby's chin.

"And I'll be a very content grandmother," Kezia exclaimed, "and I'll certainly spoil the child, as grandmothers have a right to do." Everyone laughed.

"Come, Deborah, Mary is most certainly tired from her trip, and I need to get back home. Thaddeus has plans to speak to Helah's parents about her and Rufus becoming betrothed later today. She must be a nervous wreck by now."

"Rufus, where's your mind, lad?" hollered Thaddeus. "Be quick about going after that stray lamb over there."

Rufus quickly came to his senses and looked in the shrub to his left where a stray lamb had become entangled in its branches. He slowly approached it and reached down, freeing its spindly legs from the sharp thorns. He gently lifted it in his arms and brought it back to the flock, where it hurriedly found its mother, who seemed to scold it for wandering off. Rufus looked at his father for support, who smiled at him from across the wooly backs of the flock.

Eleazar was soon beside Rufus. "So, I hear Father is going to speak to Helah's parents tonight." He jabbed Rufus playfully in his side with his staff. "You'll be an old married man before I'm even betrothed, you rascal."

Rufus looked at his brother, surprised at his friendly tone of voice.

"I'm truly happy for you, Rufus; in fact, I envy you. Helah is a very nice girl, and I'm sure she'll make you a good wife."

Rufus watched his feet traverse the rocky terrain, unable to keep his mind on his work knowing that Father would be speaking to Helah's parents in a matter of hours. Once the betrothal contract was signed, it was as binding as a marriage.

"I'm very glad that it's Helah I'll be marrying. Father and Mother have been very open to us choosing our own wives rather than picking for us. One day soon, you'll find the right girl for you, too, Eleazar."

"I suppose you're right, but if that doesn't happen before too long, I'll simply have one picked out for me. I don't think I'll like very much being the last to get married, excluding Simon, of course."

"I heard Uncle Reuben talking to Father the other night, and he's seriously thinking about picking a wife for Benaiah. Of course, the marriage contract wouldn't be signed for several years after the betrothal contract, but he is seriously considering it. You have to remember that Benaiah's already one year past the legal age for marriage. But you're right – if you don't marry soon, you might not find anyone who wants you!"

Eleazar punched his brother playfully in the arm as they laughed.

Soon, they arrived at the grazing land chosen for the day. As they ate lunch, Thaddeus addressed Rufus. "After our evening meal, I'll be going to town and speaking with Helah's parents, or Caleb, if need be." He glanced up at his son from his sitting position with a wry smile. "That is, I'm going unless you've changed your mind."

"No, I've not changed my mind, Father."

"Good. I'd hate to go all the way into town for nothing. On the serious side, Rufus, I'll be paying Helah's father a tidy sum of money for the mohar. Of course, he isn't allowed to spend the money itself, only the interest, and that money will return to you and Helah when her father dies. Sadly, it appears that time won't be long in the offing. It doesn't seem possible that either parent will live much longer. It's good that the two of you are becoming betrothed. It will give her parents peace of mind that their daughter will be taken care of, and Helah won't have to be concerned about her future. The timing is right."

"Even if Helah's parents survive until the wedding day, it doesn't seem possible that they would be strong enough to attend the feast. I'm sure it will be hard on Helah not to have them there."

"Well, Son, we'll just have to take one day at a time, and it all starts tonight when I see them."

"I wonder how Helah is holding together," queried Benaiah. "She's probably as nervous as a fox in a hen house." He laughed at the thought.

"And what would you do if I informed you that you might be next to be betrothed?" interrupted Reuben as he playfully kicked his son.

"What!?" shouted Benaiah. "You can't do that to me, Father! Eleazar is next, not me! I'm not ready to settle down with a wife!"

"Well, you'd better start thinking along those lines. I'm not getting any younger, and I'll not have you still living under my brother's roof when I'm dead and buried. You must have your own roof by then."

"But you're not going to die soon. Besides, Uncle Thaddeus loves having me around, don't you?"

"Now, don't drag me into this conversation," Thaddeus pleaded. "I've got my hands full enough." He took a long drink from the flask by his side. "Speaking of roofs, Rufus, have you decided where you want to build your house? I still need you to help with the flock and farm, so I hope you don't want to move away. Feel free to choose any spot on our property, and we'll help you build your house."

"Of course Helah and I will stay here. Where else could we possibly go? I've already chosen a place, and I'll point it out to you tonight or tomorrow, whichever is more convenient."

"Good. Then that's settled. Now we can start looking for wives for Eleazar and Benaiah!" Thaddeus and Reuben laughed loudly as the young men protested profusely.

* * * * * * * * * *

Helah spent the day cleaning the house after she returned from the market in town, noting that Kezia still hadn't returned from her visit with Deborah when she started cleaning the kitchen area, giving it a particularly good scrubbing. She had to stay busy or she would go crazy with excitement and anxiety. By the end of the day, she would be betrothed to Rufus! And then the wedding ceremony would take place, probably in about six months or so. The only thing that troubled her was the lack of a sizable dowry for her father to give to Thaddeus.

Kezia finally returned from town as Helah was feverishly cleaning the fire pit, scraping the ashes into a bucket to discard outside. Helah was filthy from the ash and dust, and Kezia couldn't help but laugh when she saw her.

"Here, let me help you, Helah. You look as if you've rolled around in the ashes." Together they finished the job as they talked of the coming betrothal and what it would mean.

"I've always considered you not a servant, but another daughter," stated Kezia as they washed the ashes from their hands and arms. "And soon you'll be just that – a daughter, married to my son, Rufus, who will give me grandchildren. That makes me very happy."

Later, the men came in from the fields after securing the flock into the folds for the night. Rufus and Helah continually exchanged glances, and the atmosphere was alive with anticipation. Thaddeus was soon on his way down the hillside into the town of Bethlehem, where he made his way to the humble home of Helah's parents, Achim and Jael.

He found them sitting around the table eating the last of a simple meal prepared by Caleb, who greeted him at the door. Achim and Jael nodded their greetings as Caleb motioned for him to be seated.

After greeting them, Thaddeus spoke. "I'm sure you know the reason for my visit."

Achim nodded slowly, his eyes gleaming.

"I've come to ask for permission for your daughter, Helah, to become betrothed to my son, Rufus." He reached into a pack he had brought along and withdrew a parchment and a bag of money, both of which he placed on the table in front of Achim and Jael.

"I have the betrothal contract, as well as the mohar, the bride-price. As you know, by law you are not permitted to spend any of the mohar, but you may invest it and use any of the interest in any way you see fit. Because I have a high regard for Helah and have been able to observe her fine character for many months, I'm presenting you with a mohar of 25 pieces of silver." Taking the money bag, Thaddeus opened it and poured the coins on the table.

"I know the father of the bride usually states the bride-price, but I also know you would never ask for this amount of money. However, I believe Helah is worth all of it, and so I offer this much to you for your daughter."

Achim and Jael were speechless as they gazed at the coins shining in the light from the oil lamps. With a shaky and hoarse voice, Achim said, "We're very honored to have Helah marry Rufus. He's a fine young man."

Turning to Caleb, he said, "Son, retrieve the chest, please."

Caleb turned and lifted a small chest from the floor to the table and placed it in front of his father, who gingerly released the latch. With tears in his eyes, he removed numerous coins of varying value and spread them on the table next to the pieces of silver.

"Jael and I have squirreled away these coins in anticipation of Helah's betrothal. They don't amount

125

to much, but it's the best we can do under the circumstances. I wish we could give you much more, Thaddeus. Rufus is certainly worth it." Achim's dark eyes glistened with the tears he tried to hold back. Jael couldn't contain hers.

Achim continued. "My wife and I are both very ill, as you well know, Thaddeus. Caleb is going to take us to Bethany to live with him until we die. We cannot stay here by ourselves any longer."

"Does Helah know?"

"No, she doesn't," interjected Caleb. "It's something we decided just today. It's better that Father and Mother come live with me; they're unable to care for themselves, and I can't stay here any longer. I must return to Bethany and my work there."

Thaddeus looked into the sad eyes of Helah's parents, old before their time from whatever unknown malady was destroying their bodies. He knew they would never live to see any grandchildren; his heart lurched at the realization.

Reaching across the table, Thaddeus covered Achim's shaking hand with his own strong one. Achim was probably no more than ten years older than he, and Thaddeus cringed at the thought of becoming debilitated, dependent on others for one's care. Shaking the depressing thoughts from his mind, he picked up the parchment and took a quill, ink bottle and pen from his pack. He signed the contract, and then slid the parchment slowly across the table to Achim, who slid it to Caleb to sign for him. They smiled across the table at each other. It was done.

Jael spoke for the first time, and her voice was so weak that Thaddeus had to strain to hear it. "Thank you, Thaddeus, for your generosity. Helah will be a good wife to Rufus, I promise you." She was exhausted from the strain of sitting up for so long, and his heart was burdened for them and for Helah.

Thaddeus sighed. He placed the parchment, quill and ink into his pack, and then slid the coins in also. It made no difference to him that the dowry was small; he didn't need the money. He wasn't losing anything by having Rufus marrying Helah; Rufus would be staying with them and working as usual, after the required time off work for his honeymoon. He was gaining a daughter in the process. It appeared to him that Jael and Achim were the ones losing everything – the dowry money, their daughter, their health, their home, and probably their lives very soon. His heart was heavy as he bade them goodnight and retraced his steps up the hillside.

As he returned to his comfortable home, with its multiple chambers and ample dining area, he felt extremely rich compared to Achim and Jael. Achim had worked all his life as a weaver of fine rugs, and several of his creations, which had withstood the steps of many feet through the years, adorned the stone floor under Thaddeus's feet. Achim had provided well for Jael and their two children, but his failing health had affected his ability to work and, without regular income, their financial status had declined rapidly. The two rooms in which they now lived were owned by a distant cousin who let them live there without charge, and soon Caleb would be taking them to Bethany where he could care for them, taking away the last vestiges of freedom and independence that they had known.

He found his family reclining and conversing in the dining room, where Simon was the center of attention, a frequent occurrence. He was telling the story of how he and Obed had quite an adventure while taking Joseph's donkey out for exercise the other day, and everyone in the room was laughing hysterically.

"So Obed and I finally just left the donkey, figuring we would come back and try to get him off his rear later, but as we walked away, we heard these little footsteps behind us. It was the donkey!" he shouted. "All we had to do was leave him alone and he got up on his legs and followed us! I wish we'd known that before we wore ourselves out pushing, shoving and pulling to get him to stand up!"

The laughter slowly subsided when everyone noticed Thaddeus, the pack that contained the contract still in his hand. A hushed silence fell over the heretofore boisterous group until Kezia asked, "Is it done, Husband?"

"Yes," Thaddeus simply stated as he looked around, his eyes settling on Rufus. "Rufus and Helah are officially betrothed." Clapping and cheering filled the room.

Helah was in the kitchen doorway when the pronouncement was made, smiling across the room at Rufus as he endured the physical pounding of his male family members.

"Well," loudly proclaimed Thaddeus, "we need to start planning and building a house for the bride and bridegroom. We will begin tomorrow. Rufus has shown me where he wants it built. Simon, your share of the work is going to increase, especially the care of the sheep, so be prepared. Tomorrow will be the start of more work for you. I hope you're up to it."

"Oh, yes, Father, I'm up to it."

Kezia rose from her sitting position and approached Helah, took her hands in hers, and kissed her on both cheeks. "Welcome to our family, Helah. You are our daughter now."

Rufus watched from the other side of the room, the glow of love warming his heart.

Chapter Ten

STRUGGLES AND OPPRESSIONS

Working on the house for Rufus and Helah became the main focus of Thaddeus and his family during the coming weeks, which quickly turned into months. Even though all the preparation for the wedding was occurring right in front of them, Rufus and Helah hardly had any time to see each other. Helah worked at the house during the day, but she stayed with Deborah at the inn during the night to ensure there was no hint of impropriety.

The house being constructed was located about 100 yards from the main house. It wouldn't have an interior well, but would get its water supply from the outside well which also provided the water for the sheep. The house would have a main room that would also serve as the dining area, a small kitchen, and two ample sleeping chambers. Rufus and Helah were at the construction site daily, and most of the construction was accomplished during the evening hours because the daily herding and farming chores still needed to be done. Materials for the house itself came from the land, the foundation being made of stone and the walls constructed of bricks. Conifers were used to make the beams to support the roof, which was composed of matting and covered with plaster consisting of straw, mud and lime. There was also a set of stairs leading up to the roof, which would be used for eating and sleeping during hot weather.

Caleb had taken his parents to his home in Bethany, located very close to Jerusalem, the day after the betrothal contract was signed. He resumed instruction in pottery with Laban, and then immediately took Laban's younger sister, Rizpah, as his wife.

Helah had a difficult time letting her parents go, even though she knew it was best. Now, as she worked in the vegetable garden the following spring caring for the young, tender plants, she still thought back to that day and often had to hold back the tears that gathered in the rims of her eyes. She and Rufus had been to visit them twice since the move, and every time they went, Helah knew that she might never see them alive again. Rufus had been compassionate and understanding, allowing her to grieve and cry at every goodbye.

During the last visit to Caleb and Rizpah's home to see her parents, Helah had seen a dramatic decline in their health, noting that they seemed to be dying together. Neither was able to walk, and both were confined to bed much of the time. Rizpah had said that on the good days, they were able to get up and sit outside in the sunshine or at the table, but those days were few and becoming fewer. Rizpah and Helah became as close as sisters, the bond of love for the same people cementing their relationship.

Pouring water from the jug into the dry soil around a plant, Helah knew that the inevitable would happen very soon, and that knowledge put a pall over her life despite her upcoming marriage. Being with Rufus lifted her spirits, at least for the time she was with him. His zest for life and his love for her often made Helah forget her parents' illness, and she would go for hours without thinking about them, but at the end of every day when she put her head on her pillow, she knew that she was one day closer to losing them.

Carrying the jug to the outside well, Helah lowered it into the darkness until she heard a splash and then hauled it back up again. As she lugged it over to the garden, Kezia appeared and offered to help.

"Here, Helah, let me help you with that jug; I know how heavy it is when it's full." Together they carried the jug to the garden, where they poured its precious contents into two smaller jugs and set about watering the young plants.

"I see that the house is coming along very well," observed Kezia as the cool liquid saturated the ground.

"Yes, it is. I still can't believe that I'll have such a big house in which to live and all this wonderful land on which to walk and work also. How can I thank you for all you've done for me?"

Kezia put down her jug as she tapped some of the watered soil firmly around the roots of one of the plants. "There's no need to thank me and Thaddeus. God has blessed us, and now we can bless our children. That's what it's all about – family. I could lose all this and it wouldn't matter to me as long as I still had my family."

Helah's smile faded. "Even though my parents are dying, I know that I'm loved and am part of your family. Deborah and Gedaliah have been so kind to me, putting me up in one of their rooms. I insisted that I sleep on a pallet in their living quarters, but they refused. They could be making money on my room each night, but they said that family was more important than a few extra coins."

"Money's necessary, but when someone puts money ahead of family, God will not bless them, and God has blessed us in spite of the special taxes the Romans collect just to enrich their own lifestyles."

"I heard that King Herod's palace in Jerusalem is very beautiful."

"True," replied Kezia as they moved down the rows of plants with their watering jugs, "but Herod has also used some of the money he's collected to rebuild the temple, our most holy place of worship, returning it to its original splendor. He's a strange mix; from what I've heard, he's marginally Jewish and even abides by our strict dietary laws. Why, I have no idea."

"I heard he's an absolutely horrible person."

"True again. There isn't much good that can be said about King Herod other than that he rebuilt our temple."

"When Rufus and I have our first male child, we'll present him to the Lord at the temple," mused Helah, "just as Mary and Joseph have done with Baby Jesus."

"Speaking of Mary, it's time we visited her again. I'll go into town with you, and then we can stop and see Mary after we get Deborah. Jesus is almost four months old now, and Deborah's baby will be here in less than two months. I'm so excited about becoming a grandmother! So let's finish this job and get going. The men won't be back from the fields for hours yet. We'll still have time to prepare the evening meal when we return."

Once in town, they found Gedaliah and Deborah arguing with a guest over the price of a room, but they finally came to an agreement, and Deborah showed him to his room while he complained about the high cost of a decent room.

Gedaliah waited a moment before he greeted his mother and Helah. "Deborah will be right back," he said as he placed a kiss on the cheeks of each of the women. "She doesn't walk as quickly as she used to."

"And I can easily see that you're quite pleased," smiled Kezia. "How happy men are when they impregnate their mates." Helah's face turned crimson, and Gedaliah simply laughed.

"Selma is doing most of the cleaning and heavy work now. I insisted that Deborah start taking it easier, and Selma is a good worker. She and Deborah get the work done together very quickly now that they've developed their own system."

As Gedaliah finished speaking, Deborah waddled back into the room, holding her hand on her enlarged abdomen. She fondly greeted her mother and Helah.

"I thought it would be good to pay a visit to Mary, if you have a few minutes," Kezia suggested. "It doesn't have to be a long visit; Helah and I must return home soon to prepare the evening meal."

The three women were soon at Mary's door and found her mending one of Joseph's tunics while the baby napped.

"We've come to see you and little Jesus," explained Kezia. "Can I peek in his basket?"

Mary nodded, and Kezia quietly tiptoed over to the basket and gazed tenderly at the infant.

"Deborah," greeted Mary, "you look well."

"I'm feeling wonderful and getting more excited with each passing day," replied Deborah as she sat down next to Mary.

"Oh, he has grown so much!" exclaimed Kezia as she tucked the blanket under Jesus's chin.

Mary nodded as she cut the thread and started to mend another hole as Deborah and Helah gathered around the baby's basket and joined Kezia in similar exclamations. After a few moments, they joined Mary at the table.

"Mending clothes again?" asked Deborah.

"Yes. Between the three of us, I never seem to run out of mending to do. We can't afford to purchase material for new ones just yet. Maybe in a few months after Joseph's business picks up a little bit, but not now."

"Isn't Joseph's carpentry shop doing well?" asked Kezia.

"It's doing as well as can be expected," Mary replied. "People don't spend much; they never know when Herod is going to levy a new tax and demand payment immediately. People seem to hang onto their money out of fear. They're reluctant to purchase new things unless they really, really need them. Furniture is something that can be repaired most of the time. So Joseph does more repairing than anything else."

"We could all do without the taxes," observed Deborah. "I'll never forget that poor man in front of us in the registration line. I often wonder what became of him." Her eyes glazed over as she let her mind drift back to that day.

"He's probably dead by now," imagined Helah quietly. "Old people can't survive long when thrust into slavery, especially if they are already weak and sickly."

"You're probably right. I can still hear the sound of the soldier's foot as it hit him in the side, and it almost makes me sick." Deborah put both hands over her face as the images of that day flooded her mind.

Mary reached over and patted her hand. "Try not to think about it, Deborah. Things will get better in the future."

Deborah lowered her hands and gazed into Mary's eyes. "Yes, that's true, and it's all because of Jesus. We'll have an end to Roman rule because of him."

Mary shook her head emphatically as she closed her eyes. "You don't understand."

"What don't we understand?" questioned Kezia.

"You don't understand the path that God has chosen for Jesus, his Son."

The women became quiet as they looked at Mary, Joseph's worn tunic still in her hands. Mary wondered if they would ever understand. She kept her eyes closed as she continued.

"God sent his Son to save us from our sins." She opened her eyes and looked at her dear friends, who were still clearly perplexed.

"We offer sacrifices at the synagogue and at the temple to save us from our sins, as Moses has instructed us to do. How's Jesus going to do it for us? Is he going to offer sacrifices instead of us? Will he offer one sacrifice that will satisfy God for all eternity?" Kezia inquisitively asked.

Silence hung like a water-soaked cloak over them as Mary's eyes drifted from one face to the other. How could she give an answer when she didn't yet fully understand the scope of God's plan? The baby lying asleep in the basket on the other side of the room was just like any other baby, yet unlike any other baby. Where were the answers to her questions and to those of her friends?

Mary sighed heavily as she set the tunic on her lap. "I don't know," she quietly responded. "I only know that the angel of the Lord told Joseph that the child conceived in me would save His people from their sins. That is enough for me."

The room echoed the breathing of the women as the silence continued. Finally, Kezia spoke. "Then the only thing we can do is wait and see how God will bring this to pass," she stated softly but firmly to the others. "We cannot question God."

Mary's face lit up as she patted Deborah's belly in an effort to change the course of the conversation. "I see that you're getting close to your delivery time."

Deborah smiled warmly as she rubbed a hand across her round belly. "Yes, it won't be very many weeks now."

"The last weeks are the most difficult because you get so big and the days seem to drag because you get so excited," exclaimed Mary. "You think the child will never be born!"

"This will be my first of many grandchildren," proudly stated Kezia. "With Helah and Rufus getting married soon, I'm certain we'll have another baby before long."

"How is the house coming along?" questioned Mary as she looked at Helah.

"It's almost half finished. The hardest part is done, so the rest of the house shouldn't take much longer."

The baby stirred and whimpered from his basket. "Well, it looks as if my quiet time for the day is over." Deborah walked to the basket and picked up the crying infant, who became excited to see his visitors.

"He's such a good baby," stated Kezia as she tickled the child's chin and cooed at him. "It's still beyond my comprehension that this is the Son of God, Mary; it's too great a thought for me."

"It's also beyond mine, but I know who his Father is, and it is not Joseph."

Suddenly, from outside came the thundering of horses' hooves on the hard-packed earth and the voices of those screaming as they scrambled into every doorway, every opening along the street in an attempt to avoid being trampled by the horses racing through the town. Roman soldiers, the plumes of their helmets flattened back against the wind, bore down on the town of Bethlehem. Fear rose in every heart as they hurled curses at those in their way, disregarding human life and treating it as of no more value than a fly's. Mary took her baby and held him close to her breast as the sound of thundering horses exploded in front of her humble home and then quickly faded down the street. As the soldiers rode away, Mary and her friends ventured to the door, cautiously peering out. They could tell that the soldiers had halted their sweaty beasts a few streets away.

"What's happening?" asked Deborah. "Whose house have they stopped at?"

They waited, suspended with anxiety, as the sounds of curses and orders carried on the air, followed by screams and cries. Kezia gasped.

"On, no, I think it's Gebia's house!"

"What do they want with Gebia?"

"I don't know!"

The sounds grew more intense as people of the town started shouting and hurling insults at the soldiers. The occasional crack of a whip wielded by a well-trained soldier cut through the air, followed by piercing screams. Then the air was filled with loud wailing, cries for mercy interspersed with insults and curses.

"Quick! Back inside!" ordered Kezia as the clatter of the horses' hooves and shouts of the soldiers approached them again.

Kezia slammed the door shut and secured it as Mary held Jesus tightly to her chest. She quickly carried him to the other side of the room, where she was joined by Joseph as he came in from his workshop. Protectively putting his arm around the two of them, he motioned for the others to join them at the back of the room.

The thunder of the horses' hooves again thundered past the house and gradually faded away, but the words of one angry Roman soldier could be heard as they left town. "This is what happens to anyone who harbors an enemy of Caesar! Let this be a lesson to you!"

As the noise abated and the earth ceased its shaking, Joseph quickly ran to the door and opened it and peered down the street at the disappearing backs of the soldiers. The noise of their horses disappeared with them, but the sound of wailing at the other end of town only grew more intense. Joseph turned and instructed everyone to wait in the house, and then he disappeared from the doorway and ran down the street toward the source of the unrelenting wailing.

As he turned the corner, he had to turn his head away from the sight before him. Gebia's wife was on the ground, holding his lifeless body in her arms, wailing uncontrollably as her friends mourned with her. Her husband had been impaled with a spear, and blood was still seeping from the massive wound and collecting on the rock-hard street. Gebia was dead, another victim of Roman 'justice'.

Gebia's wife tore her robe, and her children stood weeping beside her, too stunned to do anything. Finally, the oldest child, a boy of about 14 years, touched her shoulder as neighbors pulled her away from Gebia's body while others picked it up and carried it into their home.

Sickened, Joseph slowly turned and retraced his steps to his house and quietly entered it, gently closing the door behind him. Questioning eyes greeted him as he turned and faced the women.

"Gebia's dead," he softly stated with a heavy heart. The women gasped in unison, and Kezia started to sob softly as Joseph continued. "Obviously the Romans are trying to get Gebia's brother, Heber, to come out of hiding. From what I've been hearing around town, he's caused quite a bit of trouble in the countryside lately, and they must want to catch him very badly."

Kezia stepped forward as she wiped the tears from her eyes. "I must go to Hadassah. She will need help with the children." She quickly left the house.

Deborah sat down, tears pooling in her eyes, and Helah put her arm around her shoulder in a comforting embrace. "What kind of a world is this to bring a baby into?" she questioned as the tears splattered onto her lap. "What point is there in life continuing when we have to live like this, fearful that soldiers will come and kill someone for no reason?" She buried her face in her hands and sobbed.

Mary handed Jesus to Joseph and rushed to Deborah's side. "Things will be different some day, Deborah. God has not abandoned his people. The throne in Jerusalem will be returned to King David's line one day."

Joseph approached Mary and reached for her as she leaned onto his chest, the tears falling unbidden down her cheeks. The harsh reality of what had happened outside the walls of their home sunk in as the sounds of mourning and wailing continued.

Kezia reached Gebia's house in a matter of minutes and found Gebia laid out on the table, where he was being prepared for burial. Hadassah and the children were in shock and were mourning loudly, pain rising from their bellies and escaping in piercing sobs. Kezia couldn't contain her tears as she assisted Hadassah's neighbors, comforted the children, and worked her way through the burial preparation process. Her mind was a muddle of confusion over Gebia's murder, and she prayed fervently for the Christ-child to grow and ease their suffering.

Turning her eyes from her own confused thoughts and heavenward, she prayed, "Comfort Hadassah and her children in their time of need, Lord."

Chapter Eleven

LIFE CONTINUES

The entire populace of the town of Bethlehem was on edge after Gebia's brutal, senseless murder, for that was what it was – murder – all in the hopes of flushing out Gebia's brother who had become an infested thorn in the flesh of Roman power. Obviously, Heber knew the countryside well and was quite adept at disappearing, and the Romans, even with their sophisticated methods, were inept at tracking him.

Several days after Gebia's burial, Hadassah and her children packed their belongings and headed to Lydda to stay with Hadassah's sister's family, yet sorrow and fear clung to the town.

"Heber probably knows about his brother's murder by now, wouldn't you think?" Reuben asked Thaddeus several days later as they were shearing the sheep.

Thaddeus grabbed another sheep, heavy with wool, and secured it to a post, immobilizing it. Taking the giant clippers, he expertly began to clip away at the wool, dropping it in large clumps to the ground.

"I imagine so."

"Do you think Heber will ever return to Bethlehem?"

"No. It would be suicide, not only for him, but for anyone that he contacts in this town." The sheep struggled unsuccessfully against the tether as Thaddeus clipped away with expert hands.

"I've seen soldiers patrolling the hills the last few days," Reuben reported. "I don't think they've missed a day watching from a distance."

"Well, Heber isn't a fool; he won't return with soldiers bandying about the hillsides. He knows this land like the back of his hand, and he'll simply stay away with soldiers patrolling the hills. He wouldn't cause more grief to come upon his family. Besides, he probably also knows that Hadassah has returned to her family."

Reuben released the sheared sheep and stood up, stretching out his back. Sweat was pouring from his body even though the day was only comfortably warm. He took a rag from his belt and wiped his forehead with it.

"How many Zealots do you think there are with Heber now?"

"It's hard to say, but I'd venture a guess of at least a hundred men. They can't possibly do the damage to the Romans that we've heard about with just a few men. There has to be a lot of them by now."

"If I didn't have Benaiah, I'd be off with Heber right now, but I can't abandon Benaiah, not with his mother gone."

"And I, dear brother," proclaimed Thaddeus as he released the sheep, "can't possibly do without you on this land. You're needed and appreciated more than words will ever say."

Reuben mopped his brow once again, squinting against the afternoon sun, high in the sky. "I feel like two people sometimes, and one of those wants to run from all this and join Heber, to make a difference or at least feel like I'm doing something to fight the blasted Romans. The other wants to stay here and do just what I'm doing. It's a somewhat safe and secure existence, but I hate feeling as if I've submitted to them without a fight."

Thaddeus grabbed a jug and drank deeply from it. As he wiped his mouth with the back of his hand, he replied, "Ah, but we can live peacefully and quietly, going about our daily business and worshipping as we wish. Thank God that we haven't been forced to worship the idols of Rome. They still allow us to worship Jehovah God, and thanks to the notorious King Herod, the temple in Jerusalem has been restored to its former glory. We have to look at the positive things about this Roman occupation."

"That's the difficult part, finding the positive among the negative. I wonder what positive thing Hadassah and her children can find in Gebia's murder."

"God will watch over Hadassah as she travels and joins her extended family. Right now, I have other things to worry about, like shearing all these sheep and getting the wool to market."

Thaddeus and Reuben resumed the task at hand, piling the sheared wool in heaps along the stone wall. Benaiah, Rufus and Eleazar then tied the wool into bundles and stacked them in the storage barn, where they would be kept until the shearing was completed. From there, the wool would be taken to Jerusalem and sold to a fuller, who would clean the wool of its natural oils. Then the wool would be spread on rocks to dry and bleach in the sun. Finally, the wool would be spun into material for cloaks and tunics.

The work was difficult and back-breaking, and by evening everyone was exhausted and welcomed the comfort of the dining area, as well as the meal spread by Kezia and Helah.

"I wonder if Hadassah made it to Lydda safely," Kezia mused as they ate roasted lamb. "I hated to see her set off without a male to accompany her for protection."

Thaddeus tossed a leg of lamb, gnawed clean of meat, into a large bowl and licked his fingers. "I feel in my heart that God gave her safe passage. Gebia was a devout man, and Hadassah was an honorable wife to him. I believe God rewards those virtues."

"Rewards?" bitterly questioned Reuben. "How can you say such a thing when Gebia lies dead in his grave?"

Thaddeus took a drink before replying. "Rewards in the sense that He provides, even when bad people do horrible things to God's people."

"Do you think that Hadassah and her children feel that God has provided for them?" derisively questioned Reuben. "Seeing their husband and father murdered right in front of them doesn't seem to be 'providing for' them, in my opinion."

"And you're entitled to your opinion," quietly stated Thaddeus. "However, God makes the rain to fall and the sun to shine on the just and the unjust. Without his blessings, we would have nothing."

"God provided a place for Mary to have her baby," reminded Simon, memories of cleaning Gedaliah's stable with Obed, which had proved to be more demanding that they had imagined, still fresh in his mind. They had a tremendous amount of fun while they worked, including chasing the chickens around the yard, but the current conversation depressed him, and he wished they would change the subject.

"You're absolutely right!" exclaimed Kezia as she reached across the table and tousled Simon's hair. "God *did* provide a place for Mary to have her baby, and he even provided help for her through you and Deborah and me."

Simon beamed. "When is Deborah going to have her baby, Mother?"

"It should be three or four weeks from now. Then you will be an uncle. What do you think about that?"

"I think it's great! I only hope it's a boy. I wouldn't know what to do with a little girl."

"Well, whichever it is," interrupted Eleazar, "you'll be too busy with the sheep and everything once Rufus goes on his honeymoon. You won't have any time for play anymore."

Simon choked on his food, eyes bulging. He looked at Eleazar quizzically. "What do you mean?"

"I mean that you'll have to help out with everything once Rufus and Helah are married. He has to take time off to be with his bride, don't you, Rufus?" He jabbed his brother in the side, making Rufus spill his wine as his face turn crimson with embarrassment, causing everyone to laugh.

Seated next to Kezia, Helah lowered her gaze and looked at her hands on her lap as color also crept up her face as the laughter created a rush of warmth. Slowly she raised her eyes to look at Rufus, only to find him gazing tenderly at her, ignoring the taunts and irritating jabs of his brother.

"Well, I remember when your mother and I got married," quietly stated Reuben to Benaiah, who was seated next to him. "Our time on earth was all too brief, over before it had actually begun."

Benaiah swallowed the mouthful of meat with a gulp. "Father, I believe what you've said about Mother and me speaking as our souls passed, hers to heaven and mine to earth, and even though I don't recollect such a moment, I believe it because I feel I know her."

Reuben slowly nodded his head. "In that respect, I must agree with my brother, that God does indeed provide. Micalah and I were married just over one year when you were born and she died, but in dying, she produced life, and I can't exchange one life for another. It's a very strange thing indeed to love someone who died to give birth and love one that was birthed that caused the dying. It's too much for this simple shepherd to comprehend."

Rufus looked over at Helah. How was he to know what life had to offer them? What if Helah were to die in childbirth as Micalah had done? Shaking his head, he tried to rid his mind of the fear of tragedy lying around the bend. Life was unpredictable. Look at Gebia. He had been alive one moment and was dead the next. How quickly life's circumstances could change!

Helah's hand rested on her abdomen, harbor for the secret beginnings of life. Union of husband and wife was a mystery to her, and the raging longings of her body were for that union with Rufus. And a child would sooner or later be created from that union, but even that was beyond her imaginations. Seeing Mary's baby and Deborah now heavy with child made her curiosity at the physical union more intense, and she was sure her desires for Rufus were evident to everyone. She lowered her gaze again to hide her secret longings from inquisitive, taunting eyes.

Reuben broke the strained silence that had settled on everyone. "But I would not trade you, Benaiah, for all the gold in the world. You're more precious to me than anything. You were your mother's precious gift to me."

"Well," cheerily stated Thaddeus, "on a happier note, we can resume work on the house in the morning. The sooner we get that finished, the sooner we can celebrate the wedding feast."

Kezia and Helah set about cleaning up from the meal, while the others lounged and rested on the large pillows. Simon cuddled close to his father's chest, comfortable in the realization that he could do so in the presence of his family without being called a baby. He was soon sound asleep against his father's chest, worn out from the long day of work and play.

Thaddeus carried his youngest son to his bedchamber and placed him on his bed, removed his outer garment as he tried to keep him in an upright position, and then covered him with his blanket. His youngest son – for there would not likely be any other children for him and Kezia – was growing so quickly, and his own life was passing so fast, that he grieved over the brevity of it all. By the time Simon took a wife, he would be considered an old man, and that was not to his liking. He gave Simon one last pat on the head before he returned and joined the others.

"I'll walk Helah to the inn," he heard Rufus say as he entered the dining area.

"Not by yourself, you won't," firmly declared Kezia. "Eleazar will go with you."

"But Mother, I'll just walk her there and come right back," protested Rufus. "Don't you trust me?"

"It's not so much a matter of trust as it is propriety. People will talk if given the chance. Eleazar will go with you so no one can start any gossip. We don't need that sort of thing."

Helah, Rufus and Eleazar left the house and headed down the hillside toward Bethlehem. The young couple made small talk as they traversed the countryside into Bethlehem. The night was warm and balmy, sweet with the scents of a multitude of flowers which bloomed in the early summer sun. The sky was clear, forming a backdrop for the thousands of stars that speckled the heavens. They slowed their pace the closer they got to town, almost pausing completely once or twice. The sounds of people settling down for the night greeted their ears as they came within the village itself, and soon they were at the back door of the inn. Eleazar stood back as Rufus said goodnight to

Helah. Once she was inside, Rufus finally turned to face his brother.

Eleazar placed his arm across Rufus's shoulder as they started the walk home. "Well, little brother, it won't be long now, and you won't be saying goodnight to Helah at all. Instead, you will be able to crawl in bed beside her. I know I've given you a hard time about it all, but I really do wish you well. Helah is a very nice girl, and she will make a good wife for you. I guess I've given you such a hard time because I'm really jealous and wish it were me getting married, that the house we are building would be for me and my wife, but such isn't the case."

Rufus looked at his brother in the shadows of the night as he turned to face him, surprised at this sudden honest exposure of his feelings.

"To be truthful," quietly responded Rufus, "I'm actually scared to death to get married. I mean, the responsibility is enough to choke me at times. Taking care of and providing for a wife isn't a small matter, and no doubt there will be a child within a year or so, soon to be followed by another and another. It scares me, Eleazar; much as I desire it, it scares me."

Continuing in silence, the two brothers returned to the house, only to find a stranger had arrived from Bethany with the news of Helah's mother's death.

Kezia was speaking to the stranger when Eleazar and Rufus entered the house. "I see no need to upset Helah at this hour of the night with this terrible news; it will serve no good purpose and will keep her awake all night. I think it would be best to wait until morning to tell her, don't you, Thaddeus?"

Thaddeus nodded in agreement. "You're welcome to stay here with us for the night, if you wish," he said to the visitor, whose name was Amon, "and then you can relay the message to Helah when she arrives in the morning. She's usually here very early, preparing our morning meal and doing chores."

"In fact," interrupted Kezia, "I think it best to tell her after our morning meal. I don't want her so upset that she refuses to eat; she'll need the energy for the trip to Bethany."

"There may be two funerals at the same time," stated Amon. "Achim was barely alive when I left, but Caleb didn't want to waste any time in getting word to Helah about her mother's passing."

Kezia turned to Rufus. "This will be a very difficult time for Helah."

"I know, Mother, and I want to be there for her and help her through it. I know how much Helah had been hoping and praying that at least one of them would live to see us married." He stared blankly down at the floor.

"I think that all of us should go to sleep now," suggested Thaddeus. "Tomorrow will be a difficult day. Again, Amon, you're welcome to stay here for the night. You can sleep in Simon's room with him. We have an extra pallet and blanket in there."

Kezia led Amon to the kitchen area and poured him a basin of water so he could wash up before retiring to Simon's room.

"Thank you for your kindness," whispered Amon as he dipped his hands into the cool water.

As Kezia and Thaddeus lay in bed together, they cuddled close. Thaddeus wrapped his arm around her as she laid her head on his shoulder, gently stroking her hair as he had done countless times before. Kissing her forehead, he said, "Dear Kezia, you mean the world to me. It seems as if life is passing by so quickly right before our eyes. Rufus will be married soon, Simon won't be a little boy much longer, and we'll be grandparents in a few weeks.

Change, always change. I wish I had ten more lives to live with you, Kezia. One is not enough."

Kezia felt a tear of joy slide from her eyes. Slowly she ran her hand across his muscular chest, gently tugging the hairs with her fingers. She nestled closer in his embrace.

"No other man could ever make me as happy as you have made me, Thaddeus. I have loved only you and no other. If I had ten more lives to live, I'd want everyone of them to be with you."

Thaddeus cupped her chin in his hand and raised her lips to his, where they met in a tender kiss. "I can't imagine life without you, and I pray that God takes you first so you don't have to suffer being a widow. And if you do die first, I'll probably not survive many days after, for to live without you would be death to me. I can easily understand why Achim won't survive much longer now that Jael is dead. Husband and wife become one flesh, and when one dies, the survivor loses a part of himself, too."

"Death has been creeping up on Helah's parents for months now with this sickness, whatever it is, but I know she'll be strong. She's been expecting it. Just yesterday she mentioned to me that she was wondering how many more days her parents had left. I'm sure they've never been far from her thoughts."

"Do you think Rufus should go with her to Bethany?"

"Absolutely. Besides, he won't have it any other way."

"The mohar will be returned to Rufus and Helah before they're married. It will give them extra money to set up house."

"I'm sure Caleb will see that it's returned to Helah while she's there. Even if Achim lives for several more days, his death is imminent. It's so sad that this has happened just before Deborah's baby is born and before the wedding."

"God alone ordains our time of departure from this earth. And I, my love, want to grow old and gray with you by my side and many grandchildren calling us blessed. That is my prayer tonight."

Kezia rolled over more fully into his arms, safe and secure in his love, as she tried to imagine a future of growing old with Thaddeus.

Chapter Twelve

A NEW LIFE

Helah and Rufus were in Bethany for seven days, during which time, to no one's surprise, Helah's father also passed away. They arrived in Bethany only hours prior to his death, and so the days there were consumed with mourning and funerals, visitations from friends and relatives. Helah, still wearing her mourning clothes, was exhausted when she returned to the house on the hillside.

"If it hadn't been for Caleb," Rufus informed the family as they gathered around during the evening meal, "we wouldn't have been able to make it through this very difficult time."

"And don't forget Rizpah," quickly added Helah. "She was most gracious and kind to me – to us – and offered nothing but sincere hospitality and understanding. Caleb is very lucky to have her for a wife."

"Yes, she saw to it that our every need was met, and she kept the professional mourners at bay, knowing that Helah preferred it that way."

"Were your parents buried in the same tomb?" Kezia inquired softly.

Helah rubbed her fingers across her eyes, weariness evident in her gesture. "Yes, they were. I'm glad, actually, that they're gone to heaven, for they're no longer suffering. They're together with God, eternally blessed with healthy bodies, and they won't suffer any more. The time of mourning is over, and Rufus and I must get on with our lives."

Rufus reached over and took Helah's hand in his and gently rubbed it between his fingers. Slowly raising his hand, he pushed back a tendril of her hair that had escaped the shawl draped over her head, awash with love for this precious young woman who was placing her life literally in his hands. "The house will be completed soon, and then we can begin our life together, dear Helah."

"Well," stated Thaddeus as he stood up from his reclining position, "we've got a lot of work to do tomorrow, so it's off to bed with you, Simon." Reaching down, he placed his hands on his youngest son's arms and hoisted him high in the air. Simon squealed with delight. "I thought I was too big for you to lift me like that anymore, Father! Put me down before I fall!"

"Not on your life!" He pranced around the room, family members laughing as they tried to keep out of the way of Thaddeus's steps while Simon hung on for dear life.

"Be careful, Thaddeus!" shouted Kezia. "You might drop him! He's right; he's not a little boy anymore!"

"That I'm well aware of!" loudly replied Thaddeus as he raced out of the room and into the main hall, Simon protesting all the while to be lowered back down to the ground. Kezia just laughed all the more as she saw the two of them bounce along and into Simon's room.

"Goodnight, Simon!" she called.

"Goodnight, Mother! Goodnight, everyone!"

Reuben adjusted his position on the reclining pillows and crossed his legs in front of him. "Simon is growing so fast."

"Thaddeus and I were talking about that very thing just last night when we went to bed. All of you," she indicated to those seated around the table, "are grown up now, or almost so. Rufus and Helah will soon be married, and Eleazar, even Benaiah, are old enough to marry. I'm afraid I'm becoming an old woman very, very quickly."

"But Kezia," quickly stated Reuben, "don't you think old age is a state of mind? One doesn't need to be old unless they think they are old, at least that's my opinion. I'm 37 years old, and I'm just as strong, if not stronger, than I was when I was 20."

"Ah, yes, I'm sure you are," laughed Kezia in agreement.

Thaddeus reappeared and fell dramatically into the middle of the group, feigning exhaustion. Just then there was a loud rap on the front door, and Thaddeus jumped back up to answer it.

"I wonder who that could be at this hour?" uttered Kezia, her eyebrows furrowed in concern.

Thaddeus found Obed at the door, his face flushed from running up the hillside. "Gedaliah wants you to come quickly! Deborah is about to have her baby!"

"Oh, my," excitedly stated Kezia as she rushed to the door. "The baby isn't due for another two weeks. Thaddeus, please come with me! You can keep Gedaliah company while I assist Deborah. It may be a very long night since this is her first child."

"Why do babies always have to arrive during the night?" he asked.

"Babies come when they're ready. Hurry!"

They soon arrived at the inn. Kezia could hardly contain her excitement and joy as she hurried into the room where she found Deborah on the bed, her arm over her huge abdomen, and Eglah sitting by her side, gently wiping her brow with a cloth dipped in cool water. Immediately Kezia noted that everything she needed to assist in the birth was placed within easy reach. Deborah and Eglah had done a good job of preparing.

"How are you, Deborah?" she asked as she placed her hand alongside Deborah's sweaty face.

Deborah opened her eyes and sighed heavily. "I'm fine, Mother. I didn't think that it would hurt this much." Closing her eyes, she groaned as another contraction gripped her abdomen.

"Try not to think about the pain. Think instead about simply relaxing and allowing your body to do what God created it to do." She lifted Deborah's gown.

"Your water hasn't broken yet?"

"No," Eglah offered, "but the pains have become much stronger since Obed went to get you."

"We'll make you as comfortable as possible, Deborah, and help you get through this." Kezia arose and went to the other room and informed Thaddeus and Gedaliah as to Deborah's progress. When she returned to Deborah's side, she was in the throes of another contraction, moaning with pain as she threw back her head in travail.

There was a gently knock on the door and Eglah called out, "Come in!"

Mary appeared slowly as she opened the door and entered the room. "Mary, how good that you're here! But how did you know that Deborah's time had come?"

"Obed stopped by our home after he went to Kezia's. I didn't want to miss the birth and assisting if I could, especially after all that Deborah did for me when Jesus was born."

Several hours passed as Deborah's labor progressed, with Eglah, Kezia and Mary encouraging and assisting her, and finally Deborah's water broke, relieving much of the pressure.

Deborah relaxed after yet another strong contraction. She was perspiring profusely, and Eglah had loosened or removed much of her clothing, often wiping her brow with a water-soaked cloth.

"I won't be long now," Kezia exclaimed. "I can feel the baby's head."

Deborah moaned in pain as she gripped Eglah's hand, and Mary quickly sat down on her other side and picked up her left hand. Several more contractions gripped Deborah, and then she was propped up on pillows to aid the delivery as Kezia coached her.

"I can see the baby's head," she stated excitedly, "so with the next contraction, push hard." With sweat pouring off her face, Deborah gripped Mary and Eglah's hands and gritted her teeth as the next pain swallowed her.

Kezia was ready to catch the baby, wet and shiny, as it entered the world, took its first breath, and let everyone know how displeased he was at being here.

Glowing with joy and amazement, Kezia held the small infant up in her hands. "It's a boy, Deborah! You've given me a grandson!" Mary quickly spread a cloth on Deborah's abdomen for the baby, and then began vigorously rubbing it down. The child's lusty cry was heard by Gedaliah and Thaddeus in the next room, waking them from a restless sleep, and they entered quietly to see the infant.

"You have a son, Gedaliah!" declared Kezia as she tied and cut the umbilical cord. "And it appears that he has all his parts and is healthy! Praise Jehovah!"

Deborah took her baby's small hand in hers, amazed at its perfection. Tears of joy flowed down her face as she listened to the cry of her firstborn, a son. Gedaliah came over and kissed her gently.

"Isn't he marvelous?" exclaimed Deborah. "He's so small, but so perfect!"

Gedaliah was overcome with joy as he looked upon the fruit of his seed with Deborah. How the sweet union of a man and woman could produce something so perfect and beautiful was beyond description. Taking the baby's hand in his large one, he gently held it between his thumb and finger as the child continued his lusty cry.

"There will be much time with the baby," stated Kezia, "but for now you need to leave so we can clean up Deborah and the baby. Then they will need a lot of rest."

Gedaliah and Thaddeus reluctantly retraced their steps to the main room, talking excitedly. Kezia attended to Deborah as the afterbirth was passed, and then bathed her while Mary attended the baby.

"Have you decided upon a name?" asked Mary as she wrapped the baby after rubbing him down.

Deborah took a long drink from the cup that was handed to her by Eglah. "We've talked about many names, but I'm not sure which we will pick. My choice is Jesse."

"That's a good choice," agreed Eglah. "My firstborn grandchild, a son, will have a good Jewish name, one that conjures up faithfulness to God. It's a good choice."

It was early in the morning when Mary returned home. Kezia and Thaddeus returned to the darkened house, overflowing with joy at the newest member of their family.

Gedaliah lay down beside Deborah, their newborn between them. Deborah was totally exhausted from doing the most difficult work a woman can do – give birth. The baby was sleeping peacefully, and Gedaliah gently stroked its soft cheek with the back of his finger. Sensing his presence, Deborah roused and gazed up at him with drowsy eyes.

"I can't believe this beautiful little baby has come from us," whispered Gedaliah. "You've made me a very happy and proud man, my sweet wife." He leaned over and gently kissed her on the forehead.

Deborah smiled warmly at him as she fought to keep her eyes open for a few brief moments. "What name will you give him – Jesse or Omar?" she asked in a whisper.

"I think it will be Jesse."

"Good," whispered Deborah. "His name is Jesse." She closed her eyes and drifted off to sleep, Jesse and her husband by her side.

Gedaliah lay awake for some time before he reached over and turned down the oil lamp. A child, his child, had arrived, and it was now his responsibility to care for and nurture this tiny infant, to teach it the ways of God, and to feed and clothe it. Jesse was so small and helpless, utterly dependent upon him and Deborah for his care and keeping. Such a perfect little child, fresh and unblemished with the troubles and sorrows of life, and yet Gedaliah realized that there was no way he would be able to protect him from pain and suffering as he grew. Oh, if only he could! It didn't seem right that such a perfect, tiny human being must grow and suffer the hardships of living! Panic momentarily clutched his heart as the enormity of the task hit him, but it vanished as the fog vanishes with the rising sun. There were many friends and family who would also assist in this monumental task, and he rested in that knowledge as sleep finally overtook him.

Mary quietly entered her home and was surprised when Joseph woke up as she crawled in bed beside him.

"It's a boy. Deborah and Gedaliah have a little boy, just like us."

"Now Jesus will have another boy to play with as he grows up, that is, if we stay here in Bethlehem," Joseph mumbled as he hugged Mary close to him.

"I'd love to stay, if that's what God wants us to do. Deborah and I have become good friends, and it would be nice to raise our children together."

Joseph looked at his wife in the dim light of the lamp. "You do realize that we will eventually return to Nazareth, don't you?"

Mary looked away from him, avoiding his eyes. Reluctantly she answered, "Yes, but I hope it's not too soon. I've put down roots here, and I'm not ready to leave just yet. Of course, when God makes it clear that he wants us to return to Nazareth, I'll go without any hesitation. I just hope and pray that it's not too soon, especially now that Deborah has a little baby boy."

Joseph again drew her close to his chest. Turning her face toward his, he said, "Maybe Gedaliah and Deborah will want to come with us when we return."

"That isn't likely," countered Mary as she left his arms and stood by the basket cradling the sleeping Jesus. "Gedaliah and Deborah have family here, and the inn is their source of income, so it's hardly likely that they would even think of leaving when we do."

Joseph came and stood by her side as they watched the sleeping child.

"Look how big he is already, Joseph," softly exclaimed Mary. "He's twice the size he was when he was born, and he is so chubby and healthy. My heart grieves over what he must accomplish in this life, and I'll forever be astonished that God chose me to be his instrument to accomplish his purpose in bringing his Son to this earth. I marvel that he exists at all as this tiny child, seemingly similar to all other children, yet unlike any other. Often I wonder what Kezia and Deborah think about all that I've told them concerning his conception and birth, Joseph. If they think I'm crazy, I wouldn't be surprised. But they seem to believe all that I've told them concerning this child, the Son of God."

"It seems so unreal at times, doesn't it?"

Mary turned and looked up at him. "Yes, Joseph, so much so that I often forget that Jesus is different because he seems just like any other little boy growing up. Of course, everyone who believes that he is the Messiah expects him to overthrow the Roman government. Little do they know that he's come to save his people from their sins, not from the oppression of Rome."

"Many nights I have often lain awake, wondering how Jesus will achieve his purpose."

"Only God knows," responded Mary after a brief silence as she gently touched her son's curly, dark hair. "I can't fathom the depth of this task that has been set before us; it often threatens to overtake me and drown me."

"God will always be with us, Mary," encouraged Joseph. "He'll never abandon us. And every day he will guide us in raising his Son, our Son." He took Mary's hand in his. "Come, let's go to bed. It's late, and you must be very tired."

The sun rose on a very exhausted, but thrilled, Gedaliah, who woke to tend to the inn and its several guests. Upon her arrival at the inn, Selma went to the family living quarters to congratulate Deborah and see the infant, and then she assisted Eglah with preparing the morning meal for Deborah and Gedaliah. Gedaliah was grateful for Selman's assistance during the day.

"I can't thank you enough for all you've done," he told her late in the afternoon. "I know Deborah appreciates it also."

"I don't expect her to be back in full swing for several weeks," stated Selma as she filled the water jugs. "She needs time with the baby, and also time to recover. I can take care of things for her until then."

Gedaliah moved the jugs as Selma filled them. "Actually, Selma, I would like to offer you more work, if that's what you want. I'd like for Deborah to spend as much time with Jesse as she wants. I'll double your wages for the additional work."

Selma rested her jug on the table. "Thank you, Gedaliah. I'd be glad to accept the extra work. I haven't forgotten what it's like to have a newborn baby, nursing it every two or three hours day and night. It can be exhausting, to say the least. So, yes, I'll do the extra work for you."

"Good. Deborah will be glad to hear that. She didn't know how she was going to manage everything, but I kept telling her that I thought you'd be willing to take on more work."

Before long, the entire town heard about Jesse's birth, and many people stopped by the inn to offer their congratulations. Such a joyous occasion was cause for celebration, and it seemed as if the town of Bethlehem was as excited as the new parents.

Kezia wasted no time in returning to the inn the next morning. She shopped at the market for the evening meal, helped Eglah bake some of her delicious herb breads, and continually offered an assortment of food to Deborah, who had a ravenous appetite.

"I can't remember when I've been so hungry," she stated as she spread some goat cheese on a slice of bread.

"You must remember that you're feeding not only yourself, but Jesse as well. You'll have a hearty appetite much of the time that you're nursing him, so all I can say is, eat what you want to eat."

Mary and Joseph brought Jesus to see Deborah and Jesse, his future playmate, and they stayed for the evening meal at Kezia's insistence. Shortly afterward,

Thaddeus and the rest of the family arrived. Simon wanted to be first to hold the baby.

"I'm so glad it's a boy," he dramatically exclaimed as Kezia placed Jesse into his arms as he sat on a bench. "Boys are more fun than girls, at least for playing."

Benaiah was reluctant to hold the infant, afraid he would drop him, but Rufus eagerly accepted the small bundle into his arms. With Helah by his side, he held his new nephew, marveling at his tiny frame.

"Just think, Helah," he said softly to her, "we could have one of these in a year or so."

Helah blushed under his gaze and her heart raced at the thought of intimacy with Rufus. "Here, let me hold him," she softly demanded as she took the sleeping child. As he passed Jesse to her, their eyes met, and Helah saw the desire for her in his eyes, making her all the more embarrassed as her longing for him increased. Taking the child, she turned her back to Rufus, desperately trying to control her fluttering heart.

Life slowly settled back to normal within the next few days, and soon Mary and Deborah were spending hours together, taking care of their infants and sharing thoughts and hopes for the future as they watched their offspring flourish under their care.

The season changed from late spring to summer, and the heat was almost unbearable in the cramped town. Many people opted to move outside the town's boundaries to ward off the summer heat, taking refuge in tents or homes scattered on the hillsides, or slept on the top of their houses. Odors from refuse and human waste dumped outside the town became putrid as the heat increased. Mary and Jesus spent many days with Deborah and Kezia, out on the hillsides or at Kezia's house during the day. Instead of baking bread in their tiny houses, Deborah and Mary joined Kezia and Helah, and together they made bread in Kezia's large oven for all their families. Besides being a more bearable place to bake bread in the heat, the time spent with each other strengthened their bonds and developed unity between the women.

Jesus grew under the nurture and guidance of Mary and Joseph, and by the time he was six months old, he was sitting up with support. It wasn't many more months before he was standing on his chubby feet with the help of an adult holding his hands, and he brought joy to everyone. Mary and Deborah often took their babies to the brook outside town, where they cooled themselves and their little ones in the refreshing water as it bubbled and tumbled over the rocks. Rainy days were always welcome, for they were few and far between, and the cooler air ushered in by the rain brought relief to the town's citizens, as well as refreshment to the parched ground and crops.

The house for Rufus and Helah finally was completed, and the day of their wedding quickly approached. Rufus was kept occupied with the farm and flock of sheep, and even though Helah was busy with her work and baking, she was often distracted from the task at hand. It was on such a day that she found her mind wandering as she kneaded a batch of dough.

"Helah," whispered Kezia as she came to her side, "I think that dough is quite ready to set aside. I think you've been kneading it for at least twice as long as necessary."

Blushing, Helah set the dough in a bowl and covered it, turning to her future mother-in-law. "I'm sorry, Kezia; my mind must have been somewhere else."

"And where could it have possibly been?" she asked with a grin. "I mean, you're getting married in just a matter of days, so could that possibly be on your mind?"

Helah looked at Kezia, and they both laughed. "Well, it won't be long until you're baking bread only for Rufus. I don't know what I'm going to do without you around here."

"Oh, Kezia, I still want to help you! There's no way you can do everything by yourself." She dusted her hands off on her dress, sending a white cloud of flour into the air.

"Oh, no you won't," quickly retorted Kezia. "You must be alone with Rufus for several months before you even consider coming to help me again. The two of you need time alone, to get to know each other and to get used to living with each other. Then, after a while, you can help me if you wish, but not to the extent you're helping me now."

"But, Kezia," Helah began to protest.

"I'll not have it any other way," Kezia lovingly cut her off rather sharply. "Much as I need and appreciate all you do, Rufus is your responsibility from now on. And I believe you'll handle the duties of your own household very well, considering what I've seen you accomplish here. Both of you need time together with no responsibilities other than to each other. That's the way it should be."

Helah washed her hands in a bowl of water. "It will be very difficult for me to stay away from here."

"No, it won't. I've seen the way you look at Rufus, and believe me, it won't be difficult for you to stay home and be alone with him. You'll find things to do." She smiled coyly.

Helah felt the color creeping up her neck as she dried her hands, her mind drifting back to Rufus again.

The wedding preparations were finalized a week later and the feast prepared. Because Helah was residing with Deborah and Gedaliah and only working at Thaddeus's house, she waited for her groom to come to the inn when the day finally arrived. All of their friends in town had been invited, including Mary and Joseph, and they waited along the path from the town to Thaddeus's house. Rufus, along with his wedding companion, which was Eleazar, proceeded to the inn at dusk. There they found Helah, waiting and adorned with her wedding veil and jewelry which Rufus had given her. As Rufus reached the inn, Helah stepped out of the door, and after a simply ceremony performed by the priest, he removed the veil from Helah's face and draped it over his shoulder. He then escorted Helah to his father's house, accompanied by Eleazar, Reuben, Thaddeus, Benaiah, Simon, Obed and Joseph. The people in the town of Bethlehem who were invited to the wedding feast were waiting along the path with torches, and the noisy, rejoicing procession wound its way up the hillside to the house, where Deborah, Kezia and Mary had prepared the wedding feast. The evening was delightfully pleasant with a cool breeze skipping across the hillside, making the fire on the torches dance in the darkness.

The evening was lively with music and dancing, food and drink, and congratulations for Rufus and Helah, as well as wishes for Thaddeus and Kezia. Rufus couldn't keep his eyes off Helah, his new bride, and he often found his heart seemingly stuck in his throat, his desire for her almost choking him. The love he had for her was more profound than he had ever imagined it could be and caused his heart to jump inside his chest. Helah had never looked so beautiful; her wedding dress was simple yet lovely and becoming, accentuating her slender figure. Her hair was adorned with flowers from Kezia's garden, and Mary had helped Kezia make her veil, which was still draped across his shoulder. The torchlight made the entire gathering surreal, casting shadows in all directions as the revelers danced and pranced with the music.

Kezia and Thaddeus found themselves standing together outside the circle of celebration, and Thaddeus reached over and put his arm around his wife and drew her close to his side. Looking tenderly down at her, he said, "It's hard to believe that Rufus is married, isn't it?"

Kezia paused, reflecting on the scene before her. With a deep sigh, she said, "Yes, it is, Thaddeus. Life moves so quickly, and soon Eleazar will get married – at least we hope he will – and then before we know it, Simon will. One grandchild will be followed by another and another and another, filling our lives with life and love." She turned in her husband's embrace and faced him. "My dear husband, I don't regret one moment of my life with you, not one moment."

Thaddeus saw the reflection of the torch light in Kezia's eyes, deep, dark pools that washed him in tenderness. He pulled her closer and kissed her, not caring who might possibly see them. This was a night for rejoicing and celebrating, and it didn't matter to him what anyone might think of his public display.

As the hours passed, the time arrived for escorting the bride and bridegroom to their own house. Eleazar grabbed a torch from its holder and led the way the short distance to the house that he had helped construct, with Rufus and Helah surrounded by their guests and family. For Rufus and Helah, the short distance seemed to take forever to cross, and they were keenly aware that they'd receive a great deal of teasing, which was all part of the ritual.

As they approached the door, Eleazar stepped aside. Speaking in a loud voice, he declared, "I think we should all camp out around the house! Rufus may need some instruction on what he is supposed to do tonight!"

The crowd of celebrants roared with laughter as Reuben went to Eleazar's side and loudly announced, "And as his uncle, I think I should be the one to give those instructions!"

Howls of laughter filled the night air, much to the chagrin of the newlyweds. Simon, not understanding the gist of the conversation, hollered, "Instructions on what? All they're going to do is sleep together!"

His comment sent the crowd into another uproar. Taking advantage of the momentary diversion, Rufus quickly ushered Helah into their home and hurriedly shut and barred the door behind them.

"Quick!" he shouted to Helah. "Shut and bar all the windows!" They scurried through the small house, each in the opposite direction of the other, closing and shuttering the windows.

Eleazar was the first to notice that they had managed to enter the house undetected. Jumping forward and pounding on the door, he shouted, "Rufus! You've got to unbar this door! We need to tell you something!" All the guests shouted in agreement.

Standing on the other side of the barred door with his heart wildly racing, Rufus shouted back, "I'll not unbar this door until the morning, very late in the morning, in fact, so go away!"

"Go away?!" hollered Eleazar. "We're only going to go away so we can get our things and camp out under your windows. You may need to ask a question or two during the night!" With that remark, the crowd laughed again as it slowly turned and meandered back to the remains of the feast.

Rufus stood pressed against the door in the near darkness, listening intently as his heart thundered in his chest; surely Helah could hear it heart beating. As the noise outside the door abated, he relaxed his position and looked upon his new bride. Helah simply took his breath away. She was flushed from the dancing and wine, and her eyes were more alive than he'd ever seen them. He stepped away from the door and slowly approached her.

Helah prayed for the strength to stay on her feet; she thought she would faint dead away with anticipation and longing. Rufus gently touched her face with his hand and slid it down her long, lovely neck as Helah's hair slid between his fingers. With his other hand, he reached around her waist and drew her to him.

Helah melted into his embrace, and all the passion and desire that she'd felt for so many months came pouring out of her as their bodies met in an earthquake of anticipation. His kisses set her body on fire, and she lost herself to time and space and gave herself completely to him. There was no longer her and him, but just one heart, one mind, one soul, and one body.

The heat of their love seared them as the stars silently slid across the heavens, eventually cooling to sweet sleep of deep satisfaction and fulfillment.

Chapter Thirteen

KING HEROD

King Herod's palace in Jerusalem was one of unparalleled splendor. There was nothing that it didn't possess, impressive even by Roman standards, lavish and opulent beyond measure. It captured the attention of anyone who came to Jerusalem, as did the Jewish temple, which King Herod had rebuilt with the intent of appeasing his subjects.

Herod's palace boasted mosaic floors, underfloor heating and piped water, and bathrooms. Attractive geometric designs covered the walls, and the halls contained many statues of Roman gods and goddesses worshipped at the time, as gods were known to come and go through the centuries. Courtyards overflowed with fountains and plants.

Herod had been appointed Governor of Galilee by the Roman triumvir, Mark Antony, one of his closest friends, and later he had been given the title 'King of the Jews' after the death of his father, Antipater, procurator of Judea. There was not a Jew alive who paid homage to King Herod because all Jews detested the man who governed their country. True, Herod had rebuilt the temple in Jerusalem and allowed the Jews freedom to worship Jehovah God, but they despised the authority which he represented. The vast majority of the rebuilding of the temple in Jerusalem was accomplished over a period of ten years, but additional work continued for many years until it was completed. The reconstruction was done on the same plane as Solomon's original temple, but the reconstruction was grander by far. The temple itself was twice as high as the former one and was covered with so much gold that it was dazzling in the sunlight. Herod wanted more than anything to win the favor of his subjects and to impress the governing officials in Rome with the grandeur of the City of Jerusalem rather than have them think he ruled some nondescript country in the middle of nowhere.

Although reconstruction of the temple didn't alleviate the burden of Roman occupation, it did a great deal to mitigate the oppression felt by the Jews over the presence of the Romans in their land.

Herod was familiar with high society in Rome and had made friends with Mark Antony and Caesar Agustus. He used Roman politics to lay his path to fortune and fame. In all actuality, Herod was not a true Roman, but an Idumean Jew, even observing Jewish dietary laws, but more than anything, throughout his kingdom he was known for his tyranny, treachery, and cruelty, which was directed at not only the Jews, but to anyone who came against him, even members of his own family.

It was into this setting that magi, men expert in the study of the stars, arrived at the onset of the winter months. They had traveled many, many miles, following a star which had appeared in the skies, announcing the birth of the King of the Jews, according to all that they had studied. They entered the city as did others, through the massive gates, and made their way through the congested, narrow streets. Troubled that the star had disappeared during the last two nights, they arrived in Jerusalem to see the reigning King of the Jews, King Herod.

Sitting astride their camels, the men were led by their servants toward the palace, its massive size making it easily discernable from every point in the city. Looking down from his lofty position astride his camel, Gaspar gazed at the masses staring up at him. Clearly, it wasn't often that people of their position or from their country set foot in Jerusalem; otherwise, they'd be a common site and of no import, but their small procession made quite a stir as it navigated the city streets, people stepping aside to make way for the strange entourage.

The going wasn't easy as the camels were more suited to walking on sand than on hard stone and packed dirt. Those that led the camels slowed their pace, not only because of the stone streets, but also because of the noisy, boisterous crowds. Finally, after many delays in the crowds, they reached the perimeter of the heavily guarded palace and approached its entrance.

"Asamin," Gaspar called to his servant at the camel's head, "we will stop here." The servant stopped the camel and tapped its legs with a long stick, and the camel knelt down, as did the others carrying Melchior and Baltazar, the other men riding the camels. Asamin and the other servants removed small stairs from pack camels that followed behind the three magi and placed them on the ground beside the camels, and the three magi dismounted, never taking their eyes off the citizens of Jerusalem who gazed silently at them.

After a few moments, Gaspar led the other magi, and they approached the heavily-guarded entrance to the palace and were met by a soldier, dressed in full Roman military array, who looked as if he could stop a raging bull from entering.

Stepping forward as Melchior and Baltazar stopped, Gaspar bowed slightly in deference and said, "We seek the King of the Jews."

"For what purpose?"

"We have come to pay homage and worship him and offer him gifts."

The guard eyed the strange men. Clearly, they were wealthy and of importance in the country from which they hailed. He found it strange that they could speak his language.

"Wait here." The guard turned and disappeared into the palace entrance, passing several more guards in the process.

Gaspar, Melchior and Baltazar waited patiently as they tried to ignore the inquisitive stares of passersby. They knew they stood out from the drab crowds surrounding them. Their robes were adorned with gold braiding and colored fringe. They had rings of precious stones on many of their fingers. Their black beards flowed halfway down their chests, and their dark eyes were constantly on the alert for any trouble. Also keenly watching the crowds, the servants kept one hand on their camel's tether and the other on their sheathed knives, ready to defend their masters at a moment's notice, should the need arise.

When the guard finally returned, he nodded to them and said, "Follow me."

Gaspar, Melchior and Baltazar followed the guard through the lavish courtyard and into the palace itself. The floors were polished marble, reflecting everything around them. Tall columns of stone held up the vast ceilings, which were adorned with frescoes and paintings, and some of the ceilings were open to the sky in places, allowing natural sunlight to enter the rooms. Their steps echoed in the vast halls as they walked, yet Gaspar and the others were not overly impressed. They'd seen a great deal of wealth in their own country and were accustomed to it, having left such luxury to make this arduous journey in search of a baby, a young child. Yes, this was just another palace built by and for another king to satisfy his lust for luxury and opulence and was probably built at the expense of his subjects.

Shortly, they arrived at a set of heavily gilded doors where two more guards were stationed, and as they approached, the huge doors swung open, revealing a hall where audience with the king was granted. A lush carpet ran from the door to the throne, which sat atop several stairs on a platform, where a portly figure dressed in regal Roman attire was situated thereon, a scepter in one hand.

The guard stepped aside, and the three men stepped forward and bowed. King Herod indicated with his scepter for them to approach his throne, and they did so, bowing deeply again at the foot of the stairs. When they rose to their feet, Herod spoke.

"So, you've come to see the King of the Jews. You've come to the right place. I am Herod the Great, King of the Jews." Herod looked down at them as he took in their expensive garments and jewelry even as he raised his nose and curled his lips slightly. Even though they were wealthy, Herod simply didn't accede to others of similar stature, preferring to elevate himself.

Disregarding Herod's demeanor, Gaspar stepped forward. "King Herod, we have traveled numerous miles for many, many months, following a star that appeared in the sky almost a year ago. My companions and I study the stars and were informed that the new star in the night sky was to announce the birth of the King of the Jews. So with all due respect, we have come to find an infant, a small child." He lowered his head slightly when he finished speaking, keenly aware that the king on the throne in front of him was pompous and conceited and probably wouldn't take this news lightly.

Herod's crude smile vanished as Gaspar finished speaking. His eyes blazed with disgust as he adjusted his position on his throne; there hadn't been a birth among his several wives for over a year, although a few were currently pregnant, despite his advanced years and ill health.

Breathing deeply, Herod leaned forward and said coyly, "You must be mistaken about the meaning of the star. We have no child that young in the palace."

Gaspar raised his eyes to meet Herod's gaze, keenly aware that the king was upset with the reason for their visit. Slowly and deliberately, Gaspar replied, "We are not mistaken. The writings speak clearly of the birth of the King of the Jews."

Herod gritted his teeth as his belly burned, furious that these foreigners would stand before him, in front of his full court of assistants and servants, and say that there was another King of the Jews, a baby, no less! How preposterous! Wildly waving his arms, he ordered Gaspar and his companions to be removed to another room. The guards in attendance quickly stepped forward, ushering the men out with pointed spears.

The three magi followed a guard who led the way to a smaller room not distant from the throne room, and there they were served drinks and fruit while they waited to be summoned into the king's presence once again. Gaspar was confident that they were close to their destination, but Baltazar was unsure and frightened of King Herod's reaction as he paced back and forth, ignoring the food.

"What if he has us killed?" nervously asked Baltazar as he faced Gaspar and cast a terrified glance at Melchior. "We've come this far, but we have no protection here in this country. We're in a foreign land, far from home, and we could easily be executed for our actions." He nervously rubbed his hands together.

Tall and lean and energetic, Melchior tried to calm the distressed Baltazar. "We will not be executed, Baltazar. We're on a journey that has been decreed from the heavens, and we won't fail. We *will* find the child."

Gaspar looked steadily at Baltazar, who was round and thick, his face tanned from the desert sun. He hadn't wanted to bring Baltazar along on the trip because Baltazar was easily upset and dissuaded when things didn't go smoothly, but he had needed Baltazar's expertise on the stars, having studied them for many years. Many times during the strenuous trip he'd had to calm Baltazar, assuring him that they would find who they sought, but time and again, worry would spill out of him. Clearly, he needed stroking again, so he went to Baltazar and placed his hand on the nervous man's shoulder in encouragement.

"I agree with Melchior. We *will* find the child. Herod will even help us. Here," he said as he picked up a goblet of fine wine, "have some wine while we wait for Herod to summon us to his presence again."

Nervously taking the cup, Baltazar gulped deeply, hoping the wine would dull his sense of dread.

After the magi had left the throne room, Herod exploded in a rage. His face became crimson, and he broke out in a sweat as he threw a royal temper tantrum. Storming down the stairs in front of his throne, he bellowed at his assistant as saliva flew through the air.

"I want the chief priests and scribes of the Jews here immediately!" The assistant scurried to do his bidding.

Herod paced angrily while he waited, cursing his Roman gods as he did so. Who was this baby that was born to be King of the Jews? He was the King of the Jews! There wasn't another, and there wouldn't be another as long as he was alive! This was absolutely absurd, a star announcing the birth of a baby! And a baby who would take over his throne, no less! Herod was fuming by the time the scribes and priests arrived in short order, and they were quickly escorted into the throne room by the assistant, who was thanking the gods for sparing his life.

Upon their entry, Herod quickly composed himself. Returning to his throne, he watched as the scribes and priests bowed before him, which brought him great pleasure. Even if they hated him, and he knew they did, they still had to pretend that they didn't. He knew that bowing before him irritated them to no end, especially the priests.

The scribes and priests stood before him, awash with fear at being summoned so hastily into Herod's presence. Clearing his throat, Herod spoke in his most political tone of voice.

"I have been visited by three men of Persian descent, and they have told me something very intriguing." He leaned forward, his portly stomach in knots as it rested on his upper legs. "They've come to worship the newborn King of the Jews, whose star they have followed to this country. I want to know where this child has been born." His eyes blazed with intensity as he demanded an answer, and if he didn't get one, he'd personally strangle every priest and scribe standing before him and would relish watching them die.

One of the scribes, knees shaking and heart hammering, quickly stepped forward, followed by two other scribes and three priests. In unison they answered, "In Bethlehem of Judea."

"In Bethlehem?" Herod's voice choked with surprise.

"Yes," replied one scribe, "for it's written by the prophet Micah, that thou, Bethlehem, in the land of Judah, art not the least among the princes of Judah; for out of thee shall come a Governor that shall rule my people, Israel."

Herod leaned back in his throne, tilted his head back and looked down his nose at his subjects as he digested the information. He considered the Jewish nation of little value and intended to keep them subject and submissive. Even though he practiced several Jewish customs, he was unfamiliar with Jewish prophets and their prophecies. If these men were wrong, he would have them publicly executed as a deterrent to anyone trying to deceive him in the future.

With a wave of his hand, he dismissed the scribes and priests, who were more than willing to leave. He then ordered everyone from the throne room except his assistant.

"Summon the foreigners again," Herod ordered as he rubbed his chin and pondered his course of action. His belly burned with rage. His mind raced to contrive a way to assuage the foreigners and get further information.

The assistant soon returned with the magi close behind, and Herod ordered the assistant to leave him alone with the magi. Knowing he had to use all his cunning and deceit to win the confidence of the magi, the king smiled and acted benignly. He'd deal with his burning belly later.

"Were you comfortable while you waited?" he asked as nicely as he could, the smile on his face belying the anger in his heart.

"Yes, thank you, we were," replied Gaspar.

Herod noted that Gaspar was the spokesperson for the three, but he didn't underestimate the others, who were obviously well educated and articulate. He had to put their minds at ease.

Leaning forward, elbows on his knees in a relaxed, friendly gesture, Herod said softly, "What time did this star appear, the one you've been following?"

"I believe the first time Baltazar noticed it in the heavens was about a year or so ago," replied Gaspar.

"Is that correct, Baltazar?"

"Yes," meekly replied Baltazar, still terrified that he would be struck dead at any moment for no other reason than for being.

Herod leaned back in his throne and crossed his arms. In a syrupy voice, he said, "I have inquired of my people, and they tell me that this child was born in Bethlehem, which is a small town about five miles to the south of Jerusalem. I want you to go to Bethlehem and search diligently for the child until you find him, but once you've found him, you must return to me and tell me where he is. I want to go and worship him also." Leaning back in his throne, Herod breathed deeply in an effort to hold his anger.

Gaspar lowered his head, nodding. "Thank you, King Herod, for your assistance. We'll return after we find the child and tell you where he's living."

"Good," replied Herod as he relaxed his position. No one would be the wiser as to his plans; the magi wouldn't even be aware of the role they would play. Dismissing the magi with a wave of his hand, he watched them leave the throne room, their luxurious robes flowing behind them. Once alone in the vast hall, Herod seethed with anger at the knowledge that a child had been born who would take over his throne! He'd stop it from happening, and he'd use whatever means necessary. The magi would return and inform him of the child's whereabouts, and that would be all he needed. He sighed heavily as his mouth curled with contempt.

The three magi were escorted by the guard back to the entrance to the palace. The sun was quickly setting in the western sky, and once again, as they mounted their camels, they created quite a stir among the populace.

Gaspar figured that they could make it to Bethlehem shortly after nightfall, for after dark was when they did most of their traveling.

"Maybe the star will appear again," hopefully stated Melchior. "We haven't seen it for two nights, but maybe it will be here to guide us to Bethlehem."

As the sun spread a creamy wash of light over the land that slowly faded to darkness, the trio left the strong walls of Jerusalem and headed south to Bethlehem. And there, right before them, appeared the star that had wooed them into this long journey, a journey fraught with difficulties – sand storms, thieves, lack of water, blazing heat, illness, uncertainty and loneliness – but the end was finally within their reach. With renewed vigor and excitement, the magi pressed on with their servants and camels, eager to reach their destination, so close now.

Approaching Bethlehem a short time later, Gaspar suggested that they find an inn in which to stay for the night. "I don't want to disturb the parents at this hour of the night," he said. "I think it best that we find a place to stay and inquire of the people where to find this child first thing in the morning."

The small caravan wound its way into the narrow passages that were called streets. Few people were out and about at the late hour, but those that were turned suspicious eyes on the travelers. The main street passed Gedaliah's inn, and a servant was soon pounding on its door as the magi dismounted their camels.

Gedaliah was resting comfortably, almost asleep with Deborah beside him, when the pounding on the door compelled him to his feet. He quickly ran downstairs. Who in the world could possibly want a room this late at night? No one ever traveled at this hour; it was too dangerous.

Gedaliah turned up the oil lamp on the table in the entrance. He released the latch on the door and opened it slowly and peered out into the darkness. He saw a foreigner, dressed in strange clothing, with several other people standing behind him. The dim light revealed little other than that they were well-dressed and obviously very wealthy. Gedaliah opened the door widely, certain he had nothing to fear.

"Can I help you?" he asked, not sure if those in front of him would understand what he was saying.

"Yes." Gaspar stepped forward as the servant stepped aside. "We've traveled for many months, and we need three rooms for the night."

Gedaliah's eyebrows shot up when he heard them speak Hebrew. "Please, come inside. I'm sorry I took so long to answer the door. I was almost asleep with my wife and new baby upstairs."

The magi exchanged questioning glances.

"How old is your child?" asked Melchior, trying not to sound too excited.

"He's just six months old. His name is Jesse, and he's our first child. We hope to have many others." He stepped aside as Baltazar, the last to enter, swept past him. The disappointed expression on Melchior's face was unmistakable.

Gedaliah continued speaking even as he wondered at their odd questions. "I see you have camels and servants. There is a stable out back with an ample courtyard. They can put the camels in there for the night and sleep with them. There is also plenty of fresh hay and water."

"Thank you," replied Gaspar. In his native tongue, he instructed their servants where to take the camels for the night. Gedaliah had to watch the caravan as it passed his front door; he hoped the stable and courtyard were adequate enough to hold so many large animals and handlers.

"How far have you traveled?" asked Gedaliah as he led the men down the hallway to their rooms.

"We've been on a long journey for almost a year," replied Baltazar. "We've been following a star, and we've been led to this town."

Gedaliah was curious, but he noticed the men were too tired to answer questions, so he simply showed the magi their rooms and bade them goodnight. He would see them again in the morning.

Returning to Deborah's side, he found her awake. Gedaliah briefly told her the little he knew about their new guests, adding that they seemed quite excited when he'd told them that they had a baby upstairs.

"I told them how old Jesse was when they asked, and then they seemed to be disappointed for some reason. It was really strange."

"Well, we'll see them in the morning. Maybe we can find out why they're here then," drowsily replied Deborah. She kissed Gedaliah goodnight for the second time and rolled over onto her side and was soon fast asleep.

Gedaliah lay awake for quite some time. Questions puzzled him. Who were these strange travelers from a distant land? Why had they traveled for so long? What star had they followed that had led them to Bethlehem? And why were they interested in the age of their baby?

Gedaliah tried to empty his mind of these unanswered questions so he could sleep, but it was still a long time before his eyelids finally closed in rest.

Chapter Fourteen

THE VISIT OF THE MAGI

Gedaliah was up with the sun which greeted a cool, crisp morning, a hint of the colder weather to come. Gedaliah left Deborah with the baby and went downstairs, rubbing his eyes to chase away the desire for more sleep, and as he entered the common room downstairs, Selma was there to greet him.

"Good morning, Gedaliah. I see that we had late arrivals last night."

Gedaliah poured himself a drink from a flask that Selma had put out for him. "How do you know that?"

Selma pulled a grape from a cluster she held in her hands and popped it into her mouth. "The stable and courtyard are full of camels, of all things, and quite a few servants besides. It isn't often that we house people of such status."

Sighing heavily, Gedaliah said, "That's quite true, Selma. They came after I was in bed last night, and they quickly retired after going to their rooms. I know very little about them other than that they have traveled a long way for a long time to find something, or someone."

"What are they looking for?"

"I guess we'll find out today. The one thing they did say was that they had reached their destination, so whatever they are looking for, it must be here in Bethlehem. How odd that something here in Bethlehem would make them travel for almost a year. I don't understand it."

As Gedaliah finished speaking, they heard voices coming from the hallway, and soon all three foreign guests were standing in the common room with Gedaliah and Selma, who was astonished at the richness of their robes and headdresses, not to mention their jewelry. Surely these were kings, she thought to herself, but what would kings be doing in Bethlehem, a town of no importance? Quietly stepping into the background with her cluster of grapes still in hand, Selman stood and watched and listened.

"Good morning," nodded Gaspar in greeting to Gedaliah.

"Good morning, sirs. Did you rest comfortably?"

"Yes, thank you." Adjusting his colorful robe tied with a gold braided rope, Gaspar smiled broadly. "Today we will see the one whom we have sought for these many months, and our hearts will rejoice. Our journey has been long and dangerous, yet we have persisted to the end."

Baltazar stepped forward and explained how he had seen the star many months earlier and how they were told that it signaled the birth of the King of the Jews. "We've been on this quest to find him so we may offer him gifts and worship him. I can hardly believe that we have arrived at last."

Deborah quietly entered the room, cradling Jesse in her arms. Seeing her, Gaspar said, "We're

182

looking for a baby who would be close to one year in age. When I heard that you had a male child, we thought he might be the object of our intense search. However, your child is too young to be the one we seek."

Deborah glanced at Gedaliah as she came and stood by his side with Jesse. She whispered something in Gedaliah's ear, and he nodded in agreement. Jesse began to cry, and she raised him to her shoulder as she gently rocked him and patted his back.

"We know someone," Deborah quietly began, "who has a male child almost one year of age. There have been marvelous, miraculous circumstances pertaining to his birth, and I believe this is the child whom you seek. The child's name is Jesus, and his mother and father are Mary and Joseph. They are dear friends of ours."

Gaspar, Melchior, and Baltazar exchanged excited glances, the expressions on their faces full of hope. Gaspar spoke. "Where do they live?"

"Just a few minutes' walk from here."

Gaspar took a deep breath and exhaled slowly, his eyes closing in relief as a small tear of joy trickled down the side of his dark face and into his black, curly beard.

"Please," Gedaliah interrupted, "let us offer you something to eat before you go to Mary and Joseph's house to see the child." Nodding to Selma, she hurried upstairs and soon returned with a large tray laden with grapes, pomegranates, figs, and Eglah's delicious bread, with goat cheese to accompany it.

"Please be seated," indicated Gedaliah to the men as he pulled out the benches around the table in the room. "Let's eat and celebrate with you that your journey is finally over."

Deborah vanished up the stairs briefly and returned without Jesse; she then assisted Gedaliah and Selma with serving their guests.

"We're most thankful for your kindness in opening your door to us at the late hour last night," stated Melchior as he enjoyed a fresh fig. "We'd stopped in Jerusalem at the palace of King Herod, obviously thinking that the child we sought would be there, but we soon discovered that such wasn't the case."

Gedaliah gulped at the mention of Herod.

"King Herod seemed rather surprised that we sought the King of the Jews, but that we didn't seek *him*. However, he assisted us by inquiring of his people where this child was to be born, and he sent us on our way to Bethlehem," added Gaspar.

"And the star which had led us this far reappeared over Bethlehem as the sky grew dark last night. We hadn't seen it for several nights, so that's why we stopped at Jerusalem." Baltazar was clearly enjoying the food set before him as he feasted on fresh bread spread thickly with goat cheese.

"From what country do you come?" asked Deborah.

"We are of Persian descent," replied Gaspar, "but our country of origin is not important. The only thing that has been important to us is finding the child whose star we have followed, and our journey ends here in Bethlehem."

"You mentioned that this child was born almost a year ago?" posed Melchior.

"Yes," quickly responded Deborah. "Mary and her husband Joseph arrived here in Bethlehem just hours before Jesus was born, but we didn't have any rooms left here in the inn due to the census ordered by Caesar Augustus, so we put them up in the stable.

Mary gave birth to Jesus there, and my mother and I attended the birth."

Gaspar listened attentively, hanging on every word Deborah said, as joy flooded his soul like melting wax. "So the child was born in the stable," he mused. "What a far cry from a palace, yet he is to become King of the Jews."

"Mary will have many amazing things to tell you concerning her child," added Deborah.

Slowly draining his goblet of the wine mixed with water, Gaspar placed it back on the table and asked, "Is the child just like other children?"

"Yes. He's growing like all others in every way; he looks no different."

The room was quiet for a few minutes. "We've been led here to find the King of the Jews," Gaspar stated, "and I'm now certain that this Jesus is the one we seek. The star last night directed us to Bethlehem, and King Herod also told us that the child was prophesied to be born here in Bethlehem. We will go and see this child now."

Rising from his seat, the others followed suit, thanking Gedaliah, Deborah and Selma for their kindness in providing a nourishing meal. They briefly stepped into the courtyard and stable and brought back with them precious gifts they had carried over mountains, deserts, fields and streams. The boxes gleamed with gold and jewels, and Deborah gasped at their stunning beauty. Trying not to stare at the boxes the magi held in their hands, she said, "Come. I'll take you to Mary and Joseph's house."

Gedaliah held the door open as Deborah led the colorful procession out the door and into the dingy, narrow streets. The hour was still early, but several people were already beginning their day's activities. Upon seeing the magi following Deborah, all who saw stepped aside to let them pass as they lowered their heads in respect.

Making two turns in the streets, Deborah arrived at the simple house where Mary and Joseph lived. She turned and smiled at the magi, and then she stepped toward the door and knocked soundly on it.

Mary opened the door, Jesus in her arms with a piece of fruit in his clasp. Mary's eyes widened at the sight of the magi standing respectfully behind Deborah, who offered her a simple explanation. "They've come to see Jesus."

Deborah stepped aside, and Mary held the door wide open and bade them enter. The sight of them caught her off guard, but she knew that they were sent by God to see his Son. Long ago she had realized that extraordinary things would happen to Jesus as he grew, and the magi appearing to see her child was certainly another extraordinary event.

As the magi swept past her and entered her humble home, she noted that they were indeed very wealthy. Their robes were of the finest material that Mary had ever seen, and the perfumes and oils on their bodies exuded a sweet fragrance on the morning air. Their turbans adorning their heads were exquisitely decorated with jewels and beads, and they had to lower their heads substantially to pass through the doorway. After the last one entered, Deborah smiled and nodded to Mary and left to return to the inn even though her curiosity was screaming to be satisfied.

Mary quietly shut the door and sat down, placing Jesus on her lap, as she wondered at the reason for this strange visit. The three magi, now standing side-by-side, stood before her and then in unison dropped to their knees before Jesus, their precious gifts in the elaborately decorated boxes still in their hands. They worshipped Jesus, offering praise to him and honoring him for what he was and what he would become. Mary watched in awesome wonder while Jesus simply waved his arms and kicked his legs in glee at the unusual, colorful men before him.

Gaspar, Melchior, and Baltazar finally stood, tears glistening in their eyes. Gaspar stepped forward and held out his expensive box. "My gift to this child, the newborn King of the Jews, is precious gold from the bowels of the earth. May it provide for his every need." He reverently knelt down and placed the box at Mary's feet.

Melchior then stepped forward with his box and did the same. "My gift to the Christ Child is frankincense, the sweetest incense on earth. May its fragrance rise to the heavens in glory to God." He too, knelt down and placed the box at Mary's feet as she held her child.

Baltazar, his round body surrounded by his flowing robes, was last. "My gift to this Holy Child is myrrh, a precious gum used as a spice and as medicine." Placing the box with the others, he heaved himself up to a standing position and stood beside his companions.

Mary watched in speechless wonder as the costly boxes were placed at her feet, tears stinging her eyes, as gratitude flowed from her heart to God. Jesus continued talking to her in childish sounds as he clapped his hands together. He wasn't a baby anymore, but a toddler with a full head of black hair and legs and arms that were quickly growing strong.

Gaspar, overcome by the moment, whispered softly. "Do you think he would let me hold him?"

Fighting to hold back her tears, Mary stood and handed the child to him. Jesus immediately started to grab and pull the tassels and fringe on Gaspar's robe and on his turban. Everyone laughed as Jesus played with the ornaments, trying his best to pull the turban off Gaspar's head. Mary picked up the gifts, overwhelmed with their extravagance, and placed them on the table, gently caressing them with her shaking fingers. Joseph would be so surprised when he returned from outside Bethlehem where he was cutting down a tree for wood for furniture. How she wished he'd been here to meet the magi!

While Gaspar, Melchior and Baltazar played with the baby, Mary poured wine for them into simple wooden cups. She noticed that they weren't offended by the starkness of her surroundings, nor were they offended by her simple clothing and way of life. The magi treated her as if she were a queen, giving her honor and praise for being the Christ's mother and asking questions concerning his birth. Mary told them as briefly as she could about the events concerning his conception, his birth, and the announcement by the angels to the shepherds on the hillsides surrounding Bethlehem.

When she was finished, Melchior said, "We believe, Mary, that this is the Son of God, as you say. We are highly honored to have seen his star, to have followed it, and to have found him. We will return home with glad hearts and will tell all we meet of this wonderful child, the newborn King of the Jews."

Mary lowered her head and briefly closed her eyes as she took her energetic child from them and placed him on the floor on his feet, where he held onto her robe for support. He danced up and down as he stood before them, laughing at his newfound ability to stand.

"My life is not my own," quietly stated Mary. "It is God's. I wish only to do His will, whatever that may be."

Slowly the magi prepared to leave, and Mary lifted the growing child into her arms as she held the door open for them. As each one passed by, they placed a hand on the child's head, praising and blessing him.   Jesus squealed with delight at all the attention.

The magi retraced their steps to the inn as curious eyes stared at them along the way. Many villagers were out and about now and had heard of the foreigners who had gone to visit Mary. Word of the wealthy travelers had spread quickly through the town. Inquisitive children ran in front of them as they walked to the inn amidst whispers that there were kings in town.

Upon their return to the inn, Gaspar informed Gedaliah that they'd be staying another night before beginning the long journey back to their country, after stopping in Jerusalem once again to tell Herod about their visit with the Christ child. The camels were also in need of rest, as were they and their servants. Deborah hurried to her mother's house to summon Simon so he could assist with the care of the camels. She excitedly told Kezia about the rich, ornate boxes the three men took to give to Jesus.

"The boxes were so beautiful, Mother, but I don't know what they contained.   The men are obviously very wealthy and have great importance in their country, and they've traveled almost a year to get here to see Jesus. Isn't that amazing?"

Kezia wiped dry the bowl in her hands. "Yes, it is, but we know that Jesus isn't an ordinary child, don't we? We must expect these strange things to happen to him as he grows up, for he *is* the promised Messiah."

Deborah returned with Simon, who led the servants outside the town with their camels. The stable was not made to hold such large animals. The camels were grateful to be out of their cramped quarters and lounged in the sun and cool air for most of the day. While they were out, Simon and Obed, who he convinced to help, mucked out the stalls and spread fresh hay for the coming night.

Gedaliah invited the magi to take their evening meal with him and his family. Eglah was excited at the prospect of entertaining foreigners, and she spent much of the day preparing some of her finest dishes with Deborah's help. Selma took care of all the work at the inn. Deborah hurried to the market after returning with Simon and bought the freshest fruits and vegetables she could find. Everyone she met was curious to know the reason for the foreigners being in Bethlehem, and Deborah had to answer the same questions over and over while at the market.

Evening approached, and Gaspar, Melchior, and Baltazar were led to Gedaliah's living quarters on the upper floor of the inn. The meal prepared by Eglah and Deborah was delicious, and the magi were constantly asking questions concerning flavors and spices used in the food. Their country didn't have the same foods, and they were enjoying the delicacies prepared by Deborah and her mother-in-law.

Jesse slept quietly in his basket, and Deborah attended to his needs as they arose. Jesse loved to be attentive to people and responsive to them. He was Deborah's pride and joy, and Gedaliah bragged, as do most fathers, about how much Jesse looked like him. All too soon, the evening had turned to night, and the magi retired to their rooms, thankful for all the good food and hospitality.

Later that day, when Joseph returned from the hillside bearing a large log on a cart pulled by their donkey, Mary told him all about the visit of the magi. Joseph listened attentively as she placed the precious gifts in his calloused hands, and he was perplexed at the generosity of complete strangers from so far away.

"The Lord has brought these expensive gifts to us for a reason," stated Joseph as he turned the heavy box of gold over in his hands, "He'll let us know for what purpose when the time comes."

"They're so lovely that I was almost afraid to touch them at first. Such wealth isn't something to which I'm accustomed."

Joseph disappeared into his shop and returned with a plain wooden box, and they placed the elaborate gift boxes inside and put the box on a shelf in their simple home.

At the inn, Gaspar removed his heavy robe and hung it on a hook on the wall. He was weary beyond belief, yet so glad, that they'd finally found the child for whom they had so diligently sought. The trip had been much more strenuous, and certainly a great deal longer, than he'd anticipated, but the result was worth every effort, every sore muscle, every struggle. He'd held the promised Messiah, the King of the Jews, in his arms, and the peace he felt was unfathomable.

When they departed the next day, they would head back to Jerusalem to inform King Herod that they'd found the child in Bethlehem, just as he said they would. Surely King Herod would bring the child to Jerusalem, along with Mary and Joseph, and establish them in a decent house and provide for them, or maybe he'd house them in the palace, a fit place to raise a king. The near poverty in which the child lived with his parents had taken Gaspar by surprise. Certainly King Herod would see to the child's needs and give him what was rightfully his as King of the Jews. Exhausted, Gaspar finally drifted to sleep.

Gaspar, Melchior, and Baltazar slept in different rooms that night, but each tossed and turned in a fitful, disturbing sleep, waking less than rested. When they came together in the morning, Gaspar sighed heavily and stated, "I didn't sleep well at all last night. I had a very unusual dream." He looked somberly at his traveling companions. "I was warned that we should return home by another route and not go to Jerusalem."

Surprised, Melchior and Baltazar said in unison, "I had the same dream!"

The three magi exchanged understanding glances as Gaspar continued. "We cannot go back to King Herod. If we do, I feel we may be endangering the child's life. King Herod wasn't happy to hear that we were seeking the King of the Jews and that he wasn't the king we were seeking, even though he is currently the King of the Jews. We must *not* return to the palace." The joy he'd felt minutes ago evaporated and was replace with dread.

"Then we must find another way," stated Baltazar, relieved at the knowledge that he wouldn't have to see Herod again. "We'll travel east from here instead of going north toward Jerusalem."

"That's the only thing we can do," agreed Melchior. "We've seen the child and our mission is completed, but we *cannot* let King Herod know that we've found him."

"It will be several days before King Herod realizes that we won't be returning as he instructed us to do," Gaspar surmised. "By then, we can be far enough away so that he won't send his soldiers out after us to force us to tell him where the child is, or possibly try to kill us for not telling him as he ordered us to do." He stood up and headed toward the entrance room of the inn.

"Come," he said to his companions, "let's pay Gedaliah handsomely for his kindness to us, and then let's be quickly on our way."

After paying Gedaliah three times what they owed him, even though he did his best to refuse their generosity, the magi mounted their camels prepared by Asamin and the other servants for the return trip. With almost the entire village watching, they slowly made their way out of the town on the slippery, hard roads. They turned off the road that led to Jerusalem and headed east, avoiding the main road that led to the palace of King Herod.

After going a short distance, Gaspar turned in his saddle and glanced back at the tiny town of Bethlehem, a town of no significance – until now. He glanced heavenward as peace, warm and comforting, settled over his soul.

Chapter Fifteen

ABRUPT DEPARTURE

Deborah rushed to Mary's house the next morning after the magi had departed, eager to see what they had given to Baby Jesus in those lavishly decorated boxes that they were carrying when they'd left the inn. She clutched Jesse in her arms as she scurried around the corner and down the street toward Mary's house.

Mary answered the door, and before she could close it, Deborah blurted out, "What did the foreigners bring you in those beautiful boxes, Mary? I can't wait to find out!" She gently placed Jesse in a basket lined with blankets on the floor.

Mary placed Jesus next to Jesse and gave him some wooden toys crafted by Joseph. Without saying a word, her eyes sparkling, she went to the shelf along the wall and retrieved the plain wooden box and brought it to the table, grunting under its weight. Deborah came to her side and gasped as Mary removed each bejeweled box and set them on the table. Ever so carefully, Deborah placed her hand gently on each box, marveling at its exquisite beauty.

"Mary, these are so lovely! But what's inside them? Surely they didn't give you empty boxes, even though they are probably worth a small fortune themselves!"

Smiling coyly, Mary gingerly lifted the lid on the first box and revealed gold coins, and Deborah gasped again as she placed her hand over her mouth. Still not speaking, Mary opened the second box and revealed the myrrh, and then the third box containing the frankincense. The fragrant scents from these two boxes soon filled the room with aromatic freshness, making both Mary and Deborah inhale deeply, enjoying the exotic smells, beyond their ability to purchase. For several moments, they stood gaping at the boxes and their contents as Jesus played with his toys at their feet.

"Why did they bring you such expensive gifts?"

Mary simply shook her head. "We don't know, but Joseph said that God has sent these gifts our way for a reason and that he would reveal it to us when the time comes." They continued staring at the boxes for a few more minutes, and then Mary carefully closed each one, replaced them in the plain wooden box, and returned it to the shelf with Deborah's assistance.

As she turned to Deborah, Mary's eyes misted over. "Only God knows what's in store for his Son, and it oftentimes makes my heart jump into my throat. All I can do is trust him daily for his provision and care for us. And that's the most difficult part."

"But God has provided for you! You won't have to worry about Joseph not making enough money anymore! You're rich, Mary!"

"Yes, we are, but we won't spend any of the gold until we hear from the Lord, Deborah. It's his blessing, and we won't squander it."

Deborah sighed and hugged Mary. Standing back from her, she changed the subject. "Why don't we pack some food and go up into the hills for lunch. It's a beautiful day, warmer than usual, and we might not have a chance to take the babies outdoors like this for months to come."

Mary nodded enthusiastically in agreement. After she told Joseph where they were going as Deborah gathered a few things for Jesus, they went to the inn, where Deborah packed a lunch of grapes, figs, lentils in sauce that Eglah had made, and bread. They were soon on their way up the hillside, following the same path that led to Thaddeus's house. They found a large outcropping of rocks and spread a blanket down and were soon seated with their two young children close by. Jesus had to be closely watched because he was excellent at crawling, and Mary was constantly reaching for him as he scurried away from her.

The day was warm and sultry, a hint of summer past in the air. The sky was a gorgeous blue with wisps of clouds, strokes of white on a canvas of blue. Bees and bugs abounded as they flitted from flower to flower as if they knew that their time to do so was short. The young women ate and played with their babies and dreamed of their future together as they soaked up the warm sunshine. Jesus finally wore himself out and dozed at Mary's feet, a blanket for a pillow. Mary and Deborah lay down on the ground as their two children slept safely beside them.

"Mary, I can't wait for Jesse to get as big as Jesus. He's already grown so much, but I'll be happy when he can do more things for himself. It's a lot of work taking care of a small baby."

"And I wish Jesus wouldn't grow so quickly," stated Mary as she gently stroked his hair away from his eyes. "It seems like only yesterday that he was born, and now look at him, almost one year old. I can hardly believe it. He's not a little baby any more."

"Do you and Joseph want to have more children?"

Mary hesitated before replying. "Yes, we do. For Joseph, our next child will actually be his first blood child, but this child of God's is as much his as mine because God has entrusted him to raise him."

"Gedaliah and I want to have a lot of children," happily replied Deborah as she watched a hawk glide through the sky. "I know the whole pregnancy thing is rather long and difficult, as well as the labor and delivery, but when you see a child that has grown inside you and now has a life all its own, that's such a miracle. I'm eager to do it again."

"I know that we'll have other children, but I'm leaving that up to God to decide when. I know our first concern right now is Jesus and seeing that he grows up to accomplish his task in life."

The two women dozed briefly in the warmth of the sun, and when the babies awoke, they decided to continue up the hill and visit Kezia. As they climbed the hillside, babies in their arms, they saw Kezia picking some of the late summer vegetables from the garden. When she saw them approaching, she washed her hands and came to them.

"Deborah! Mary! What a pleasant surprise!"

"Hello, Mother. Mary and I were just out enjoying the beautiful day. It's not likely that we will have many more of them with winter just around the corner."

"We had lunch on the hillside and decided to come see you," Mary interjected as she shifted the growing child in her arms.

"And let me see little Jesse," cooed Kezia as she took her grandchild from Deborah's arms. "My goodness, he's grown since the last time I saw him, which was just three days ago. He's getting so big, and look at him smile at his grandmother." She held him close and rubbed his face with her nose.

"He's making sounds all the time now, and he's grabbing hold of things with his hands, and he's pretty good at that already. And he scoots on his belly in an effort to crawl."

"And he'll be crawling soon," Kezia assured her as they turned toward the house.

The two young mothers stayed until late afternoon as they visited with Kezia and adored their little ones. Kezia never tired of holding Jesse and only gave him back to Deborah when he needed to be nursed. Jesus explored the house and its many rooms on his hands and knees, often pulling blankets down on top of himself, making the women laugh at his antics.

The sun was losing its warmth when the two women said goodbye to Kezia and headed back to town.

"This has been such a lovely day," reflected Mary as they reached the outskirts of town. "Of course, there are plenty of things I could have been doing today, but I can always do them tomorrow. Thanks for thinking of doing this, Deborah. It was a great idea."

"Well, I'm glad we went, too. We need a lazy day once in awhile. One thing is certain, all my work will still be there for me to do when I get home!" They laughed and walked arm in arm.

As they came to the inn, Mary paused and said, "I'll see you tomorrow, Deborah. Thanks for a lovely afternoon. And thanks for the lunch."

"Have a nice evening, Mary. Tell Joseph I said hello."

Deborah entered the inn and went upstairs, where she found Eglah preparing vegetables for a stew.

"Hello, Deborah. Did you and Mary have a nice time?"

"Yes, we did, Mother Eglah. It was such a beautiful day that I hated to waste it inside. We won't have too many more such days." She laid Jesse down in his basket.

"I used to love to go to the country when I was a young girl," Elgah said dreamily. "My mother was always afraid that I would be eaten by a wild beast or something, so most of the time I had to sneak away. How I miss being able to go there."

Deborah came up behind her and gave her a hug. "Maybe someday Gedaliah and I could arrange for you to be carried outside the town walls again. How would you like that?"

"That would be wonderful!" exclaimed Eglah in delight. "I just hope this old body can take it, that's all."

"You're not old, Mother Eglah," insisted Deborah. "Here, let me help you prepare the stew."

Deborah worked with Eglah, and Gedaliah soon returned from purchasing straw from one of the farmers for the stable, and they sat down to their evening meal, thanking God for the abundant blessings in their lives.

* * * * * * * * *

"Mary, wake up!"

"What is it?" asked Mary as she snapped awake, her heart racing.

"We have to leave Bethlehem immediately!" exclaimed Joseph as he climbed out of bed and slipped into his tunic.

Mary sat up, clutching the blanket to her neck, perplexed. "What do you mean – leave Bethlehem?" Surely Joseph must be dreaming or sleep-walking, thought Mary as she shook the cobwebs from her brain.

Joseph tied his belt around his waist as he slipped on his worn sandals. "I had a dream, Mary, and God told me that we must leave Bethlehem immediately. Herod seeks to harm the child." His face reflected the intensity of his emotions in the feeble light of the small lamp.

Mary quickly climbed out of bed and lit another oil lamp. The soft light cast large, elongated shadows on the mud walls as Mary quickly dressed, her body quaking in fear, waves of concern slamming against her chest. Joseph gathered personal articles and placed them in large cloth sacks as Mary rolled up the blankets.

"What should we take, Joseph? Or should I ask, what should we leave?"

Joseph placed the plain wooden box containing the precious gifts of the magi into the bottom of one sack, cushioning it with a small blanket. "We'll take only what we can carry or put on the donkey. We can probably take all our clothing, and we should take all the food that we have."

Mary hurriedly slipped on her sandals and started gathering all their food supplies, as well as a small jug of water. There wasn't much to take, just cheese, bread, figs, two pomegranates, and one small bag of dates. Once she had everything in the sack, she tied it securely shut and placed it by the front door.

"Where are we to go, Joseph?" pensively asked Mary as tears pooled in her dark eyes. The sudden change threatened to crush her emotionally. This was so unexpected, but she'd do anything to save her child's life.

"I don't know. I only know we can't stay here another hour, another moment!"

"Your tools, Joseph!" Mary exclaimed. "What are we to do about your tools?"

"We have to leave them," Joseph stated grimly as he put his hand on the door latch. "There's no way we can take such bulky, heavy items." Turning to Mary, he said, "I'm going to get the donkey; get Jesus ready to go. I'll be back in a few minutes." He quietly opened the door and stepped out into the darkness, leaving Mary alone with her thoughts and fears.

Looking around the room, her home for almost a year, Mary was momentarily seized by panic as she continued to pack. What did all this mean? Why would Herod want to harm her Son? Where were they to go? How would Joseph be able to make a living without his carpentry tools? What about all the friends they had made in Bethlehem? Would she ever see them again? And Deborah, she couldn't even say goodbye to Deborah, and the tears she'd held at bay spilled from her eyes as she placed the last of their belongings in a large sack, grief overwhelming her. After placing the sack by the door with the others, Mary slowly approached her sleeping infant. He was so perfect, so beautiful! How could someone want to harm such an innocent child?

Tears trailed down Mary's cheeks as she gently placed her hands under her Son's body and lifted him to her chest. Jesus responded with a whimper as he rested his head on Mary's shoulder. Reaching down for his blanket, Mary draped it over his head to ward off the chilly, damp night air.

"My dear, sweet Jesus," cried Mary as she cradled him to her breast, "everything's going to be all right. We won't let anything happen to you. We will protect you, and so will your Heavenly Father." Holding him, Mary breathed his sweet scent as she cuddled him in her arms even as terror threatened to immobilize her.

Joseph retrieved the donkey from Gedaliah's stable and returned to the house. Opening the door, he saw that Mary was ready to go, albeit fearfully. Joseph picked up the two largest sacks – one of them containing the precious gifts -- and tied them together across the donkey's sturdy back, then bundled two smaller sacks together across the top of the first two. He then picked up the last sack containing their food and slung it over his shoulder. Looking around the room to see if there was anything else that they could take, he saw all they were leaving – the two cooking pots, several large bowls and baskets, the simple furnishings he had made, and Jesus's sleeping basket. Joseph went to Mary and hugged her gently, Jesus between them, and placed a reassuring kiss on her forehead.

"I know how difficult it is for you to leave our humble home," he whispered into her hair, "but all these things can be replaced. The child's safety is of the utmost importance."

"I know, Joseph," Mary said through her tears. "I'm just afraid, that's all. But I'll do anything necessary to keep Jesus safe. And if God says we must go, how can we stay?"

Joseph stepped back slightly and put one hand on her shoulder and with the other gently cupped her chin, lifting her tear-stained face upward. "Jehovah will lead us and guide us." He planted another kiss on her forehead and then whispered, "Let's go."

Mary slipped outside as Joseph extinguished the oil lamps. The quiet of the night greeted her, and she felt strangely calm. What Joseph had said was true – God would lead and guide them. God had a mission for His Son and He would see to it that no harm came to Jesus. Joseph joined her, latching the door behind him, and took the donkey's tether, and together they walked silently through the narrow, deserted streets of Bethlehem.

Mary held her sleeping infant close to her breast, praying that he would remain asleep. A crying infant in the street in the middle of the night would certainly draw attention. Quickening her steps to keep pace with Joseph, Mary held the blanket snugly around Jesus. The night was cool and crisp, and Mary pulled her tunic tighter around her neck.

Joseph led the donkey as Mary followed on its heels. Everything seemed surreal to Mary in the darkness of the night. The moon and stars were obscured by clouds, and the air was heavy with dew. Her sandaled feet made little noise compared to the clopping of the donkey's small hooves on the hard-packed soil of the streets. Jesus nestled into Mary's shoulder, curling his chubby legs up in her arms. Mary realized how heavy he had become and prayed for the strength to carry him as long as she needed to.

Soon they left the protection of the town and entered the uninhabited hillsides. As they climbed the hill that would obscure Bethlehem from their sight, Mary paused and turned, looking one last time at the town where she'd given birth, the town where she had been welcomed, the town that had given her wonderful friends, the town that she'd called home. What did the future hold? Where would they go, and where would they settle? Would she ever see her friends again, especially Deborah? There were no answers for Mary as her eyes misted over again.

Drawing a deep breath, Mary resolutely set her mind and her heart to trust God and the man she called 'husband' as she turned her back on Bethlehem and scurried to catch up to Joseph as she firmly held her sleeping, precious Son

Chapter Sixteen

ATTACK ON INNOCENCE

Herod awoke after a fitful night's sleep. There was little comfort for him lately, either awake or asleep. Ever since he'd had his beloved wife, Mariamme, murdered because he suspected her of adultery, he'd become psychologically disturbed and suffered prolonged delusions. No matter that he'd had ten wives and numerous male lovers when he'd eliminated Mariamme from his life – she'd been unfaithful to *him*, and that's all that mattered. Three of his male offspring had also met their end at his hand, the murderous hand of a warrior who'd spent life making his own rules and eliminating those who disagreed.

Herod was an oppressive ruler, even by the standards of the savage world in which he lived, but it seemed that his many war injuries and the effects of his lascivious lifestyle were finally catching up with him. Now in his mid 60's, Herod frequently was attacked by a mild fever, swelling of the feet, spasms in his limbs, and seizures that caused his eyes to roll back in his head. Even though he was under the care of many physicians, his condition continually worsened, and no one could help.

Swinging his legs off the bed and placing his swollen feet on the floor, Herod was gripped by a convulsive cough. It was several minutes before he was able to stop and catch his breath, cursing his gods for his abominable health as he did so. His bowels burned as he gingerly gained his footing, causing him to clutch his abdomen in agony. Each step he took caused excruciating pain in his swollen feet as he made his way to his bathing chamber.

As he was attended to by his servants, Herod's thoughts centered on the magi who had visited him five days earlier. They should have returned to Jerusalem and informed him of the whereabouts of the child they'd sought by now. Herod's blood pressure rose as he dwelt upon the unknown child, born in Bethlehem, born to be king of the Jews. *He* was king of the Jews and would remain so until his death, and then the throne would not go to some low-life Jew, but to one of his many sons. How dare those foreign travelers presume and proclaim that the throne would go to a child born in Bethlehem, a town of no consequence inhabited mostly by shepherds and farmers and tradesmen; yet that town had purportedly produced a child that would take away *his* throne.

As he was bathed and dressed in his royal robes of fine linen trimmed with gold thread, the pain from Herod's physical ailments subsided as his mind burned with rage. The magi were either still in Bethlehem 'worshipping' this child or they were on their way home by another route. They should have bowed down and worshipped *him*, not some unknown child in a nondescript town. He was the one ruling the land and dressed in royalty, not some Jewish baby who probably lived in abject poverty. There was no wealth to speak of in Bethlehem; no families of royal heritage resided there, so how could a child born to be king possibly come from there?

Yet the Hebrew scholars and priests had said that was the case. Lowly Bethlehem would be the source of one who would sit on King David's throne in Jerusalem.

As the morning progressed and Herod went about his duties as ruler, he became consumed with the need to take matters into his own hands. It was obvious that the magi had disobeyed his order to return and tell him where the child could be found, and this greatly infuriated him. How dare they defy his orders! They, or someone else, would soon suffer the consequences of their blatant arrogance!

So consumed was his mind with the magi and the unknown child that Herod found he couldn't conduct business as usual, and about mid-morning, he angrily ordered everyone from the throne room. Servants and administrators alike scurried out of the room, eager to withdraw from his presence. Many times they had witnessed Herod's foul moods, and no one wanted to cross him lest he lose his life for no other reason than simply being in the way.

Stepping down from the throne, Herod paced back and forth across the highly polished marble floors, constantly wringing his hands. All he could think about was the child, the child who would take away his throne! He mustn't let that happen! But how could he stop it? He had to get rid of the child! Somehow, someway, he had to eliminate the threat embodied in the unknown child. But how would he know which child, out of all the children certain to be in Bethlehem, was the child to eliminate?

His devious, murderous, war-calloused mind answered his own question. Eliminate them all, every last male child in Bethlehem and its surrounding area. What were they to him other than a conquered people who he could do with as he pleased? He was king, and he would do whatever it took to secure his kingdom.

Eliminate every male child – it was ridiculously simple. If he were to eliminate only some, he might not get the one that was the real threat. Eliminate every male child – that was the only answer. He didn't need to give any reason for such a cruel order, for to Herod it wasn't cruel, just necessary. He'd committed many heinous acts in his lifetime; his lust for power and luxury had birthed all of them.

Now clear in his thoughts, Herod painfully climbed the stairs back up to his throne. Loudly clapping his hands, he shouted, "Guards!"

Two high-ranking guards immediately entered the room, quickly approached the throne and knelt down before him, swords at their sides. Herod paused not an instant.

"Take a regiment south to the town of Bethlehem," he placidly stated as he stared straight ahead, "and there I want you to find every male child two years old or younger and slay them. Not one male child is to be spared. Is that understood?" He glared at the guards kneeling at his feet.

The guards lifted their faces to their ruler, eyes unflinching, and replied, "Yes, Honorable King."

Herod motioned for them to rise to their feet, and as he looked at them, his eyes projected his evil intent. "Then go, and do your business in Bethlehem and the surrounding areas. Report back to me when my orders have been carried out."

The guards bowed again as they slowly stepped back from Herod's throne, then turned and left as a sly, evil smile crept across Herod's face. There would be no child born to be King of the Jews by the end of the day, and if the magi were still in Bethlehem, they would see first-hand the consequences of their disobedience.

He touched his robes, imagining the slaughter to come, as relief washed over him in the knowledge that his throne would soon be secure from an insignificant, low-life Jew.

* * * * * * * *

Deborah had risen early, eager to be about her business for the day. Now that Jesse was six months old, he didn't require such frequent feedings as when he was a newborn, and Deborah's strength was returning. She loved being able to once again assist Selma with work at the inn and to spend more time with Gedaliah.

Leaving Jesse in Eglah's care, Deborah hurried to the town market to buy her fresh purchases for the day. Mary was usually there with Jesus firmly propped on her hip, but Deborah couldn't find her. Presuming that Mary had been earlier than usual for whatever reason, Deborah hurried to Mary's house.

Upon her arrival, she noticed that the covers on the windows were still drawn, even though it was mid morning. Puzzled, she knocked firmly on the door.

"Mary!" she called out as she knocked again. When no response was forthcoming, Deborah placed her hand on the latch and turned it, pushing the door open.

"Mary! Joseph!" Deborah called as she quickly walked from the living quarters into the shop, concern welling up inside her as she noted that the bedding was missing, as well as several other items.

Worried and confused, Deborah grabbed her tunic and held it up as she hurried from the house, leaving the door ajar. Basket in hand, she scurried toward the inn, and people stared at her as she pushed them aside, but she paid them no heed. Mary, Joseph and Jesus were gone, simply gone, and she didn't know why.

Reaching the inn, Deborah burst through the door, slamming it against the wall. Gedaliah was nowhere to be seen, but Selma was in the entry way.

"Where's Gedaliah?"

"He just went to the stable to check on the animals," Selma replied, wondering at Deborah's anxious expression.

Deborah dropped her shopping basket and fled out the back door of the inn, only to run into Gedaliah returning from the stable. She grabbed his shoulders as she tried to control her emotions.

"Gedaliah, Mary and Joseph are gone! Mary is usually at the market when I'm there, but she wasn't there this morning, so I went over to her house. Their personal things are gone, Gedaliah, but Joseph's tools are still in his shop. Where could they be?"

Gedaliah placed his hands on Deborah's arms, removed her hands from his shoulders and took them in his. "Their donkey is gone, too." His eyes reflected Deborah's concern.

"Where could they have gone?" questioned Deborah as her voice became tense with anxiety. "And more importantly, why are they gone? Mary never mentioned anything about them leaving in all the time we spent together yesterday."

Gedaliah started walking back to the inn as he turned Deborah around and put his arm around her waist. "I don't know any more than you do."

"Why would they leave in the middle of the night?" Deborah wailed. "Why would they leave without telling us? Do you think they'll be back soon?" Questions raced through her mind as she tried to unravel the mystery of their abrupt departure.

Entering the inn, Gedaliah took Deborah in his arms, comforting her as best he could, but her trembling body refused to be consoled. She suddenly jerked away.

Quickly wiping away her tears, Deborah exclaimed, "Maybe Mother knows something. I'm going to see her. Tell Eglah that I'll be back in time for Jesse's feeding." She turned and ran out of the back door, fear, frustration, and uncertainty propelling her forward.

Gedaliah almost called out to her, but thought better of it at the last moment. There was no way he'd be able to change her mind. He rubbed his brow, perplexed and concerned.

Deborah held her dress high as she ran over the trail. She stubbed her toe on a rock and almost fell down, but it didn't slow her pace. She passed the very spot where she and Mary had sat the previous day with their young sons, and her heart lurched at the thought that they might never enjoy each other's company again. Exhausted and out of breath, she reached the crest of the hill and saw the house where she was birthed and raised. No one was in sight, and she panicked as she raced for the house. She didn't know why, but she had a feeling of impending doom as she tried to escape from the phantom of fear that chased her.

Throwing open the door, she loudly called. "Mother!" She frantically ran through the house as tears began to run down her face. Finding no one, she ran from the house into the yard, where she saw Helah and her mother gathering late-season flowers on the slope behind Helah's new house. Hiking up her dress again, Deborah ran toward them as she called.

Upon seeing Deborah, Kezia quickly handed the flowers to Helah and hurried toward her daughter, her heart in her throat.

"What is it, Deborah? Has something happened to Jesse?"

"No," Deborah exclaimed as she gasped for air and tried to slow the frantic pace of her heart. "Jesse's fine. But Mary, Joseph and Jesus are gone. They've just disappeared, Mother, without even saying goodbye. It looks as if they left in the middle of the night."

Kezia opened her arms to her grown child, and Deborah fell into them and buried her face on her mother's shoulder.

"Deborah, dear, what makes you think they're gone?"

"Because all of their personal things are gone from the house, and the donkey is gone from the stable. Oddly, Joseph's tools are still in the shop."

"Maybe someone came with news, possibly bad news, of one of their relatives, and they had to return to Nazareth."

"If that were so," countered Deborah as she wiped her eyes, "wouldn't they have told us? Why would they simply take the donkey and leave in the middle of the night without saying a word?" Suddenly she gasped and placed her hand over her mouth as her eyes grew large. "Maybe someone robbed them of those precious gifts they received from the wealthy foreigners and then forced them out into the countryside and killed them!" The thought sent her heart into a frenzy of terror.

Kezia cast a glance at Helah, who was standing close by, her arms loaded with wild flowers. "Helah, please put those in water and join us at the house." Helah nodded and left, looking back at them over her shoulder.

Kezia consoled Deborah as they walked back to the house, where she had Deborah wash her face, and then Kezia cleansed her injured toe. "They must have left for a very good reason, Deborah. Mary isn't the kind of girl to just disappear without a just cause. Surely she will send a messenger soon with the reason why they left and where they are. I'm sure we'll hear something before too long." She finished wrapping the bandage around Deborah's injured toe. "Remember, Joseph's tools are still at the house; he can't make a living without them, so I'm sure they'll come back."

Deborah sighed heavily, her energy spent, her tears dried up. "I suppose you're right, Mother. I just wish they'd taken the time to knock on our door when they got the donkey instead of leaving us wondering. It would have only taken a moment of Joseph's time, and it could have prevented all this anxiety and concern."

Kezia emptied the bowl of water used to cleanse Deborah's injured toe, then she brought her a drink of wine mixed with water.

"Where are Father and the others?" Deborah asked as she drank deeply of the refreshing drink and tried to focus on something other than the disappearance of her best friend.

"They're at the south pasture."

"Rufus joined them today," Helah offered as she entered the room. "He was tired of being lazy."

"Men can't stand being idle too long," stated Kezia, "even when they have a beautiful new bride. God has instilled in them the drive to provide for their families, and that certainly isn't a bad thing."

Deborah smiled at her new sister-in-law. "How do you like being married?" she asked in a desperate attempt to focus on something other than Mary being gone.

"I like it very much."

"Do you miss Rufus?" explored Deborah. "He's only been gone half of the day, but do you miss him?"

Helah paused briefly. "Yes and no, but when he's here, I can't get any work done, if you know what I mean. I still have meals to prepare, cleaning to do, clothes to wash, bread to bake, but all Rufus wants to do is . . . . well, ... you understand what I mean." She let her voice fade as she giggled and placed her hand over her mouth as a rush of warmth flooded her face.

"Stay for a few more minutes and have a bite to eat," Kezia suggested to both Deborah and Helah as she started gathering bread, cheese and fruit on a tray.

"Okay, Mother, but I won't stay long. Jesse will need to be nursed soon, and if I'm not there when he's hungry again, Eglah will have her hands full with a very angry baby."

After an enjoyable lunch, during which Deborah forced herself to remain calm and keep her mind focused on the conversation, she prepared to return home. As Kezia and Helah walked with her toward the path that led to town, Kezia noticed a large cloud of dust rising from the road that led to Jerusalem.

"What could be creating such a large cloud of dust?" she wondered, her two daughters by her side.

Soon the thunder of many horses' hooves traveling at a full gallop reached their ears as a large number of mounted soldiers came into view, their shields reflecting the afternoon sun through the dust. Puzzled, the three women watched as the soldiers bore down on the town.

"Why are soldiers going to Bethlehem?" questioned Deborah. "Has Heber returned?" She grabbed her mother's hand as anxiety gripped her heart. All thoughts of Mary were pushed aside. Gebia's murder was still fresh in everyone's mind.

From their vantage point, the women watched as several small groups of two soldiers each broke away from the main contingent and started riding toward the houses in the hill country surrounding Bethlehem, a pair of them heading their way. The women shook in fear as the two soldiers barreled toward them, regally mounted on their massive steeds, spears in hand. There was no possible way of escape. Kezia placed herself in front of Deborah and Helah as they watched the sweat-drenched horses pick their way through the rocky path.

"Don't run away," nervously ordered Kezia. "If we try to run, they will surely kill us. We must stand our ground and wait."

As the two mounted soldiers approached, the women were taken aback by the size of the horses they rode. Only the very wealthy, and the war machine of Rome, could afford such beasts, and the size of the snorting, sweating animals bearing down on Kezia made her step back, afraid they'd trample her to death.

The muscular soldiers reined in their steeds. Kezia's legs trembled beneath her dress, terror gripping every fiber of her being, yet the trio of women fearfully held their ground.

Suddenly, shouts of terror and screams drifted through the mid-day air and echoed in the hills. Momentarily diverting her eyes, Kezia shot a glance toward Bethlehem, but the soldier's rough voice brought her back to his commanding presence. Lean and muscular and well-equipped, Kezia instantly realized that they would have no way of defending themselves if the need arose. Quaking in fear, she prayed for strength.

"You!" shouted the soldier as he pointed beyond Kezia to Deborah and Helah. "Do either of you have any young children, male children?" The horse he straddled pranced around, fighting against the restraining hand of his rider.

Deborah and Helah exchanged frantic glances. Helah replied first. "No, sir. I'm newly married."

Deborah choked, unable to respond as a wave of nausea washed over her. Confused, Kezia quickly turned around and looked at her daughter, and then stepped toward the soldier.

"Why do you ask such a question?"

Without warning, the soldier's sandaled foot came up and kicked her in the chest, knocking her to the ground. Instinctively, Deborah and Helah rushed to her aid, only to be intercepted by the second soldier. Kezia was sprawled on the rocky ground, her elbows skinned and bleeding, shaking in terror as the screams and shouts from the town reached a terrifying crescendo.

"Answer me!" shouted the soldier as he placed the tip of his spear on Deborah's chest, "or I'll drive this through to your back, which wouldn't bother me one bit!"

Sharp steel against her skin, Deborah cried out, her voice coming in broken gasps. "Yes, I have an infant son!" Deborah felt as if she would faint. Why would he ask such a question? What did it matter if she had an infant son?

"Where is he?!"

Fighting to gain control of her trembling body and desperately trying to keep from losing her lunch, Deborah looked down at her mother, bruised and bleeding on the ground. Eyes wide with terror, she glanced back at the soldier as she shakily responded, "He's at my house with my mother-in-law." Tears appeared in her eyes and fell unchecked down her cheeks as her body went limp. Surely this strange question could mean nothing good! With the horrifying cries coming from the village echoing in her ears, Deborah felt as if her life was draining away.

Helah choked back a sob, and Kezia started weeping as she hid her face on the ground.

"And where is your house?" demanded the mounted soldier. The point of the spear pierced Deborah's clothing. "This isn't it?"

"This is *my* house," wailed Kezia. "There are no young male children here!" Her face soiled and tear-stained, she glared up at the soldiers with angry, tear-filled eyes. Suddenly, her instincts understood the reason for the cries, the reason for the odd question, and her belly burned with rage.

All expression and color drained from Deborah's face, and she appeared as though dead as she returned her gaze to her mother's face. The thought that crossed her mind was too horrible, too horrific to even consider, but she couldn't deny it; her mother's countenance even spoke of it. Life seemed to stop and her eyes glazed over as she simply whispered, "At the inn in Bethlehem."

"Where?! Speak up, or I'll cut your throat!"

Trancelike, Deborah again replied, "At the inn in Bethlehem." Frozen in fear, she stared at her mother, whose eyes ran rivers of tears.

Suddenly, the soldier jerked the tip of the spear away from her chest, deliberately cutting her dress with its razor-sharp edge. Laughing at her, he sneered back, "Then he's probably dead by now!"

Collapsing to the ground on her knees, Deborah released a mournful wail that was birthed in her belly, crawled up her throat and escaped into the air. She felt shredded and torn, lifeless. Her cries rose from the utmost part of her being, encapsulated her overwhelming terror, echoed through the countryside and joined the cries from the town. She grasped her dress where the spear had cut it and tore it as she groaned in deep, unfathomable despair.

Turning their horses, the solders set off at a gallop toward the next farmhouse, eager to participate in Herod's ordered killing spree. A bloodless spear was nothing to brag about.

Stunned and speechless, her mouth agape, Kezia lifted her bruised body from the ground and crawled to her daughter, who was now wailing and weeping and pounding the ground with her fists. As Kezia reached for her, Deborah snapped her head up, tears streaming down her face.

"My baby! My baby!" she frantically screamed as she bolted into action. "Mother, I've got to save

Jesse!" Rising so quickly that she tripped on the hem of her torn dress, Deborah ran down the path to the town, screaming as she ran. "Jesse! Jesse!" Totally consumed by the instinct to protect her child, she ran carelessly down the hill toward the carnage in the town that was her home.

Kezia watched her go as fear stabbed her heart, knowing that Deborah wouldn't be able to prevent anything even as she prayed that Deborah's life would be spared. Reaching for Helah, whose eyes were moist with tears, she cried, "Helah, run to the south pasture and get Thaddeus and the others! Hurry! Go quickly!"

Shaken and trembling, Helah turned and ran, familiar with the route through the hills to the south pasture. Hadn't she and Rufus walked it many times in the lovely days after their marriage? Hadn't they played hide and seek between the rocks, laughing and loving as only young lovers do? The beauty and magic of those moments were lost to her now as she raced along the trail to get help, but what could a simple family of shepherds possibly do against a contingent of Roman soldiers bent on completion of their murderous deeds? Suddenly, the day didn't seem real as her feet flew over the ground.

Kezia watched Helah disappear around a group of rocks, and then glanced back toward Bethlehem, a town under attack. Rising despite the pain in her body, she moved as quickly as she could, thanking God that Simon was with the others today and not at the house. The thought of what might have happened had he been home made her sick, and she vomited beside the path. Stumbling along the rocky trail, she followed Deborah's steps toward the town as the cries of those suffering assaulted her ears and grew louder.

Deborah entered Bethlehem even as many people were running away, trying to escape the swords and spears wielded by the mounted soldiers. Terrified parents were carrying frightened children as they ran, many falling down in their haste. It was against this flood of humanity that Deborah pushed, desperate to reach her infant son.

Finally bursting through the back door of the inn, she ran down the hall, hysterically screaming, "Jesse! Jesse!" She catapulted herself up the stairs covered with drops of blood and ran through the open door and into the living quarters, leaving the chaotic streets behind, only to be greeted by personal chaos.

Deborah froze, paralyzed by what she saw and heard. Gedaliah, a gaping, bloody wound on his head, was hunched over the mutilated, lifeless body of little Jesse. His painful cries combined with Eglah's wails as she reached her injured son's side. Her dress was blood-soaked, and her tears mingled with Jesse's blood as it pooled on the floor.

Spasms of unimaginable grief sucked the air from Gedaliah's lungs as he gently lifted the broken body of his son, and he threw back his head and released a blood-curdling scream.

Through her tears, Eglah saw Deborah, frozen in the doorway, shaking her head in disbelief. "I'm so sorry, Deborah!" she cried loudly in utter despair. "I tried to protect him, but there was nothing I could do!"

Gedaliah turned on his knees, his child clutched close to his chest, as his eyes met Deborah's. Feeling as if she was having a horrible nightmare, Deborah hesitantly took a step toward him. Surely this grotesque image would change any second, she thought, for this couldn't possibly be real. Jesse was just a little baby, full of life and promise, unable to harm anyone. How could it be possible that someone would kill him? Deborah took another step and then another, as time seemed suspended, and then she collapsed onto the floor next to Gedaliah, who reached out and broke her fall with his free arm.

When her knees hit the floor, the reality of the slaughter penetrated her numbed mind, and Deborah cried as only a mother who has lost a child can cry. She wrapped her arms around Gedaliah's neck, and he pulled her close, Jesse's tiny body between them. Their love had created him, and now their love surrounded him in death. Something – or someone – unspeakably evil had destroyed his precious, innocent life. Their peaceful, loving home had been shattered, and they'd been given no chance to protect themselves or their precious, sweet, innocent baby!

Deborah felt Gedaliah's body shaking with convulsive sobs as intense as her own. Even though she wanted to take Jesse from his arms, she couldn't yet bring herself to hold him. Her precious, beautiful baby was mutilated, gouged by a spear through his tiny chest. She'd never seen so much spilled blood in all her life, not even at the crucifixions commonly performed along the roadsides by the soldiers, and it all came from this small child she had birthed, nursed and loved.

Shaking and bleeding, Kezia made her way through the stable yard as the pounding of horses' hooves echoed through the town. The warm sunshine and beautiful sky overhead belied the horror that was occurring under its canopy. The thunder of the horses' hooves receded as the soldiers left, their horrific task accomplished, but the screams and cries of weeping mothers and fathers, grandparents and siblings pierced the air and cut at the heart of the small town.

Kezia gingerly approached the stairs in the inn. She knew Jesse was dead from the cries that descended the stairway. How was she to comfort her daughter when she herself needed comforting? How could she even find the strength to climb the stairs before her?

Her grief was so heavy she felt as if she were carrying a ton of stone on her back as she put one foot in front of the other, going ever closer to the incomprehensible.

Drops of blood on the stone steps greeted her as she climbed, her body screaming with both pain and rage. Who had ordered this slaughter? Who could possibly do such a thing? And why?

Her heart heavy with blinding grief, she reached the doorway and saw Deborah and Gedaliah embracing and weeping, Jesse's bloodied, lifeless body between them. Eglah was behind Gedaliah, her head resting on his back as she wept uncontrollably. A rush of silent tears poured from Kezia's eyes as she went to Eglah, who was trembling with grief and horror, and embraced her.

Kezia choked through her tears, "Here, Eglah, let me help you get up and seated in a chair."

Eglah moaned with pain as Kezia, momentarily forgetting her own suffering, helped her rise and walk slowly to a chair. Once seated, Eglah grabbed Kezia's tunic and pulled her face close to hers, hoarsely whispering between her cries, "I tried to keep him safe, Kezia, I really tried, but once they found out he was a male, they killed him!" Sobs shook her body as she tried to continue, her chest heaving. "They pulled him from my arms on the spear and threw him off on the floor, laughing as they did so! They laughed, Kezia, at the murder of an innocent baby!" Eglah covered her face with her hands, and Kezia gently stroked her hair as her tears splashed onto Eglah's bloodied dress.

"They wounded Gedaliah when he tried to save Jesse! Thank God they didn't kill him, too!" The two grandmothers of little Jesse embraced and mingled their tears, grief so intense that it sapped the life from their bodies.

After several moments, Kezia pulled herself away and asked, "Were you hurt, Eglah?"

Eglah shook her head as she tried to dam the river that rushed from her eyes, but it was impossible.

Kezia lifted her heavy body and went to the table, where she poured water from a jug into a basin. She dipped a cloth into it and took it to Eglah. "Here, wipe your face. There is much we need to do."

Resolutely, Kezia moistened another cloth and approached Gedaliah and gently placed it on his head to stop the flow of blood. His grief spent momentarily, he looked up at Kezia through red, swollen eyes. She gazed at him in her sorrow, this man who was her son-in-law, her daughter's husband, the father of her first grandchild. Kezia feared what the loss of his first son would do to him. She'd seen violent deaths of loved ones change people forever, and she worried what this would mean for Deborah's future.

The role that now lay before her was one from which Kezia would rather walk away. It was up to her to prepare the body of her grandchild for burial, to tend to the gaping wound in his chest, to wash his bloodied, torn and broken body. How was she going to do that? Her own grief was more than she could bear, yet she had to be strong for Deborah, Gedaliah and Eglah, who'd been holding Jesse when the attack occurred. Moving woodenly as if in a dream, she couldn't see beyond the present moment, for to think of the future without Jesse was impossible. Only the grace of God would be able to provide her with strength for what lay ahead.

"Hold this to your head," wearily ordered Kezia as she placed the cloth on Gedaliah's head. "We need to get the bleeding stopped."

Slowly, Gedaliah released Deborah from his embrace and placed his hand on the cloth, aware of the deep gash on his head for the first time. Deborah gently grasped Jesse and took him from Gedaliah, holding him close to her breast as fresh sobs convulsed her body.

"My baby! My baby!" she sobbed, her face flushed with grief and wet with tears. "Why have they killed my baby?" She rocked back and forth as she held Jesse, her hands becoming soaked with the blood that still oozed from his mangled body.

Kezia knelt down and gently whispered, "Deborah, let me take the child. Please, let me take him."

Slowly Deborah released her hold on Jesse and allowed Kezia to lift him from her arms, and then Deborah gave a soul-wrenching cry as she tore her clothes again. Gedaliah stood to his feet, his legs shaking, and utilized his last ounce of strength to lift Deborah off the floor. They embraced and wept as Kezia carried Jesse to the basin of water she had prepared.

With loving hands and tears splashing into the basin of water, Kezia removed Jesse's torn, blood-drenched wraps. The color had already drained from his face. No longer was he pink and warm, but white and cool. As she removed the last of his wraps and exposed the wound that had caused his death, she almost vomited again. A fresh river of tears dropped onto Jesse's naked body as she placed him into the basin and began to wash him. Just yesterday she'd held him and played with him, had lavished kisses on his cherub cheeks, and now he was no more! It didn't seem possible!

After she finished bathing him, she packed the gaping wound with cloth, dried him and placed him on the table on a blanket. He was such a beautiful child, and now he would never grow up. His life had been extinguished in an instant. It was all so utterly senseless!

Kezia felt a hand on her shoulder, and she turned her head to see Deborah standing beside her. "Thank you, Mother," she whispered. "I'd like to rub him with oil."

Kezia wiped her eyes to stop the flow of tears as Deborah, acting far older than her years, retrieved a small bottle of scented oil. After pouring a few drops into her hands and rubbing them together, she took one of Jesse's arms and rubbed it with the oil. She began to sing as she lovingly caressed him and slowly rubbed the oil onto his arms, his legs, and his abdomen. Gedaliah came and stood by her side and took one of Jesse's hands in his fingers and tenderly caressed it as his tears flowed unceasingly.

Broken and in shock, Deborah marveled at the body of her child as she rubbed the oil over his body, which had grown inside her with seed from her loving husband. She had enjoyed every moment of her pregnancy and was continually amazed at the girth of her abdomen as the child inside her had grown. The agony of labor had been well worth giving life to Jesse, and she would never regret it, but now she was preparing his body for burial, and he was only six months old! He should have grown into manhood, not be murdered in infancy! Where was the God of Abraham, Isaac and Jacob when this horrible blow had been inflicted? How could he have allowed this to happen?

Weeping quietly, Deborah smoothed Jesse's dark hair in place with her hands, and then she placed kisses on his forehead and cheeks, her tears dripping into his hair. There wasn't so much as a scratch on his face, and Deborah hoped that the fatal wound was something she had imagined as she placed the another kiss on his forehead. Surely a mother's kisses could heal any hurt! Surely he would turn his head and smile at her at any moment!

But this, this was too much for even love to heal! Jesse was dead!

Kezia handed Deborah clean wraps for Jesse, and when she was done wrapping him, Deborah held him in her arms. The wound that had torn his heart asunder was no longer visible, and Jesse looked normal. Deborah lifted him to her face and placed his cheek on hers, crying loudly, "Oh, my dear son, how I love you! I will never stop loving you! How my breasts long to feel your tiny mouth suckling them! How I long to see your bright eyes and happy smile! I'll never see you walk; I'll never hear you talk; I'll never see you grow as tall as your father! But you will always be in my heart, my Jesse, my first-born son!"

Gently kissing his tiny cold lips, Deborah held him to her breast, fresh tears streaming down her cheeks.

Just then there was a loud commotion downstairs and Gedaliah, his head now bandaged, bolted to the doorway. Upon hearing Thaddeus calling for him, he answered and shouted for them to come upstairs.

Thaddeus, Reuben, Benaiah, Eleazar, Simon, Rufus and Helah rushed up the stairs and into the living quarters, but their advance was halted when they saw the scene before them. After standing for a brief moment in the doorway, Thaddeus slowly approached Deborah as tears spilled from his eyes.

Through her tears, she whispered, "They killed Jesse, Father. They just killed him."

Thaddeus embraced his daughter and grieved with her, wanting to comfort her yet knowing such a loss was inconsolable. He'd been frantic to get to town when Helah had arrived at the south pasture and told them of the carnage being visited on Bethlehem. He couldn't run fast enough, and the entire time, he was keenly aware that he'd be powerless to change the course of events once he arrived. His heart broke, not only for the loss of Jesse, but for his daughter and her suffering.

Thaddeus ran his calloused hand gently across Jesse's tender skin, wiping away the tears deposited there by Deborah as she held him. Never would he hold this child again, nor would he ever teach him the ways of the sheep as he had taught his own sons. All dreams of the future with Jesse were crushed in one split second, the second the spear tore his chest open and extinguished his life. After leaning over and placing a kiss on Jesse's cold cheek, Thaddeus held Deborah's head in both his hands and gently kissed her forehead, and then he turned and looked at his family surrounding him. Head hung low, he went to Kezia and held her close as she wet his tunic with her tears.

Taking her aside so the others couldn't hear, Thaddeus whispered through his grief and tears, "From what we've seen on our way here, apparently every young male child around 2 years old and younger who lived in or near Bethlehem was killed today. A common gravesite is being readied outside town; all of the children will be buried together."

Kezia rested in the strong arms of her husband, weary with grief. "Why, Thaddeus? Why would someone order all the male babies to be killed? And why in Bethlehem?"

"I don't have an answer to the 'why,' but it could be none other than Herod who gave the order. He has command over all the soldiers who did this horrible deed."

In a fog of grief, Thaddeus and Kezia watched as everyone in the family said goodbye to Jesse, lifeless in his mother's arms.

Deborah and Gedaliah, as well as Eglah, changed into mourning clothes. All the other family members spread ashes over their bodies and clothes.

Just before sunset, the entire population of the town of Bethlehem converged around a freshly-dug mass grave on the outskirts of town. Not one family was left untouched by the atrocities committed that day, and the sound of weeping and wailing and great lamentation echoed back from the hills, and 11 mothers wept for their children and could not be comforted, because they were no more.

Chapter Seventeen

NO REASON

Mourning for the slaughter of the innocents in the town of Bethlehem seemed to be unending. Every day, mothers went to the mound of earth that contained the remains of their young ones and drenched the soil with their tears. Empty arms longed to caress their babies, and swollen breasts, engorged with milk, ached exceedingly to be suckled. But there were no young male babies to suckle their mothers any longer, and the cries of the mothers were not only emotional, but physical as well.

The gravesite never lacked for a visitor, for there wasn't one family in Bethlehem which wasn't affected by the slaughter, either by blood relation or friendship. Women who'd lost babies tried to console each other at the mass grave, their only comfort knowing that many others understood their grief because it was their grief also. Mourning mothers often prostrated themselves on the mounded, rocky soil, heedless of the dirt that clung to them from head to toe. Even though their grief was overwhelming, the necessity of attending to the needs of their other children forced them to accomplish minimal chores. Hugs from older children brought a portion of comfort to those who'd lost infants, but nothing could ease the anguish.

Fathers tried to console their grieving wives, trying to remain strong when what they really wanted to do was take revenge. The unspeakable crime of killing innocent babies demanded revenge. Reason dictated that the 11 innocent lives lost not be forgotten and that the perpetrator of the insidious crime be remembered, not as one to be admired, but as one to be hated forever and ever. Even though many fathers, such as Gedaliah, had tried to protect and save their young and had been seriously injured in the process, many were despondent that they hadn't done enough. If they had, they would also have been killed, or so they thought.

For a time, all activity in Bethlehem came to a standstill. The merchants and farmers didn't display their wares or produce for sale at the market for several days. One farmer pushed a cart full of produce through the narrow passageways in town, giving his produce away. Better to give it away, he said, than to let it rot in the fields.

The men of Bethlehem often gathered and discussed what to do. Revenge was the main subject of conversation, but how could a small town which couldn't even defend its babies rise up and take on the Roman army? The desire to do so was a raging fire in the men, and the sheer impossibility of it fueled the flames all the more.

Four days later, Thaddeus and his family gathered for their evening meal and found themselves talking about the desire for revenge once again. Kezia, her face shallow and dark circles under her eyes, quietly cleared the table as the men began to talk. Even though Helah was no longer there to help her, Kezia didn't mind much. The work gave her something to do. If she didn't keep busy, she felt as if her grief would kill her. Granted, the men would talk and contrive ways of getting revenge, but Kezia knew that it was talk and nothing more.

Reuben was speaking as Kezia refilled their glasses with a mixture of wine and water. "We have to find Heber and his men. They'll be willing to join us in an attack."

"And where will this attack happen?" probed Thaddeus.

"Wherever there is a Roman soldier."

"And what will you attack them with?"

Reuben was momentarily silent. Thaddeus saw his frustration. His fists kept clenching and unclenching by his side.

"That's the most difficult problem," Reuben finally replied. "We can melt down our farming tools and make weapons out of them, I suppose."

"And how many swords could we get out of a plow?" irritably queried Thaddeus. "Four? Five? Six?"

Reuben's fist hit the table, startling everyone. "I don't know, Brother, but we've got to do something! We can't just let them come into our town and slaughter our babies and do nothing about it!"

Thaddeus's face was intent as he loudly replied, "I agree, Reuben, I agree! But maybe the timing isn't right. We may have to wait years before we can make them pay for what they've done."

"You're referring to the Messiah, aren't you, Father?" Quiet until now, Eleazar finally spoke.

Reuben glared at him, angry at the idea of having to wait.

"That's right," Thaddeus calmly replied. "We know that the Messiah has come, but we also know that he's just a baby right now. It will be years before he can lead an army against our oppressors."

"That's true, Father," replied Eleazar, "but I'm not going to wait until then. I'm going to do something now." Everyone looked in his direction. "I'm going to find Heber and join the Zealots."

Listening from the other room, bile rose in Kezia's throat. Hurrying into the common room, a towel in her hands, she cried out, "No, you will not join Heber! I've just lost my grandchild! I'll not have my son slaughtered, too!" Her body shook from head to toe and tears cascaded down her tired face. "Why do men always think killing is the only way to solve problems? Why are the young always so ready to die?" Unashamed of her outburst, Kezia continued her tirade. "Why don't we all just go to Herod's palace and ask his guards to kill us – wouldn't that be quicker and easier? For you will end up dead if you join Heber, and if the Romans find out, they may kill your father as they killed Gebia! Do you want his death on your head, Eleazar?" Her face was flush and her body shook uncontrollably. "Do you!?"

Thaddeus rose and came to her and put his arms around her. "We're all dealing with our grief differently, Kezia. Men want to fight when something such as this happens."

Kezia put her hands on his chest and abruptly pushed him away. "So you condone and sanction what Eleazar wants to do?" Eyes blazing with anger and dammed with tears, she glared at her husband.

"If I were 20 years younger, I would want to do the same thing. But I'm not, and I have you and Simon to provide for and this farm to run and sheep to tend. I don't have the freedom to make such a choice anymore."

Kezia spit angry words at her husband. "And Eleazar does?"

Thaddeus simply nodded his head.

Kezia quickly glanced at Eleazar, so sure of himself, a young man not quite 20 years old. She saw no fear in his eyes, only determination. Kezia fought to hold back her sobs.

"I should have insisted on picking a wife for you years ago, and then you wouldn't be so eager to leave."

From the corner of the room came Simon's young voice, "I'm staying, Mother."

Kezia glanced his way and retorted, "And well you should; you're just a lad."

"But when the Messiah gathers an army," Simon continued in an almost monotone voice, "I'm going to join it because he will win."

"Yes, he will," quickly agreed Reuben, "but we don't even know where the child is now. Hopefully, we'll hear something about why Mary and Joseph left Bethlehem and where they went before too long. It's a good thing they weren't here that day or Jesus would have been slaughtered, too."

"I hate the Romans," Simon added. "They killed little Jesse and so many other baby boys. I'm glad Obed's mother had a girl, not a boy, or she would have lost a baby, too."

Kezia sighed heavily as the anger drained from her. She had no strength left with which to argue the ways of men. She felt as if she had aged 100 years since Jesse's death. Weariness so great it came from her bones and spread through every muscle was all that she could feel. When would she stop crying and enjoy life again? When would she look at the morning sun and feel hope for the day? Her shoulders slumped as she turned toward the kitchen, unable to look at her grown son or at Thaddeus.

"I can't stop you from doing what you feel you must do, Eleazar, but I only ask that you strongly consider the consequences before you leave." She shot a piercing glance over her shoulder at him and retreated to the kitchen once again, her heart weary and worn.

Thaddeus sat down with the others again, fondly looking at each one of his family members. Simon, almost ten years old, now knew the burning rage of hate. Eleazar, determined to join the Zealots,

231

was in the prime of his life. Benaiah, son of his brother Reuben, just entering manhood, but apparently was not filled with the zeal to take revenge as was Eleazar. And Reuben, his younger brother, so strong and opinionated, was eager to take up arms without counting the cost. All of them were precious to him, and he couldn't imagine life without one of them. To lose just one would change the whole family dynamics dramatically. Jesse's death had affected all of them even though he was just an infant.

Everyone looked at Thaddeus. What could he tell them? Their quiet world had been turned upside-down four days ago, and there was nothing he could do about it. Even if they could acquire arms, there was no one to lead them, no one to teach them how to fight. The Romans were highly-trained, skilled in the ways of war, and they possessed weapons far superior to anything an opposing force could possibly come up with. Going to battle was not the answer, at least not for now. Thaddeus still believed their only true hope was the Messiah.

The ache in his heart for his little grandson was still acute, sharp as a knife in his chest. Family was by far the most important thing on the face of the earth, and to have such small, innocent lives so brutally destroyed cut at the very heart of Bethlehem's existence. He had to do what he could to stem the flow of blood and the desire for revenge or the town's streets would become a river of blood, and most of it would be from its citizens, not from Roman soldiers killed by Jews.

Clearing his throat, Thaddeus began. "All of us want to see those that did this to suffer terribly, but such hatred can only bring sorrow and death. Jehovah says that vengeance is His, He will repay. I don't know why God allowed this horrible event to take place, but I do know that we must trust Him and allow Him to deal with Herod.

"Wanting to join the Zealots, Eleazar, is a noble thing, but you must consider what your mother said. You must also think of how a decision you make affects the rest of the family. If you go, it will be extremely hard on your mother, your sister, me, all of us. Each one of us is important to the family operation here, and if you leave, we would have a difficult time getting along without you.

"Decisions like this should never be made in the heat of the moment. The pain of losing Jesse is still too fresh for any of us to make rational decisions. We need to give ourselves time to heal, time to seek God and His will for us. The Messiah has come, and in due time, He will grow up and accomplish His purpose on earth."

"But that means at least 20 more years under Roman rule!" thundered Reuben. "What kind of a life is that? You and I, Thaddeus, will probably never live to see the day when freedom is gained!"

"True, but Benaiah will, and so will Eleazar, Simon, Rufus and Helah, Gedaliah and Deborah. Wouldn't the wait be worth it for all of them and their future children, our grandchildren?"

Reuben ran his hand through his curly, tangled hair, exasperated. He closed his eyes, nodded his head and simply said, "Yes."

Thaddeus motioned for Simon to come and sit by his side, and when he did, Thaddeus put his arms around him. "I want Simon to see the day the Messiah frees us from the Romans. I don't know how that's going to be accomplished, but God is a mighty God and can do what we think is impossible. Didn't he part the Red Sea for Moses and our forefathers? Didn't he speak to Moses from a burning bush? Didn't he give Sarah and Abraham a child in their old age?

"We'll have to wait until the Messiah reappears and takes the throne in Jerusalem. We can do nothing else." He pulled Simon close to his side and rested his chin on his boy's head. "We must wait for the sake of our children and our children's children."

Standing in the doorway, Kezia caught a tear with the back of her hand as it slid from her eye.

* * * * * * * * *

Sitting on a cushion at a window, Deborah gazed out over the town from her second-story home. Life had almost returned to normal, or so it seemed. The market was open every day, the local priests went about their business, and women were busy baking bread, spinning and weaving, making clothes, cooking and cleaning. Yet at the same time, nothing was the same in Bethlehem and never would be again. Even now, almost three weeks since the slaughter, the mothers of those killed still wore mourning clothes, and their daily chores were carried out in a daze, hiding their pain under a veil of busyness.

Word of the senseless slaughter had spread far and wide, and it was rumored that the order for such had been issued by King Herod. The people continually questioned what motive Herod had in doing so. Further, what kind of a king would inflict such a heinous act upon those he ruled? Herod had a reputation of killing, even members of his own family, but he always had a motive for what he did. This edict issued against defenseless children and babies seemed beyond the boundaries of human understanding and even beyond Herod's ruthless personality.

Deborah pulled her knees to her chest and sighed heavily. Her heart was as empty as her arms. The passing days had done little to ease her sorrow, and she really had no reason to go on living. She was the only mother in Bethlehem to lose a baby who did not have an older child already. Her only child was taken, and she had no one to ease her pain. Oh, Gedaliah tried, and she loved him for it, but he couldn't take the place of little Jesse. Deborah truly felt there was no reason to continue to live.

She hadn't eaten anything substantial since the time of the slaughter, the meal with her mother and Helah being the last one she had enjoyed. Eglah prepared all of the meals for Gedaliah, and often friends in the community would bring over a prepared dish for them. But she had no appetite; just the thought of eating made her feel nauseous. A few small bites were the most she could eat at one time, and that only once or twice a day.

Eglah sat across the room, throwing the shuttle back and forth through the loom, weaving a rug. Deborah watched her briefly and then let her gaze drift back to the scene outside her window. She knew Eglah blamed herself for Jesse's death, but Deborah didn't blame her. She blamed herself. If she hadn't become so upset at Mary's disappearance, she wouldn't have gone to her mother's and would have been at home when the murderous soldiers arrived. Even if she couldn't have saved her son's life, she would have died trying and would be in heaven with him now instead of living without him in a world gone mad.

Deborah ran her hand across her breasts, bound tightly with a band of cloth. They'd been engorged and extremely painful for days after Jesse's death, and oftentimes her milk would flow, soaking her dress. Those had been the most difficult times for her, when she wanted her little child to ease the terrible discomfort of her body. Even now, she remembered his chubby cheeks and the way he smiled at her while he was nursing as he rested his hand on her breast. But those moments were gone forever. Her milk was drying up, the discomfort diminishing with each and every passing day.

"Deborah."

It was Eglah speaking, and she turned and looked at her holding a small dish of food in her hand.

"You should eat something. You've lost a lot of weight." Eglah's deep concern for her daughter-in-law was clearly etched all over her face.

Deborah resumed staring out the window. "I know I should, but I can't, Mother Eglah. I just don't have any appetite."

Eglah placed the dish of bread, cheese and grapes close to Deborah. "I'll leave it here in case you get hungry or change your mind."

Deborah gave the plate a cursory glance and then gazed out the window again. She saw people passing in the streets, even entering the door to the inn, but she seemed to be in another world. She heard the sounds of voices and children playing, but they all seemed so very far away. She smelled the familiar aromas of cooking, but smelling them almost caused her to be sick. She was living in her body but yet seemed to be out of it, watching life pass her by and go on without her. And so she sat for hours at a time, day after day.

Later that night, Gedaliah tried to coax Deborah into eating something. She knew she should eat, but she just couldn't and told him so.

"I understand, but I need you, Deborah. I can't lose you, too, or I'll die of a broken heart. My heart is no less broken over Jesse's death than yours, but I go on because I still have you. Please go on because you still have me. Here, please eat a few grapes for me. Please." He held up a cluster of plump purple grapes as he pleaded with her, his eyes deep pools of concern.

Deborah reached for one, knowing her husband was right, and noticed how gaunt her hand had become. It didn't look like it belonged to her, but to someone else. The veins showed through the pale skin, which was so thin it looked as if it was stretched over a skeleton. Surely this couldn't be her hand, but it was. She carefully pulled off two grapes, placed one in her mouth, then another, and then looked up at Gedaliah as tears welled up in her eyes.

"I'm sorry, Gedaliah!" she lamented. "I want to die; the pain of living is just too great!" She put her hands to her face, sobs shaking her body.

Gedaliah quickly embraced her and pulled her close as he tenderly stroked her hair while he desperately attempted to control his own grief. .

Suddenly Deborah stopped crying and jerked herself from his arms. She began to pace the floor, eyes blazing with anger. "I've sat up here day after day, dear husband, trying to make sense out of all this madness, but I've found none. Where was Jehovah God when Herod gave his gruesome orders? Was He sitting in the beautiful temple that Herod rebuilt for Him, enjoying its grandeur? And if so, did God not want to offend the one who had given Him His new temple? Did God favor Herod over the male babies of Bethlehem, Gedaliah? Why didn't He do something to stop it? Has God forgotten His chosen nation, Israel, and gone over to the camp of the Romans in gratitude for the rebuilding of the temple? I'm so very, very angry at God! He took my best friend away and then took my child, all in the same day! I'll never forgive Him! Never!"

Deborah's face was red and she was shaking all over. Clenching her fists by her side, she glared at Gedaliah.

Startled at his wife's angry tirade against God, Gedaliah listened as Deborah spewed out the venom that had been brewing in her. When she finished, he went to her and embraced her again, rocking her gently.

"I don't have any answers for you," he whispered into her ear. "I have no answers at all."

"I'm so broken," gasped Deborah between renewed sobs. "Life has no meaning anymore. I can't make myself do anything. All I can think about is Jesse lying dead out there with all the other little babies. Every time I close my eyes, I see him with his chest ripped open and blood spilling out through the huge hole made by a spear! My heart races so fast that I'm afraid it will beat itself out of my chest, and I get hot all over and start to cry again! When will this end, Gedaliah? When will I want to live again?"

Gedaliah shed his own tears as he lovingly embraced his sobbing wife.

PART II

Jerusalem – 32 Years Later

Chapter Eighteen

CELEBRATION

Jerusalem, the Holy City of God, was never more crowded than at Passover. Devout Jews from all over the Roman Empire and surrounding world came to Jerusalem to celebrate, and the burgeoning city population was suffocating to those who lived there. Inns were crammed to capacity and the streets were continually clogged with masses of people. Traveling from one place to another was a superb challenge, for the throngs of people shoved and pushed, jostling everyone about and often carrying them in a direction they didn't want to go. The normal population of approximately 40,000 swelled to 150,000 during Passover, and the stench of so many unwashed people, as well as the waste they produced, was often unbearable.

The celebration of Passover itself was often obscured by the merchants who sought only to profit from the influx of people. Even the temple court was not off limits to those profiteering from the need of thousands to offer required sacrifices, and money-changers set up tables therein to convert the coins of foreign travelers into local currency. Chaos abounded, and Pilate, the Roman Governor, saturated the city under his command with hundreds of soldiers to discourage any thought by the Jews under his authority of gathering to form a rebellion.

Clinging to each other as they followed their husbands, Deborah and Helah stayed as close to them as possible as they wove their way to Caleb and Rizpah's house. Caleb had established himself in Jerusalem about 20 years earlier and was now a well-known maker of fine pottery. He and Rizpah had raised two daughters, who were now married with children of their own.

As they snaked their way through the crowds, the four travelers from Bethlehem were amazed at the huge masses of people that had descended on Jerusalem. It seemed as if Jews from every nation were there, and the sounds of strange words and languages mingled with the Hebrew language. There were Parthians, Medes, Elamites, and people from Mesopotamia, Cappadocia, Pontus, Asia, Phrygia, Egypt, Libya, Rome, Crete, and Arabia, all trying to exist inside the walls of Jerusalem.

Deborah and Helah clung to the tunics of their husbands, fearful of being separated from them in the swelling crowds. Even though they lived a mere five miles outside Jerusalem, they seldom came to this noisy metropolis, mostly because of the pronounced Roman presence. Back in Bethlehem, soldiers were seldom seen, but here in Jerusalem at Passover, there were numerous soldiers. The women's greatest fear was that they would get separated from their husbands and be unable to navigate the streets by themselves. Even though they had been to Caleb's house a few times, it had been when the city was at normal population levels, not during the mass invasion that occurred at Passover.

As they pressed their way through the crowds, they circumvented the temple area, and the density of the crowds lessened and walking became easier. Deborah thought that her toes had been stepped on more than once, and she was sure that she would have bruises where she had been jabbed by elbows of people pushing their way past her. Helah felt the same way, and it was with great relief that the women finally were able to walk beside their husbands rather than behind them.

As he reached for Deborah's hand, Gedaliah said, "Now that the crowds have thinned, it should take us much longer to reach Caleb's house."

"I've never seen so many people in one place at one time in my entire life!" exclaimed Deborah as she gladly grasped his hand.

"Just think of it," posed Rufus, "thousands of Jews from all over the world are here right now, and all to celebrate the Feast of Passover. I've heard so many languages that I'm astounded! I didn't know that there were so many different tongues." He placed his arm around Helah's still-slender waist and drew her to his side as they pressed toward their destination.

Helah kept as close to Rufus's side as she could. "I don't like such huge crowds of people; it terrifies me, to be honest with you. I like our little town of Bethlehem and all the beautiful surrounding countryside. There are too many walls for me to be happy living here."

"I feel the same way," agreed Rufus.

"Caleb and Rizpah are very happy here," Gedaliah reminded them.

"Of course they are," somewhat tartly replied Deborah. "They've become accustomed to towns such as this and have forgotten the freedom of the open earth and sky."

"When Caleb and I were small children growing up in Bethlehem," reminisced Helah, "we'd often escape the confines of the town and wander out onto the hills. That was when I fell in love with the countryside and all its beauty. Caleb, on the other hand, always wanted to get back to town and work with Father, and when he was grown, he went off to Bethany to learn his trade. He's never loved the countryside as I have."

The four visitors climbed the hill, navigating the narrow streets, toward Caleb's house. Gedaliah and Rufus carried packs containing their personal belongings they needed for the week, and their weight often caused them to shift it from shoulder to shoulder.

"Well, we should be thankful that Caleb has a home in Jerusalem and can accommodate us for the Passover celebration. If not for that, we might not even be here. I couldn't imagine having to deal with finding a room in all this madness," stated Gedaliah.

The noise of the crowds lessened with each step. The cobblestones which made up the street were worn smooth by the thousands of feet that had walked upon them for countless years. Shadows from the buildings and houses cast their shadows across the streets and were a welcome relief from the open spaces and sunshine. Noises of families and friends wafted to their ears as they passed through the narrow streets, as well as delightful aromas of dishes being prepared for the evening meals.

Soon they were at the door of Caleb's house, which was set on a hillside and did not share walls with other houses. It was large and spacious, but not ostentatious, and contained several small pools and smooth stone floors which Rizpah kept highly polished. Several large potted plants adorned the entranceway, and various plants were scattered about the small bit of land around the house. Gedaliah stepped upon the doorstep and pounded hard. Within a few seconds, the door was opened and an excited Rizpah greeted them with open arms.

"Gedaliah! Deborah! Rufus and Helah!" she exclaimed as she hugged and kissed each one. "Please, come in out of the heat and the crowds. You must be exhausted from your trip!"

The two couples entered the home and were swallowed up in its cool dimness. The small windows along the wall did little to let in light but did a great deal in keeping out the heat. Promptly removing their sandals, they stepped onto the cool stone and sat down to wash their feet. Rizpah, although wealthy enough to afford a servant or two, preferred to take care of her own home, and she already had basins of water prepared for her expected guests. Gedaliah and Rufus set down their bags, happy to be freed from carrying them.

After freshening up, they were soon seated on cushions around a large table. Rizpah chattered the entire time, eager to catch them up on the latest news. "Caleb is still at the shop. He had a customer coming by today to pick up some vases that he made. He is getting a fine price for them, but of course, they are absolutely beautiful and worth every coin. He will be home shortly. Leah and her husband, Lamech, will be here tomorrow, along with my two grandchildren. Seth is already five years old, and Dinah is three. She is such a sweetheart; I like to tell everyone that Dinah takes after me." She laughed as she continued her narrative. "Keturah and Jabal will also be over with Micah, who just turned two. He's a little rascal, full of energy and life, always wanting to get into everything. You can't take your eye off him for one minute or he's off somewhere he's not supposed to be. So we'll have a full house for Passover, but that's good. I wouldn't want it any other way."

As they settled themselves on the cushions, Rizpah went to a counter along the wall and lifted a beautiful pitcher, obviously Caleb's work, and brought it to the table. Goblets were already spread about on the table, and she poured a mixture of wine and water into them for her guests.

"Please, tell me about your trip. You arrived earlier than I thought you would."

Helah thanked Rizpah for her drink and, after taking a sip, said, "We got off earlier than expected, which was a good thing. The roads were very congested, and our pace slowed considerably as we approached Jerusalem."

"Did you see any soldiers?" asked Rizpah.

Gedaliah answered. "Yes, many, especially at the entrances to the city."

"It seems Pontius Pilate is very concerned about uprisings among the people with such huge numbers under his nose, so to speak. Of course, that's impossible, as we all know."

The sound of the front door opening and closing interrupted them, and all eyes turned to see Caleb entering the room.

"Greetings!" he shouted to everyone. "It's so good to see all of you!" Caleb immediately went over to his sister and gave Helah a kiss on each cheek and then affectionately slapped Rufus on the back.

"So, how have the two of you been?" he asked as he sat down and took the goblet of wine that Rizpah handed to him.

"Very well, thank you," replied Helah as she smiled coyly at her husband of almost 32 years. "As I knew when I married this man, he has turned out to be a fine husband and father of our three daughters."

"Who would have known that we would have three daughters while Gedaliah and Deborah had three sons?" questioned Rufus as he rubbed Helah's back.

Deborah's eyes darted to Rufus as she gently reminded him, "Four sons, Rufus, not three. Everyone seems to forget about little Jesse."

An uneasy silence fell on the group as memories of long ago came flooding back. "I'm so sorry," Rufus apologized softly. "I didn't mean to forget Jesse. It's just that he was with us such a short time that it's difficult to even remember him at all."

"Well, I remember, and I'll never forget," emphatically stated Deborah as her eyes stared at nothing in particular. "He would be 33 years old now, but his life was cut short at six months. I'll never forget him; never."

Caleb cleared his throat in an effort to break the uneasy silence that ensued. "How are all of your other children, Deborah?"

Gedaliah looked at the wife of his youth. She had aged well. Her face was wrinkled with laugh lines and creased with years of worry over her children, as well as over the unspeakable death of Jesse. Her dark hair was streaked with gray in places, yet her eyes still held the same sparkle they had when she was young. Gedaliah thought Deborah was more beautiful now than when he had married her. They'd suffered much together when Jesse was killed during the rampage on Bethlehem, yet they'd rejoiced over the birth of each additional child. Now their three sons were married with children of their own, most of them living within a day's walk from Bethlehem. He waited for Deborah to answer Caleb's question.

"They're all well. Joshua and Damaris, Horab and Martha, Judah and Rebecca, and all of those precious grandchildren of mine, are doing well. My sons have brought a great deal of joy to my life, and I'm happy to be a grandmother now. It keeps me busy and fills my life."

"And she still helps at the inn," interjected Gedaliah as he affectionately patted her gnarled hand. "When Selma died a few years back, Deborah insisted that she do the work herself since the last of our sons had just married, and she's done it since then. Of course, since our son Joshua and his wife, Damaris, began helping us, we do less of the work."

"Without Mother Eglah to keep me company any longer, I had to have something to do to keep myself occupied," Deborah explained. "I can't stand being idle."

"Rufus, how are all my nieces?" asked Caleb as Rizpah placed bowls of lentils, bread and large clusters of grapes on the table and then sat down beside him.

"Very well. As you know, Jael and Philip live on the farm with us. Dorcas and Levi live in Gazara, and Sarah and Mahlon settled in Hebron to be close to Mahlon's family. All of the children are well also, and it's difficult not to be able to see them regularly. Of course, Jael's two little ones are with us, and that helps a great deal. When we do get to see the others, we hardly recognize them because they grow so much between visits."

"And will everyone be celebrating Passover in their own towns?" Rizpah inquired.

"Yes," Deborah replied. "They wanted us to celebrate with them, but we haven't been to Jerusalem for Passover for many years. Now that there are no children at home, we made the decision to come here for a change."

"Tell me," asked Gedaliah, "what's going on in Jerusalem these days?"

Caleb dipped a piece of bread into the lentils and ate it before replying. "Just the usual Roman presence that lurks in the background like a snake ready to strike its prey. They're more visible than ever with the Passover celebration, and they shadow everything that goes on in this city. Nothing seems to escape their notice."

"The Pharisees are in an uproar about a man who is turning the people against them," interjected Rizpah. "Don't forget that, Caleb."

Caleb popped a grape into his mouth. "That's right. How could I forget?"

"Who is he?" Helah asked.

"Someone they call Jesus," replied Rizpah. "He speaks daily in the temple court and teaches crowds everywhere. We've even heard that he's healed many diseases that are incurable. He apparently arrived here several days ago, and he has a huge following."

Deborah's hand stopped in mid air with a grape between her fingers. Allowing her mind to drift to the distant past, she finally connected to the time when she knew the name, so long ago now that she had nearly forgotten it.

She looked up at Gedaliah and caught his attention with her eyes. "Don't you remember, Gedaliah?" she asked. "Don't you remember when we knew an infant named Jesus? Mother and I delivered a baby who was given that name, before Jesse was born. Don't you remember?"

Conversation around the table ceased as Deborah's questions caught everyone's attention. "Has everyone forgotten that time in our lives, or is it just me who remembers because of Jesse's death?" The mood in the room suddenly became somber.

Deborah continued. "The child Jesus was born to Mary and Joseph in our stable, and angels announced his coming to you, Rufus, out on the hillsides tending the sheep. Certainly you haven't forgotten that night?"

Rufus looked at the table and his hand as it held the goblet, which was almost empty now. "No, I haven't forgotten. How can one forget seeing the skies filled with angelic beings?"

247

Gedaliah took Deborah's hand in his. "We'd hoped at that time that the child Jesus would be the promised Messiah. We all did. But he disappeared, along with Mary and Joseph, and we've heard nothing about him since then."

"Until the day he died, Reuben hoped to hear that the Messiah was gathering an army," stated Rufus. "He truly believed that the Jesus we knew was the Messiah, as I believe all of us did. But somehow nothing ever became of him."

"This man that's speaking in the temple courtyard may not be the same man," offered Helah.

"True," replied Deborah, "but I want to find out if it is. He'd be just a few months older than Jesse would have been, and maybe his mother, Mary, is still alive. I would hope so. She was just about my age."

"Why do you want to find out?" asked Gedaliah. "If I remember correctly, Mary and her husband.... ah, Joseph, and their baby disappeared just before the slaughter in Bethlehem. Why do you want to find out?"

Deborah stared across the room at the wall, wondering that same thing. If they had left town early that day, they may have been far enough away to escape the swords and spears, but if not, Jesus would also have been cut down and murdered. But why did she want to find out?

Somberly gazing at her husband, she said softly, "If this is the Jesus we knew back in Bethlehem, he'll be able to tell me where to find his mother. I just want to know why she left without telling me goodbye."

The only sounds that could be heard were sounds that came into the house from outside, and everyone sitting around the table flashed back to the town of Bethlehem 32 years earlier, a lifetime ago. Each person recalled the horror of that day in the way they remembered it. It seemed like an eternity had gone by since that time, and even though it had happened, it was almost as if it had never happened at all. The pain of the slaughter had greatly diminished with the passing of time, and the reality of it had been pushed back into the recesses of their minds so that they could continue on with life. It was too horrible, too shocking, to bring to mind on a regular basis. And now here they were, sitting in Caleb's house in Jerusalem, wondering if the Jesus that was speaking in the temple was the one whom they had known as an infant a lifetime ago.

Helah cleared her throat, rose from the table and came over to Deborah, who was still staring at the wall across the room. Taking her hand, she said, "Deborah, is it wise to reconnect with someone from your past? If this is the same Jesus, surely seeing his mother will only make you recall horrible things."

Deborah pulled her gaze from the wall and looked at her sister-in-law. "Mary and I were close friends before the slaughter, Helah, and I don't think that seeing her will upset me. The image of Jesse's mutilated body is still in my mind; it will never leave. It was years before I could sleep without being haunted by that image. Seeing Mary again will help me understand why she abandoned me, leaving me alone on that horrible day. Who knows but that Mary lost Jesus outside the town's walls; if they headed toward Jerusalem, they would have encountered the soldiers. The answers to my questions can only come by finding out if this is the same Jesus and if so, where I can find his mother."

Helah gently patted Deborah's hands as she released them and returned to her seat. The heaviness of the moment broke when Rizpah stated, "I'll be going to the market in the morning. I'll ask around and see what information I can gather for you,

Deborah. One way or another, we'll find out if this is the same Jesus. It's a common name, you know."

"Thank you, Rizpah," replied Deborah as she ate the grape that she had set down on the table moments earlier.

"You said that this Jesus is turning people against the Pharisees," reminded Gedaliah. "How's he doing that?"

"From what I've heard, he teaches things that simply anger the religious leaders, and they've tried to get the people to pay no attention to him, but to no avail."

"You'd think that he would be telling people to go against the Romans, not the Pharisees," Gedaliah stated sarcastically. "Why would he want to turn people against religious leaders?"

"I don't know. I hear only bits and pieces while at the market every day, and I've even tried to find this Jesus, but all I've been able to do is see him from far away. He draws huge crowds continually. In fact, about four or five days ago, he entered Jerusalem on a donkey, and people were waving palm branches and throwing their robes on the ground in front of the donkey. They were all shouting hosannas and praises. Some were shouting 'Hosanna to the Son of David! Blessed is he that comes in the name of the Lord!' It was really quite exciting."

"My wife loves to know what's going on in town," laughed Caleb, "and it irritates her to no end when she can't find out the latest gossip." He gently nudged Rizpah with his elbow.

"That isn't true," saucily replied Rizpah with raised eyebrows. "I've just been wondering about this man Jesus because the entire city is talking about him now."

"Can I go to market with you tomorrow?" softly questioned Deborah.

"Certainly. We'll go early in the day so we have more time to ask questions and look for this man."

"Thank you, Rizpah."

"So, Caleb," posed Rufus as he changed the subject, "how are things at your shop? Rizpah told us that you were meeting a special customer today."

"Things are going very well. The pottery I sold him was some of the finest I have made, and I commanded a high price for it, and he was more than willing to meet it."

"Good," nodded Rufus. "You've become one of the best potters in Jerusalem, from what I hear."

"And you are absolutely right," interjected Rizpah. "Caleb is the finest potter, in my opinion."

"Of course he is," laughed Gedaliah. "He's your husband and you're supposed to have that opinion." Laughter filled the room.

The rest of the day was spent in visiting and in preparing for the Passover. The women worked together in the kitchen while the men talked and made a short trip to Caleb's shop to see his newest creations. Deborah kept busy with her hands and contributed to the conversation as they worked, but her mind kept drifting back to her early years as Gedaliah's wife in Bethlehem and the events that had occurred. Oddly enough, she hadn't thought about Mary and Joseph for years, and now suddenly they were all she could think about. The possibility that she could find Mary after all these years was more than she had ever hoped for, but to locate her among the masses teeming through the streets of Jerusalem would be a monumental task indeed.

As Gedaliah and Deborah were preparing for bed that night, Deborah nestled into the crook of her husband's arm as she always did. She rolled over onto her side and put her arm across his chest. The years had begun to age her husband, and the realization that they had lived most of their lives made her heart jump into her throat, choking her with sadness. She loved this man who had stood by her side and given her children and provided for her. She loved him for his strength of character and his good business mind. She loved him for his gentleness and faithfulness to her. To live without him would be unimaginable. Losing Jesse had been unspeakably horrible, but to lose her husband would be simply unbearable. She touched his beard with her hand and placed a kiss on his lips.

"What was that for?" Gedaliah asked softly as he embraced her.

"Just because I love you."

Gedaliah kissed her tenderly and wrapped her more fully in his arms. "Something's bothering you, isn't it? I'm sure it has something to do with this man called Jesus who you want to find."

Deborah paused briefly before replying. "Yes, it does. I have so many questions that have no answers, and if I can find Jesus and he's the same one from years ago, I might be able to find Mary, and hopefully she'll be able to give me answers. Strangely enough, I haven't thought about getting answers for years, but hearing about this Jesus has stirred up everything all over again."

"What will you do if this isn't the same Jesus we knew?"

Sighing heavily, Deborah replied, "I don't know, Gedaliah, I don't know. I can only hope and pray that he's the same one and that I'll be able to find Mary. Joseph was older, so I won't be surprised if he's no longer alive, but Mary was my age. She should still be alive unless some tragedy befell her. As you know, I felt so abandoned when she left without saying goodbye, and then the soldiers came and took little Jesse from us. It was the worst day of my life; nothing can ever compare to that day. I just want to find out why she left and where she went. And I want to know why she never came back to live or to visit so I knew where she was and that she was okay." Deborah stroked the hair on Gedaliah's chest, twirling it between her fingers.

Gedaliah was quiet for a moment. He was surprised to hear that, all of these years, she had wondered where Mary and Joseph had gone and why. He chided himself for not speaking to her more often about that day so long ago. Rather than talk about it, he'd wanted to push it out of his mind, to forget that it had ever happened. But Deborah still had questions and still wanted answers. He pulled her closer in his arms as he kissed the top of her head.

"My dear wife," he whispered, "I'll do anything I can to help locate this Jesus and find out if he's the one we knew as a child. If that can be done, we'll be able to find out about Mary. I want you to have your answers."

Deborah felt a tear escape her eye, and it slid down the side of her face and into the hair on Gedaliah's chest. Surely tomorrow would bring some answers her way.

Chapter Nineteen

THE QUEST

Rizpah wrapped a shawl around her head and draped it across her shoulders as she prepared to go to the market. Deborah was soon by her side, and together the two women left the house and headed down the sloping street into the business district of Jerusalem in the early morning light. Even though the hour was early, the streets were already filled to capacity with people, and once again navigating was difficult. Rizpah clung to Deborah's hand, and they slowly made their way through the throngs of people and into the market. Talking to each other was practically impossible because of the noise of so many others shouting and talking at once. When they reached the market area, Rizpah turned to Deborah.

"Keep your ears open for Jesus's name," she shouted. "I've heard him mentioned every day for the last several days, so we should be able to locate someone who knows something of his whereabouts."

Deborah nodded as she continued to walk beside Rizpah. They slowly wound their way through the market, looking at jewelry, finely-woven cloth, pottery, rugs, spices, fruits and vegetables, bread, a variety of grains, and perfumes. Deborah was fascinated by all of it. The market in Bethlehem was much smaller and offered only the essentials of life, not perfumes and exotic spices. Despite the throngs, she had a marvelous time holding fine jewelry, smelling sweet perfumes, and sniffing spices from different lands. Through it all, she and Rizpah kept their ears open, seeking someone who would mention the name of Jesus.

"Oh, Deborah, smell this perfume!" exclaimed Rizpah above the din. "It smells like a garden of fragrant flowers!" She lifted a bottle to Deborah's nose.

"That's wonderful!" Deborah replied as the scent filled her nostrils.

Suddenly, Rizpah had an idea. "Let me buy this for you!" she exclaimed as she dug into her purse. "It will be my gift to you, and I'll also buy one for Helah. Both of you deserve to have something costly once in a while, and Caleb and I can certainly afford to buy it for you!"

Deborah held up her hand in protest. "I couldn't take such a costly gift! That's far too much money."

"I won't let you deny me the privilege of spoiling you with this gift," replied Rizpah as she handed the coins over to the merchant, who carefully wrapped two vials in a piece of velvet and handed it to her. "Every woman should have an expensive bottle of perfume at least once, and I won't allow you to say no." She tucked the cloth containing the costly vials into her tunic pocket.

Deborah simply smiled at Rizpah as she shook her head in disbelief. "Thank you very much, Rizpah. I only hope Gedaliah doesn't get angry."

"Why should he get angry? He's the one who gets the ultimate benefit from the perfume. Right?"

The two women laughed as they continued through the market, each table they passed containing more costly items than the previous one. As they were admiring some fine linen fabric, they overheard the conversation of two men standing next to them.

"I tell you that this Jesus is a miracle worker unlike any of the prophets!" loudly stated the tall man.

"But the Pharisees and Sadducees aren't pleased with him at all and want him to leave Jerusalem immediately." He shoved his way past Deborah and Rizpah with his friend close by his side.

Rizpah pushed her way through the gap left by their passing and followed closely on their heels as Deborah grasped her tunic to keep from being separated. The men in front of them were speaking about Jesus! They had to catch up to them and ask them questions!

The men's forward motion stopped momentarily, and Rizpah pounced on the opportunity to catch their attention. "Sirs!" she shouted. "I heard you speak the name of Jesus. We're looking for him. Please tell us where he is!"

The tall man turned around and pulled the arm of his companion to inform him that he also needed to stop. He gazed down his beard at the two women.

"You want to know of Jesus?"

"Yes," replied Deborah as she stood by Rizpah's side, her heart pounding wildly.

"He was at the temple courtyard, as he has been for several days," replied the tall man. "I'm surprised he's still teaching there, especially after what he did when he entered the temple courtyard four days ago. Don't you agree, Elah?" He turned to his companion.

"Absolutely."

Rizpah pressed forward with her question. "Why? What did he do?"

The two men looked questioningly at each other, and then Elah asked, "You haven't heard?"

Deborah and Rizpah emphatically shook their heads.

"Well, about four days ago, Jesus went to the temple courtyard after entering Jerusalem riding on a donkey as people waved palm branches and threw their coats on the ground in front of him. Everyone shouted hosannas and blessings on him. We were part of that crowd and followed him into the temple courtyard." He looked around in frustration. Noise from the shoppers in the market was unbearably loud, so he motioned for them to step aside in a doorway in hopes of hearing each other more clearly.

When they were situated, Elah continued. "That morning when Jesus entered the temple courtyard, he took off his tunic and then began angrily flipping over the tables of the moneychangers in the temple. We'd never seen anything like it before! Jesus is usually so mild-mannered and quiet, but that morning, he was angry, very, very angry! He overthrew the tables of all who did business there, scattering their money on the ground. People scattered like sheep without a shepherd, but the moneychangers crawled around on the ground, trying to collect all the coins Jesus had scattered about. He even opened the cages of the doves being sold for sacrifices and the gates of the pens that held the sheep and goats."

Rizpah asked, "Are you sure it was Jesus who did this?"

"Absolutely," replied the tall man. "We've been to the temple courtyard several times to hear him teach, and we know what he looks like. Besides, we'd just seen him enter Jerusalem."

"It really was quite comical in a way," laughed Elah. "Just imagine if you can, merchants frantically trying to retrieve their coins on the courtyard floor with doves flying out of their cages and sheep and goats running around! It truly was a chaotic scene, and I personally thought it was a bit funny. The moneychangers and merchants always raise their rates during Passover, and the poor find it difficult to afford even a dove for sacrifice. I guess the money changers got what they deserved. Most of those who had followed Jesus to the courtyard scattered in a thousand directions when the melee broke loose, but we managed to step back a few paces between some pillars where we had a good view of the whole incident."

"Why was Jesus so angry?"

"Who knows? Jesus shouted something after he had turned every table upside-down, but I can't quite remember what it was. Can you, Naan?"

"Yes. I believe he said, 'Isn't it written, my house is a house of prayer; but you have made it a den of thieves.' That's what I understood him to say."

Deborah and Rizpah looked at the men, puzzled. "What did he mean by saying it was *his* house?" questioned Deborah. "He was in the courtyard of the temple; it belongs to the nation of Israel."

Naan and Elah simply shook their heads. "I'm only telling you what I think I heard," responded Naan. "I could be wrong, but his words were clear enough to me from where I was standing."

"Do you think Jesus is in the courtyard today?" questioned Deborah anxiously as a knot of anticipation formed in her stomach.

"I think so," replied Elah. "He's been there every day since he cleared it out; he won't even let anyone carry a vessel through the courtyard anymore."

Rizpah took Deborah's hand and stepped back from the two men. "Thank you for your time and information." The men nodded and returned to the crowds and their shopping.

Deborah pulled on Rizpah's arm. "Let's hurry to the temple. Maybe Jesus will still be there."

Once again they joined the masses swarming through the streets, and it was only by perseverance that they finally reached the temple courtyard, but they couldn't get inside because so many people were already there, huddled together in a hushed mass of humanity. Pressing forward, they stood on their toes in an attempt to see over the heads of those in front of them, but to no avail. Rizpah finally pulled on the tunic of a woman in front of her and asked, "Is it Jesus teaching in the courtyard?"

The woman replied, "Yes. So many people come to hear him that it's almost impossible to get close enough to hear his voice."

The two friends looked at each other. Deborah could hardly contain herself, knowing that Jesus, possibly the same person she had known as a small child, was just beyond their reach.

Deborah asked Rizpah, "Can't we work our way through the crowd and get closer?"

"I don't know. The crowd is so tightly packed that it may not be possible."

"Well, let's try," pleaded Deborah. "I've got to find out if this is the same person I knew; I want to find out about my friend, Mary. Please, let's try."

Rizpah nodded, and the two women gripped hands as they started pressing through the crowd, but their attempt was in vain. They were only able to go a few yards beyond where they had stood. The crowd was so tightly packed that there was no room for turning around, much less moving forward, and even though they were pressed together, they weren't pushing and shoving as those at the market had done. These people stood quietly as they strained to hear the voice of the one they had come to hear. Deborah and Rizpah soon found themselves whispering rather than shouting to each other in the stillness of the crowd.

"Can you hear anything, Rizpah?" whispered Deborah as she stood on her toes.

"I hear his voice, but I can't hear it well enough to be able to understand what he's saying." Rizpah stretched her neck high.

And so they strained to hear the voice that captivated the crowd. Not very many minutes had passed when the crowd suddenly became agitated, swelling and moving in frustrated anticipation.

"The Master is leaving!" someone shouted.

"Where's he going?" questioned another.

Several voices rang in unison as they tried to follow Jesus. Deborah became frustrated that she was so far away, too far to see or hear anything, and she found herself becoming angry. Her frustration soon gave way to tears, and Rizpah noticed them as they were pushed along with the flowing masses. Gently taking her hand, Rizpah took Deborah and pulled her out of the crowd and into a side street, allowing the masses of people to push past then and leave them behind. She gently encircled Deborah with her arms.

"Don't cry, Deborah," she comforted. "We'll find out one way or another, but we were too far back to be able to do anything about it today." She lifted Deborah's face with her hand.

Deborah wiped away the tears that were flowing down her creased face. She couldn't understand why she was so upset or even why she felt she had to find Mary. Maybe it would be better just to forget the whole thing and return to Bethlehem after the Passover. Bringing up the painful past would certainly open old wounds that had never completely healed.

"I'm sorry. I didn't mean to cry," she softly sobbed as she dabbed her eyes. "I feel like an old woman in a young girl's body, and sometimes I act like that young girl, impetuous and energetic. Ever since I heard about Jesus, I've had an indescribable urge to find Mary. It's so difficult to explain. Mary and I were such good friends. Best friends don't part without saying goodbye, but Mary left without even telling me she was going to leave. I've just got to find out why she did that to me, Rizpah. I won't rest until I have an answer."

Rizpah closed her eyes as she nodded her head. "I understand completely, Deborah. We'll find out if this Jesus has a mother named Mary, and if so, we'll find her. If she's alive and in Jerusalem, we'll find her. I promise." She gently placed both hands on Deborah's shoulders. "Let's go home. Our husbands are probably worrying; we've been gone a long time."

Together the two women returned to Rizpah's house on the hillside, where they found Helah working in the kitchen. Rizpah presented Helah with her gift of perfume, much to Helah's delight. Helah told them that the men were out and would return later in the day. Rizpah set about assisting Helah in the kitchen while Deborah went to her sleeping chamber and laid down to rest. Helah noticed Deborah's somber face and asked Rizpah about it after Deborah went to her room.

Rizpah relayed the day's events to Helah. "She's just disappointed that we couldn't get close enough to Jesus today to ask him if his mother's name is Mary. Deborah's intent on finding out, and I've promised her that we would help her all we can." She filled a bowl with water from a large jug and filled it with fresh vegetables.

"I just hope she doesn't have her heart set on something that could ultimately disappoint her," quietly stated Helah. "It's been years since Mary left, and Jesse was killed the same day. If I were Deborah, I'd want to leave that part of my life shut. There's a high probability that Jesus was killed that day also."

Rizpah washed the vegetables and started cutting them for cooking. "Didn't everyone in Bethlehem think that Jesus was the Son of God?" she asked in retrospect. "I mean, from what I remember hearing, all of you believed that Jesus was the Messiah.

If that's true, don't you think God could protect his own Son?"

Helah stopped what she was doing and looked at her sister-in-law. "Yes, we did, but the Messiah was sent to deliver his people, and even though there were miraculous signs and wonders at the birth of Jesus, there has been no deliverance of the people of Israel. This Jesus may be a miracle-worker, but so were many of the prophets of old." She wiped her hands on a towel looped through her belt.

Rizpah sighed. "Maybe our husbands will have more information about Jesus when they return home. In the meantime, we'll let Deborah rest while we'll get ready for the arrival of the rest of my family. They should be here by later this afternoon."

The two women busied themselves with preparing food for the entire family, which would consist of seven additional people by day's end. They carried on a casual conversation the entire time, but their hands were as busy as their lips.

Deborah rested on her bed, troubled and confused at her jumbled feelings. Mary's disappearance was a lifetime ago; why did she need to find her now? Even though Jesse's murder happened 32 years ago, it seemed like it had just happened yesterday. The distant memory often plagued her nights, and even Gedaliah couldn't comfort her when the nightmares came, images of her small son's body spilling blood reviving the memory. No reasonable explanation had ever been found for Herod's order to slaughter the babies, all male, in Bethlehem, and to this day, everyone still questioned its purpose, although they knew that Herod was responsible for the slaughter. Yet here she was, reliving the whole horrific event as if it had just happened. Surely this man in Jerusalem couldn't possibly be the Jesus she sought; or could he be?

Deborah tossed and turned, unable to sleep in spite of her fatigue. It was absolutely silly of her to try to find Mary after all these years. Mary could be dead by now. Many women didn't live as many years as Deborah had already lived. Disease, child birth and maladies that had no name often took people in the prime of their life, but Helah, Rizpah and Deborah had all lived well into their forties, and each had grandchildren, so it was possible that Mary was also still alive. But how was she to find her in a city swelling with over 100,000 people? Deborah shook her head in dismay as she got up and went to help Rizpah and Helah.

The men soon returned from their walk around the city, and the conversation soon turned to Jesus, for his name seemed to be on everyone's lips.

Gedaliah spoke. "We heard about this Jesus today, and he's apparently made quite a few enemies, especially among the Pharisees and Sadducees. From the talk around the city, Jesus cleaned out the temple courtyard of people and animals several days ago, turning over tables and driving everyone away in a rage."

Deborah nodded her head. "We heard the same thing while out this morning, and then we made our way toward the temple courtyard where we heard he was still teaching, but we couldn't get close enough to see him. We heard he's been teaching there every day."

"Shortly after we arrived, Jesus left and the crowds moved with him," interrupted Rizpah. "We tried to get closer, but the crowd was so tightly packed that we got pushed even further back." She put her arm around Deborah. "And that was when Deborah became overwhelmed, and we simply came back home. We'll try to find him another day."

"It's rumored that he went to Bethany today," offered Rufus.

Deborah turned as disappointment slid down her face. "Then we won't be able to find him unless he returns to Jerusalem before we go home," she sadly stated as her gaze dropped to the floor.

Gedaliah took her in his arms. "We'll find him. I promise you that we will find him and ask him about his mother. It may just take a little time, that's all."

Deborah sighed heavily and returned to the task at hand, disappointment settling heavy on her soul.

Caleb and Rizpah's children and their spouses and children arrived later in the day. The evening meal was joyous and festive, and everyone was glad to see each other after such a long separation. Caleb and Rizpah's three grandchildren, Seth, Dinah and Micah, were soon in bed and fast asleep. The trip to the city had been much too exciting for them, and they were simply exhausted.

The adults convened and reclined around the dining table, and once again, the subject of conversation was Jesus. It seemed that there was nothing else to talk about but him because his name was heard no matter who one talked to or where one went.

Caleb told of what he had heard from customers during the last few days. "This Jesus certainly is a miracle-worker. There doesn't seem to be anything that he can't do, at least according to the stories I've heard. People tell of how he took a young lad's lunch and fed 5000 men with it, and women and children besides. And then there are countless stories of healing people who were blind, lame, paralyzed, and even those who had leprosy, and I've even heard tales of him raising people from the dead, one in particular named Lazarus, who lives in Bethany. Apparently he's gone to Bethany to visit Lazarus and his family."

Deborah listened intently at the conversation while her mind regressed to a former time and place, recalling the many wondrous signs from the heavens, including an announcement of Jesus's birth to her family in the fields as they watched their sheep. The years had dulled her memory of those days, but all the talk about Jesus now sent memories that she hadn't thought about for years rushing to her mind in crystal clarity. She interrupted Rufus with a hand on his shoulder.

"Don't you remember?" questioned Deborah loudly as she broke into the conversation. "Doesn't anyone remember that night when Jesus was born?"

The room became oddly quiet. "Of course I do," Rufus replied, "and as I told you before, it's impossible to forget being visited by a host of angels in the sky. It was a sight I'll remember until I die."

"Gedaliah," questioned Deborah as she looked pointedly at her husband, "don't you remember anything about that night?"

Gedaliah looked at her, puzzled. "Well, I remember that Joseph, the baby's father, came to the door of the inn very late at night, while we were getting ready for bed, in fact. He was seeking a room for his wife, Mary, who was ready to give birth. We had no room because of the census ordered by Herod, and so I told them to go to the stable behind the inn."

"That's right, but you're wrong about one thing," insisted Deborah. "You said Joseph was the baby's father, but that isn't true. Mary told me that Jesus was conceived by the Holy Spirit of God and that she was still a virgin when she gave birth to him. If what Mary said was true, wouldn't that make God the Father of Jesus?"

"How can that be?" questioned Leah, Rizpah's oldest daughter. "We all know how children are conceived."

265

"But that's just the point," excitedly stated Deborah, her thoughts finally becoming clear in her mind. "If Mary was a virgin when she gave birth to Jesus and God is his Father, then that makes Jesus the Son of God. And don't you think that the Son of God would have powers to perform miracles of all kinds?"

"But if Jesus is the Son of God, that would make him the Messiah, and the Messiah was sent to deliver God's people. Jesus hasn't done anything to deliver us from the Romans," cautiously reasoned Caleb.

"That's right," agreed Helah. "Jesus has done many miracles, and because of that, most people think that he's a great prophet, probably greater than any that has ever lived, but he's done nothing to free us from Rome."

"It's clear to me," offered Rufus, "that he hasn't attempted to come against Rome in any way. From the talk around the city, it appears that the only enemy he's made has been with our religious leaders. There's talk that the Pharisees and Sadducees are planning to have him arrested."

"Where did you hear such a thing?" questioned Lamech, Leah's husband.

"Oh, just keep your ears opened while walking around; you're sure to hear it, too. And I heard it more than once."

"But why would our religious leaders want Jesus arrested?" asked Rizpah.

"I've heard from customers into my shop that Jesus has called them all sorts of names, including white-washed sepulchers, vipers and snakes, and the like. They've constantly tried to get Jesus to say something specific that they can arrest him for, but they've been unsuccessful so far. Jesus even proclaims himself to be the promised Messiah, and the crowds of people in the city support him. They believe in him as such. But the religious leaders argue that Jesus is not from God, that he doesn't observe the Sabbath, and that he's turning the people against them."

"Not all people believe Jesus is the Messiah," stated Lamech. "We heard talk while out this afternoon that there's a great division among the people because Jesus is from Nazareth, and the scriptures say that the Christ will come from the seed of David and from the city of David, which, of course, is Bethlehem."

"But he *did* come from Bethlehem!" excitedly stated Deborah. "He was born in our stable and lived in Bethlehem for almost a year. Don't the people know that?"

"They only know that Jesus comes from Nazareth," quipped Caleb. "He's known as the son of Joseph, a carpenter, and he even learned to be a carpenter under his father's instruction."

Deborah stood up and started pacing back and forth along the side of the room.

"It's all coming back to me now! Joseph, Mary's husband, was a carpenter, and they came to Bethlehem because of the census ordered by King Herod. Don't you understand? Can't you see?! Joseph came to Bethlehem because he was a descendant of David, which would make Jesus from the seed of David, too! When they left abruptly during the night, maybe they returned to Nazareth, which would explain everything! But Jesus *was* born in Bethlehem, not Nazareth! This Jesus preaching in the temple has to be the same one I knew when he was born!"

Deborah became more excited as she paced the room, heedless that all eyes were on her. Finding Mary suddenly seemed possible! Her face glowed with hope and optimism.

"Deborah." Gedaliah's voice called her back to the present. "Please sit down, or you'll wear yourself out. You've had an exciting day."

Deborah stopped her pacing and looked at her husband, the man who'd stood by her side all these years. He'd been more than faithful to her; he'd been devoted to her. Even during the time after Jesse's death, when she couldn't find the strength to get up each morning, he'd been there for her, supporting her, encouraging her, and sharing her grief. They'd aged together, raising three additional sons and running the inn. Their lives had stayed simple, only leaving Bethlehem on occasion, content with the quiet life with which they were blessed. Looking at him now, she saw the years written on his face, the character lines etched there, the skin no longer glowing with youth. How she loved him! And she knew he would support her now as she sought to find Mary. This might be her only opportunity, and she knew her husband would do everything in his power to help her.

Deborah reluctantly sat down beside Gedaliah, suddenly somewhat embarrassed by her ambitious quest. Lowering her head and closing her eyes, she said, "I know in my heart that this Jesus is the one I knew when he was a small child, and I know he is the promised Messiah. Mary privately told me things that she wished to keep secret those many years ago, and I don't think that she would lie to me. I believe the things she told me, and I believe that her son is the Son of God. I will find Mary," Deborah stated, "and when I do, each of you will need to make a decision about Jesus. I can't make it for you. I can only tell you that I know in my heart that Jesus is the Christ, the Son of God."

Chapter Twenty

PASSOVER

Deborah arose from her bed earlier than everyone else the next morning and wandered into the small garden behind Caleb's house after she was dressed. She needed time to be alone with her thoughts. The Fourteenth of Nisan started at sundown that day, and she could see the lamb in the small pen behind the house, the lamb that would be slaughtered in a matter of hours and roasted for the Passover feast later that evening. Even after seeing numerous animals slaughtered for sacrifices throughout her lifetime, her heart still lurched at the thought of the poor, helpless animal giving up its life so that she could be reconciled to God. When would enough animals be killed to satisfy God's need for spilled blood? It seemed endless to her, and the small, perfect lamb that she watched with misty eyes was totally unaware of what would happen to it later that morning.

She pulled her gaze from the innocent animal and focused on the flowers in Rizpah's small, compact garden. Such beauty could only be created by God, the same God who demanded animal sacrifices year after year after year. Without the sacrifices, there was no forgiveness of sins, and so the Passover feast, the Feast of Unleavened Bread, took place every year for a period of eight days. She and Gedaliah had traveled to Jerusalem only once before to observe the Passover with Caleb and Rizpah, and all other times had observed it in Bethlehem. Because they hadn't been in

Jerusalem, they couldn't sacrifice a lamb, but instead had to have a shank of lamb for the Passover feast. Lambs could only be sacrificed in Jerusalem and at the temple, so the men in the family would be taking the lamb to the temple later that morning, where they would kill it in the presence of the priests. The lamb would then be brought home and roasted for the feast in the evening, which would last well into the night.

With a heavy heart, she sat watching the sun rise above the horizon; she wouldn't be able to search for Jesus today, which meant finding Mary would have to wait yet another day. Frustration had driven her early from her bed, and frustration would keep her hands tied until Jesus returned to Jerusalem. Even then she might not be able to find Mary because today was the First Seder and tomorrow was the Second Seder. Many people observed the First Seder, but a large number of Jews observed the Second Seder on the Fifteenth of Nisan.

Deborah placed her head in her hands and her elbows on her knees as she sighed heavily, despair and sadness seeping through every bone in her body. Suddenly, she felt very old.

When she'd arrived in Jerusalem, she'd had no idea that things would turn out this way. The trip was to be a simple celebration of the Passover, the Feast of Unleavened Bread that had been celebrated by the Jews for centuries. It was nothing new, yet this trip had now turned into a desperate search for a dear friend from long ago. Celebration was far from Deborah's mind now; all she wanted to do was find Jesus, speak to him, and then locate his mother. She desperately needed answers to questions that were raised 32 years ago. She was sure that her family was beginning to think her quest was illogical and ridiculous. But what did she care? Her desire to find

Mary was beyond her control. She'd have so much to tell her when they finally met again.

The first rays of the sun filtered through the trees and warmed Deborah's body, as well as her soul. This little space that Rizpah called a garden was a reprieve from the congestion of the city of Jerusalem. Even though she had lived in the inn ever since marrying Gedaliah, Deborah still frequented the hillsides outside Bethlehem, as well as visiting the house in which she was raised, which now belonged to Rufus and Helah. When she was surrounded by walls for any length of time, Deborah felt the need for open spaces again, for flowers and wind and sunshine on her face. This space provided by Rizpah filled that need.

"There you are," sounded Gedaliah's voice as he slid onto the bench and sat beside her. He put his arm around her and placed a light kiss on her cheek, which she acknowledged with a smile. "Are you alright?"

"Yes. I just wasn't able to sleep very well last night, that's all."

Gedaliah kept his arm around her thickening waist and pulled her close to him. "We'll find Jesus, and then we'll find Mary," he reassured her. "As I said, it may take a little time, but we will find them."

Deborah turned to look into his eyes, the eyes which she had come to read so very well through the years. She saw her reflection in them as she responded, "I know, Gedaliah, I know. I'm just frustrated that we have to wait another day or two to continue our search. We can't possibly do it on the Passover."

"That's true, my dear. So let's try to put it out of our minds for today as we celebrate with our family and have a wonderful time. This is a time for celebration, not weeping and mourning."

Deborah cocked her head at his tender tone and looked at him from under lowered eyelashes. "You're right, my sweet husband, you are absolutely right. Jesus went to Bethany yesterday, so who knows when he will return. He may stay there for the celebration and return in a few days. We'll just have to wait and see."

"Let's go inside," suggested Gedaliah. "I think everyone is up and getting ready for the morning meal. We won't want to miss it."

After the morning meal, the women cleaned up the dishes while the men in the family gathered together and dressed to go to the temple. The women and children solemnly watched as Caleb opened the door to the pen containing the lamb and gently lifted it into his arms. After being purchased five days ago, the lamb had been cared for and tended by the family, and everyone knew that his blood would soon be spilled so they could be forgiven and reconciled to God. Having known the lamb, each family member felt a certain degree of sadness that it had to die in order for them to be made right with God.

Caleb held the lamb in his arms as each family member touched it, some kissing its woolly head, and then Rufus opened the front door as Caleb walked through it. No one made a sound, not even the children, as they watched the lamb as it looked back at them and loudly bleated. Rizpah stood at the door as they watched Caleb, Rufus, Gedaliah, Lamech, and Jabal leave the house and head down the street to the temple. When they returned, the lamb would be dead, slain for their sins.

A solemn atmosphere settled over those in the house, and the remainder of the work for the Passover meal was performed with little talk and much thought. Even the children were subdued when they were told what was going to happen to the lamb and why it had to happen. Dinah, only three years old, cried profusely when she understood that the little lamb would be killed at the temple. Leah spent much of her time consoling her daughter and trying to explain why it was necessary, but getting a three-year-old to understand was simply impossible.

Rizpah had a fire going in the roasting pit when the men returned from the temple, the lamb limp and lifeless in Caleb's arms. Blood covered his hands, and even though the lamb was dead, he still carried it gently and lovingly. Rizpah soberly removed the lamb from his arms and carried into the kitchen, where it was prepared for roasting.

The afternoon was spent reading the Holy Scriptures as they prepared their hearts for Passover.

As the sun set, the First Seder began.

With the family gathered around the table, the first of four cups of wine, the cup of sanctification, was blessed by Caleb. "Blessed are You, Lord our God, King of the Universe, who creates the fruit of the vine." The cup of wine was passed around the table, and each person drank from it.

Next came the ceremonial washing of hands.

Afterward, Rizpah placed bowls of green vegetables on the table, accompanied by salt water, and each person dipped a vegetable into the bitter water and ate it.

Next, Caleb took the middle piece of matzah, or unleavened bread, from a plate that had been set on the table. Each of the three pieces was separated by a napkin from the other. Breaking the middle piece in two, he wrapped a napkin around the larger piece and set it aside as the afikomen, to be eaten at the end of the meal. He then passed the smaller piece around to everyone, who broke off a piece and ate it.

When this was done, Caleb told the story of the Exodus of the people of Israel from Egypt. The

Maggid was long, but Caleb had a way of telling a story and was able to keep the children's attention until the end. The second cup of wine, the cup of wrath, was poured out on the table when Caleb recited the plagues visited upon the Egyptians by Jehovah God.

The washing of hands with a blessing, the Rachtzah, was next.

Caleb then offered the Motzi, the blessing over the bread. "Blessed are You, Lord our God, King of the Universe, who brings forth the bread from the earth." The matzah, the unleavened bread, was then blessed and eaten.

Bitter herbs were then blessed and eaten with the matzah.

The feast of the meal itself then began, and the lamb that had been slaughtered and roasted was eaten. Every person ate until they were full, and the entire lamb was consumed by the family. The solemn start to the meal became festive at this point in time, and laughter and lively conversation accompanied the meal. The hour was getting late, and the children were getting sleepy as the next phase of the meal began.

Caleb found the afikomen, the piece of bread that was hidden in the napkin, and passed it around to his family members to be eaten.

Then Caleb offered grace after the meal, and at the conclusion of the Barech, the third cup of wine was blessed. This cup, the cup of redemption, was filled to overflowing and was then passed around and drank.

Hallel, the chanting of psalms to God, was a joyous time, and that joy was reflected on the faces of those who reclined around the table. When the four psalms were completed, the fourth and last cup of wine was filled, and a door was opened for Elijah to enter and announce the coming of the Messiah.

A final song was sung, and everyone said in unison, "Next year in Jerusalem!"

The Passover meal was completed, and Leah and Keturah, Rizpah's two daughters, quickly scooped up their sleeping children and put them to bed. The hour was late, almost midnight, and the dishes had yet to be washed and dried and the kitchen cleaned.

The men continued to recline around the table as the women set about cleaning the table, and soon everyone bade goodnight to each other and retired to their sleeping chambers. Rizpah and Caleb lingered in the dining area, straightening up and talking quietly. The light from the oil lamps cast a soft glow in the room, and the exquisite pottery crafted by Caleb reflected the dancing flames.

The town had been unusually quiet that evening; because of the First Seder, many people were celebrating, and those that weren't honored the feast. No shops were open, and people retired early to their homes in preparation for the Second Seder.

The hour was late, well past midnight, when Caleb and Rizpah finally settled down on the cushions and reflected on the day's celebration.

"It was so good to have the children here today, and our grandchildren, how they've grown since we last saw them!" exclaimed Rizpah.

"They'll be grown before we know it," solemnly replied Caleb.

"The sad part is that we won't live to see them as adults. At least, that's very unlikely." Rizpah's face became downcast at the thought. Caleb reached out and took her hand.

"Dear wife, life here is all too short, but we'll be in heaven with the Lord God Almighty when we leave this world."

Rizpah slowly raised her eyes to meet his. The amber tones of light from the oil lamps revealed the depth of his caring. How had she been so fortunate to find such a good man? Many of the women she knew were married to men that neither cared for them nor provided well for them. Caleb did both and did both exceedingly well. Many times as a young girl, she'd worried to no end about her future and whether she would have a good husband, but her parents had been wise in choosing Caleb, and she soon fell deeply in love with him. Their years together had their share of trouble and hardship, but overall, they were blessed far beyond measure.

"I know that, Caleb. It's just hard to understand why our lives here are so short. Before the Great Flood, people used to live hundreds of years before they aged. But now, fifty years old is very old for someone, and we're almost there. I truly feel very blessed to have you still living and taking care of me. Many men your age are infirmed or blind or lame. God has truly blessed us."

"Yes, he has. And today was a celebration of our freedom that God gave us those many years ago, and we're blessed to be able to celebrate our feasts even though we're still governed by Rome." Caleb dropped his gaze and stared at the walls, adorned with woven tapestries that warmed the cold, stark walls. "As long as we stay in line and don't rebel against our conquerors, we can celebrate our feasts as we have for hundreds of years."

"But when will we be able to celebrate them without anyone ruling us? When will the Romans be removed from our land, and how will that happen?"

Sighing heavily, Caleb rose to his feet and went over to a window, where he looked out at the sleeping city, the center of which was the temple. The stars in the heavens twinkled with unusual brilliance while the surrounding hillsides were black by comparison, but his gaze was quickly captured by a cluster of flickering lights. At first he thought they were also stars, but they were too low in the sky to be stars. After a moment, he realized that they were torches in the area of the Garden of Gethsemane. He drew his brows together, puzzled.

"Rizpah, come here," he softly stated. When she was by his side, he directed her gaze to the area in which he saw the flickering lights. "Do you see those torches over there?"

"Yes." Rizpah watched the lights as they seemingly danced among the trees in the garden.

Silently the two watched for several more minutes, and then Caleb said, "They must be from people staying there for the night. Why would anyone be in the Garden of Gethsemane at this hour of the night?"

Rizpah yawned and placed her hand over her mouth. "Well, all I know is I'm very tired, and I'm going to bed now. Everyone will probably sleep in a little late in the morning, at least, I hope they do." She shrugged her shoulders at Caleb as he continued to gaze at the flickering torches on the hillside.

"Well, I guess it's nothing to be concerned about," he quipped as he turned and followed his wife to their bed.

Lying on her bed in another room, Deborah had done anything but sleep after her head rested on the pillow, even though she was exhausted from the day's activities. All she could think about was Jesus and how she was going to find him. With tomorrow being the Second Seder, he still wouldn't be in the temple teaching, so she would have to wait until the next day.

Rolling over onto her side, she released a tired sigh as she attempted to make herself comfortable while still doing her best not to disturb Gedaliah. The more she reflected on those years long ago when Mary lived in Bethlehem, the more she remembered. Through the years, she'd almost forgotten about the visit of the wealthy foreigners to Bethlehem; they had worshipped Jesus and given him gifts, very expensive gifts. What where they? Oh, yes, gold, frankincense and myrrh. The glint of the gold coins and the smell of the fragrant herbs flooded her memory. Afterward, she and Mary had spent the day with their two small sons on the hillsides outside the town to enjoy the beautiful day, surely one of their last before winter set in, and they had visited Kezia, her dear mother, dead many years now.

Deborah tried to sort out the jumble of thoughts in her mind as she shifted her position again. Was it the very next day or a day later that Mary and Joseph disappeared with Jesus? She couldn't remember, and she tried to convince herself that it didn't really matter. All she wanted to do was find Jesus, who could tell her where his mother lived so she could see her and talk to her. The mere thought that she could possibly go to her grave not knowing why Mary left without saying goodbye filled her heart with deep sorrow. Even though she'd lived her entire adult life not knowing the reason, the possibility of finding an answer had become an unquenchable, passionate urge that she couldn't ignore.

Turning over yet another time, Deborah looked at her sleeping husband. Gedaliah had lost much of the hair on the top of his head, and what he had left was peppered, more gray than black. His beard had followed suit, and the hairs had become coarser with his advanced years. His eyebrows were bushy. Many of his teeth had fallen out, especially during the last few years, and so had many of hers, but she loved the man sleeping soundly beside her and didn't care that he had wrinkles and creases on his face or that his body wasn't as strong as it used to be.

She wondered if Mary's husband, Joseph, was still living. He'd been somewhat older than Mary, so Deborah doubted that he would still be alive. Of course, it was possible, but not probable. When a husband died, the widow had to depend on her male children to take care of her until her own death. Was that the case with Mary? Was Jesus, as the oldest male child, taking care of her, or did Mary have another son who was fulfilling the obligation? She had so many questions.

Cobwebs finally began to spin themselves in Deborah's mind and sleep overcame her as a small group of Roman soldiers entered the city with one lone prisoner in tow as their torches cast dancing shadows on the streets and walls.

Chapter Twenty-One

HOPE LOST

"Caleb! Wake up!"

Startled from a restful sleep, Caleb threw off his cover and sat up.

"Why? What's the matter?"

Rizpah was sitting up in bed, her eyes wide open and her ears straining to hear the strange sounds in the distance that had wakened her minutes before, and she couldn't go back to sleep because of them. Usually, she would have been up by now, but the festivities and all the work had drained her and caused her to sleep much later than usual.

"Don't you hear it?" she asked in a strained voice. "It sounds like a mob of people, doesn't it?"

Chasing the last vestiges of sleep from his brain, Caleb rose and went to the window. The sounds carried through the early morning mist, dissonant shouts that reverberated through the city. He listened for a few moments more and then turned to Rizpah as he started getting dressed.

"You're right. I only hope and pray that it isn't a bunch of fanatical Jews trying to revolt against the authorities. We don't need bloodshed at this time, at the Passover feast." He quickly tied his belt securely around his tunic.

Rizpah stepped out of bed and frantically dressed, fear gnawing at her insides, twisting her stomach into knots. A mob rising against the Romans would only mean certain death and destruction to anyone who participated, and the mere thought of such an event made her absolutely terrified. The Romans weren't particular about punishing only those who participated in an uprising but would, without hesitation or remorse, kill everyone they could, including women and children.

Quickly tying back her graying hair with a small cord, she tried to subdue the panic threatening to overtake her, but to no avail. Surely this could not be happening at Passover; there had to be another explanation for the angry sounds drifting on the early morning air.

Caleb left their sleeping chamber and almost bumped into Gedaliah, who'd just come into the common room. The expression on Caleb's face belied his attempt to remain calm.

"What's going on?" Gedaliah anxiously asked. "What's all the commotion about?"

Soon all of the adults were gathered in the common room as they anxiously listened to the distant shouts in the streets.

"I'm going to find out what's happening," Caleb firmly replied as he headed for the front door.

"I'll go with you," insisted Gedaliah as he stepped toward him.

"No, you'll stay here with the rest of the family. We have no idea what's happening, and until I find out, we must consider that all of us are in danger." He somberly continued instructing his family. "Gedaliah, Rufus, Lamech and Jabal, you are to stay here and defend this house if the need arises. If I'm not back in the hour, bolt all the doors and windows and protect yourselves if there is any threat." Caleb turned his gaze to Rizpah, who had tears pooling in her eyes.

"Don't worry, Rizpah, I'll be fine." He went to her and took her hands in his and gently kissed her on the cheek.

"God be with you!" she cried as he turned and unlatched the door.

The sound of the raging crowd was even louder and fiercer when Caleb opened the door. His heart was racing as he stepped across the threshold and pulled the door closed behind him. He heard it being latched and bolted securely on the other side. His legs trembled as he headed toward the sound of the crowd, weaving his way through the streets of Jerusalem. Many people were anxiously looking out their windows and doors or standing in their doorways, fearful of the unknown.

The mid-morning air was still cool and crisp, and it helped Caleb keep from overexerting himself as he quickly strode through the city. His stride was not as long as it used to be, nor was his walk as vigorous as in earlier days, and he felt his heart beating wildly in his chest, causing him to stop and catch his breath to slow its frantic pace. It would do absolutely no good for him to drop dead on the streets of Jerusalem.

Several other men from various houses joined him as he followed the shouts of the crowd, which grew louder with each step. Finally, rounding one last corner, he was almost caught up in the mob as it pressed its way through the street. Men, and even women, were angrily clenching their fists and beating them in the air. Caleb stretched to see what was at the center of this flowing, angry mass.

Finally, he saw the source of all of the anger. A group of Roman soldiers surrounded a badly beaten prisoner. The skin on his back was shredded, exposing his bones. Blood oozed from the multiple slashes, and Caleb was repulsed at the sight. He was surprised that the man could still walk in that condition. Clasping his hand over his mouth, he wondered what deed this obvious criminal had committed to be dealt such a harsh sentence. This man must have committed murder or rape to be sentenced to death, for that was surely to be the outcome.

The man with the shredded, bleeding back was carrying a cross, the instrument of death utilized by the Romans. Only the Romans could ever conceive of such a horrible way to kill someone. Caleb viewed it as totally inhumane. Death by stoning, which had been used for centuries by the Jews, seemed a much more humane way to execute someone, but this man would be crucified and would hang for hours before death took him, and he would certainly welcome death when it came.

Death by crucifixion was the cruelest punishment imaginable, for it meant hours of hanging on a cross, naked and bleeding, thirsty and dehydrated, until the body could endure no more and succumbed. But why was this man being crucified during the Passover celebration? Couldn't they have waited a day or two to carry out their gruesome sentence?

The crowd was apparently excited about the impending crucifixion. It was thirsty for blood.

Behind the bloodied man, sneering soldiers prodded him on his way. Every time the prisoner fell beneath the weight of the heavy wooden cross he dragged, he was dealt another blow across the back with a whip, which opened a fresh wound, if that were even possible, and drew more blood. Looking with horror on the man, Caleb couldn't understand why he wasn't already dead from the monstrous lashing that he'd already received. It didn't seem possible that he was still alive.

Following a short distance behind the man were two more criminals carrying crosses, but it was clear that they hadn't been whipped and beaten. They would suffer longer on the crosses, Caleb knew, because it would take them longer to die. He turned his head to shut out the gruesome scene before him as he turned to retrace his steps home, but found himself caught up in the crowd as more people came to see what was happening. He was no longer at the back of the shouting mob, but was now in the center of the burgeoning mass of angry people, which grew continuously.

Hemmed in on all sides, Caleb had no choice but to allow himself to be pulled along with the crowd. Soon they were outside the city walls and heading to a place known as Golgatha, the Place of the Skull. This was the most prominent site for Roman crucifixions, as it could be seen from almost anywhere as it was set on a hillside. Straining to see the men who carried crosses, Caleb was finally able to catch a glimpse. To his surprise, the badly beaten man was no longer carrying his cross, but someone else who was obviously not a prisoner was carrying it for him.

The pressing, angry mass surged forward and surrounded the prisoners as they left the narrow streets of the city and headed toward Golgatha, and Caleb was able to move about freely again. It was then that he noticed that not everyone in the crowd was screaming for this man's blood; there were a few people who were crying unashamedly. Slowly approaching one such woman, he quietly stood before her and looked at her until she noticed him.

"Who is it they are crucifying today?" Caleb asked as kindly as he could.

A fresh river of tears streamed down the woman's face, and the young man standing next to her firmly placed his arm around her. Answering Caleb's question, he choked, "Jesus of Nazareth."

Caleb felt as if he had been hit with a sledge hammer as he gasped in complete shock.

"No! It can't be!" Staring at the ground as he shook his head, he was glued to the ground, unable to move or even think as his blood pounded in his heart as he tried to wrap his mind around the information. There had to be some mistake! He stood for several moments, his mind a tornado of confused thoughts.

Frantically looking up again, the woman and the man were no longer before him, and he was being passed by as people pressed toward the site of the crucifixion. Caleb, in an effort to confirm the horrible news, joined the crowd that was pressing forward, hungry for death, thirsty for spilled blood, driven by the strength of its numbers.

Suddenly the mob slowed its forward movement, and Caleb heard guards ordering the crowd to stop, which only caused many people to scream louder for blood, but as they watched, their cries subsided when they realized that their wish would be granted momentarily.

And then he heard it. The unmistakable, sickening sound of a hammer driving a nail into the flesh of the condemned man, which was instantaneously followed by a painful, unpalatable cry which made Caleb's heart stop as it reached his ears. Soon, the first blow was followed by another and another and another, and even the noise of the cheering crowd couldn't mask the ghastly, gruesome sounds. Caleb winced every time the hammer met the nail. He felt sick and faint as he lowered himself onto a rock, cold sweat breaking out on his forehead. His mind swirled with confusion as he listened to the heartbeat of the mad mob as it exulted over the gruesome work of the soldiers.

More shouts from the Roman guards moved the crowd further back, compressing the people more compactly. Caleb felt as if he was participating in the atrocities being committed by simply being there and doing nothing to stop it. But what could he possibly do?

As the crowd was forced back by the guards, Caleb saw the crosses of the three condemned men being raised. As the cross which suspended Jesus above the mob was dropped into a hole and secured, the crowd cheered and laughed, scorning him and denigrating him even as his body writhed in excruciating pain, every breath a monumental effort.

As time passed, the crowd slowly began to thin out, and Caleb was able to work his way closer to the guards. He'd seen Jesus before and would know for sure if this was the same man, for he had to see it with his own eyes to believe that it really was Jesus being crucified. Slowly he approached the perimeter of the guards' circle, and fearfully, tearfully, he raised his eyes to look at the face of the man suspended above him.

His heart lurched and he clutched his chest. It *was* Jesus! His face was covered with blood, and a crown of thorns had been pressed into his skull. A soldier was hanging a sign at the top of the cross which said, "Jesus of Nazareth, King of the Jews." Upon seeing the sign, those in the crowd who could read laughed and pointed accusing fingers at Jesus. One man came close to where Caleb was standing and challenged Jesus, "If you are the Son of God, come down from the cross!"

Caleb turned and stared at the man, who simply laughed and walked away. Suddenly, Caleb felt sickened and faint, and he was desperate to get as far away from Golgatha as he could. His body flashed hot as he turned and pushed his way through the crowd and toward the city. Gasping for breath, he hurried down the hill, frantic to put as much space between him and Golgatha as he could. It seemed as if the world had suddenly gone mad!

Turning briefly, he gazed back with eyes brimmed with moisture to the scene he'd left behind.

The three dark crosses stood out starkly against the blue sky of mid morning. Caleb leaned against the city wall and cried unashamedly. No one noticed; they were too caught up in the drama being played out at Golgatha.

Caleb's tears grew in intensity when he realized that he had to go back and tell his family the horrible news. And Deborah! How was she going to receive such news? Fresh tears tracked down his face and into his curly beard as he tilted his head back and cried out in grief to God.

Back at the house, Caleb's family patiently waited for him to return. Rizpah set about preparing a light morning meal with the help of Helah, and soon the children were up and playing, which alleviated some of the tension and uncertainty that permeated the house.

Occasionally, Rizpah went to the window and looked out, wondering what was taking Caleb so long. He'd said he would be back within the hour, and surely it had been longer than that by now. Deeply concerned, she tried to busy herself with work in the kitchen to bide away the time until Caleb returned.

Suddenly there was a loud knock on the door, and Gedaliah, who had been standing close to it all morning, was instantly behind it.

"It's me! Caleb! Unbolt the door!"

Gedaliah quickly unbolted the door, and Caleb slowly entered his house and bolted the door behind him, sick with the knowledge that he possessed. Leaning heavily into the closed door, he fought to gain control of his emotions.

When he turned and faced his family, he saw the questions in everyone's eyes as they gathered around him. The silence that enveloped the room was suffocating, for it was clear to everyone that Caleb didn't bring good news.

Caleb sucked in his breath as he stood by the door. Rizpah came to him, put her hand on his arm, and asked haltingly, "What is it, Caleb? What's happening?"

Caleb shrunk at her touch, feeling as if his life was being drained from him. Avoiding Rizpah's eyes, he cast a quick glance at Deborah and then sat down on a bench near the wall, and everyone gathered around him, anxiety and concern etched in their faces.

"Caleb," gently urged Rizpah, "please tell us what you know. Please."

Caleb sighed heavily and wiped his age-spotted hand across his perspiring brow. Tears filled his eyes and fell unheeded to his beard. Every time he opened his mouth to begin, the words caught in his throat and lumped there. He couldn't speak.

"Helah, get a glass of water, quickly!" ordered Rizpah. Caleb drank deeply of the glass handed to him, quenching his thirst and wetting his lips and throat. He wiped the tears from his face with the back of his hand, and then pulled himself together as best he could.

"There is a crucifixion today," he simply stated, finally finding his voice even as more tears threatened to spill over.

"Today?!" exclaimed Jabal. "This is the Passover! Why are they crucifying someone today? Couldn't it have waited?"

"But why are you so upset?" inquisitively asked Rizpah. "There've been many such crucifixions by the Romans. Why has this one upset you so?"

Lowering his gaze to the floor and furrowing his eyebrows together, Caleb softly replied, "It's who they are crucifying that's upset me so."

Rizpah glanced up at her family as she placed her arm around her husband. Gently prodding Caleb,

Rizpah encouraged him to continue. "Who's being crucified, Caleb? Please, you must tell us."

Caleb's heart was heavier than he could ever remember it being as his eyes found Deborah's and locked into hers. Deborah's heart skipped a beat as a feeling of doom settled on her.

Choking back his sobs, Caleb tearfully whispered, "Jesus of Nazareth."

Deborah's hands went to her face and a gasp of disbelief escaped her lips. "No!" she cried out. "No! I don't believe it!"

Gedaliah went quickly to her side and tried to console her. He looked at Caleb, and his eyes begged him to explain his answer further.

Tears poured down Caleb's stricken face. "I'm so sorry, Deborah, but it's true. I saw it with my own eyes. When I reached the mob, I got caught up in it and was carried outside the city to the Place of the Skull. There I heard that it was Jesus who was being crucified, and then I saw him with my own eyes. It's true!" He cried unashamedly.

Deborah gasped and collapsed into Gedaliah's arms, and she had to be carried to a cushion where the women ministered to her by giving her a sip of wine. She started sobbing uncontrollably, and even Gedaliah couldn't assuage her tears. Caleb felt as if he had brought Deborah's world to an end and said so to Rizpah.

"It wasn't you who brought it to an end, but those that cried for Jesus to be crucified," she assured him. "You had nothing to do with it."

Gedaliah embraced his weeping wife and cried along with her as he held her, and she found a degree of comfort in the strength of his arms. Through her pain, her body wracked with sobs, she cried into his shoulder, "I'll never find Mary now, Gedaliah. I'll never find her! I'll never have the answers I so desperately seek."

"Shhh, Deborah, everything will be all right. There's nothing we can do, Deborah, but I know everything will be all right."

Jerking her head back from his shoulder, she resolutely stated through her tears, "But there is something I can do, Gedaliah. I can go to the crucifixion and see Jesus. I can pay my respects to him even though I never got a chance to talk to him."

"No, Deborah, I don't think that's a good idea," opposed Gedaliah.

Deborah pushed herself to her feet and wiped away the tears that cascaded down her deeply wrinkled face. "I'm going, and there's nothing you can do to stop me. I've not seen Jesus since he was a small child, and I want to see him one last time."

"But why?"

"Just because I need to, that's why!" Deborah resolutely pushed her way through the family members and headed for the door with Gedaliah at her heels. "I'm coming with you," he stated as the others watched them pass through the opening.

Caleb stretched out his arm as if to stop them, but Rizpah grasped it and pulled it down. "Deborah needs to go, Caleb. We mustn't stop her."

Her heart in her throat, Deborah placed one foot in front of the other as she walked along the streets of the city with Gedaliah by her side. Everything seemed surreal. Her feet were touching the ground, yet she felt as if she wasn't in her body. Fear gripped her insides and twisted them into a knot that threatened to squeeze the life out of her, yet she kept breathing. Every so often she heard a groan escape her lips. Sobs from deep within her welled up to the surface of her soul and spilled over into the tears that constantly moistened her cheeks. With every step, she thought about all the questions that would never be answered. There would be no opportunity to put to rest the desertion of years ago in Bethlehem.

Her feet were like iron weights as she struggled to set one in front of the other. Each step brought her closer to accepting the inevitable, but she still plodded along.

Gedaliah's heart was torn in two for his wife. He kept fighting the lump in his chest, the gnawing inside that sapped his strength. He feared for Deborah when they finally reached the cross, feared how she would react when she saw Jesus on the cross.
Swiping away a tear that escaped his brimmed eyes, he firmly clasped Deborah's hand in his as they walked.

Leaving the city by way of one of its gates, they were able to see the gruesome sight on the hillside from a distance. They paused at the sight of the crosses against the pale blue sky, and Deborah choked back a sob and wiped away fresh tears as she sighed, gathered her courage, and pressed on.

Approaching the crowd, they weaved their way in and out of people sitting on the rocky ground and standing around and made their way close to the restricted area. The guards were unaffected by the sight of the crucified men, and Deborah realized that their hearts must be made of stone to be able to carry out such a gruesome assignment without a hint of remorse or pity. Some of the soldiers were tossing coins over one crucified man's clothing, laughing as they did so, oblivious to the pain they were inflicting on those suspended and impaled just yards from them. *Is there no sanctity of life in the Roman world?* Deborah thought. *Are lives so easily and carelessly disposed of that soldiers can toss coins while their prisoners writhe in agony right next to them?* She shook her head in horror that such was the case.

Deborah gazed up at the three crosses. They were close enough now to plainly see the faces of the condemned men. She had resigned herself to the fact that what Caleb had said was true and that the man she was now looking at was indeed Jesus of Nazareth, son of her friend Mary. The man hanging before her, naked and bleeding, appeared to be the right age for such, and her heart skipped a beat when she realized that Jesse would have been that age had he lived. The other two men were much younger, just lads, really, and were on either side of Jesus.

"This is close enough," she whispered through clenched teeth as she grabbed Gedaliah's robe. She sat down on a rock and pulled her knees to her chest and laid her head on her knees, disappointed, shocked, and dejected.

Several groups of people stood around the crosses, as close as they were allowed. Oddly enough, none of them paid any heed to the two other men crucified with Jesus, but often someone would approach the cross on which Jesus hung and hurl challenges and insults his way. Every time this happened, Deborah felt righteous indignation rise up in her, and if she had been a man, she would have slapped the men in their faces.

Occasionally, she looked at Gedaliah, and she could see the muscles in his face throb with anger at the ribald accusers. When some of the religious rulers stood up and derided Jesus as he suffered and bled, Deborah rose to her feet in protest, but Gedaliah restrained her, saying that it would only cause trouble and wouldn't help Jesus. She cast him an angry glance and reluctantly resumed her hunched position.

The sun climbed higher in the sky, and still the men on the crosses clung to life. The crowd dissipated as the day passed, apparently losing interest, but Deborah refused to leave her spot on the hard rock.

Several times Gedaliah implored her to return to Caleb's house with him.

"No," she vehemently shook her head. "I'll stay here until he dies. That's the least I can do. I saw him come into this world, and I'll see him leave it. I will *not* leave him alone with these hateful men who falsely accuse him." Her throat was parched and cracked with the intensity of her emotions.

Gedaliah patiently waited with his wife, his thoughts confused. It was obvious that Jesus was *not* the promised Messiah. They had been sadly mistaken. Gedaliah sucked in his breath in grief.

And so they waited. As the day approached the sixth hour, the sky became inexplicably dark with clouds that rolled across the land. Deborah pulled her robe close around her as the temperature dropped with the incoming clouds. Rain threatened.

The day headed toward mid afternoon, and still the three men on the crosses had not died. Deborah watched as Jesus heaved in agony with each breath, pushing himself up by his impaled feet so his lungs could expand. His hands and arms turned white from the loss of blood even as his blood continued to drip onto the dry ground, creating a pool that congealed quickly on the dry soil, creating a dark gelatinous puddle. Deborah saw Jesus speak with great difficulty to a soldier, and the soldier raised a sponge soaked in a liquid to his lips, but upon tasting it, Jesus turned his head away and refused it. The crowd that had been so angry was now quiet and much smaller, but it seemed to Deborah that there was a group that refused to leave until they saw Jesus breathe his last breath.

As the afternoon progressed, the darkness that covered the land deepened. The crucifixion scene became oddly quiet. The strange darkness drove many people back to the city in fear, for it was the middle of the day and the sky was almost as black as night.

Deborah felt a strange sense of anticipation which she couldn't explain. Gedaliah felt it, too. As the crowd thinned, Deborah noticed a small group of people approach the crosses. The darkness prevented her from seeing anything clearly, but she whispered to Gedaliah, "Those people over there must be friends of Jesus, for it seems to me that they are weeping, not railing him." The sadness in her voice reflected the darkness in the skies.

Suddenly, Jesus pushed himself up with all his remaining strength, and with a loud voice shouted, "Eloi, Eloi, lama sabachthani?"

His cry pierced the heavy air as a sword cuts through cloth. Deborah and Gedaliah, as well as those still remaining, jerked their heads at the sound of his voice, amazed that he had the strength in him to call out so loudly. Many thought that Jesus had just called upon Elijah, but Gedaliah said that it sounded like Jesus had just spoken in Aramaic, but he was uncertain of the meaning.

Jesus slumped, weak and near death. All again was quiet. The waiting continued, and the strange darkness over the land intensified. Deborah slowly rose to her feet, her aching body refusing to cooperate. Her joints were stiff and sore from sitting for so long. Gedaliah slowly rose also, hoping she'd want to return to the house soon. They couldn't possibly stay there for the rest of the day.

Once she gained her footing, Deborah slowly made her way closer to the crosses, with Gedaliah reluctantly behind her. Gazing at the bleeding, suffering men, she felt a fresh wave of grief wash over her. Silently standing, she wondered how much longer Jesus could possibly survive.

Suddenly, Jesus raised his battered, bloodied head, looked heavenward, and exclaimed, "It is finished." His body went limp. Deborah clutched her stomach.

It was over, at last it was over.

Without warning, the earth beneath them shook violently, and Deborah and Gedaliah were thrown to the ground, terrified. People screamed and ran. Rocks on the hillside slid and tumbled down, causing a great deal of panic as they bounced toward the city walls. People fled in spite of the shaking, desperate to seek shelter from the ominous, unexplained darkness and the quaking ground. When the shaking stopped, most people still on the hill raced toward the city, all interest in watching the crucifixion vaporized.

Deborah was shaking all over; her heart was racing, but she stood and continued to gaze upon the surreal scene before her.

The other two men crucified with Jesus were still alive, so a soldier came along and broke their legs. Seeing that Jesus was already dead, a soldier took a spear and thrust it into his side, and Deborah and Gedaliah saw body fluids pour out. Deborah groaned and turned her head in revulsion of unnecessary mutilation to his body.

"Why don't we go home now," cautiously suggested Gedaliah. "Jesus is dead. There's nothing we can do."

Deborah stood quietly. Stubbornly, she replied, "I don't want to leave just yet."

Gedaliah sighed deeply. He would wait, however long that it took Deborah to be ready to return home.

Slowly, the clouds disbursed and the sun shone on the few people still remaining at Golgotha. Deborah settled her weary bones on the rock again.

Within the hour of having their legs broken, the other two criminals also died. The soldiers then began removing the bodies from the crosses, and the piercing sound of mournful wailing reached Deborah's ears. The women who had stood off to one side and cried during the crucifixion were begging the soldiers to allow them to approach Jesus's body. Deborah watched as a well-dressed man handed the head centurion a piece of parchment. The soldier then granted the women and men access to the body.

Deborah stood again and slowly came nigh to the cross. As she watched, the body of Jesus was lowered to the ground, and one of the women embraced it. Her cries were obviously that of one close, very close, to Jesus. Curious, Deborah cautiously stepped forward. No one held her back.

The woman holding the lifeless, battered body of Jesus wept uncontrollably. Heedless to the blood that was soaking into her tunic and robe, she lovingly touched and kissed the face that bore the marks of countless wounds. She stroked the strong arms that had been impaled by nails. *Could this possibly be the wife of Jesus?* Deborah wondered. She hadn't heard that he was married, but that didn't mean that he wasn't.

As she came closer, Deborah noticed that the woman's hands weren't young hands, but old ones, hands that looked a lot like her own. Her heart jumped and she clutched her chest! This could be Mary! It had to be! Eyes wide with astonishment, Deborah quickly turned to Gedaliah, her breath coming in quick gasps.

"Gedaliah! That has to be Mary!" she exclaimed excitedly. "That must be Mary, his mother!" She turned her eyes back to the woman on the ground, who was still weeping and caressing Jesus.

Deborah shed new tears as she watched the woman she now believed to be Mary mourn the loss of her son. The other women and men with Mary allowed her this time alone with him as they stood and knelt around the body, weeping profusely. Mary finally reluctantly released the body to a few of the men, who wrapped Jesus in a large cloth and carried him away. The women in the group then surrounded Mary and tried to comfort her.

Deborah continued to observe as a young man from the group approached Mary and assisted her to her feet. She rested in his arms for several moments, and when he said something softly to her, she nodded her head, leaned on his arm, and started walking. At that moment, Deborah *knew* that it was Mary. Yes, she was older, but Deborah was certain it was Mary. She just had to see her! She just had to talk to her!

She tried to say something to Gedaliah, but the words got stuck in her throat. The group of mourning men and women were moving now, heading down the hillside to return to Jerusalem. Quickly gathering her emotions, Deborah stepped toward them and intercepted their path. Her eyes stinging with tears, she reached out an arm to stop Mary's progress.

The group of people stopped abruptly and looked at Deborah, obviously upset that she would intrude upon them so rudely in their private time of grief. Mary lifted her head and looked at the woman standing before them, perplexed at her actions. She stopped walking and put out her arms to stop her friends. Tilting her head, she wiped the streaks of tears from her face and gasped as she recognized Deborah.

Reaching out a hand covered with blood from her slain son, Mary whispered through her tears, "Deborah, is it really you?"

Deborah's eyes brimmed with moisture as she nodded her head. Words were lost in her throat as the tears spilled over.

Simultaneously, the two women, friends from long ago, fell into each other's arms and let their tears flow anew. Deborah clung to Mary, and she felt her body shaking with both grief and unexpected joy.

After several moments, Deborah and Mary looked at each other as they clasped each others' arms. Her voice choking with emotion, Deborah whispered through her sobs, "I'm so very sorry, Mary, so very sorry about your son's death."

Mary, her eyes red from weeping, closed her eyes briefly and took a deep breath in an effort to gain control of her tumultuous emotions. It was obvious to Mary that Deborah had been on the hillside most, if not all, of the day. Mary was simply overjoyed that she was here.

Resolutely setting her face toward Jerusalem, she said to Deborah, "Come, dear, old friend. We have much to talk about." Putting her arm around Deborah's waist, they turned and headed back to Jerusalem side by side.

Deborah abruptly turned and searched for Gedaliah, saying to Mary, "My husband, Gedaliah, is with me." Mary turned and followed her gaze.

Gedaliah smiled broadly at Mary, and she momentarily left Deborah's side and approached him.

Placing both bloodstained hands alongside his face, she joyously stated, "Gedaliah, I'm so very happy that we meet again after so many years." He gently took her in his arms and held her close.

Releasing Mary, he said to Deborah, "I'll go and tell our family that you've found Mary; they will be overjoyed for you."

Mary nodded to the young man who'd been by her side. "John will see that Deborah is returned to your home safely after we've had time to visit. Is that all right with you, Gedaliah?" He assured her it was.

Mary continued. "At sundown, the Feast of Unleavened Bread begins. Would you like to stay and celebrate with us, Deborah?"

298

Deborah nodded her agreement after she questioningly looked at Gedaliah for confirmation.

"Good. Then it's settled. Come, Deborah, we have so much to tell each other. It's been many, many years." Once again, the two women intertwined their arms and wearily plodded down the hill to Jerusalem, the others with Mary following closely behind.

Tears of joy stinging his eyes, Gedaliah watched them go, relieved and grateful that some good had come of this horrible, tragic day. He turned and hurried back to Caleb's house, eager to relay the news that Mary had been found.

Chapter Twenty-Two

TRUTH REVEALED

Deborah and Mary walked slowly through the streets of Jerusalem. They didn't speak to each other but simply marveled at being together again after a lifetime apart. Deborah felt Mary's pain as if it were her own. She remembered how long it had taken her to worship God again after Jesse's death, to attend services at the synagogue, and to truly celebrate with her heart the Jewish festivals. Her anger raged for many years. Would it be that way with Mary, too?

Recalling what Mary had told her about Jesus when he was born only caused a ball of anguish and fear to form in her stomach; surely Mary would see the truth today, see that she had been disillusioned. Until now, Deborah had believed with all her heart that Jesus had been the promised Messiah, but now he was dead, being laid that very moment in a tomb owned by someone named Joseph of Arimathea. Surely Mary would see that Jesus had been no more than a prophet. Her own disappointment at the realization was acute.

The group of people that had been on the hill with her at the crucifixion followed the two women. A few women in the group were still wailing and crying loudly, but Mary held her tears in check and walked with a dignified, although weary and worn, posture.

The man named John stepped in front of them and opened the door to the house when they arrived. Mary motioned for Deborah to enter first, and soon the entire group of people was in the house. The heavy, subdued atmosphere was punctuated by Mary's soft and steady voice. "Hazael, please bring us something to drink. I wish to speak with Deborah alone, and we wish not to be disturbed. We have a lot to discuss after all these years."

Hazael nodded her head and went to do Mary's bidding. Mary motioned with a sweep of her arm for Deborah to walk down a short hallway and into a small room. It contained a bed, two benches, and two small tables, one which held a basin and jug of water. Hazael soon entered the room with the drinks and a small lighted oil lamp.

"Thank you, Hazael. Please tell the others to prepare for the Feast of Unleavened Bread. We'll partake with you when it's ready." Hazael nodded and retreated from the room.

Mary quietly poured water from the jug on the table into the basin, pulled up her tunic sleeves, and dipped her blood-stained hands into the water, which immediately turned crimson. Silent tears splashed down Mary's face into the basin as she rubbed her hands and rinsed her son's blood from them. When she was finished, she dried them on a towel hung on a peg in the wall as spasms of grief shook her body.

After a few moments, she took a deep breath, wiped the tears from her face, and turned to face Deborah, who immediately realized that the years had been rather kind to Mary; Deborah still thought she was lovely and gracious, even though she had aged just as she had.

"I can't believe that you still want to celebrate the Feast of Unleavened Bread, Mary, after what happened today." The knot in Deborah's stomach refused to untie. "After all you've suffered, how can you still worship God?"

Mary gazed at the floor and then back at Deborah. "I choose to worship God for who he is, Deborah. He never promised me that I wouldn't see sorrow." She walked to the small window and looked out at the setting sun. "Many years ago, when I took Jesus to the temple when he was a baby, I was told that a sword would pierce my heart."

Deborah struggled with her tumultuous emotions. She was confused, utterly confused. "You must be in shock, Mary. You haven't come to terms with your son's death. I understand completely."

Tears gathered in Deborah's eyes as Mary turned from the window and sat down on one of the two small benches in the room. She motioned for Deborah to sit across from her; the table, on which rested the lighted lamp, was between them.

Mary reached across the small table and clasped Deborah's hands. Deborah thought that she should be comforting Mary, not the other way around. Astonished, Deborah looked at her, confused and perplexed.

Mary saw the questions in Deborah's eyes and asked, "What's wrong, Deborah?"

Deborah shook her head, trying to find the words to express what she was seeing and feeling. "Your son was killed today, yet here you are, talking to me as if nothing has happened. I don't understand, Mary."

Mary gently patted Deborah's hands, and as she did so, she laughed softly. "Look at us, Deborah, two old ladies now. Our fingers are gnarled, our hair is gray, our faces creased with wrinkles, and our eyesight dimmed. Time has taken its toll, hasn't it?"

Deborah nodded as she attentively watched Mary.

"This day has been extremely difficult for me, Deborah, as you can well imagine. You apparently witnessed most of it, but I'd rather hear about your family than talk about today's pain. Do you live in Jerusalem now, or do you still live in Bethlehem?"

Deborah gazed into the eyes of her friend, troubled at the turn of conversation, but she cautiously answered Mary's inquiry.

"We're here visiting Helah's brother – you remember Helah, don't you?" In response to Mary's nod, she continued. "We came for the feasts and will return to Bethlehem at the end of the week. We still operate the inn in Bethlehem, but our son, Joshua, and his wife, Damaris, now help us run it. Now that we're older, we need the help; it's too much to operate it on our own anymore."

"I'm so glad to hear that you still operate the inn," smiled Mary. "I have so many questions concerning your family. Let me start with your mother and father and work my way down to your children; I'm sure you have more than one now."

Deborah's heart lurched. She forced a smile at Mary as her palms began to sweat.

"Your mother's name was Kezia and . . . I don't remember your father's name. ."

"Thaddeus."

"Yes, Thaddeus; I suppose they're gone home to be with the Lord?"

Deborah's stomach turned upside-down as fear rushed through her veins. The line of questioning would ultimately lead to Jesse. She stuffed the fear away and tried to focus on Mary. "Yes. Father was injured by a lion while watching the sheep one day, and he was never the same after that. He wasn't able to do much of the work that he'd done all his life, and it frustrated him continually. Mother took care of him, but his wounds were more than even she could mend completely, and he died several months later." Deborah's voice dropped as she remembered that day, but it in no way compared to losing Jesse. Her father had lived a full life – Jesse hadn't. Pushing thoughts of Jesse aside, she lifted her voice and said, "Mother lived another nine years, and she died peacefully in her sleep. That was about 12 years ago, I believe."

"You had a younger brother, didn't you?"

"Yes, Simon."

"What's become of him?"

Deborah's countenance changed, and her eyes became dark and sad. "Simon left home when he was 17 years old and joined the Zealots so he could fight the Romans. Mother and Father tried their best to keep him from going, but they couldn't stop him. Do you remember when the Roman soldiers murdered Gebia?" *And they murdered Jesse, too!* Deborah wanted to shout, but she held her tongue as her heart raced. Did Mary even know of the slaughter of the babies in Bethlehem? Pulling her mind away from the past, she listened to Mary's response.

Mary nodded. "I remember the incident, but I didn't remember the name."

"Well, Father and Mother were terrified that the Romans would discover that Simon had joined the Zealots and would kill one of our family, so they argued with him for weeks when he first mentioned what he wanted to do. But he went anyway, and thankfully, no one else but our family knew where he'd gone and what he was doing. We kept it a secret from everyone." She looked down at her gnarled hands, spattered with age spots and calluses; when had she gotten so old? "We never heard from him after that. We don't know if he's alive or dead." A lump gathered in her throat and caught there, causing her to swallow hard in an effort to eliminate it.

Mary whispered, "Life isn't always what we want it to be, is it, Deborah?"

Deborah shook her head, trying to dislodge the jumbled cobwebs of the past. "I often lay awake at night wondering what became of him." She bit her tongue to keep from telling Mary that Simon had joined the Zealots to take revenge on little Jesse's death. She cast her gaze to the floor as she fought the demons of long ago.

"Do you believe in miracles?" gently asked Mary as she interrupted Deborah's thoughts.

Deborah raised her eyes and gazed into Mary's face which was bathed in the soft amber light. "Yes, of course."

"I believe it's a miracle that you found me today, don't you?"

"Yes."

"Then have faith, Deborah, that God can bring another miracle to you someday where Simon is concerned." She patted Deborah's hands affectionately. "Now, what about your other brother? I believe he was older."

Deborah gulped and took a deep breath. *Why doesn't she ask about Jesse? Maybe she does know!* Stumbling over her words, she responded. "Oh, yes, Eleazar. Father and Mother were resigned to the fact that Eleazar would also join the Zealots, but to their surprise, he didn't. In fact, about a year and a half after Rufus and Helah were married, Eleazar took a wife. Her name is Miriam, and oddly enough, they're the ones who operate the farm and tend the sheep now. They have so many children that I've lost count! Gedaliah and I spend quite a bit of time with them on the hillside." She forced a smile as she pulled her hands away and slid them onto her lap, where they balled up into fists under the tiny table.

"I remember your parents' house with a great deal of fondness," reminisced Mary as her eyes glazed over. The light from the lamp revealed deep pools of wonder as Mary's mind slipped into the past. "Your parents adored each other so much, and they always made me feel welcome in their home."

"Yes, they loved each other very much."

"And your uncle and his son . . . "

"Reuben and Benaiah. Reuben died about two years before Mother, and Benaiah took a wife and moved to a house on the other side of Bethlehem. We see him quite often, as well as all five of his children," she replied, agitated that Mary was taking so long in asking about Jesse. Her agitation festered and turned into anger. She bit her lip to control her tongue.

Deborah quickly stood up and walked to the small window in the room and looked out at the street, which was now practically deserted. She wrung her hands together as she fought to control her tumultuous emotions, the battle to blurt out the questions that haunted her.

Mary, sensing that something was wrong, looked at
Deborah's back, puzzled.

Suddenly Deborah turned around and released all of her suppressed anger, her eyes blazing balls of fire.

"Mary, for years and years I've kept inside all the hurt that you caused when you left me without saying goodbye!" Her voice caught and crackled, and she had to cough to clear it before taking a drink from the goblet on the table. Mary cocked her head and watched her, puzzled at the turn in the conversation. She held her tongue and let Deborah continue, keenly aware that she was greatly disturbed.

"Do you remember taking our babies out on the hillside and making plans for our futures?" Deborah's eyes burned with tears and her belly burned with anger.

Mary nodded. "Yes, of course. How could I forget?"

"We did that on a beautiful day, just when the weather was turning colder, and the very next day, you were gone. I've never understood why you left

306

without even telling me you were leaving or without saying goodbye!" Deborah tried to hold back the tears that pooled in her eyes, but to no avail. "Why, Mary, why did you leave without saying anything? And why didn't you ever come back?" Tears streaked down her face even though she fought to contain them.

Mary's eyes probed Deborah's, which were ablaze with anger and dark with pain, as she stood in the amber light.

Mary lowered her gaze as she stared at the table. Deborah's heavy breathing was the only sound in the room. "Do you remember what I told you about Jesus?" She flashed her eyes at Deborah.

"I remember that you told me things that I believed then, but now I don't think they're true."

Mary's heart lurched inside her chest. "Do you remember that I told you I was still a virgin when I gave birth to him?"

"Yes."

"And do you recall that I told you that I was visited by an angel who told me that what was conceived in me was of the Holy Spirit?"

"Yes, I remember all that."

"You believed it then. What makes you doubt it now?"

Deborah's heart was racing, and she felt as if it would pound itself out of her chest. She was too old for this kind of stressful conversation, too old to demand answers to questions that should remain unanswered. Why had she found Mary? She'd been warned by her family that to do so would only make her relive the nightmare of Jesse's death. Why hadn't she listened to the warnings?

Wringing her hands, she staunchly replied, "Because your son Jesus died today. If he was the Son of God, he would not, could not, have died. Man cannot kill God, but man can kill man. Since Jesus died today, there is no way he could have been the Son of God as you say he was." Her voice faded away as she finished her sentence. She clenched her jaw and turned once more to stare out the window.

Mary's voice didn't waiver as she replied, "There's much you don't know about the night we left, Deborah. We had no choice but to leave."

Swiftly turning around to face Mary, Deborah blurted out in anger, "Why, Mary, why?!"

Mary offered a prayer to God for the right words to speak. Many nights she'd tossed and turned on her bed, worried about Deborah, wondering how she was dealing with her sudden and unannounced departure as her own heart ached and bled anew for the loss of such a beautiful, tender friendship.

Steadying her voice, Mary chose her words carefully and slowly. "Because an angel of the Lord spoke to Joseph in a dream and told us to leave immediately and go to Egypt."

"Oh, another angelic visit! But *why* did you have to leave?" insisted Deborah as she returned to her bench and stared into Mary's face. "I need to know why you had to leave. Did the angel give you a reason?"

Ever so slowly, Mary hesitantly replied, "The angel told us that Herod would try to destroy Jesus."

"Destroy him?"

Mary slowly nodded.

Deborah's face turned ashen in the soft light, and her mouth dropped open in shocked realization. Her gaze flitted around the room. Her breath came in quick gasps, and her eyes blinked rapidly as she tried to hold back the flood of tears that gathered there. Sudden spasms of ice cold reality gripped every fiber of her being. She felt as if she was going to die at any moment, and then she froze, unable to say or do anything but stare straight ahead.

Mary watched her, troubled and confused at her strange reaction. She cautiously reached out a hand to touch Deborah's arm, but when she did, Deborah pulled it back as if she'd been bitten by a snake, causing Mary to jump in surprise.

Deborah bolted to her feet, sending the bench toppling to the floor, and stared at Mary. Still gasping for breath, she heaved out her words in one agonizing breath at a time. "Do... you ... remember ... my ... son, Jesse?"

Confused and troubled, Mary nodded slowly. "Of course I remember sweet Jesse! How could I forget him? I was going to ask about him last so you could tell me all about him."

"He's dead, Mary! He should have grown into a man and given me grandchildren, but he was murdered by Roman soldiers who drove a spear through his tiny heart the same day you left!" Deborah's voice didn't sound like her own. Her body heaved with agonizing sobs as she continued. "All these years, no one ever knew why the soldiers came to Bethlehem and killed all the male children two years of age and under! But now I know! Now I understand everything! They were looking for Jesus! Herod wanted to be certain Jesus was killed after the wealthy foreigners went to him and told him they were looking for the King of the Jews! My son, Jesse, died because Herod wanted to kill Jesus! My son died instead of yours!"

Mary gasped and moaned in agony as Deborah threw the painful words at her, and they tore fresh wounds in her heart. More tears leaked from eyes that were still swollen from weeping all day. Her pain was so intense, so acute, that she felt as if her heart had been pierced by the same spear that had been thrust through her son's body earlier in the day.

Deborah wasn't finished yet, and she angrily continued her verbal assault as she paced back and forth in the small room. "Your son, who you claimed to be the Son of God, was spared all those years ago, Mary, but look at him now! Where is he now?! He's as dead as my Jesse! You must be crazy to think that God made you pregnant and that Joseph wasn't the father of your child! Jesus is dead, Mary! If he was the Son of God, he wouldn't have died! God can't die!"

Stunned and shaken, Mary listened as Deborah vented. Bracing herself and crying to God for assistance, Mary gathered her thoughts and boldly proclaimed through her tears, "God had to spare Jesus at that time so he could accomplish his purpose on earth. God had to spare Jesus for this day."

"What do you mean by that?" Deborah bitterly asked.

Mary's voice fell to a whisper. "Jesus knew he was going to be crucified today; he'd been warning us for months that it would happen, but he won't stay in the tomb. He's also prophesied, and I believe him, that he will rise from the dead."

Deborah's tears ceased flowing and she cocked her head at Mary. Mockingly, she spit out her words. "Come back to life? How absurd! You just can't accept the fact that your son is dead." She walked around the table and stood behind Mary and looked down at her. "My son, my precious baby, died when a soldier put a spear clear through his chest, and he never came back to life. Can you begin to imagine how horrible that was for me? I had to accept the fact that he was dead, and he was my first-born son, Mary. Do you know how much I hated God for what he did to my Jesse? Do you know how much I wanted to die? It took years for me to be able to enjoy life again, and having three more sons helped, but not one of them ever replaced my little Jesse. At least you got to see Jesus become a man; my little Jesse was only six months old when he was killed. I can't even remember what Jesse looked like, Mary. I can only remember that he was a beautiful, happy baby, and I loved him very, very much."

The anger drained from Deborah's voice as she slowly walked to the other side of the table and gazed down at Mary, who met her stare. "All these years I've secretly wanted to find you, hoping against hope that I would, so I could ask why you left without saying goodbye. Now I wish that I'd never laid eyes on you again." Her voice was empty and void of all emotion, her eyes dry. She wouldn't shed any more tears. It was time to walk away and put it all behind her.

Mary sat where she was, dazed and stunned, numb with grief. Memories of tender moments shared long ago with Deborah were lost in the hopelessness now at hand, and she couldn't think of anything to say or do which would comfort Deborah. Her words came broken as she cried. "The slaughter of the babies in Bethlehem is something I haven't heard before, Deborah. Upon leaving Bethlehem, we were directed by the angel to travel to Egypt and stay there until he appeared to us again. And so we did. The expensive gifts the foreigners had brought paid for our travels and our time in Egypt. When the angel told us to return, we feared returning to Bethlehem because we heard that Herod's son ruled in his stead, so we settled in Nazareth and reunited with Joseph's family, raising Jesus and several other children. All these years, I knew nothing about your great loss, Deborah. Knowing of this horrible tragedy breaks my heart."

"Your heart can't break like mine did." Deborah's words cut like a knife.

Mary hung her head as tears dripped from her eyes. She could find nothing else to say.

Deborah slowly approached the door, and then she turned and looked at Mary, still sitting on the bench. "I was so very, very happy when I saw you today, even under the tragic circumstances that brought us together, but I wish now that I had listened to my family and had not pursued finding you. Realizing that Jesse was killed because of Jesus, my best friend's son, has laid waste to my bones. God in heaven have mercy on my soul, for I cannot pray to him or worship him any longer. He is not worthy."

She grasped the latch with her hand and slowly opened the door. With glassy eyes, Mary watched Deborah step through the doorway and into the other room, and she heard John offering to take her home. Undoubtedly, the others in the house had heard Deborah's loud voice and were concerned at the turn of events. Deborah's feet dragged as she shuffled across the room and through the front door and into the darkening street, heedless of John's offer. Mary slowly stood and motioned for John to follow Deborah anyway, and he left the house and stayed close to Deborah's heels as she made her way home.

Deborah was so numb she felt dead. Her best friend had deserted her, had not warned her about the coming attack, and had allowed her child to be killed. It was no wonder Mary never returned to Bethlehem. She would have been terrified to return and face her friends who had lost sons. Selfish, that was what Mary was, and Deborah hated her now more than she had loved her. Deborah even took pleasure in the fact that Mary's son had died a horrible, humiliating and excruciatingly painful death. How absurd! God had saved him so he could accomplish his purpose on earth! What purpose could there possibly be in dying by crucifixion? Mary had to wake up and face the fact that her son was now dead for absolutely no reason!

Deborah meandered through the streets of Jerusalem, unsure of where she was or even how to get back to Caleb's house. The streets were almost deserted, people celebrating either the Second Seder or the Feast of Unleavened Bread. Soft light filtered through windows and doors left ajar to allow in cool breezes, and joyful sounds of laughter and music reached Deborah's ears as she shuffled along, numb from her ordeal. It seemed like ages ago now, not just hours, that she'd been told that it was Jesus who was being crucified. Finding Mary had turned out completely opposite of what she had envisioned it would mean for her. The knowledge of the circumstances surrounding Jesse's death was simply too overwhelming. She simply wanted to lie down and die; what point was there in living one more day?

She became aware of someone following her, and fear briefly stabbed at her heart, but then quickly vanished. She didn't care if someone harmed her; she really didn't care. Eventually Deborah came to the area outside the temple courtyard, and she knew the way to Caleb's house from there. She continued to shuffle along, not desiring to face the other members of her family with the knowledge she now possessed. How was she going to tell Gedaliah and the other family members the truth about Jesse's murder? She should have left well enough alone. Losing Jesse had been horrible, but this new revelation was more than she could bear. She felt as if she had been sliced into little pieces and scattered in the wilderness for the vultures to devour. Her grief was excruciating, but she took consolation in the fact that Mary had lost her son earlier that day. If Jesus had been the Son of God and if he was the promised Messiah, he would have freed his people from captivity. He was nothing but a mere man, and Deborah scorned herself for having been so gullible to have believed that he was anything more.

Finally reaching the rise on which Caleb's house was located, she crept up the cobbled street, struggling to put one foot in front of the other, each step more agonizing than the one before. As she stood at the front door, she wished she could die. Family would be waiting on the other side, she knew, and she had nothing but shocking news to tell them.

Stepping onto the threshold, she grasped the latch and turned it and slowly walked into the house. The voices that she had heard as she entered suddenly ceased as she turned and closed the door behind her. It was then that she saw John; he had been the one following her, probably to see that she arrived home safely. Well, she was home, but suddenly she wished she was anywhere else but home.

Shoulders slumped and heart in her throat, she turned and looked at her family.

Once they saw her countenance, the joyful expressions on their faces evaporated. Gedaliah reached her first, and Deborah collapsed into his arms, unable to stand any longer. He guided her to a seat as concern for her caused his heart to race.

Her face was white; her eyes were red and puffy. Her mouth was set in a thin line, and her countenance relayed that something had gone terribly amiss in her reunion with Mary. Rizpah quickly took off Deborah's shawl and gave her something to drink, while Gedaliah kept speaking softly to her, telling her everything was going to be all right.

Deborah surprised herself by eagerly drinking the refreshing drink Rizpah handed her. Everyone stared at her as she drank, confused and concerned.

Gedaliah sat down beside his wife and held her hands after Rizpah took the empty goblet. Eyes rife with concern, Gedaliah stroked her hands and anxiously asked, "Deborah, what happened? Gedaliah told us you were so happy to find Mary. What happened to make you return like this?"

Her face drawn and her voice monotone, she said, "I found out why Mary left Bethlehem those many years ago." Her words drew everyone to her as silence filled the room. Deborah struggled to form the words that threatened to choke her. Why was life so cruel, she wondered as she looked at the faces of her family members. What was the point of sharing her acute grief and feelings of betrayal with them? Was there really any purpose? But she wanted everyone to know the kind of person Mary really was, not what they thought her to be, so Deborah found the words as she answered her own question.

"She told me that she left because an angel of the Lord told her that King Herod was going to try to kill Jesus. So she and Joseph left in the middle of the night and didn't warn anyone about what was going to happen. When the soldiers came, in an attempt to make sure they killed Jesus, they slaughtered every young male child. Little did they know that he'd already left and would live another 32 years." Her voice dropped to a mere whisper. The truth had been told, and now everyone would understand her pain and that Mary had betrayed their friendship.

Gedaliah's face turned ashen as Deborah's voice faded away. He dropped his hands to his side, certain his heart was going to stop at any minute. A rush of heat flashed through his body, and he clutched at his chest with his right hand as he held himself upright with his left while unheralded gasps and sobs tore through him as he struggled to digest the news.

Deborah watched as the others fussed over Gedaliah, afraid that he would die right before their eyes, but she was so numb that she didn't even care. What was left worth living for? She was old, worn out, and very weary. She'd had a good life with Gedaliah, and it would soon be over anyway, so what did it matter if either one of them died today? Death was prevalent in this city, where its citizens were crucified on crosses and tossed to the wild dogs. Rome had brought savagery to their civilized land. And God?! What was he doing about it? Absolutely nothing! He was still residing in that beautiful temple that she'd just passed, which King Herod, who had ordered the murder of her son, had built for Him!

Gedaliah finally recovered, but the shock of what Deborah had just told him gripped his soul. Everyone stared at Deborah, who simply offered a blank expression, and muttered, "I was so very, very sad for Mary when I saw her son die today, but now I'm really very glad he died. Now she knows what it feels like to have a son murdered for no reason."

No one in the room spoke, and the silence that wrapped around everyone was like a cloak heavy with ice water. The joy of celebrating the Passover and other feasts had evaporated and only a dark, foreboding atmosphere remained.

Slowly rising to her feet, Deborah straightened her dress and vigorously rubbed her face with both hands. As her arms fell to her sides, she mumbled, "I have nothing to live for any longer. My best friend betrayed me and allowed my baby to be murdered."

She forced her bent, aging frame to move toward her room. She could feel the stares of her family members on her back, probing and wondering, anxious for her to turn and talk with them, but she shuffled into her room, where she laid down on her bed and stared at the ceiling. She kept replaying and replaying the conversation with Mary over and over again in her mind. The real reason she had searched for Mary was obscured by her current pain. The result of her insistent search had brought her a truth that she couldn't bear.

Stiff and weary, Deborah changed her position as tears fell unbidden and wet the pillow beneath her head. She tried hard to imagine what the day would have been like if she'd never found Mary, for it had turned out to be the longest of her life, even longer than the day Jesse had been killed, and it still wasn't over. She wondered how she got to the scene of the crucifixion in the first place. Her mind was so muddled, so cloudy, so cluttered with thoughts that couldn't be separated. Oh, yes, the mob woke everyone up in the morning, and Caleb had gone to find the source of all the commotion. The discovery of the person being crucified had changed the course of her life, finally bringing her face to face with Mary, her dear friend of so long ago, and had filled her with such joy. Yet all that had evaporated in an instant, vanished just as quickly as Jesse's life had been snuffed out. Life could change so quickly.

Deborah sighed heavily and felt a smug sort of satisfaction that Mary had watched her son die; it was only right after what Jesse had suffered. Jesse had done no wrong, but Deborah knew people weren't crucified unjustly. Surely Jesus had committed some horrible crime that had brought him to such an end. She'd felt pity for him while on the hillside, but now she felt only disgust. If he was the Son of God, he would not, could not, have died. The people were justified in railing and taunting him while he hung on the cross! He had called himself the Son of God, but he couldn't even stop his own crucifixion! He had deceived so many people, including her, and Mary had been simply disillusioned.

Deborah rolled onto her side as Gedaliah entered the room. She closed her eyes, wanting to shut him out. She couldn't bear any more today. She felt

317

him sit down on the bed beside her and place his hand on her back.

"Please come and join us for the Feast of Unleavened Bread," he gently whispered as he stroked her back.

Through clenched teeth, she seethed, "I don't want to see or talk to anyone, not even you. Please leave me alone."

Gedaliah sucked in his breath as he began to respond, but without a word, he arose and slowly and quietly left the room.

Deborah was still awake when he came to bed some time later, but she neither acknowledged his presence nor spoke to him. Her pain was her pain, and even Gedaliah couldn't possibly understand the depth of her sorrow and grief. If she had believed in God, she would have asked him to end her life while she slept, but she didn't believe in him any longer, so there was simply no point in even asking.

Chapter Twenty-three

RECONCILIATION

"She can't remain in her room forever," insisted Rizpah two days later. "She has to eat sooner or later. She can't stay angry forever!"

"It's much more than anger; it's unfathomable pain," murmured Gedaliah. "I truly think that finding out why Mary left and why Jesse was killed will be the death of my wife. It's more than she can bear."

Rizpah poured a fresh goblet of wine for Gedaliah. He looked as if he had aged ten years in two days. His face was haggard, his eyes puffy from lack of sleep and worry, and his mouth drawn downward in a tight line. What had begun as a time of celebration and feasting had turned into a season of profound sadness.

"Well, if she doesn't come out of that room and eat with us by this evening, I'm going in there and forcing her to eat. She can't go without eating! She'll die!" exclaimed Rizpah.

"I tell you, that's what she wants to do. She says she has nothing left to live for, not even me or our sons and our grandchildren. Nothing matters to Deborah any more."

They were sitting outside in the garden at the back of the house, one of Rizpah's favorite spots. The butterflies and bees abounded, flitting from flower to flower, drawing life from the nectar and pollen. The day was warm and the sun was slipping away in the western sky. Rizpah had coaxed Gedaliah to sit outside with her for a while; he'd been wasting away inside, fretting over Deborah's refusal to eat or come out of her room. Even he hadn't been able to convince her to eat, which distressed him to no end.

The sun warmed their bodies as they sat on the garden bench, but Rizpah noticed that it did little to warm Gedaliah's soul. The other family members had gone out to shop and visit some friends, taking the children with them to stretch their legs and burn off energy, but Gedaliah had refused to go with them, wanting instead to stay home in case Deborah needed him, but apparently Deborah needed no one, not even her husband. Her refusal to eat had spilled over into her refusal to talk to anyone, and that included Gedaliah. Rizpah saw the hurt and confusion and deep sense of utter helplessness on Gedaliah's face.

A song bird lighted on a tree branch and chirped, bringing a smile to Rizpah's face. Watching the birds and butterflies was one of the reasons she so loved her garden; she considered it her little Eden on earth. Oh, the bugs sometimes got the best of things, but not usually.

Gedaliah sighed and placed both hands over his face, rubbing it fiercely. "How are we going to go back to Bethlehem and run the inn? Deborah won't eat; she won't talk to anyone. She's shut herself away in a room, both physically and emotionally. How are our children going to react to all this? What will they think when they hear that their oldest brother, whom they never even knew, was killed because of Deborah's best friend?" His arms dropped to his lap in utter and complete dejection.

Rizpah put her arm across his shoulders. "God will take care of things, Gedaliah. I'm sure He'll make a way for Deborah to return to her old self in a few days."

Gedaliah turned an angry face toward her. "God!? What has God ever done to help us?" He rose to his feet and started pacing through the small garden.

"Years ago, when Jesse was killed, Deborah vented her anger and rage at God, wondering how he could have let something as horrible as the slaughter of the innocent babies in Bethlehem to occur. And you know what? I didn't agree with her then, but I agree with her now. I used to try to persuade her that evil people do evil things, that it wasn't God's fault, but now I'm really beginning to wonder! God could have stopped the horrible massacre, but he didn't! And now to find out, after all these years, that an angel of the Lord told Mary to leave Bethlehem because Herod was going to kill her child. She could have wakened us and told all of us to leave too, but she didn't. I remember now how Deborah was so upset because Joseph took the donkey out of our stable right behind the inn, but he didn't even have the courtesy to knock on our door and tell us they were leaving. And Mary now insists that Jesus had to survive then so he could die the other day! That's ridiculous!"

He ceased his pacing and sat down by Rizpah again, slouching on the bench. "I don't have any strength left with which to help Deborah. I'm an old man now, and I'm tired of all the brutal killing and unnecessary death I've seen in my lifetime. We had so hoped that Jesus would be the promised Messiah and that he'd save his people, Israel. But he didn't. He died on a cruel Roman cross instead, just like a common criminal! I don't have any hope any more!"

Rizpah reached around him and patted his shoulder. Silently, the two sat for some time watching the bees and the butterflies, and then Rizpah got up and went into the house to prepare some food. She left Gedaliah in the garden alone, hoping that he would find some solace there.

She busied herself in the kitchen, humming a tune as she worked. She'd wanted to go out with the others, but on the other hand, she hadn't wanted to leave Gedaliah alone with his thoughts and an unspeaking, bitter, angry wife, so she'd stayed behind. Besides, her old feet hurt her terribly when she walked very far.

There was a loud knock on her front door, and she answered it as quickly as she could. Whoever it was most certainly was impatient, she thought as she scurried to the door. She pulled the latch and opened the door a crack. Three women stood before her, but she didn't know any of them. All of them were dressed in mourning clothes, yet their faces were radiant and they were full of excitement and laughter – an odd combination for people dressed in mourning attire.

"Yes, may I help you?" she asked.

"We've come to see Deborah of Bethlehem. Is she here?" one of the women eagerly inquired.

Rizpah opened the door further and stood in front of the women. "May I ask who wants to see her?"

One of the women, the one with seemingly the most radiant face, if that were at all possible, stepped slightly forward. "I'm Mary, her friend from long ago. I desperately need to speak to her."

Rizpah frowned. Hesitating, she looked over her shoulder and then back at the visitors and replied, "Deborah isn't feeling well; she's taken to her bed."

Mary's expression didn't change, nor did those of the other women. Mary persisted. "I must tell Deborah something that will make her very happy. I believe I know why she isn't well. She told you about our conversation the other day, correct?"

Rizpah reluctantly nodded. So this was the woman who had caused the murder of Jesse. Her eyes stared and she drew her mouth into a tight line.

"She has to hear the news of what happened earlier today, and apparently is continuing to happen at this very moment. We *must* see her!"

Gedaliah suddenly stood behind Rizpah. He recognized Mary instantly, and his face became sullen and drawn. Stepping up to the door, he firmly stated, "Mary, I know you mean well, but what you told us the other day has brought us great grief. Deborah hasn't spoken to anyone or eaten anything since she came home and told us what you said, and I fear seeing you again will only cause her to draw her last breath. Please, return to your house, you and your friends. Seeing Deborah won't do any good."

Mary reached for Gedaliah and took his hands in hers and looked into his eyes. What he saw there startled and puzzled him, for her eyes were no longer full of anguish and sorrow, but were now filled with unmistakable joy instead. He looked at her, confused.

"Gedaliah, we *must* see Deborah, for what we have to tell her, and you also, will change the world forever! Please, take us to her!" Mary's insistence and expression caused him to pause.

Gedaliah turned and looked at Rizpah, who shrugged her shoulders. It wasn't her decision. Stepping aside, Gedaliah motioned for the three women to enter the house.

"Thank you, Gedaliah. These are my dear friends, Mary Magdalene and Salome. They saw something this morning that we must share with Deborah. Please, where is she."

Rizpah started walking. "Follow me."

They were soon at the door of Deborah's sleeping chamber, and Rizpah knocked softly and the opened the door slowly despite a lack of response from Deborah.

"Deborah, some people have come to see you. They have something they want to tell you." She stepped aside and allowed Mary to enter the doorway.

Deborah had turned her head to see Rizpah in the doorway as anger welled up inside at her audacity in bringing people to visit. When she saw Mary step in front of Rizpah, the anger and rage reared up like a wild stallion. Gathering all her strength, she sat up in bed and hollered, "You!? Get out of here! I told you I never wanted to see you again!"

The simple act of sitting up in bed was too much for her, and she collapsed onto the bed again. Refusing to be prostrate before her 'visitors', she swung her feet to the floor and sat up with a great deal of effort, her eyes blazing and her heart racing. She was surprised at how weak she'd become due to lack of food for several days; however, there was no way she was going to appear weak and suffering in front of Mary.

Mary wasn't discouraged or dissuaded by Deborah's reaction. She slowly approached the bed as Deborah sat upright. How she still loved her!

Reaching the side of the bed, Mary knelt down and took Deborah's hands in hers, and surprisingly, Deborah didn't pull away. Mary's eyes glistened with joyful tears as she said, "My dearest Deborah, God has been so good! We have something wonderful beyond anything to tell you! But please, you must eat first. There's no reason to be in mourning like this. Please, come out of this room and eat."

"I'm not in mourning," Deborah croaked as the warmth of Mary's hands touched her heart. She gazed down at the woman who knelt at her feet, surprised that she would posture herself so. Deborah felt only emptiness. The anger had suddenly drained out of her when she'd shouted at Mary. All the hours she'd spent lying on her bed, refusing to talk to anyone, had given her plenty of time to think, and she'd finally realized that it wasn't Mary's fault that Jesse had been killed. Back then, everyone knew Herod wasn't in his right mind. He'd thrived on his own brutality, and those under his thumb had suffered because of it. Even though she realized that Mary wasn't responsible for Jesse's death, Deborah was still in too much anguish to tell her that she'd arrived at that conclusion and ask her forgiveness. She just couldn't do it.

And now Mary knelt at her feet, her face glowing and radiant. Jesus had been killed three days ago; what could possibly bring such joy to Mary's heart? Deborah's thoughts returned to the present as she realized that Mary was pleading with her to eat.

"Please, Deborah, eat something. You can't go without eating. Gedaliah loves you and so do many others, myself included." Mary nodded to Rizpah, who headed off to the kitchen, eager to prepare a quick meal for her unexpected guests.

"Here, let me help you up," offered Gedaliah as he reached for Mary's arm. After Mary was on her feet, much to everyone's surprise, Deborah tried to get off the bed! Gedaliah quickly held his arms out and assisted her, and she readily accepted his assistance. Her knees shook and her legs felt as if they'd give out at any moment, but she leaned into Gedaliah and slowly made her way out of the room.

Everyone, including Mary Magdalene and Salome, returned to the living area. After a few short minutes, Rizpah had food spread on the table, and Deborah seated herself, relieved to be off her shaking, wobbly legs. She realized that she really didn't want to die after all; she still had a lot to life for. Her temper tantrum had run its course.

Gingerly, Gedaliah filled a plate with a fresh pomegranate, lentils, a thick slice of cheese, fresh bread, and a cluster of grapes. Deborah protested, "I can't possibly eat all that, Gedaliah."

"That's all right. Eat what you can." He placed the plate in front of her.

Slowly, Deborah began to eat, first one bite and then another. Gedaliah couldn't have been more pleased. They engaged in small-talk as they ate, but soon the conversation turned to the reason for the women's visit.

"What news is it that you must tell Deborah?" asked Rizpah.

Mary smiled at her two friends, Salome and Mary Magdalene. "Yes, of course, I don't think we can put off telling this much longer." She emptied her hands of food and excitedly looked at Deborah as she wiped her hands on her cloak.

"Where should we begin?" puzzled Mary as her eyes searched those of her friends.

"Maybe I should start," offered Mary Magdalene.

Mary nodded, anxious for them to begin.

"You were at the crucifixion of Jesus, and you saw how he suffered and died," Mary Magdalene said to Deborah. "He was punished for crimes he didn't commit. After he died, he was placed in a tomb belonging to Joseph of Arimathea, where he has lain since then. This morning, Salome and I, as well as Mary, the mother of James, planned to go to the tomb to anoint his body. Well, I was very distraught about Jesus's death, for he had delivered me from many things. My grief was acute, and I got impatient and couldn't wait for Salome and Mary to get ready, so off I went to the tomb in the early hours of the morning by myself, even though I knew soldiers were guarding the tomb."

Deborah looked puzzled. "Soldiers? Why soldiers?"

"Apparently our religious leaders were certain that one of us, those who followed Jesus and believed that he was the Christ, would come and steal away his body during the night and then tell everyone that he had risen from the dead, as he said he would." She paused and looked around. "Anyway, as I walked through the garden to the burial place, I remembered the huge, heavy stone across the tomb and hoped the soldiers would roll it away from the opening so I could anoint his body, but when I reached the sepulcher, there wasn't anyone there! No one! All the soldiers' belongings and such were still there and the fire was still burning, but they were gone! That made me even more upset! Without the soldiers to roll the stone away from the tomb, I wouldn't be able to anoint the body. But when I went toward the tomb, I found the stone *was* rolled away! Who had rolled it away?! Had someone come and taken his body away?! I became terrified and ran back to the city to tell the disciples what I'd seen."

"I think I should take over here," excitedly interrupted Salome. "Mary, the mother of James, and I had made our way to the tomb, a few minutes behind Mary Magdalene, to anoint the body with her. When we came close to the tomb, we saw her running away. Even in the early morning light, we noticed that she was terribly upset about something. At first, we thought that some of the soldiers might have troubled her, but as we came to the sepulcher, we also saw that the soldiers were gone and that the tomb was open." She paused to catch her breath, her face glowing.

"Mary and I cautiously stepped into the tomb, not knowing what to expect, and we discovered that it was empty! Jesus's body wasn't there! We looked at each other, confused and frightened, and simply didn't understand what was happening! And then......" Her face was so radiant that it seemed to shine, and her eyes sparkled and danced with joy as she held her hands to the sides of her face. Her voice became choked with emotion as she looked heavenward.

"Out of nowhere, two men suddenly appeared in the tomb, and their clothes were so brilliant that the tomb was bathed in radiant, heavenly light. Mary and I fell down to the ground, terrified! Even though we were afraid, we were also very excited. We knew something wonderful had happened, something beyond our wildest dreams! And then the two men spoke to us. They said, 'Why are you looking for the living among the dead? He's not here; he's risen! Remember he told you when he was with you in Galilee that the Son of Man would be delivered into the hands of sinful men, would be crucified, and would rise again on the third day.' And then they told us to go and tell his disciples and Peter -- who felt terrible because he had denied he was a follower of Jesus the night he was arrested -- that *Jesus* would see us in Galilee. Then the light slowly faded from the tomb, and Mary and I stared at each other in amazement!" She paused and gazed at Deborah as her heart raced with the vivid memory.

Deborah sat transfixed as she listened, confused and perplexed. She'd seen Jesus crucified, as had the other women. Maybe they still weren't able to accept the fact of his death, but somehow, as she sat quietly, she began to feel a deep, unexplainable urge growing inside her to hear the entire story – and to hope that it was true.

Mary Magdalene once again took up the narration. "When I left the tomb, I ran back to the house and found Peter and John and immediately told them that the tomb had been opened. I couldn't stop crying! I was so upset that I think I frightened them! Anyway, they left me and ran to the garden to see for themselves if what I said was true. I was told by others in the house that I should wait until they returned, but I was too upset and distraught at the thought that someone *had* taken Jesus's body, so I didn't listen to them and headed back to the tomb, hoping beyond hope that Peter and John would find out what had happened. I was so confused and worried that I took a wrong turn in the garden, and it took me a little longer to find my way. When I was approaching the tomb again, I saw Peter and John running away! That only caused me to be more upset, if that was even possible, for they obviously hadn't been able to find out anything more than I had. I slowly approached the tomb and cried uncontrollably as I leaned against the stone that had covered the opening!" She sucked in her breath quickly and closed her eyes in an effort to stop the tears that streamed down her face.

The room was hushed. Deborah glanced at Gedaliah. He was staring at Mary Magdalene and hanging on every word she spoke.

"And then I went closer to the tomb and looked into it," Mary Magdalene continued in a whisper, "and as with Salome and the Mary, I saw a great light. I saw two angels sitting in the tomb, one at the head and one at the feet of the place where Jesus had lain. I was still so upset and my eyes so full of tears that I didn't even realize they were angels at the time. And then one of them asked me, 'Woman, why are you crying?' I replied, 'Because someone has taken away my Lord, and I don't know where they've taken him.' My grief was so deep that I couldn't stop crying! I stood up and moved away from the tomb, only to find a man standing in front of me. I couldn't see anything clearly, mind you. And then the man in front of me asked me the same question, why was I crying, and he also wanted to know for who I was looking.

"You must remember that, at the time, I was still certain that someone had stolen his body. I thought the man standing in front of me was the one who attended the gardens, and so I asked him if he'd taken the body, and if so, would he be so kind as to tell me where he'd taken it, and I told him I would take it away."

Mary Magdalene opened her eyes as a broad smile spread across her face, which shined with a heavenly light, and paid no heed to the tears that were running down her cheeks. "And then the man said my name. He knew me! All he said was my name, and I instantly knew that it was *Jesus*! I looked up at him and lunged to touch him, to see if he was real, when he told me that I mustn't touch him because he hadn't yet ascended to his Father in heaven." Her voice faded to almost a whisper as the tears splashed onto her tunic. Her eyes were transfixed heavenward, and Deborah sensed that Mary was seeing something, or someone, that she couldn't see.

Lowering her head and fixing her eyes on Deborah, Mary Magdalene resumed speaking. "After Jesus told me to go and tell his disciples that he had risen, I hurried back to the house, where the other Mary and Salome were already in a heated discussion with Peter and John and others at the house about Christ's resurrection. What I had to tell them convinced them that it was true! Jesus, the Christ, the Messiah, has risen from the dead, just as he said he would! Of course, we didn't believe what he was telling us before he was crucified; we didn't want to believe that he would be killed in such a horrible way! We loved him! We didn't want him to die! But he did die, yet he's alive again!"

A sweet, heavenly presence enveloped the room, an awesome wondering, at the events that were shared. Deborah shook her head as she tried to absorb the account and sort things out.

"I don't understand! If Jesus was the promised Messiah, the Son of God, how could he be killed? And now you tell us that he's alive again! How can that be? I don't know what to believe!" Her brows furrowed as she shook her head in confusion and ran her hands over her face.

Mary came to her friend's side and took Deborah's hands in hers. She knelt down in front of Deborah and looked up at her with eyes full of love. "Deborah, do you remember when I told you that Jesus didn't come to this earth to free his people from Roman oppression, but rather to save us from our sins?"

Deborah slowly nodded.

"If I remember accurately, when I told you that so many years ago, your mother asked me how Jesus was going to save us from our sins. She wondered if he was going to offer sacrifices for us so we wouldn't have to do it any more. She even asked if Jesus would offer up a lamb that would satisfy God forever. I didn't have an answer at that time because I didn't know the path God had chosen for his Son, but Jesus died the other day at the same hour that the High Priest was slaying the Passover lamb for the nation in the temple. And with his last breath Jesus said, 'It is finished.' Those are the same words spoken by the priest when the lamb dies, as has been done for centuries. Deborah, God has made his Son, Jesus, to be the perfect sacrifice for our sins. He was the perfect lamb slain for all of us. He knew no sin. We no longer have to shed the blood of lambs, goats, doves and oxen; Jesus has shed his blood and saved us from our sins. I didn't know how God's purpose was to be accomplished when he was a small child, but now that it's been done, it's all very clear to me. His resurrection this morning has proven to everyone that he *is* the Son of God, just as he said. Not even death can claim the Son of God!" Mary looked into the eyes of her friend and watched as the tears began to flow down her cheeks.

Deborah quickly glanced at Gedaliah and noticed that tears were also coursing down his weathered face. She opened her mouth to speak, but no words came out. She wanted to believe, but it seemed so impossible – to be dead and come back to life! But God could do anything, and if she believed that Jesus was God's Son, how could she not believe that he could come back to life after being dead.

Deborah gazed at Mary, still on her knees before her. The truth began to seep into her soul and flow from her spirit as she found her tongue.

"I'm sorry for not believing you, Mary," Deborah cried as she grasped Mary's shoulders. "I believed you years ago, but when we spoke the other day after Jesus died, I couldn't believe any more. Lying in bed these last few days, my mind has been replaying everything, even why Jesus had to be spared from Herod's soldiers' swords." Her body began to convulse with sobs so great that they took her breath away as the dam of pent-up emotions broke in a torrent of tears, tears of release and belief and forgiveness.

"Oh, Mary, please forgive me for blaming you for Jesse's death! How could I have imagined such a thing?" She hid her face behind her hands in shame as sobs wracked her body.

Mary slid onto the bench next to Deborah and wrapped her arms around her, holding her close as Deborah's tears dripped onto her mourning shawl. Taking Deborah's face in her hands, Mary smiled tenderly as she wiped away the tears with her thumbs. "Deborah, Herod was a horrible person, one that thrived on brutality. God has punished him eternally for what he did to Jesse, but I want you to know something. Jesse is with God, right now, even as we speak. He's not hurting, he's not sad, he's not angry, he's not wounded. Jesse is happy and joyful in the presence of the Lord! I know in my heart that God in heaven cried the day the babies were slaughtered. I believe that with all my heart! God didn't condone Herod's actions, but the enemy of our souls is full of evil and hate for all of God's children. Please, Deborah, take comfort in the fact that Jesse played a vital role in God's plan for redemption and that his brief life was *not* in vain. Someday soon you will be with Jesse in heaven. You will sit with him and eat with him and discover the wonders that God has in store for you with him. There will be no heartache there for you, dear Deborah, only joy!"

Deborah's tears were unending as all the anger and malice that she'd held in her heart melted away as Mary held her. Gedaliah cried as he watched. Just a few hours ago, he'd been so fearful that Deborah wouldn't live out the week, and God was now bringing her healing and release from all the pain she'd suffered, and he was receiving healing, too. There wasn't a dry eye in the house! As his eyes met Salome's, he started laughing from sheer joy, and soon everyone was laughing and hugging each other in joyful, exuberant celebration.

Wiping her eyes, Deborah smiled at Mary and asked, "How did you keep on believing all these years, especially when Jesus was crucified?"

"I had no choice *but* to believe, from the angelic announcement, to his birth, to his first miracle when he changed the water to wine, and to all the miraculous healings Jesus performed. I had no choice but to believe with all my heart. Remember, I knew the identity of his Father."

Quickly rising to her feet, Mary exclaimed suddenly, "When I get back home, I'm taking off these mourning clothes! There isn't anything to mourn about! Jesus has risen from the dead, just as he said he would! He was dead, but is alive again!"

Deborah embraced Mary again and, greatly relieved, stated, "I don't know how to thank you for coming here today. If you hadn't, I probably would have gone home to Bethlehem and carried all this anger with me to the grave. Thank you, Mary, for not giving up on me."

Mary clasped her face in her hands and kissed her on each cheek. "I felt so absolutely terrible the night we had to leave Bethlehem, Deborah. You were my best friend, and I had such a difficult time without you. I prayed for you every day and hoped that someday we'd be able to see each other again, and when our paths crossed the other day, I felt horrible the way our conversation ended. But now a great deal of good has come from all of this. Your faith in God and in his Son has been restored, and the anger and loss that you have carried all these years over Jesse's death have been washed away. It has truly been a wonderful day!"

Deborah smiled weakly. "You're right about seeing Jesse very soon," she chortled. "This old body won't hold up much longer!" Together, they laughed through their tears of joy.

Gedaliah came to his wife's side and pulled her close to him. "Because of Jesus and his resurrection from the dead, this day has become one of celebration!"

Salome offered, "We weren't the only ones to see Jesus today," she said excitedly. "Two of his followers, while walking on the road to Emmaus, also saw him. They didn't know it was him until later, but Jesus walked and talked with them for some time. We are so excited, not knowing when or where he will appear again!"

A few moments later, Mary and the others said goodbye to Deborah, Gedaliah and Rizpah. Mary and Deborah held each other close for a long time, wanting to stop time from moving and to delay their parting, but Mary stressed that she would be over to see Deborah again before she returned to Bethlehem at week's end. With their faces damp, they said one final goodbye, and Mary and her friends left as Deborah stood in the doorway.

Gedaliah came to her side and placed his arm around her waist, drawing her close. They quietly watched the women become lost in the crowd that swarmed the streets. Deborah rested her head on Gedaliah's shoulder as she heaved a sigh of relief as one final sob escaped her lips.

Turning his wife to him, Gedaliah said, "Come, dear wife, it's time to help Rizpah prepare the evening meal."

Later in the day, the rest of the family was informed of the day's events, and the house that had been in mourning, fearful for Deborah's health, even her life, burst into joy with tumultuous celebration at the news.

The very next day, Mary again returned to see Deborah to tell her that Jesus had appeared to all of his disciples, except one, Thomas, while they were gathered for their evening meal in the same room in which Jesus had celebrated Passover with them. No longer was Mary wearing mourning clothes, but she was dressed in her usual way. The radiant light beaming from her face reflected the joy within her heart at the sudden turn of events, events that had been foretold by her Son, the Son of God, but which hadn't been believed by his followers. They couldn't believe the things He was telling them at the time because they were simply incomprehensible; they were beyond the scope of human understanding. As Mary told of

Christ's appearing to all the disciples in the upper room, save one, her heart knew no greater joy. Mary felt as if she was a child again, and her steps were not those of an aging woman, but of one who was once again full of life.

Mary and Deborah spent many more hours together, both alone and with Deborah's family, and they praised Jesus, God's Holy Son, as they sat in the garden behind Rizpah's house on the hillside in Jerusalem.

During the next few days, Deborah and Gedaliah fellowshipped with the disciples of Jesus and gained many new friends as they grew in knowledge and in faith.

* * * * * * * * * *

Several days later, as they were walking back to Bethlehem, Deborah said to her husband, "I thank God for this Passover celebration and all it's done for me. The truth about Mary's departure almost devastated me, but Jesus was . . . is, the Son of God, as Mary said, and he has risen from the dead.

"Our Jesse played a part in this story, which is surely to change the course of history forever. I may never see Mary again on this earth, but I know we'll meet again in heaven, and we'll both play with Jesse, who is in the presence of God, at the feet of Jesus." Her sandaled feet kicked up the dust as she placed one foot in front of the other on the rocky road back to Bethlehem. Her steps were no longer heavy and slow but quick and sure and purposeful. She had a reason to live now; she had to tell others the truth.

Gedaliah looked at his wife with eyes full of love and tenderness, and then he put his arm around her shoulder and hugged her just as the town of Bethlehem, their home, came into view. His emotions had run from one extreme to the other over the previous days. For a time, he'd thought that he'd lose Deborah and that she wouldn't return to Bethlehem with him. So many experiences had jolted his soul and made him realize the important things in life. The love he felt for the woman by his side welled up inside his heart, and he swallowed the lump that formed in his throat as he held her tightly with his arm. He was truly a blessed man.

Deborah quickened her steps at the sight of Bethlehem. This was where her children, including Jesse, had been born, and it was the birthplace of Jesus, the Son of God! Humbled by the fact that she'd been chosen by God to play a role in the events that had unfolded those many years ago stung her eyes with tears, but she abruptly brushed them away. Deciding that there would be no more tears of sadness, she reached for Gedaliah's hand as she quickened her steps on the dusty road.

"I can't wait to tell everyone about Jesus, Son of Mary, Son of God, and the great sacrifice He's made for all of us," exclaimed Deborah as she took his hand. "Let's hurry, Gedaliah. There are so many that need to know the truth."

Hand in hand, Gedaliah and Deborah walked the remaining steps to Bethlehem with renewed energy, faces glowing, and hearts at peace.

Acknowledgements:

First of all, I'd like to thank my husband for bearing with me through all of the hours of creating and editing this work. Thankfully, he's a patient man!

I'd also like to thank my dear friends, Steve and Martha Bollinger, for reading this novel while in rough draft and encouraging me to fine-tune it and publish it. Without their encouragement, I don't know if I would have done it.

Also to thank is another friend, Michelle Buckmier, who helped with the proofing and editing. Thanks, Michelle!

But above all, I want to give all praise to God because He is the true author of this story. All of my writing is inspired by Him, and when He tells me to write something, the work isn't tedious, but a joy. Studying the word and creating a story around a true biblical account is easy for me because it's from God. His ideas are always the best!

Barbara Stewart lives in North Carolina with her husband, Bob, where she enjoys gardening, biking, crocheting, hiking, camping, and entertaining when she's not writing, as well as spending time with their five children and six grandchildren, all of whom live in the area. Having enjoyed writing all of her life, she's now taking the time to do what she loves. She utilizes the writing of biblical fiction to study the Word and strives to make the characters in the biblical account come to life, all in an effort to draw people who've never experienced the touch of God into His presence.

Barbara has also written "A Cat's Tale", the account of life from one of her Maine Coon cat's point of view (available at www.createspace.com/3369283), and "A Horse's Tale", the true story of Sassy, a miniature horse that was lifeless and unresponsive when rescued by the United States Equine Rescue League in the Triangle Region of NC (USERL) (available at www.createspace.com/3394742). A portion of the profits from the sale of this book is donated to USERL to assist with the cost of rehabilitation, both physical and mental, of abused and neglected horses.